THE PHOTOGRAPHER'S WIFE

Also by Robert Solé
and soon to be published in English translation

BIRDS OF PASSAGE

(*Le Tarbouche*)

Robert Solé

THE PHOTOGRAPHER'S WIFE

Translated from the French
by John Brownjohn

THE HARVILL PRESS
LONDON

First published with the title *La Mamelouka* by Editions du Seuil, Paris, in 1996

First published in Great Britain in 1999 by
The Harvill Press
2 Aztec Row
Berners Road
London NI 0PW

www.harvill-press.com

3 5 7 9 8 6 4 2

Copyright © Editions du Seuil, 1996
Translation copyright © John Brownjohn, 1998

Published with the assistance of the French Ministry of Culture

A CIP catalogue record for this book is available from the British Library

ISBN I 86046 549 8 (hbk)
ISBN I 86046 550 I (pbk)

Designed and typeset in Centaur at
Libanus Press, Marlborough, Wiltshire

Printed and bound in Great Britain by Butler & Tanner Ltd
at Selwood Printing, Burgess Hill

To Caroline

THE PHOTOGRAPHER'S WIFE

I

"Milo! Milo!"

The little girl raced down the steps of the villa and made for the beach. Alerted by her cries, the other children tore themselves away from their sandcastles and followed hard on her heels. Ten or twelve of them went galloping off to meet the young man in the jaunty white suit.

"Milo! Milo!"

Émile Touta's arrival was greeted with the same rapturous cries every morning. Smiling as the children clustered round him, he gave their cheeks a familiar pat, ruffled their hair, playfully punched them in the ribs. Then, at the top of his voice, he would hail the new day with an aria from *La Traviata* or *Rigoletto*. He sang a trifle off-key, but no matter: anything Milo did delighted his nephews, his nephews' cousins, and all the other children at Fleming. He was the only denizen of the grown-up world to take an interest in their games, the only one who not only tolerated their antics but actually encouraged them.

Tall and regular-featured, Milo had instant appeal. Women were suscept-ible to his glib tongue and the air of amusement with which he regarded people and things. A somewhat brash but engaging bachelor of twenty-five, he always had a fund of stories to tell — sensational anecdotes that never appeared in the newspapers. He was adept at presenting them and quick to applaud them himself, being the first to laugh if they were funny. He also punctuated them with exclamations — for they all evoked cries of wonderment — even more loudly than his audience.

Milo could put a name to every face on Fleming beach, near Alexandria, where his family had holidayed for years. So he was all the more intrigued, on this particular morning in July 1891, to see a strange girl in a white dress seated at her easel in a secluded spot.

"She's been there for ages," the children told him, "but she hasn't done much painting."

Milo left them to get on with their game and sauntered in the girl's direction. She had installed herself at the far end of the beach, several yards from the water, her face shielded from the sun by a big straw hat. Nothing could be heard but the whisper of wavelets breaking on the shore. The nearby rocks gave off a faint smell of seaweed.

The girl was dabbing her canvas with various shades of blue, using the very tip of her brush. Milo watched her with a smile.

"You reinvent the sea, mademoiselle," he said. "I reproduce it exactly."

The girl turned to look at the author of this boorish intrusion. Milo smiled, delighted by the effect he had produced.

"Émile Touta, photographer."

"Congratulations."

Taken aback, he fell silent for a moment, looking at the girl's hand. Long and slender, the fingers that held the brush formed a right angle with the palm. It was a superb hand – a queen among hands.

Then he caught sight of the bootees beside the easel. She was barefoot beneath her dress! Milo pictured her skin caressing the warm sand.

"To whom do I have the honour?" he asked, rather abashed.

Her dark eyes gazed into his.

"Sarah Bernhardt, amateur painter."

Milo burst out laughing. The pert young thing had already readdressed herself to her palette. He almost returned to the attack but thought better of it.

"I won't take up any more of your time," he said loftily. "However, I'm sure we'd have plenty to say to each other on the subject of painting and photography. Another day, perhaps . . . "

* * *

Émile Touta had chosen the photographer's profession much as he would have elected to become a lawyer, grocer, or baritone: with nonchalance and enthusiasm, convinced that he would shine at it. He spoke of his future exploits with such assurance that people were tempted to congratulate him on them right away. He had rented a modest but well-situated shop in Ezbekiyah Square, close to some bigger establishments. It was just across the way from that of Maloumian, who styled himself "Photographer to the British Army of Occupation", and a hundred yards from that of Jacquemart, a medal winner at the World Exhibition of 1878, who was photographer to the khedival family. To keep his end up, Milo had devised a title as flashy as it was unverifiable: "Photographer to the Consulates".

Truth to tell, his only regular customer was the Jesuit school in Cairo. The Fathers authorized him to photograph the junior classes every year in return for a small sum. The Photographer to the Consulates recouped this outlay by imposing a very idiosyncratic tariff on the parents. He charged them ten piastres per group photograph if their sons were stand-ing, twenty if seated alongside the teachers, and twice that sum if they belonged to the privileged few who reclined on the carpet in the foreground.

Émile Touta had given up producing picture postcards because the shops in the big hotels were already cluttered with sphinxes, pyramids and feluccas of all kinds. He had, however, contrived to render other, less overt services to the tourist trade. On three or four occasions, with the aid of a New Hotel bellboy who picked them up in the Ezbekiyah Gardens, he had sneaked women of easy virtue into his studio, where they gracelessly bared their breasts for the camera, or, in return for a few extra shillings, adopted more improper poses. One of them, who smelt of stewed beans, had even deemed it her duty to join the photographer under his black cloth . . . But the odd commission for these rather risqué photographs did not make much money. Milo felt that his vocation lay elsewhere, and besides, he was far too fond of women to sell such grotesque images of them on gelatinized paper.

In summer he closed his shop for several weeks and joined the holiday-makers' exodus to the coast. Put up at Fleming by one of his brothers, he worked as a beach photographer in the environs of the Hôtel-Casino San Stefano. The yearly floral bicycle competition was always good for several commissions.

Once Milo had returned to his pitch near the sun umbrellas, it took him only a couple of minutes to discover that the girl's name was Dora Sawaya, that she was nineteen years old, and that she had come to stay with her newly married girlfriend Lita Tiomji the day before. He also ascertained the profession of her father, a Cairo estate agent, and the maiden name of her mother, a distant cousin of the Falakis. He was careful not to approach her again, however, and confined himself to devouring her with his eyes when she folded up her easel and headed for a nearby villa.

Dora's slender form was swathed in a flimsy muslin dress with a bodice fringed with white gauze. Her steady tread, almost unaffected by the easel and paintbox beneath her arm, lent her an air of poise and strength. Her eyes were as dark as the curls that escaped from her hat, but it was her mouth that made the most immediate impression: a coral mouth whose full lips contrasted with the delicacy of her features. Milo found her wildly attractive.

Next morning he went down to the beach a little earlier than usual and stationed himself a few yards from the spot where Dora had been paint-ing the day before. He was surrounded by several children by the time she appeared.

"I trust we aren't disturbing you?" he said.

Her only response was a sardonic stare.

"Allow me to come and admire your canvas later on." Without giving her time to reply, he continued, "Let's go, children, Mademoiselle Bernhardt wants to work. Personally, I'm going to take a dip." And he went off, followed by his little retinue, to change in one of the beach huts.

Half an hour later, with his hair still damp, he strolled up to Dora in a striped bathing costume whose lack of sleeves showed off his muscular shoulders.

"Your picture is a great success, mam'selle, though I myself would have made the sea less dark, possibly by inserting some green highlights."

"Even though photography doesn't allow you to reproduce colours?" she said sarcastically.

"Photography possesses other attributes. Were you aware that many painters use it as an aid to composition?"

The hem of her dress, which was slightly rucked up, afforded a glimpse of her bare feet half buried in sand. In an abstracted voice, Milo launched into a rambling dissertation on painter-photographers.

Dora shook the drips off her brush like someone briskly ringing a bell. She might have been summoning a servant to escort an unwelcome visitor from the premises.

2

Every year in August Milo would photograph the whole of the Touta clan augmented by several members of connected families. To feature in this ritual photograph, some sixty persons of all ages stationed themselves on the steps of one of the villas.

This year Milo suggested bringing the date forward. "The light is better in July. We could do it tomorrow – on the beach, for a change."

One or two protests rang out, but they were swiftly drowned by the children's cries of delight: to abandon the steps for the beach would lend the operation even more excitement. Getting ready for the annual photo was one of the summer's biggest treats.

Milo appeared at nine that morning, wearing a white tie and jacket. The family photograph was a solemn occasion that required appropriate dress. No one could have imagined him officiating in casual attire, still less in a bathing costume. He removed his jacket, loosened his tie, and transported his equipment to the site with the children's help. As if by chance, he chose the spot where Dora Sawaya had been painting on previous days. By the time she turned up a quarter of an hour later, a large tarpaulin had been spread out on the sand to protect his apparatus.

Without a word, without so much as a glance, Dora installed herself a short distance away.

"Pay attention, children," called Milo. "First I set up the tripod – firmly, like this – and tighten all the screws to prevent it from vibrating. The camera mustn't budge a millimetre. The slightest movement would ruin everything.

Photography is precision work – half-measures won't do . . . Right, who'll hand me the camera? Careful! It's fragile, that thing, what do you think! Now I fit the camera on to the head of the foot . . . What are you laughing at, you idiots? That's the correct expression: the head of the foot."

Just then Dora had a fit of the giggles, which she hid behind her hand.

"Now watch: I'm installing the camera. I screw the bolt right down. What am I doing now? Honestly, children, I don't *know* what I'm doing – you're confusing me with all your questions, I can't work and answer them at the same time. Very well, now I release the hooks so the camera can slide along the base. That? That's what holds the focusing screen . . . No, I'll explain about the focusing screen later. Where are the holes in the carriage? Fix the camera at the second hole. The second, I said! Good, now step back, all of you, for the preliminary focusing. No, no, I'll explain about focusing later . . . "

Dora, unable to concentrate on her work, was watching her disruptive admirer with an amused smile. Milo took advantage of this to give her an embarrassed little wave, as if apologizing for his inability to quit the spot with so many children around.

The family were beginning to arrive. An amiable state of chaos reigned. Not enough chairs had been brought for the oldest members, and the ladies made a fuss before taking their places.

"What about me, *ya* Milo, where shall I go? Oh no, please not – not in the front row, I look so awful in photographs . . . "

Milo, who had resumed his jacket and adjusted his tie, orchestrated the ceremony. It occurred to him, rather belatedly, that the absence of steps would prevent him from arranging his subjects in the manner of a school photograph, as he did every year, with the result that those at the back were threatened with invisibility. He went over to the children several times, instructing them to close up, sit down or kneel, as the case might be. Deprived of their parasols and fans, the ladies began to complain of the heat. The youngest children grew fidgety. An over-hasty smack made one of the little girls burst into tears, but Milo consoled her and order was finally restored.

Returning to his post behind the tripod, he spent long minutes adjusting the focus. Now and then he would withdraw his head from under the black cloth to shout instructions. At last, taking the bulb in his right hand and the cloth draped over the lens in his left, he called:

"Ready now! Quite still!"

Soon afterwards, when the grown-ups had dispersed and the children were playing football, Milo walked over to Dora.

"I'm afraid we disturbed you . . . "

"Don't flatter yourself," she said drily.

"But mademoiselle, I see you're putting in some clouds. Why, when the sky is so unutterably blue?"

"Why not? An ordinary paintbrush can do more than all your mechanical and chemical processes put together."

"You're mistaken. I could add some clouds to the family picture I took just now by retouching it. Photography can lie too. Photography, too, is an art."

Dora smiled. "I didn't know that lying was definitive of art."

He acknowledged her riposte with a courtly bow.

Moments later a piercing cry from little Yolande made them turn to look. She was kneeling on the sand, having taken a football full in the face. Milo hurried over to her, bent down, and took her gently in his arms. Dora saw her tearful face disappear into the hollow of his shoulder. Encircling Yolande with his big hands, he patted her in a maternal way and whispered something in her ear. Before long she began to smile through her tears.

Thoughtfully, Dora moistened her brush and went back to mixing the paints on her palette.

3

Émile Touta came over to me every morning from then on, asking the children not to follow him. "You'll disturb her, it's only natural. She needs to concentrate."

I wouldn't say that he'd changed – it was doubtful if he could – but I found him a little less forthcoming and a little more on his guard, as if watching himself. I kept my eyes fixed on my picture or on the sea in front of me. From time to time I would turn towards him and burst out laughing despite myself. The children were jealous.

To say that I was painting the sea would be an overstatement. Its ever-changing highlights contrived to elude me. No mixture of blue, green and white was equal to the task. Perhaps I should have stopped peering at it, abandoned my laborious experiments, and painted some imaginary waves instead. The young man's presence distracted me. His laugh, his voice . . .

Émile Touta never spent longer than ten minutes beside my easel before plunging into the waves. He could not prolong our tête-à-têtes without compromising me. Fortunately, his visits tended to coincide with those of one or two inquisitive spectators who could not resist the temptation to come and inspect my progress.

During these snatches of conversation, which were devoted to painting, photography, and small talk, Milo told hilarious tales of his family, the Toutas, whom I had seen on the beach the day of the group photograph. His descriptions were so vivid that I almost felt personally acquainted with these characters. Fat Aunt Angéline, for example, the inveterate matchmaker who had succeeded in thrusting her three daughters into the arms of the three Dabbour brothers, civil servants all. Or Cousin Lolo, a simple soul and man of his time, who had disguised himself, in turn, as a French engineer during the construction of the Suez Canal, a barrister of the Mixed Courts at the time of the law reforms, and an English tourist at the outset of the British occupation. Ever since Gaston Maspéro's discovery of the royal mummies at Deir al-Bahari he had posed as an Egyptologist, complete with outsize solar topee, pince-nez, and puttees.

One morning, when I had finished painting, Milo took my easel and put it under his arm. The children came running up, and we headed for the Tiomjis' villa in a kind of procession.

I was carrying my bootees in my hand, heedless of the hot sand and what people might say. Halfway across the beach I sat down on my folding stool and put them on while the children formed a circle round me. Milo's steady gaze unnerved me.

"Till this afternoon, then," he said when we reached the villa a few minutes later. I responded with an evasive smile.

"Why this afternoon, Uncle Milo?" little Yolande could not help asking. He put a finger to his lips. "This afternoon there's a tea dance at San Stefano. I'd have liked to take you along, but you know they don't admit children."

I had hesitated when Lita, a bride of barely six months, invited me to spend the holidays at Fleming. I didn't feel entirely at ease with Richard Tiomji – in fact I wondered how my childhood friend, a dainty china doll of a girl, could live with an uncouth man whose thickset body was as hairy as an ape's. But Lita had insisted, and I wasn't averse to getting away from my family for a week or two.

At the drop of a hat, Richard would deliver dogmatic pronouncements on minor matters in a loud, authoritative voice. He alone held the floor, his self-assurance boosted by material success. To hear him hold forth about his ostrich farm at Matariya, near Cairo, was an experience in itself.

Lita's husband might not be very refined, but he did have flair. In 1885, the year Khartoum fell, he managed to exploit the cessation of trade between Egypt and the Sudan. Consignments of ostrich feathers no longer arrived by caravan, so he decided to set up an ostrich farm of his own. Notwithstanding a few setbacks, for he knew nothing about the strange creatures, Richard very soon succeeded in rendering his business profitable. He even channelled part of his output into a workshop in the Moski, and it was as a fan manufacturer that he had won the hand of dainty Lita early in 1891.

Having gradually become inured to Richard Tiomji, I no longer attached any importance to his bombastic effusions. I even found him reassuring, in a way, and amusing despite his lack of humour. All in all, I was enjoying my stay at Fleming more and more.

Richard thought it improper to permit a girl to paint unchaperoned at the other end of the beach. He said as much the very first week, but the look on my face promptly put him in his place. He made up for this by rebuking his wife with a proprietorial air. "Have you seen that young man chatting with your friend?" he asked her one evening. "He's a Touta," she replied. "I know he's a Touta, but there are Toutas and Toutas. That one isn't worth a piastre. He's a humble photographer from Ezbekiyah Square."

Lita didn't pass on that remark until some months later.

4

The orchestra at the Hôtel-Casino San Stefano was outstanding, like everything to do with that luxurious establishment, which had opened some
years before and become a prime feature of the Alexandrian summer. At
night it could be seen from a long way off, thanks to the electric lights
installed in all of its rooms.

The dark-suited musicians had not yet begun to play. They were tuning
their instruments while a buzz of conversation arose from the tables
covered with embroidered tablecloths, on which waiters were depositing
silver teapots.

Milo came over, looking very dapper in a cream linen jacket and striped
trousers.

"Excuse me," he said, "but aren't you Richard Tiomji, who owns the
farm at Matariya?"

Rather surprised, Lita's husband pricked up his ears.

"Yes. Why?"

"I have to talk to you about ostriches," Milo said with an air of mystery,
after bowing to the two young women.

And he sat down.

Dora stifled a fit of the giggles. Lita saw this and almost gave way, but
she managed to control herself.

"Come, *chérie*," she said, "I want to show you the new carpets in the main
lounge."

When they returned fifteen minutes later, ostriches had ceased to be the topic of conversation. Richard Tiomji was listening, enthralled, to some astonishing revelations about the British authorities' secret plans to prolong their occupation of Egypt.

"Well, really!" he kept saying.

"And I haven't told you everything," Milo added in a confidential undertone. "But enough of that! May I have your permission to ask Madame Tiomji to dance?"

Although Richard detested waltzes, he felt duty-bound to offer Dora a hirsute hand and join the other two on the dance floor.

The musicians had their backs to the sea, which was visible beyond them through a big bay window. The orange sunset was becoming tinged with violet.

At the next intermission, Milo turned to Dora.

"Go ahead," said the ostrich farmer, "we'll sit this one out. Lita's tired."

To loud applause, the violinists rose and struck up *The Blue Danube*.

Milo's previous partner had been slightly built, limp-wristed, and so politely submissive to his lead as to seem non-existent. Dora, by contrast, was very much "there". Supremely alert to the music, she might almost have been leading the dance.

They moved in time, in perfect accord. Milo had never danced better. He looked into the girl's face now and then, as if to reassure himself that his pleasure was shared. Her eyes were half closed, and there was a faint smile on her lips. They found it hard to let go of each other when the music stopped, but the orchestra launched into a mazurka, so they abandoned themselves to it.

From half-past midnight onwards the Tiomjis' villa was rocked by Richard's snores — powerful snores whose varying rhythms Dora could hear from her bedroom.

Opening the door carefully for fear of waking Lita, she tiptoed along the passage, which was lit by a small oil lamp. Fortunately, the front door opened without a sound. It was very warm outside.

Milo was waiting, as arranged, beside a low wall twenty yards away.

Emotion overwhelmed her at the sight of him. Her bare feet sank into the sand as she walked towards him with her stomach in a knot and her head spinning.

He took her hands and bent to brush them with his lips. She shivered. When he folded her in his arms and drew her close, her last defences crumbled. Tears sprang to her eyes.

Glued together, they strolled along hand in hand, pausing every few steps to kiss with feverish intensity.

"I must go back," Dora murmured half-heartedly.

"Yes, yes, you must," said Milo, holding her even closer.

He accompanied her to the steps of the villa. Suppressing their laughter at the sound of some exceptionally violent snores, they exchanged a last kiss, and another. They released each other's hands, only to clasp them again and again.

5

Émile Touta and Dora Sawaya announced their engagement in mid September.

"I fell for him the very first day," Dora confided to Lita. "By the time I saw him the next morning, I was in love. That voice, that smile . . . He's so gentle, too."

"Gentle?" said Lita, raising her eyebrows. She found Milo loud-mouthed, if not brash, and capable of sudden outbursts.

"Yes, gentle. And there's that way he has of being one step ahead, of opening doors without having to force them. Besides, he's so amusing. I shall never get bored when we're together, I can sense it."

The Touta children were dismayed. They felt they were suddenly losing an irreplaceable being. Who but Milo could allow them to fish for crabs with their bare hands, to take over the coachman's reins while going full tilt or consume two vanilla cornets in succession? "I once ate three on the trot, believe me!" he told them with his mouth full and his lips smeared with ice cream.

Once married, Milo would cease to understand them. He would form part of their world no longer.

"And all because of a picture!" said little Yolande, wrinkling her nose in disgust. "Anyway, what exactly *was* she painting?"

Léon Sawaya was only half convinced by his daughter's suitor's brilliant dissertation on photography in general and his future as a photographer in particular. The young man seemed likeable enough, however, and he did have the merit of belonging to the Toutas, who rated as one of the most distinguished families in the Greek Catholic community. Although Milo's father, who had died ten years earlier, had left no particular mark, other members of the family, who originally hailed from Syria, like the Sawayas, but had been resident in Egypt for a century-and-a-half, were persons of importance. One of Milo's uncles, old Dr Touta, enjoyed universal esteem. Thirty years after the event, people still spoke of his heroic conduct during the cholera epidemic of 1863. The doctor's two sons, Maxime and Alexandre, had also succeeded in their different ways, one as editor in chief of the *Sémaphore d'Alexandrie*, the other as a timber merchant. But the Touta most widely admired and cited as an example to children was Rizqallah Bey Touta, founder of *Touta et Fils*, the chain of department stores. His resounding financial success, albeit of questionable origin, commanded respect.

Milo greatly entertained those present at the wedding dinner in Cairo with accounts of happenings in the corridors of power. The beaming bridegroom had a whole stock of anecdotes about the worthy Khedive Tewfiq, generally considered to be a figurehead whose sole acknowledged function was to lend the British occupation a semblance of legality.

Dora never stopped laughing. She had shocked her sisters-in-law by removing her tulle veil as soon as she emerged from the church and limiting herself to the aigrette in her hair. In contrast to the formal attire of the ladies present, she wore a simple white satin gown unadorned with brocade or lace.

"You look quite naked," Milo told her in an admiring whisper at the start of the meal.

Bemused by all the voices and laughter, the bewildering sea of unfamiliar faces, the ladies' perfumes, the glittering candelabra, Dora felt she was on a cloud.

Milo recounted the exploits of his lone employee, a simple-minded young man named Bulbul, who had a peculiar habit of guffawing when addressed. Although the Photographer to the Consulates had ceased to notice this himself, new customers found it somewhat disconcerting. "I've come to have my photograph taken," was their customary preamble on entering the shop. Bulbul, having scrutinized them for a moment, would roar with laughter.

Halfway through dinner, when universal good humour reigned and arrack fumes were relaxing the starchiest faces, Lita Tiomji recalled an incident from her days at boarding school.

"One afternoon, Dora and I and some friends of ours had hidden at the bottom of the garden to smoke a cigarette. Suddenly we heard a noise: a nun was coming in our direction, jingling her bunch of keys. 'Quick,' Dora hissed, 'follow me!' We were too petrified to move, but Dora made a dash for the garden wall and scrambled nimbly over at the risk of tearing her dress. She'd vanished by the time Mother Marie des Anges appeared, sniffing suspiciously. The rest of us, who hadn't had the sense to escape, were put on bread and water for forty-eight hours. Isn't that right, *chérie?*"

"You took a leaf out of the Mameluke's book," old Dr Touta told Dora with a smile.

"Which Mameluke?" she asked.

"I'm talking about the famous incident at the Citadel. It happened in 1811, the year of my birth. Don't trouble to work that out: it's exactly eighty years ago."

Milo's uncle was only too pleased to recall this chapter in the history of Egypt, which he did with his customary regard for accuracy.

"Muhammad Ali had grown tired of the Mamelukes' encroachments on his authority and decided to get rid of them. One day he invited all those unruly princes to the Citadel to witness the appointment of his son, Toussoun Pasha, as commander in chief of the troops of Arabia. He welcomed the Mamelukes warmly, had them served with *shishahs* and coffee, and then invited them to join the official procession. Preceded by a military band, the Mamelukes set off along the old sunken road, hewn out of the rock, that leads down to the city. At a given signal, they were fired on by soldiers stationed on the walls. Several of them managed to get as far as the palace, but there they were captured and beheaded. Only one of their number contrived to leap on to his horse and escape over the battlements. He was never seen again. You, my dear Dora, acted like the Mameluke – in fact you did even better, because you're with us today."

The guests applauded, then drank the bride's health.

The boarding-school anecdote went the rounds of the children during the days that followed.

"Not bad," Yolande said meditatively. "She ought to be called the Mameluka."

6

"This is the mistress of the house," Milo told his factotum.

Bulbul looked Dora in the eye and roared with laughter.

She was disappointed by the shop of which her fiancé had given her such a glowing description. The lobby, which boasted a greyish counter and half a dozen shabby armchairs, was as welcoming as a prison visiting room, and the handful of cracked and faded prints on the walls seemed to have been languishing in their frames since the invention of photography. Customers who pushed open the door emblazoned ÉMILE TOUTA STUDIO, PHOTOGRAPHER TO THE CONSULATES were greeted by a bell that clattered like a bunch of saucepan lids, creating the disagreeable impression that all this ironmongery was about to descend on their heads.

The studio proper was situated at the rear of the lobby and on the left. Painted iron grey, it was lit by a large skylight and pervaded by a vaguely theatrical odour of leather, velvet, and varnished wood. The camera, massively enthroned on a heavy walnut tripod, was equipped with a crank and a handwheel that adjusted the height and the angle of inclination respectively. With its bellows, shiny brass fittings and big, convex lenses, it had already seen honorable service: the Italian who had sold the shop to Milo three years earlier had acquired the contraption from a Viennese manufacturer in 1875.

"If madame would care to take a seat," the Photographer to the Consulates said ceremoniously, waving Dora into an armchair whose back was adorned with arabesques.

Certain customers preferred to pose on a two-seater ottoman upholstered in green silk. They could select their décor from a range of heterogeneous props: a chunk of Roman column in moulded plaster, a fake stairway with four steps, pieces of armour, animal skins – even a stuffed crocodile. Various panels done in trompe l'œil could be slid along rails in the background to suggest a desert, a pine forest, some rocks, or a stormy sea.

The studio was connected with the darkroom by a small padded door.

"Take care," said Milo, "there's some dangerous stuff in here."

A smell of acetone and ether stung Dora's nostrils. The tables were littered with flasks, test tubes, funnels, and dishes of all sizes. The darkroom had no running water, so Bulbul regularly fetched buckets of water and lined them up along the walls, which were painted black. Milo developed his plates after dark, as a rule, but he sometimes did so in broad daylight. To show Dora how he operated, he drew an imitation leather curtain over each of the two windows, having first lit a red glass lantern.

"Sensitive plates will only tolerate red," he explained. "They're the opposite of bulls."

Beside the darkroom was a cubbyhole equipped with a desk for retouching. This diminutive room gave on to a sunny courtyard where Bulbul kept his buckets beside a cistern. Some laundry was hanging out to dry, and a cockerel could be heard crowing intermittently on a terrace near by. It was easy to forget that one was in the very heart of Cairo, quite close to Opera Square.

The upstairs apartment was accessible from the shop by way of a spiral staircase. Dora got a shock when she saw her husband's lair, with its greenish-yellow walls. The furniture and knick-knacks, scattered around at random, were in appallingly bad taste.

"This is your domain," Milo said magnanimously. "Do what you like with it."

He didn't recognize his apartment. Over the next few weeks, the premises were completely transformed by warm colours and a handful of new

acquisitions. Dora furnished as she dressed: with a disconcerting simplic-
ity that did not preclude the odd, eye-catching flight of fancy. In one
corner of the drawing room, for example, she decided to install a monu-
mental plant with thick, fleshy leaves. Bulbul had a devil of a job getting
it up the spiral staircase.

"What's the point of that?" demanded Milo, looking bewildered.

"None, that's just it."

Next, Dora made it her business to lend the lobby a more prepossess-
ing appearance. She refurnished it with a low table and three squat little
armchairs, had the walls repainted, and replaced the framed photographs
with some watercolours.

"Watercolours in a photographic studio!" Milo expostulated.

"It's less overwhelming. Bankers don't paper their walls with banknotes.
Have you ever seen a dentist display jawbones in his consulting room?"

He smiled, then smothered her with kisses. However, Dora had to
restrain her redecorating ambitions because most of her dowry had already
been spent.

She experienced an intoxicating sense of freedom during those first few
weeks of marriage. She was done with her father's lectures, her mother's
qualms, the daily irritations inflicted by her five younger brothers and
sisters. Sharing Milo's bohemian existence made her feel she was perma-
nently on holiday. She awoke each morning with her heart aglow and her
body still throbbing from the night's caresses, not knowing what pleasant
surprise or source of wild amusement the day would bring.

Although business was far from brisk, Milo overrode such concerns
with his infectious gaiety and indomitable self-confidence.

"Once I get my double drop-shutter," he would say, "I'll work wonders.
Maloumian will be trounced. Even Jacquemart will have to watch his
step!"

Milo liked to brand the Frenchman a mediocre photographer, it being
his habit to denigrate well-established competitors in a way that never
failed to surprise and sometimes impress. If Milo was to be believed,
Jacquemart owed his success to his nationality alone.

"Believe me, if I were French like him . . . We Syrians labour under two disadvantages: the Europeans despise us and the natives are jealous of us."

In his dreams Milo already saw himself as photographer to the khedive. He told Dora how Napoleon II, when setting out for the battle of Solferino in the spring of 1859, had paused at Disdéri's celebrated Paris studio to have himself photographed.

"Imagine, the whole French army was waiting at attention on the pavement! The emperor couldn't have paid a lightning visit to a painter's studio, could he?"

This sparked off yet another argument about the relative merits of painting and photography.

"A painted portrait requires lengthy sittings," Milo would say, "whereas a plate can be made in half an hour and developed within the day. Photography has another advantage: it enables you to produce an infinite number of copies. Disdéri employed ninety people, did you know that? Guess how many prints he could turn out in a day? Go on, guess . . . Two thousand! Two thousand prints a day! His studio became a regular portrait factory."

"You can keep your factory," Dora retorted. "I prefer my easel. Besides, one painting by a master is worth more than two thousand photographic prints."

Having little left to do in the apartment, and not being the sort to window-shop or gossip away whole afternoons over cups of tea, Dora spent much of her day downstairs. Her presence there did not go unnoticed. Instead of encountering Bulbul, who was largely relegated to household tasks, customers were greeted in the lobby by an elegant young woman whose "consular" associations they could readily imagine. Many gentlemen were sufficiently charmed by her to spread the word, and this brought in additional business.

No one entered the studio itself without a trace of apprehension. Certain customers refused to come unless accompanied by a friend. Milo would sit them down in the arabesque-adorned armchair and immobilize them by fitting their necks into the jaws of a patent clamp. He left them there throughout the lengthy focusing procedure, rigid and incapable of more than a few grunts of approval at the conclusion of his protracted monologues.

"Quite still, please!"

The patient would tense himself a little more and hold his breath, looking as if he'd swallowed a ramrod.

"Smile!" commanded the photographer.

A grimace appeared on the paralysed face, and Milo pressed the bulb.

"You moved!" he would say on occasion. "We'll have to start again from scratch."

That was worse still. Wide-eyed and distraught, the luckless subject resembled a corpse.

Dora discovered that her husband specialized in flattering portraits: he used to retouch all his plates with a liberal recourse to pencil, scraper, or paintbrush. This he did not only to eliminate the jaws of the metal neck-clamp that sometimes made an untoward appearance in his photographs; wrinkles were dissipated, scars filled in, cheeks slimmed down. There were no more furrows around the mouth or crow's-feet in the corners of the eyes. On emerging from Émile Touta's studio, the most withered grand-mother resembled her girlhood self.

Not all his customers took kindly to this excessive embellishment. One of them, endowed by nature with a hooked nose, complained of the classical Greek profile he'd been given.

"If you wanted a mere likeness, monsieur," Milo told him haughtily, "you should have said so."

Dora, who was at the other end of the lobby, found it hard to keep a straight face.

7

It was through photography that Dora got to know the Touta family a little better. In October she accompanied Milo on his traditional round of visits to sundry brothers, sisters and cousins, its purpose being to deliver their copies of the summer photograph. The children were very attached to this ritual, which had for some years occupied a place in the calendar between Easter and Christmas, on a par with Sham en-Nessim, the spring festival.

Milo had a very characteristic way of knocking on the door. His nephews would rush to answer it, stampeding along the passages with cries of delight.

The print was removed from its capacious envelope with extreme care. Impatience rose to fever pitch among the actors of the summer, who had now become spectators of their own performance.

"Have you washed your hands properly?" the materfamilias would ask. "With soap? Let me smell."

She would then drape a cloth over her knees to receive the precious object, and everyone, young and old, formed a circle round her. Exclamations rang out, together with comments on this aunt's dress, that uncle's moustache, or the unruliness of some youngster who had turned his head away at the last moment. Certain faces were scrutinized for the "Touta look", a mysterious form of resemblance which no one had ever managed to define in a convincing manner. The photograph was then passed from hand to hand, balanced on the palm to avoid touching it with sweaty fingers. Later, it would join those of previous years in a padded leather album interleaved with tissue paper.

This time the surprise was even greater because the photograph had been taken on the beach instead of on the steps of Dr Touta's villa. The persons seated in the front row made a tense impression. Some of their chairs had dug into the sand a little, notably that of Angéline Falaki, who looked as if she was sinking into a quagmire. Comments flew thick and fast. Impudent youngsters were called to order, but Milo encouraged them by roaring with laughter. One or two faces in the back row were obscured by those beside them and hard to distinguish, even though the photographer had tried to pick them out when retouching. He promised their unfortunate owners a prime position in next summer's photograph.

That October Dora made the acquaintance of Oscar Touta, one of Milo's uncles, who presented himself at the shop some three times a year. A rouged and powdered sixty-year-old complete with walking stick and bowler hat, he gave his hair a final, feverish pat in the big oval mirror at the entrance to the studio. Then, trembling all over, he took his place in the arabesque-adorned armchair. Oscar was genuinely terrified of the camera, convinced that it would belie his appearance or steal some part of his precious person. He was more than usually apprehensive on this occasion.

"Are you going to photograph me face-on?" he asked Milo.

"If you wish, uncle."

"If I wish, if I wish!" snapped Oscar. "*I'm* not taking the photo, *you* are!"

Milo suggested a three-quarter-profile portrait, but that only earned him a fierce retort:

"Three-quarter-profile? Why? What's wrong with my face? Answer me, I insist!"

Milo tried to pacify him, but Oscar's agony of mind only intensified as the minutes went by. His lower lip quivered, his cheeks twitched.

"Why are you tilting the camera like that? You're going to take my bad profile, I can sense it!"

"No, uncle, I assure you —"

"He assures me, he assures me! You can assure me all you like, you hypocrite. Do you think I'm blind?" His voice rose to a shout. "You'll never fool me! Never, you hear?"

Abruptly overcome with panic, Oscar Touta leapt to his feet before the photograph could be taken. Snatching up his hat and cane, he rushed out of the room, leaving Milo stranded. Two seconds later the shop door slammed with a deafening clatter of saucepan lids.

"There goes my most faithful non-customer," Milo sighed.

8

One night in December, when the young couple were having a romantic dinner at Santi's in the Ezbekiyah Gardens, Milo broached the subject point-blank:

"There's a growing demand for photographs in colour. Maloumian tints his work. You're a painter, why don't you try your hand at it?"

That, Dora replied briskly, was at odds with her conception of painting.

"Let me talk you into it," he said softly.

While Milo was speaking, her thoughts went back to her parental home eight years before. Who had he been, that amateur painter? A friend of the family, no doubt. She well remembered his big, blunt-fingered hands and dirty nails, which contrasted so markedly with his little brushes. Eleven years old at the time, she'd spent an entire afternoon sitting for him in a corner of the drawing room. The man hadn't said a word. At last he put away his paints and held out the miniature for her inspection.

What a shock! The sight of that huge, crimson mouth had robbed her of speech, rendered her incapable of thanking him.

"Bravo, it's a perfect likeness!"

No one quarrelled with her father's verdict, not even when the artist with the funereal fingernails had taken his leave. The miniature was framed and hung in the drawing room.

Dora could not stop scrutinizing herself in the mirror for days thereafter. Dumbfounded and close to despair, she discovered that her lips were thick. Closed, her mouth looked big; open, it seemed alarmingly disproportionate. How to disguise it? She tried hard to suck in her lips and took to putting her hand over her mouth when she laughed, as though smothering a sneeze or a yawn.

How greatly she had envied Lita from then on – Lita of the thin, pale, almost invisible lips. Back at boarding school the next term, she told her about the miniature in a spuriously offhand tone. She referred more than once to her oversized mouth but failed to hold her friend's attention. She should have wept, shouted, unburdened herself to Lita or someone else, but she was paralysed by a mixture of fear and pride.

"No," she said to Milo, "colouring isn't the same as painting."

"You aren't listening! That's just what I said."

A waiter brought some *mezze*. Little by little, Dora took in the arguments her husband was patiently expounding. She hadn't set up her easel once since the summer, doubtless because she found Cairo uninspiring. Added to that, she was becoming bored in the shop, where business was still far from brisk. Given the state of their finances, any supplementary source of income was worth considering.

"I might give it a try," she said at length, and earned herself a kiss.

A preliminary experiment in oils on linen-grained paper did not strike her as conclusive in spite of Milo's admiring exclamations. It looked less like a photograph than a poor painting. She carried out further experiments in the days that followed, this time in watercolour on albuminized paper. These were a distinct improvement. The prints were trimmed with a cutter and mounted on stiff cardboard. To lend them a glossy finish prior to framing them, Dora used a wad of flannel impregnated with wax polish.

Her first efforts were well received, and she was encouraged to persevere by several new commissions. Her portraits looked rather like miniatures in oils but were far less expensive, even though the Photographer to the Consulates charged twice the usual price for a coloured print.

Whenever a customer requested it, therefore, Dora would come into the studio and jot down particulars in a notebook. She recorded the colour of the sitter's eyes, hair and complexion. Then, at the end of the morning or early in the afternoon, when the light was at its best, she would settle herself at the retouching desk in the cubbyhole and start painting with the aid of a large magnifying glass.

She always began by tinting the cheeks with a little rose madder or red ochre. Then, toning down the initial tint as she went, she extended this treatment to the entire face. Next she proceeded to colour the hair, eyes, eyebrows, and lips, which she stressed with a hint of vermilion. A second print of the photograph, pinned to the wall above the desk, enabled her to keep a running check on her painting's resemblance to the original.

"You're making life difficult for yourself," Milo told her. "Most colourists work without ever having seen their subjects."

Dora devoted just as much care to her backgrounds. She eschewed unduly bright colours for pale-skinned people and children, but would happily use warm brown as an accompaniment to dark complexions. Frequent glances at her guide-print ensured that the light and shade on her drapery was correctly positioned and its form and depth faithfully preserved.

"I'm not painting," she kept saying, "I'm colouring."

She reverted to the face to strengthen the flesh tints and the greys, then gave the eyes their highlights and ended by lightening the shadows in the hair. All that remained was to make any jewels sparkle by applying a few dots of Naples yellow with the tip of the brush.

"Superb, absolutely superb!" Milo exclaimed from behind her. She shivered as he planted a kiss on the nape of her neck.

It was all she could do not to hurl herself into his arms, but, if his hand caressed her breast, she would half close her eyes and abandon herself to the moment.

9

It was a radiant Milo who joined the family outing to Helwan in April, accompanied by the Mameluka. Cheerful, voluble, and a pleasure to behold, he massacred *La Traviata* with his usual blithe abandon. Compared to this young man in love, his four elder brothers and two sisters might have been creatures from another planet.

Helwan, a peaceful watering place some twenty kilometres from Cairo, was the children's term-time paradise – the counterpart of Fleming Beach during the summer holidays. A joyful, jostling crowd of them would depart from Bab al-Louq station on a Sunday morning. The train set off to the sound of shouts and singing, but the hubbub died down once it passed Sayyida Zeinab and Saint George's and entered the desert. The passengers were overwhelmed by the gigantic panorama unfolding before their eyes: on the left, a sand-covered limestone massif and the Citadel; on the right, a forest of palm trees and an array of big white sails gliding along the Nile.

At Tourah the platform was invaded by youthful vendors of sesame-seed biscuits who clustered round the carriage windows like flies. Scuffles broke out and coins went rolling along the ground. A blast on the whistle, and the locomotive ponderously resumed its progress in a pall of black smoke. It gradually picked up speed before coming to the military installations, passed the quarries and the explosives factory, then left the river and climbed, whistling and puffing, until it reached Helwan Spa.

A scent of eucalyptus greeted the travellers as they emerged from the station.

"Breathe deeply!" the children were told. "Fill your lungs with that bracing air! You're thirty metres above the Nile!"

Milo's mother owned a big house tucked away in the trees beyond the Casino. She had lived there, with only two maidservants for company, ever since her husband's death. Helwan's ultra-provincial existence seemed to agree with Nonna. She never spoke French except with members of the family when they visited her on certain specified Sundays; the rest of the time she spoke Arabic and consorted with the Copt or Muslim ladies who occupied the houses near by.

Each of them had her at-home day. That was when the sleepy, shuttered drawing rooms came to life for the space of an afternoon. The lady guests were joined by women of lower rank. These cloth sellers, nursemaids or former slaves removed their heelless slippers on entering, then squatted on woollen mats beside the armchairs. Formidable gossips, they filled the room with their chatter until the mistress of the house silenced them by claiming that she couldn't hear herself speak.

Nonna's provincial lifestyle did not prevent her from being a very emancipated woman notorious for her outspoken manner – one who insisted on downing a good, strong glass of arrack before every meal. It was a mystery how she had managed to produce four sons as conventional as Aimé, Joseph, René, and Albert. She had rather more in common with her daughters, Irène and Adrienne, but her favourite child, beyond a doubt, was Émile, the youngest, whose fanciful notions sometimes perturbed her.

The ladies of Helwan thought Milo adorable. They still considered him a child, so they had no qualms about receiving him in their drawing rooms, which were out of bounds to men, whenever he happened to be passing through. He was always ready with a smile, a compliment, or a spicy anecdote. They greeted his bold sallies and apt imitations with little squeals of delight, convinced that they were being flirted with by this charming young man whose good humour and wholesome appearance made them forget, while he was with them, their diabetes, varicose veins, and other worries.

"Tell us what's happening in Cairo, *ya* Milo," they would say, gorging themselves on sweets and barley water.

He complied with good grace, adapting himself to his audience by taking a few liberties with the facts.

Nonna, who was affectionate and indulgent with her grandchildren, could be detestable to her daughters-in-law, on whom she was forever heaping groundless accusations.

"Your wife doesn't like me," she told Joseph. "No, no, I can sense it. One can sense these things, believe me."

Or again, to Aimé, Albert and René in turn:

"It's good of you to have come. I know your wife can't bear to spend Sunday at Helwan."

All their expostulations were in vain.

"But honestly, *ya Mama* –"

"No, don't deny it, I've got a pair of eyes in my head! One can sense these things, believe me."

The family were spending Sunday at Helwan for the first time since Christmas. As usual, Nonna had had two enormous tables laid, one for grown-ups and the other for children. Anxious not to miss any of Milo's stories, the youngsters competed for the places nearest him. Dora's presence at his side rendered competition keener still, because at least half a dozen of the older nephews, fascinated by her mouth, had already fallen in love with her. The Mameluka's shapely lips were a positive invitation to sin in thought, and possibly in deed . . .

Nonna's terrace afforded a view of the palace where Khedive Tewfiq had died four months earlier. His sudden and unexpected demise remained an enigma. In whose interest could it have been to eliminate such a self-effacing man, who wielded no real power and had endeared himself to the British because of his docility? Wasn't it more likely that he had succumbed to his physicians' negligence? The first bulletin, issued on the morrow of New Year's Day, announced that His Highness had simply caught a cold while walking in the desert. This was doubtless a consequence of the influenza epidemic that had confined half Cairo to bed and sentenced every child in the Touta family to countless spoonfuls of prophylactic cod-liver oil. Tewfiq's court physicians initially prescribed him a diet and infusions of violet. Having subsequently treated him for a cough and constipation, they ended by diagnosing infectious pneumonia with nephritic complications.

"At about three o'clock in the morning," Milo's mother recalled, "some palace guards knocked on my door and those of several other private houses, asking for a catheter to help the khedive to urinate. No one possessed such a thing, so they had to fetch one from Cairo by special train. Panic reigned. Before long the khedive's ministers came hurrying to Helwan, each accompanied by his personal physician, but it was too late. The Casino and the Grand Hôtel turned off their electric lights. The khediva fainted when told of her husband's death. Two ladies-in-waiting thought it incumbent on them to throw themselves out of the window. One of them broke her arm. She's a fool, I know her."

Nonna took a swig of arrack, then added, in a mysterious tone:

"Tewfiq was born on a Thursday. He was appointed khedive on a Thursday. After 'Arabi's rebellion in 1882 he returned to Cairo on a Thursday, under the protection of British bayonets. And guess what day of the week he died?"

"Holy Mother of God!" exclaimed Aunt Angéline Falaki, crossing herself.

The peculiar circumstances surrounding the succession had been the talk of Cairo for weeks. 'Abbas Hilmi, the crown prince, was not yet eighteen and could not, therefore, have ascended the throne at once. Would a regent be appointed? The British authorities were strongly opposed to this, fearing that the sultan in Constantinople might take advantage of such an interregnum to regain control of Egypt.

"The British were clever," Milo observed. "They contrived to calculate 'Abbas's age in a different way."

"How do you mean, in a different way?" asked Aunt Angéline.

"By altering the calendar. It occurred to them that there are only 354 days in the Muslim calendar. On that reckoning, the crown prince was already eighteen. The ulemas were instructed to turn a blind eye. It only remained to wire the Theresianum in Vienna and invite 'Abbas to return to Cairo in double-quick time."

"I don't understand why the boy had to go to school in Austria."

"Austria is neutral territory, *ya Tante*, that's why! By sending his son to Vienna, instead of Paris or London, the khedive offended neither the French nor the British. Incidentally, did you know that the prince's return to Egypt went very badly?"

Ears were pricked on all sides, at the children's table as well as the adults'. The clatter of cutlery on crockery died away. Milo could always count on an attentive audience.

"Yes, the journey was an ordeal. The Emperor of Austria had put an old ship at 'Abbas's disposal, commanded by an admiral. They sailed in stormy weather, and the heavy swell made the crown prince seasick. His request to put into Brindisi was politely rejected: the admiral's instructions were to get to Egypt as quickly as possible. 'Abbas twisted the ends of his little moustache, as he always does when thwarted. The sea was as rough as ever when they skirted the Greek coast. Again the khedive asked to put into port, and again he was refused. The youngster flew into a rage. He has a violent temper."

"In other words," Dora said with a smile, "Tewfiq's reign was brought to an end by urine retention and 'Abbas's began with a tempest."

Her sisters-in-law pulled a face at this remark. As for Nonna, she stared at Dora with a kind of amused surprise, almost as if she were seeing her for the first time. Milo's mother appreciated a touch of imagination — something she had yet to discover in any of her other daughters-in-law. Milo had presented her with a *fait accompli* when announcing his engagement six months earlier, but he was so much in love and she so anxious to see him married that she gave her consent before even making Dora's acquaintance.

The dish of steaming *molokhiya* made another circuit of the table. Voices were loudly, heatedly questioning the new khedive's ability to govern a country occupied by the British and dependent, even now, on the Ottoman Empire.

"No country can have three masters," Albert decreed. "Look at that business with the firman."

"What business?" asked Nonna.

Everyone tried to speak at the same time. Milo's voice finally quelled the hubbub.

"It's simple, *ya Mama*. Technically, 'Abbas wasn't the khedive because he hadn't yet received an official firman from his sovereign, the sultan of Constantinople. The sultan proposed to take advantage of the succession to redraw Egypt's Red Sea frontier. The British got wind of his intention and firmly opposed it."

"Why should the British interfere?"

"Because they're the guarantors of Egypt's territorial integrity. They've promised to return the country intact."

"They never will!" growled the old lady.

There followed a confused debate about the intentions of perfidious Albion. Aimé and Joseph functioned as spokesmen for Queen Victoria, whereas Albert, whose relations with his English superior at the Ministry of Public Works were strained, was a confirmed anglophobe. The waters were further muddied by noisy interjections from the jeweller Alfred Falaki, who spoke only in figures.

"I don't understand a word of it!" cried Nonna. "Let Milo explain."

With relish, Milo embarked on an account of the tragicomedy that had kept the whole of Cairo in suspense for several weeks: the firman, which no one dared to open for fear of finding that it contained bad news; the postponement of Jacquemart's official photograph of the new sovereign; the *bakshish* of six thousand pounds discreetly remitted to the sultan; the bogus public reading of the firman, carefully arranged so as to save his face . . .

Nonna began to laugh. Then she raised her glass of arrack.

"To the health of the new khedive!"

Milo produced a newspaper cutting from his wallet and unfolded it. "Firman from his August and Imperial Majesty the Sultan!" he declaimed in a loud voice.

Loud cheers greeted these words. Milo had a hilarious way of reading out official announcements.

"To My enlightened vizier 'Abbas Hilmi Pasha, appointed to the khedivate of Egypt with the exalted rank of sadara, decorated with My imperial orders of the Mejidiya in diamonds and the Osmaniya first class, may the All-Powerful perpetuate his splendour, et cetera, et cetera."

The children's table burst into applause.

"In consequence of the decrees of Providence, Khedive Muhammad Tewfiq having departed this life, the khedivate of Egypt, together with the former provinces indicated in the imperial firman dated 2 Rabi'a al-Akhar 1257, has been bestowed upon you in accordance with My imperial edict dated 7 Jemmazi al-Akhar 1309, in token of My exalted benevolence, and having regard to your services, your rectitude, and your loyalty both to My person and to the interests of My empire, blahblahblah, blahblahblah . . ."

The orator skipped the purely formal passages and came to the nub of the document:

"All the revenues of the khedivate of Egypt shall be collected in My imperial name . . . The government of Egypt shall ensure regular payment of the annual tribute of 750,000 Turkish pounds . . ."

Each of the sentences intoned by Milo called forth exclamations.

"The coinage shall be minted in My name. In time of peace, eighteen thousand soldiers will suffice to guard the Egyptian interior. That figure must not be exceeded. This, My imperial firman, adorned with My imperial signature, has been drawn up and dispatched with an eye to the full implementation of the above measures . . ."

The rest was drowned by shouts of laughter.

After lunch, Milo suggested that they all go for a walk to the edge of the desert to watch the British hitting little balls about.

"Helwan's golf course is the only one in the world to be laid out on sand," he reminded them.

The children, who needed no second bidding, rushed outside. The grown-ups, who were averse to going so far, decided to take a stroll beneath the trees outside the palace railings.

"I shall stay here," said Nonna. "Dora will keep me company."

She was clearly eager to take a closer look at the young woman who had captured her favourite son.

"I don't know the golf course," said Dora, draping a shawl round her shoulders. "If you don't mind, I'd very much like to see it."

There was silence for a few seconds. The sisters-in-law couldn't believe their ears. Even Milo seemed embarrassed: people weren't in the habit of thwarting Nonna. The old lady looked Dora in the eye. Then, without a word, she went off to supervise the maids who were clearing away the lunch things in the dining room.

IO

Bent double, Milo was rummaging under the counter in search of a missing invoice. He straightened up to find himself face to face with a young British officer in uniform.

"Are you the proprietor?" the newcomer asked. His manner was rather aloof.

"I am."

"I've come for a portrait."

Milo could not conceal his surprise. "Maloumian is just across the way, why not go to him? He's the photographer to the army of occupation."

"I'm not a member of the army of occupation," the officer retorted sharply. "I'm in the Egyptian army."

Milo refrained from pointing out that no one in Cairo drew such a distinction. To quote old Dr Touta's sarcastic *bon mot*: "There are two armies in Egypt: the British army, which is commanded by the British; and the Egyptian army, which is under British command."

Tall and fair-haired, the Englishman looked about twenty-five. His athletic figure was enhanced by his cavalry officer's close-fitting, pale-blue tunic, with its white collar and double row of buttons.

"Aren't you the son of Elliot Bey?" Milo asked.

The other man stiffened.

"How did you know?"

"My family have spent the summer at Fleming for a number of years. I think I once saw you on the beach."

Milo was too interested in people not to have an unrivalled memory for faces. It was only the uniform that had given him a moment's pause for thought. Everyone on the beach knew Elliot Bey by sight. A senior official in the customs authority at Alexandria, he owned a villa on the other side of the dunes: a massive figure of a man who never mixed with the holidaymakers and was accompanied everywhere by a black bulldog. Unlike him, his son seldom came to Fleming.

"Do sit down," said Milo. "May I offer you a coffee? Do you take sugar?"

"Yes, *mazbout*," the Englishman replied. He installed himself in an armchair, stretched his legs, and casually propped his boots on the low table.

"One *mazbout* and one with extra sugar!" Milo called in Arabic to Bulbul, whom he dispatched to the corner café on a dozen such errands a day.

Delighted to be entertaining a British officer, Milo launched into a knowledgeable survey of the beach at Fleming, which now boasted some twenty villas. He spoke of his uncle, Dr Touta, who still went swimming in the sea at the age of eighty. Then there were the doctor's two sons, Maxime the journalist and Alexandre the timber merchant . . .

"They all appear in our annual family photograph. Permit me to show you the one I took last summer." He produced a big cardboard box from under the counter. "Look, Dr Touta is seated in the middle. We should have taken the photograph on the steps of his villa, but exceptional circumstances compelled us to use the beach instead. That's my cousin Alexandre with his two little girls, Yolande and Maggi. Maxime Touta, the journalist, is standing behind them. The woman beside him isn't his wife. She's Madame Mancelle, wife of the director of the Suez Canal Movement . . ."

The Englishman cast a perfunctory glance at the photograph.

Milo's purpose in showing it may have been to mollify him, but he was also proud to associate himself with Dr Touta, with his cousins Maxime and Alexandre, and even more so with Étienne Mancelle, who was regarded as one of the Suez Canal's foremost engineers.

In the course of conversation, William Elliot revealed that he was serving in the 1st Cavalry Regiment and held the rank of captain. Milo gathered that he had joined the army in 1885, just after General Gordon and his men were massacred in the Sudan. The Englishman clenched his teeth when referring to that defeat, which had left such a mark on his fellow countrymen.

"When I think that Khartoum was under siege for nine months, and that we sent him no help in all that time!"

"Yes," Milo said politely, "you've been unlucky in the Sudan."

That was a tactful way of summarizing Britain's series of disasters there. Milo not only knew them in every detail but had added sundry refinements of his own, having told the story a hundred times. The British had only just occupied Egypt in 1882 when a revolt headed by the Mahdi broke out in the Sudan. An Anglo-Egyptian force under General Hicks was sent off to Kordofan to suppress it but was cut to pieces: all that remained on the battlefield was a huge pyramid of skulls. Another force commanded by Baker Pasha was no more successful: only a few hundred men escaped. It was then decided to abandon the Sudan, and General Gordon was appointed to supervise the withdrawal. It was already too late, however: the Mahdi, spurred on by his victories, had encircled Khartoum. Famine reigned inside the walls. The inhabitants ate donkeys, dogs, even rats. "Gordon descended the steps of his residence," Milo's description ran. "A solitary figure, he went to meet his enemies halfway. One of them rushed at him and ran him through with his sabre. The general's head was cut off and taken to the Mahdi. Several hundred warriors thrust their spears into his corpse. Nothing was left of it but a gory, unrecognizable mass."

Bulbul served the coffees, guffawing loudly. Milo gestured to William Elliot to take no notice and changed the subject by asking what he thought of the new khedive. The Englishman gave a sarcastic little smile. He took a sip of his scalding coffee before replying.

"He seems a very well-mannered, very civilized young man. Too civilized, perhaps, if you know what I mean. 'Abbas has the look of a schoolboy fresh from Eton or Harrow. He speaks several languages and has visited several countries — he's even been to the North Pole, it's said — but he's never climbed the Great Pyramid. I doubt if the new khedive is very popular with his subjects, but we couldn't care less about his popularity. Just as long as the country remains peaceful and 'Abbas proves as cooperative as his father . . . "

All that remained at the bottom of William Elliot's coffee cup was a sludgy deposit. It was time to revert to the purpose of his visit.

"What type of portrait would you like?" Milo inquired.

"I want a photograph to send to some cousins in England."

"In that case I recommend a full-length portrait. With a military man like yourself, the effect is superb. The photograph could be in colour, I might add. My wife, who is a painter, takes care of the colouring. It costs more, of course . . . "

At that moment Dora came down the stairs. The Englishman looked pleasantly surprised. He removed his feet from the table and stood up. Then, going over to her with a rather nonchalant air, he shook her hand.

"Captain Elliot is a regular visitor to Fleming," said Milo. "He's here to have his portrait taken. A full-length portrait, correct?"

"Yes, and in colour."

"Please step into the studio, then."

Dora did not like the way the officer had looked at her. His offhand, self-assured demeanour was that of a young European in a conquered country — a handsome man, moreover, and one who took everything for granted. She made a mental note: "Lavender-blue eyes, hair Venetian yellow, very pale complexion." For a full-length portrait, however, she needed full details of the subject's uniform, so she followed the other two into the studio. "Crimson tarboosh," she jotted down in her notebook. "Tunic pale blue, trousers ditto, white piping, gilt buttons with crescent."

"This forest background won't do," said Milo. "I'm going to photograph you in front of the seascape with rocks. That will do admirably, you'll see."

He adjusted the officer's position several times. Then he made him strike a pose: right hand on hip, left hand on the back of a chair, left leg crossed over right. Going up to him for the last time, he raised his chin, then disappeared under the black cloth.

"Quite still, please!"

Captain Elliot froze. All expression drained from his face. He remained rigid for several seconds, staring fixedly at the lens.

Milo took a second photograph of him, this time with the tarboosh in his hand. It was rather an abnormal pose, but no one would find fault with that in far-off Yorkshire.

Afterwards, having relaxed, Elliot asked Dora to disregard the colour of his boots. He usually wore black boots but had put on brown ones for a few hours because the others were being repaired.

"But of course," Milo said gaily. "We can do whatever you wish, that's the advantage of photographs in colour. I mean, if you'd sooner have mauve eyes and ash blond hair . . . "

Captain Elliot burst out laughing. Irritably, Dora wondered if her vocation was to be a British officer's bootblack.

II

Some days later, when Milo had gone to show the Jesuits a school photograph he'd taken, I went into the studio and quietly closed the door behind me. It was late afternoon, and the light had begun to fade. The camera looked big and black in that silent room, which was dimly illuminated by the glass roof overhead. I remained standing just inside the door, breathing in the scent of leather and varnished wood and feeling like the perpetrator of some forbidden act. The studio was Milo's personal domain.

I remembered my forays into the boarding school's deserted chapel. I would sneak in there before supper to savour the smell of incense, the sight of candlelight dancing on silver, and the still more pleasurable sensation that I was defying a prohibition. Kneeling on a prie-dieu, I prepared to bury my head in my hands and feign prayer at the least sign of trouble: Mother Marie des Anges might well have emerged from a side door at any moment, big bunch of keys and all. I had once talked Lita into accompanying me on an illicit visit to the chapel, but she was so mortally afraid that she vowed never to do so again.

Bulbul's heavy tread on the stairs jolted me out of my daydream. I hurriedly left the room, already trying to concoct the explanation I might be called upon to produce.

In the course of the next two weeks I devised several pretexts for entering the studio. Armed with a feather duster, I dusted the camera and gently polished its brass fittings with a piece of silk. I fingered the crank and gingerly operated the handwheel that adjusted the angle of inclination. I endeavoured to tame the monster, unwilling to acknowledge that I found it irresistibly attractive. "It's a docile beast," the Italian had whispered to Milo when relinquishing the shop to him. "It does as it's bidden, but you have to know how to address it." Although Milo had made a joke of that remark when he passed it on, it set me thinking. Photographers weren't mere adjuncts of their instrument, as I had always thought: the initiative was theirs, and the camera could see nothing without them. It was simply a mechanical eye which they could operate as they pleased. But did that reduce the photographer to the status of a mechanic?

"Photography reproduces reality," I had said to Milo some weeks earlier, "whereas painting transfigures it. That's the essence of artistic creation." I no longer believed that either. To capture a face or a landscape on paper by reducing it to black and white — wasn't that a transformation in itself? I was beginning to wonder if the medium of expression I had vainly sought in painting would be granted me by photography.

Painting . . . I was fourteen when my father decided to redecorate the drawing room. All the objects on the walls were removed, among them the fateful miniature, which lay forgotten in a boxroom when the decorators had finished work. Nobody noticed its absence but me, of course, and I was careful not to remark on it.

My mouth had grown no smaller. I continued to loathe my face and contemplate its reflection with dismay, firmly convinced that I was ugly.

A year later, when invited to choose myself a Christmas present, I asked for a paintbox and some brushes. I hit upon the idea quite spontaneously, without giving it any real thought. Besides, I proposed to paint landscapes rather than portraits. Being unable to treat the wound, I tried to scratch its edges.

My modest efforts displayed not a trace of red. That was a colour banned from my palette. In the baskets of fruit I painted, the apples were yellow and the cherries non-existent.

I watched my husband very closely while taking notes for coloured portraits during sittings. When the customer had gone, I always questioned him on points of detail. He replied in the humorous, offhand manner typical of him. "A good photographer's secret," he used to say, "is ten per cent technique, ten per cent artistic sense, and eighty per cent commercial flair."

An old French handbook on photography was gathering dust on a shelf under the counter. The few pages I read one evening gave me a sudden insight into all that Milo had failed to explain. If you make a small aperture in the shutter of a darkened room, the author wrote, the image of objects outside will show up on the opposite wall. For the image to be distinct, the hole must be a fair distance from the wall, and all one needs to capture that image is a sheet of glass coated with silver nitrate, which darkens when exposed to light.

Enthralled, I proceeded to devour the book in bed every night. Milo would snatch it out of my hands with a laugh, blow out the lamp, and smother me with caresses I could not resist, so I contrived to read it during the day. Being limited to technique, however, this handbook supplied no answers to the other questions that puzzled me. How to apportion light on a face? How to emphasize the subject's personality?

"We ought to subscribe to *L'Amateur Photographe*," I told Milo one day. "They say it contains a lot of interesting tips."

"I'm not an amateur," he said irritably.

"It's for me . . . "

He stared at me in surprise.

"Be nice," I said in a coaxing voice. "It would please me so much." He shrugged his shoulders but agreed to indulge me to the tune of twelve francs.

My first copy of *L'Amateur Photographe*, a Paris publication, reached the shop early in May. Its arrival filled me with as much delight as my first doll. I bore it off to the bedroom and leafed through it with feverish excitement, but I was loath to read it too quickly because I knew that the next issue would not turn up for another two weeks.

* * *

L'Amateur Photographe advised beginners not to tackle portraits right away. It was better to familiarize oneself with the properties of light by starting with landscapes. This advice pleased me. After all, even my painting had hitherto been limited to exteriors. I begged Milo to teach me how to operate the field camera. Amused and flattered, he suggested a photographic excursion to the Pyramids the following Sunday.

I chose my outfit several days in advance and prepared two hampers of provisions. For his part, Milo shut himself up in the darkroom on the eve of our departure to load his plateholders. He removed the plates one by one, dusted them with a shaving brush, then numbered them and stowed them in a special bag.

We left on donkeyback at sunrise. Bulbul trotted along in the rear, holding the bridle of the fourth donkey to which our field equipment was secured. Qasr al-Nil Bridge, guarded by its cast-iron lions, was alive with people even at that early hour. Men and beasts passed each other on the metal walkway in complete chaos, making a thoroughly aimless impression. Laden camels were almost invisible beneath their huge loads of firewood.

We soon reached the outskirts of Cairo and set off along the road to the Pyramids. "We'll be there in less than two hours," said Milo, and proceeded to tell me the story of the narrow thoroughfare, which had been hurriedly constructed for Empress Eugénie's visit to Egypt in 1869.

I was intoxicated by the open countryside. This first photographic experiment would leave me with enduring memories of the scent of maize and lucerne, the sound of muffled hoofbeats on a dusty road flanked by acacias. Scattered clumps of palm trees jutted from the plain, which was threaded with little canals. One or two water buffalos grazed beside the road, heedless of the few passers-by.

"There they are, I can see them!" cried Milo. The grey shapes of the Pyramids were coming into view through the branches of the acacias. Cultivated fields had given way to golden sand. Eugénie's road was no more than a narrow track through the desert.

We passed not far from the Mena House, the luxurious oasis where wealthy tourists breakfasted in the shade of eucalyptus trees. Some early risers were already treating themselves to a drive in a so-called sand cart, a broad-wheeled trap drawn by a pony.

Seen in sunlight from nearby, the pyramid of Cheops looked pink and violet. I was struck yet again by its majestic appearance. This was the third or fourth time I'd seen the gigantic mass of stone at close range, but each visit inspired the same thrill.

Some Thomas Cook tourists were just beginning the ascent. Their *galabiya*-clad guides insisted on helping the female members of the party to hoist themselves from stone to stone by seizing handfuls of their ample posteriors. The ladies seemed delighted. I wondered what lunatic had thought up the idea for a funicular to the top of the Great Pyramid. The scheme was said to be ready for submission to the cabinet. Milo, who knew all about it, discoursed on the details with customary enthusiasm.

We set up the tripod some sixty metres from the Sphinx, which I proposed to photograph in three-quarter profile. The strange beast crouched there with its paws embedded in the sand, staring at the horizon. Its time-worn human features were reminiscent of an Egyptian peasant. This wouldn't be a landscape, I told myself, but a portrait.

Having ensured that the camera was perfectly horizontal with the aid of a plumb line, Milo invited me to put my head beneath the black serge cloth.

"I can't see a thing," I said. "It's very blurred."

"Of course it is. You must adjust the focus. Turn the knurled wheel slowly." He guided my hand.

"That's it, that's it!" I cried. "But . . . the Sphinx is upside down."

"That's normal," Milo said, smiling. "With practice, the photographer's eye automatically inverts upside-down images."

I had never read of such a thing in the photographic handbook. Dejectedly, I withdrew my head from under the black cloth. "Oh no," I said, "I'll never get used to seeing a landscape upside down."

"Go on," said Milo, "get under there again."

When I was back under the cloth he placed a small mirror at the foot of the focusing screen, and the Sphinx righted itself. "Ah, so that's it," I said, much relieved. He roared with laughter. I proceeded to turn the wheel with one hand while vainly trying to hold down the cloth, which kept flapping in the wind, with the other. "I think it's all right," I said at length in a hesitant voice.

Milo replaced the lens cap and removed the focusing screen, for which he substituted a sensitive plate. "There," he said, "it's all yours." Controlling the tremor in my hand, I removed the lens cap as carefully as possible to avoid jogging the camera. I counted up to six, but I was so excited that I took an additional second to replace the cap. "I waited too long," I kept saying, very disappointed. "Better overexposed than under," I was sagely informed by the Photographer to the Consulates, who never worried about the odd second either way.

I was eager to photograph the same view with a different exposure, but some Bedouin came up, leading their camels: it wasn't every day they saw a female photographer. Convinced that they were dealing with a tourist, they insistently offered their services in a mixture of French and English. Bulbul tried to shoo them away, but without success. Milo lost his temper and threatened them, but they only smiled. That was when I harangued them furiously in Arabic.

"*Kifaya kidda!* Enough of that now! Go away and leave us to work in peace!"

The Bedouin were dumbfounded that a local woman, who spoke the language of the Prophet, should devote herself to such an activity with her head under a black cloth. Other curious spectators joined them soon afterwards, compelling us to cut our photographic excursion short.

I had, for all that, managed to take half a dozen shots. Milo promised to develop the plates during the week. "Oh no!" I protested. "You must do them tonight. *L'Amateur Photographe* says it's best to develop them the same day, while the impression you meant to convey is still fresh in your mind."

"*L'Amateur Photographe* be damned," snapped Milo, whose one desire since we returned home had been to coax me into the marital bed.

He finally yielded to my insistent demands, knowing that I would refuse him if he didn't.

"But I warn you," he said, "it'll take quite a while!" He retired to the darkroom, grumbling. Having lit the red lantern and called Bulbul all the names under the sun for leaving a bucket of water in the wrong place, he put three dishes on the table and filled them with different solutions. An acrid smell made me sneeze. "You see?" he growled. "It isn't cinnamon tea!"

He removed a sensitive plate from its holder and immersed it in the first dish. The liquid washed over the gelatine. From time to time he lifted the protective sheet of cardboard to see how the image was progressing. I myself, standing on tiptoe, could see nothing. All at once the plate began to go cloudy. Little by little a big dark shape appeared: against a black sky, a mirror image of the Sphinx slowly emerged.

"The Sphinx!" I muttered excitedly. Without a word, Milo removed the plate and let it drip into the dish, then rinsed it liberally in water. "Come over to the fixing bath," he said. I hastened to comply. "No, no! The fixing bath, I said, not the alum bath!" I got the various dishes mixed up, too excited to try to understand. All I could think of was my broken-nosed Sphinx, which had emerged from the darkness.

The plate gradually lost its milky coating in the fixing bath. When it was completely transparent Milo took it out and placed it in the alum bath. "Light the lamp," he commanded. My work was not yet done. "The negative must be left·to soak for two hours," he said brusquely. "Change the water every fifteen minutes. I'll get on with the second plate."

At nine that night the first print, completely dry, was placed in contact with the glass of the positive. Milo inserted a sheet of bromide paper and closed the hinged back of the printing frame. "The negative's too faint," he decreed after a while.

Fearful for my Sphinx, I tensely watched his subsequent procedures. Still ostentatiously annoyed with me, he rinsed the print in a bucket, then immersed it in the toning bath, agitating it continuously. It gradually lost its chocolate hue. My hopes revived.

"Pass me the hydrosulphite!" he called suddenly, as if the sky were about to fall in. "No, not that bottle, the one beside it." He steeped the print in this new bath for another fifteen minutes, then swore: the print was too pale, the printing process would have to be repeated from scratch.

It was past midnight when I finally had all my negatives. "Thank you," I said, throwing my arms around his neck. "I'll look at them calmly tomorrow morning." Then, having given him just enough time to wash his hands, I hustled him up the spiral staircase and into the bedroom. Taken aback by my impetuosity, Milo was all smiles once more. I had never enjoyed our lovemaking as much as I did that night.

"Not a single decent photo," I said the next day, with a pout of annoyance. "They're all overexposed, quite apart from the composition. I mean, look at that horizon."

"What's wrong with the horizon?"

"It runs right across the centre line!"

"So? That's fine."

"No, it isn't! From that point of view, photographs and paintings are the same: the horizon should never be exactly on the centre line. It should be either higher or lower – lower, as a rule, so as to bring out the sky. In *L'Amateur Photographe* . . . "

Milo shrugged. He was beginning to regret that subscription!

Had it been up to me alone, I would have returned to the Pyramids at once, Bedouin or no Bedouin. I'd have beaten them off with my parasol and started all over again.

12

At Fleming that summer, Dora's rounded belly prevented her from accompanying most of the other holidaymakers to Alexandria to witness the khedive's solemn arrival. Dr Touta, who had been consulted, was quite categorical: his nephew's wife, being in her eighth month, could not risk being jolted around on the road to the station, still less jostled by the crowds that would throng the processional route. She would therefore spend the afternoon with her sisters-in-law at Aimé's villa, where she and her husband were staying.

Milo himself had taken a gaggle of children to the Place des Consuls. He was even more excited than they at the prospect of seeing 'Abbas Hilmi.

"The khedive is only nineteen. No sovereign of Muhammad Ali's dynasty has ever come to power so young."

The children had some difficulty in understanding this. To them, nineteen was an advanced age – to some, in fact, it sounded older even than twenty. Yolande, who had just celebrated her tenth birthday, was more puzzled than most.

The khedive was coming to spend the hot season at Alexandria for the first time since acceding to the throne five months earlier. Always well organized, the Europeans of the city had formed themselves into a reception committee, and the fabulously wealthy Monsieur Antoniadis had opened the fund with a subscription of one hundred pounds. As for the native dignitaries, they had failed to agree among themselves and left the decoration of the Arab districts to the goodwill of the inhabitants, who had adorned their balconies with palm fronds and home-made red flags bearing the white star and crescent.

Yolande and her cousins had managed to perch on the edge of one of the fountains to watch the procession approach. The square was ringed by three rows of Chinese lanterns suspended from the trees. To kill time Milo sang excerpts from *Rigoletto* in his own inimitable fashion, attracting sour looks from two European ladies.

"Did you know, children," he said, to enliven the wait still further, "that 'Abbas is a polyglot?"

Their first thought was of some physical disability. It appeared, however, that Tewfiq's successor not only followed opera in Italian but spoke German with his former Viennese schoolmasters, English with the British consul, Turkish with the sultan's representatative, Arabic with his servants, and French with the members of Cairo's high society. That seemed a lot of languages, even to young Syrian residents of Egypt, who switched from French to Arabic and back within the same sentence, knew a few words of English and one or two coarse expressions in Italian, and could say *kalimera* in Greek.

Milo told the children how, in the summer of 1882, ten years earlier, the British fleet had bombarded Alexandria before landing there.

"This handsome square you see now, the Place des Consuls, was just a heap of rubble. Only the statue of Muhammad Ali remained standing. Our cousin Rizqallah seized the opportunity to buy several ruined buildings and replace them with the big store you see before you. A stroke of genius!"

As though in confirmation of his statement, the sky was punctured by the gunfire that signalled the long-awaited arrival of the white viceregal train at Sidi Gaber station. The crowd stirred restlessly, but another good half-hour went by before an immense clamour made itself heard: the khedive's carriage and four was entering the square by way of Franc Street, preceded by forty lancers and a mounted detachment of Egyptian police with a British officer at its head. The whole of the processional route had been strewn with fine sand.

Moving at a walking pace, the carriage had some difficulty in forging a path through the crowd. Milo and the children shouted *"Ya'aish Effendina!"* and showers of multicoloured confetti rained down from the balconies. 'Abbas was resplendent in his white *fariq's* attire. Raising one gloved hand in a leisurely gesture, he saluted the members of the Khedival Society, who were assembled on a balcony with their families.

Following the cortège, which included a closed landau occupied by the dowager khediva, came a band and one battalion of the Egyptian army, then a British military band and a contingent of troops drawn from the army of occupation. A few people jeered as the latter marched past, but their voices were drowned by the band of the Frères des Écoles Chrétiennes, whose pupils were arrayed on a stand.

"I saw the khedive! I saw the khedive!" cried Maggi, Yolande's little sister, from her vantage point on Milo's shoulders.

When darkness fell, Sherif Street lit up like a trail of fire: the Lebon Gas Company, the Anglo-Egyptian Bank, the Châlons department store, the palace of Mazloum Pasha. Overhead, rockets exploded into multi-coloured showers of sparks.

"Did you know that Queen Victoria will be celebrating her seventy-third birthday in London tomorrow?" said Milo as he shepherded the rather sleepy children to the station for the train ride back to Fleming.

Seventy-three against nineteen . . . The khedive did indeed seem young by comparison. The newspapers had just announced that Sir Evelyn Baring, the British consul general in Cairo, was to be elevated to the peerage in Her Majesty's birthday honours. The most powerful man in Egypt would henceforth be known as Lord Cromer. It was an inexhaustible topic of conversation.

"Why Cromer, Uncle Milo?" asked young Maggi.

"It's the name of the place where he was born, sweetheart."

She thought for a moment, then: "So will the Mameluka's baby be called Lord Fleming?"

Dora's labour pains began at three on the morning of 10 August. Panic reigned. Milo, accompanied by one of his brothers, took the carriage and whipped the horse into town. The midwife awoke with a start and haggled over her fee. The brothers resorted to entreaties, threats, promises. By the time they got her back to Fleming, little Nelly had already been born. Aunt Angéline's injunctions were still ringing in Dora's ears:

"Push, my angel! Push, my love! Push, I said! In the name of God, push!"

On seeing the baby at Helwan some weeks later, Nonna took care to ward off the evil eye by making repeated allusions to its ugliness:

"*Wihsha! Wihsha!*"

As for Milo, he never tired of extolling his daughter's beauty. As thrilled as he had been when announcing his engagement the previous summer, he held the swaddled infant on high as if posing for an invisible camera.

"Milo's overdoing it," murmured his sisters-in-law. "She's only a girl, after all."

The family photograph of 1892 shows a smiling young woman seated on the left of the front row with a little bundle in her arms. The photographer has obviously based his composition on her alone: to her right, Alexandre Touta is short of an arm and Angéline Falaki has lost half her ninety kilos.

At that age, Nelly was neither ugly nor beautiful. The boys of the family took absolutely no interest in their young girl cousin. It was her mother on whom they bestowed all their surreptitious glances, hoping to catch a glimpse of brown flesh at feeding time. They forgot to breathe when the Mameluka slowly undid the buttons of her bodice, cupped her slender hand around a breast heavy with milk, and proffered it to Lady Fleming's ravenous mouth.

While the Touta clan was being enriched by a new addition, the khedive spent an agreeable summer at Alexandria. The newspaper regularly reported his activities of the previous day at the head of the gossip column. 'Abbas Hilmi had gone sailing outside the harbour . . . 'Abbas Hilmi had gone riding out at Abukir . . .

To get from one palace to another the sovereign himself drove a light conveyance, and the children were always hoping to find themselves on his route. They sometimes spent whole hours waiting beside the gravelled road on the other side of the dunes, knowing that he had a special liking for Montaza Bay. After all, rumour had it that he intended to build a chalet there.

"A chalet? You're joking!" said Milo. "It'll be a regular palace in the middle of a vast estate."

"But there are three khedival palaces at Alexandria already," it was pointed out. "The one at Ras at-Tin, the one at Ramlah, and the one on the Mahmoudiya Canal, aptly known as Palace Number 3."

"'Abbas doesn't care for any of them. He wants a Palace Number 4."

In accordance with custom, the entire court had accompanied the khedive to Alexandria and taken up its summer quarters there. The round of receptions and parties was endless. Several members of the government including Tigrane Pasha, the Armenian minister of foreign affairs, were staying at the Hôtel-Casino San Stefano, whose reputation had steadily increased as the years went by. Even the cabinet had taken to meeting there.

"Only an operetta cabinet would meet in a casino," growled old Dr Touta.

13

The operetta almost turned into a drama some months later, when 'Abbas unexpectedly decided to change prime ministers. Change prime ministers without the say-so of the British consul? Lord Cromer was flabbergasted. He politely explained to His Highness that such things weren't done. In any case, the khedive was wrong to have chosen Tigrane Pasha: he was a Christian and, as such, unacceptable to the people. But the khedive stood firm, knowing that Tigrane's principal demerit in Lord Cromer's eyes was that he didn't happen to be an anglophile. This unprecedented clash was the talk of Cairo.

"Who does 'Abbas think he is?" said Captain William Elliot, when he visited the shop to order another photograph. "We could depose him at any moment. Without our support, that boy would lose his throne in three months flat."

Several pashas were sufficiently alarmed to call on the youthful khedive and remind him that the British consul in Egypt was the country's real master. His impulsive act fell little short of a *coup d'état*, they pointed out, but 'Abbas remained adamant.

"It'll end in tears," said Milo.

A compromise candidate for the premiership was finally found, but the specious façade that had been maintained for ten years was cracked beyond repair: the British could no longer claim that they were occupying Egypt to buttress the khedive's authority.

"Lord Cromer has managed to get an additional British battalion sent to the banks of the Nile," Captain Elliot told Milo. "It's a warning. Sooner or later, His Highness will need a good hiding!"

By holding out against the British authorities, 'Abbas had become a national hero overnight. Delegations from all over Egypt flocked to the palace to pay their respects. Students attending Cairo's law school gave him an ovation, while those at the school of medicine went on strike against their British teachers.

"I've never known such a thing," said Nonna. "Up to now, whenever people came out on the streets, it was to boo the khedives, not defend them. Young 'Abbas amazes me."

Some young Egyptians tried to bear him along in triumph during prayers at the mosque. The next day he was expected at the opera house, where *Aïda* was to be performed in the presence of the entire diplomatic corps. Every seat was snapped up, and some of the boxes held as many as nine operagoers — even the side aisles were jam-packed with standing figures. 'Abbas arrived just as the curtain fell on the first act. The audience leapt to their feet and broke into thunderous applause. The khedival anthem had to be played four times.

The French residents of Cairo were delighted that the British should have suffered such a rebuff. This Milo learned from a new customer, Norbert Popinot, who had come to be photographed with his wife. A short, plump man in his late forties, Popinot was an export–import merchant with a shiny bald pate and the serene and cheerful countenance of someone beloved of his bank manager. He dressed smartly, and his handshake left one's palm smelling faintly of vetiver.

"What do you expect?" he said with a spuriously sorrowful air. "The British have failed to win the hearts of the Egyptian people. It's ten years since they landed here, and they're still exactly where they were. They've brought a little order into the country, made the system of taxation a little fairer, and distinguished themselves as engineers where irrigation is concerned, but the people have no love for them. The fact that no one wants to learn their language proves it. The country's finest schools are French. You yourself, I imagine —"

"Yes, I'm an old boy of the Frères."

"Of course, of course."

Milo wanted to add that he was also photographer to the Jesuit Fathers, but Popinot had the bit between his teeth.

"When you consider, my dear sir, that in order to attract enough readers the *Egyptian Gazette* is compelled to print half its pages in French! Some comedown for an English newspaper, you must admit! Even British civil servants are obliged to write in the language of Molière when addressing notes to Egyptian government departments!"

A Parisienne, Madame Popinot was self-evidently younger than her husband – she looked no more than thirty – and far from unattractive. With her rippling laugh, sensual mouth and ample bosom, she seemed to carry all before her.

The couple wanted a double portrait in black and white, so Milo seated them on the ottoman side by side. He had no need to ask them to smile: Monsieur and Madame Popinot displayed the gaiety of people who enjoy life to the full. Being lovers of novelty, they had pushed open the door of the Studio Touta rather at random. It struck them as more amusing than to have themselves photographed by Jacquemart, who received customers by appointment only.

"You work for the French consulate?" asked Norbert Popinot.

"No, not the *French* consulate," Milo replied, without dwelling on the subject.

A baby's cries could be heard as they emerged from the studio.

"My daughter," Milo explained proudly. "If you can spare a moment, I'll introduce her to you."

He hurried upstairs to fetch Nelly. The Popinots, who had no children, declared themselves charmed by the baby. She was panting a little with a dummy in her mouth.

"May I offer you something to drink?" asked Milo, indicating the spiral staircase.

Dora greeted them in the drawing room. They were still there an hour later. Solange Popinot much admired the huge plant that occupied one whole corner of the room. Quite spontaneously, she sat down at the piano, which was very seldom touched, and played a brief waltz. Milo amused the visitors by recounting some details of life in the civil service, which he knew from his brothers.

"It's true that a British civil servant gets through twice as much work as an Egyptian," he said, "but why should he be paid three times as much?"

"Well said, well said!" exclaimed Norbert Popinot. He went on, in his mellifluous voice, to present an account of the consular High Mass that he and his wife had just attended.

"The French minister had invited all our compatriots to assemble in the Agency's reception rooms, as he does four times a year – yes, four times a year, at Christmas, Easter, All Saints, and Whitsun. Even the freemasons make it their duty to attend. At this distance from the motherland, the dispute between Catholics and laymen becomes nonsensical. I mean, could the Third Republic have a finer advertisement in Egypt than the religious colleges and boarding schools we spoke of just now?"

The Popinots proceeded to describe the High Mass in a kind of duet.

"A long line of carriages was waiting outside the consulate. The French minister boarded the first of them, and the procession set off."

"You should have seen the faces of a party of English tourists as we drove past! How they stared at us! The inhabitants of the Arab quarter are used to such spectacles."

"The minister entered the Roman Catholic church in the Moski preceded by eight *kawaases* wearing baggy blue trousers and little gold waistcoats."

"They struck the flagstones with their silver-topped canes. It was charming."

"The minister was flanked by two national deputies. He was brought the Gospel and the crucifix to kiss."

"All the same," said Solange, "two hours of sung Mass is on the long side."

"Yes, my dear, but what a thrill it was to hear the *Domine salvam fac rem publicam Gallorum* sung three times on Egyptian soil by the whole of the little French phalanx!"

The Popinots, who entertained a great deal, invited Milo and Dora to a soirée at their home the following Sunday. Milo, gratified by this chance to consort with the French, accepted on the spot.

"You might have consulted me first," Dora told him when the others had left.

But she, too, felt attracted to this easygoing couple who were suddenly expanding her horizons.

14

The Popinots' home was a luxurious apartment opposite the Khedival Club in Manakh Street. Their guests were welcomed with warm smiles and a few words of French by grizzled Egyptian servants belonging to that breed of exceptionally devoted retainers whom the French of Cairo seemed to have handed down from generation to generation.

The décor of the reception rooms mirrored their owners. Norbert's affluence was detectable in the thick carpets and fine pieces of furniture, whereas the profusion of knick-knacks bore the mark of Solange, with her fanciful nature and thirst for novelty.

This party at the Popinots', of which Milo had expected great things, proved a thorough disappointment. No one took any notice of him. Being accustomed to attentive audiences who hung on his every word and laughed at all his jokes, he felt completely ignored. Norbert and Solange made a point of introducing the couple to all their other guests and mentioned that Émile Touta was a photographer, but it was a waste of breath.

"Oh, so you're a photographer," drawled more than one elegant Frenchman, looking him up and down. "Personally, I go to Jacquemart."

Milo would then feel obliged to utter some trite remark about his illustrious competitor and pay him a reluctant compliment. His listeners barely heard him out before turning to some other guests as if resuming a conversation begun at another party the night before. The only person to linger at his side, having learned that he belonged to the Greek Catholic community, was an elderly professor from the French law school. The professor, who took a keen interest in the history of the oriental patriarchates, asked a number of questions about the origins of the Melchite Church. Milo was quite unable to answer them, nor did they interest him in the slightest. He made three attempts to change the subject and mentioned in passing that he was a photographer, but the monocled academic, who was intrigued by certain aspects of the imperial firman of 1848, wanted to know why Greek Catholic priests had for so long worn hexagonal headgear, whereas those of their Greek Orthodox counterparts were perfectly round.

"Because the Greek Catholics have always been more elegant than the Greek Orthodox," explained Milo.

The old jurist gave him an odd look and walked off, shaking his head.

Although a centre of attraction, Dora felt like a fish out of water. She was still too young and inexperienced to be interested in such a social set. A Frenchman of about forty, who had been watching her intently from the other end of the drawing room, came over, introduced himself, complimented her on her dress, and asked if she had any children.

"Yes," she replied, "have you?"

Soon afterwards a young man with curly fair hair tried to engage her in a rather risqué conversation about the nudity of oriental danseuses. Having told him quite curtly that the subject didn't interest her, she went for a solitary stroll on the veranda.

"I'd like to go home," she told Milo a little later.

This rather suited Milo. He went to make his excuses to the Popinots, pleading that his wife was tired. Sorry to see the young couple go, Norbert and Solange saw them out and promised to get in touch again at the first opportunity.

"My coachman will drive you home," said Norbert. "No, no, I insist. We mustn't let Madame Touta catch cold."

Once in the carriage, Milo regretted having left so soon. After all, he had just lost an opportunity to make himself known and expand his clientele. He told himself that he ought to have been himself, shown more courage, criticized Jacquemart – indeed, torn him to shreds. Back home he remained in a foul mood for the rest of the evening.

"You're not even looking at me," said Dora, pouting provocatively.

She was seated at her dressing table in a lace nightdress with a very low neckline that barely concealed her breasts. Milo caught sight of her reflection, and his face relaxed at once. Slowly, he came up behind her, rested his hands on her bosom, and bent to kiss her neck.

"We mustn't let Madame Touta catch cold," he said softly.

A long tremor ran through Dora's body as she watched Milo's hands caressing her in the mirror. She shut her eyes from time to time, and her face tensed. A first wave of pleasure engulfed her even before he carried her over to the bed.

15

We awoke later than usual. The maidservant was already busy with Nelly, and Bulbul had opened the shop. Snatches of conversation drifted up from below: Oscar Touta had come to have his photograph taken. Milo hastily got dressed and went downstairs.

"Here I am, uncle!"

"What's the meaning of this?" the ageing bachelor demanded angrily, seeing him descend the spiral staircase. "Have you given up working on Tuesdays?"

When I came downstairs twenty minutes later, Oscar had just flounced out of the shop and slammed the door behind him. Unable to endure the eye of the lens upon him, he had panicked yet again.

"Why are you tilting the camera like that?" he had asked Milo in an apprehensive voice.

"So as to centre you, uncle."

"Oh, so you're centring me, are you? If you think you can hoodwink me just like that . . . "

The shop door was still vibrating. Milo shook his head and smiled, then launched with gusto into an excerpt from *La Traviata* that threatened to shatter the windows.

Having restrained myself for two days, I thought this a good time to broach my request.

"You were wondering what to give me for my birthday. Well, I've had an idea . . . " Then, after a moment's embarrassment: "I'd like a plaster bust."

Milo stared at me. "To photograph, I mean. A plaster bust to practise on."

He almost lost his temper. Not that I knew it, he had just committed a secret extravagance in the shape of some diamond earrings. Alfred Falaki, his jeweller uncle, had agreed to be paid in three instalments, interest-free, but in order to pay the first of them Milo had parted with a watch bequeathed him by his father, and he didn't really know how he would raise the other two.

A plaster bust? Yet another whim undoubtedly inspired by the magazine to which he had been weak-minded enough to subscribe on my behalf! "Not even I, a professional," he said in an erudite tone, "needed a plaster bust to help me learn my trade. Neither a bust *nor* a magazine, for that matter!"

He found it incomprehensible that I could devote so much energy to a mere pastime, so much care to setting up the field camera on our little terrace when taking views of Cairo. All things considered, however, he preferred to see me amuse myself in this way rather than argue with him over the relative merits of painting and photography.

That was a subject on which I pondered alone from then on, aided by my reading matter and my practical experiments. "The same landscape photographed by two different people will produce two unrelated negatives," stated *L'Amateur Photographe*. I was now convinced that the said difference stemmed less from technique than from the operators' sensitivity.

"Photography doesn't just record the world," I told Lita Tiomji. "It beautifies and elucidates it, so to speak." My friend continued to fan herself in silence. She was clearly devoid of ideas on the subject.

In accordance with the magazine's advice, I had started to keep a photographic diary in which I carefully recorded the date and time of each shot, the lighting, the exposure, the type of plate employed, and, last of all, a remark such as "Overexposed, rather grey" or "Jogged it, reshoot on isochrono". Milo found this particularly amusing. "My sisters and sisters-in-law keep cookery notebooks," he said. "At least they're good for something!"

I continually had to remind myself that photography and painting were two different things. I was more than once led astray by colours, rhapsodizing over the green of a palm tree or the orange of a sunset, neither of which would contribute to the photograph when developed. As time went by I learned to see nature in black and white, light and shade, as if it were a monochrome drawing.

I was now impatient to try portraiture. Writing in *L'Amateur Photographe*, a distinguished member of the Photo-Club de Paris explained the extent to which faces could be modified by the judicious use of lighting. He suggested practising on a plaster bust, which had the advantage of never altering its expression. This enabled one to make an exact comparison of the results obtained by different shots.

Would I have suffered less as an adolescent had I sat for a photographer rather than a painter?

My first dance at the age of sixteen. I was cured of my agony of mind by a pimply youth whose name I cannot even recall. "You've got the loveliest smile I've ever seen!" he told me. "Don't make fun of me!" I retorted angrily. The stupefaction on his face spoke volumes. I hurried to the cloakroom to examine myself in a mirror. My mouth was unlike any other. My fingertips caressed it with a kind of affection. It struck me as vital, vibrant, sensual. I decided that I was beautiful, and from then on I saw myself as such whenever men looked at me. Later on, Milo confirmed this feeling every time he laid eyes on me, caressed my cheek with the back of his hand, or kissed me full on the lips.

When my birthday came he handed me a little package. "I'd already bought you these earrings," he said, almost apologetically. So he was giving me two presents. I wept despite myself.

I was forever practising on my plaster bust during the exhilarating weeks that followed. Early in the morning before opening time I would hurry to the studio and place Apollo, as I christened my model, on a high stool.

I studied it through the lens from every angle, tilting the camera and varying its proximity to the subject. Seen at very close range, Apollo had a big mouth and wide-set eyes; at a distance, these characteristics were reversed. Again, depending on the camera's angle of inclination, the figure became either spinning top- or pear-shaped. At other times I would tilt the bust itself by means of a chock. Seen from above, the nose became elongated; from below it looked shorter, but the nostrils showed up in an unsightly manner. "I haven't got one Apollo," I told myself enthusiastically, "but twenty!"

I discovered yet another twenty by experimenting with light. All I had to do was vary the main lighting by means of the glass roof's sliding curtains and the secondary lighting cast by the reflectors. I now knew how to emphasize or efface individual parts of the bust and lend it a three-dimensional effect. "Light can do anything," I kept telling myself. "Light is a magician."

I had often been struck by a paradox while watching Milo at work. On the one hand he immobilized his sitters and reduced them to corpselike rigidity; on the other, he strove to "animate" them by compelling them to smile and photographing them against an artificial background. My plaster Apollo, lit with care in front of a plain backcloth, looked far more animated than one of my husband's customers stiffly posed in front of a raging sea.

"I'm ready," I said one Saturday morning.

"Ready for what?" asked Milo, who was shaving with his big cut-throat razor, his cheeks still covered in foam.

"Ready to take some portraits. Would you sit for me when you've finished?"

"But I'm not dressed."

"You'll do just as you are, I promise you."

He regarded me with a smile. "What do you propose to do, photograph me like a monkey in front of a forest background?"

"No, no forest, no background at all. The grey curtain will be enough."

"I'm flattered."

I sat him down in the arabesque armchair and undid the top two buttons of his shirt. His amusement steadily increased. He had difficulty in concentrating, not that this worried me overmuch. He was astonished to see me press the bulb on two occasions without getting him to strike a pose.

"That's an odd portrait you've taken of me, I must say. Shall we begin again?"

"No, that won't be necessary."

He shook his head, looking thoroughly perplexed.

I was anxious to develop the photographs myself. I spent half the day in the darkroom, breaking off only to feed Nelly or satisfy myself that the nursemaid was taking good care of her. I was very upset to find, after rinsing the first negative, that it was hazy. Had the exposure time been too long? Trembling, I added a little hydroquinone to the dish, and – heaven be praised – the next plate did not mist over.

In high excitement, I saw Milo's face gradually take shape. The lights and shades were very well defined, the only fly in the ointment being the shirt collar, which was askew. Although tempted to retouch the negative, I decided to leave it as it was.

My husband reacted like most of his customers: he thought he looked awful, whereas I thought the opposite. "I should have retouched your nose," I told him with a laugh. "I should have tip-tilted it and put a blob of lather on the end. I could also have rouged your cheeks and turned you into a complete clown – and charged double."

16

Dora was steadily losing interest in colouring portraits. "I feel as if I'm making up dead bodies," she said.

She knew from *L'Amateur Photographe* that this hybrid technique was going out of fashion in Europe, where pioneers were endeavouring to perfect genuine colour photography. The shop was not doing well enough to warrant a reduction in its takings, however, so she continued to wield her brush in the cubbyhole with dwindling enthusiasm but growing dexterity. She was busy at the retouching desk one morning in February 1894 when the shop door opened with its customary clatter of saucepan lids.

"I've come to have my picture taken," a man's voice said in Arabic.

Bulbul emitted a guffaw, but Dora was quick to appear.

"Do you take portraits?" asked the young man who had just entered, this time in French.

"Yes, of course. My husband is out, but he won't be long. Perhaps I could begin by taking down your name and address."

"My name is Seif 'Abdel-Latif, and I live at 42 Clot Bey Street," the young man said gravely.

The sight of Dora had clearly thrown him out of his stride. A scrawny youth of about twenty, he had a thin moustache that failed to mature his boyish features, but there was an almost disconcerting hint of steel in his piercing gaze.

"What type of portrait would you like?" Dora inquired.

"The simplest and quickest possible. I need it for an administrative formality."

She could have dealt with the matter herself, but Milo would certainly have been annoyed. Besides, how would this young, austere-looking Muslim have reacted to the sight of a woman operating a camera?

While Bulbul trudged to and fro in the background, laden with buckets of water, she tried to engage the visitor in conversation. He proved to be a law student.

"Was it your school that welcomed the khedive?" Dora asked, for something to say.

Seif 'Abdel-Latif's face lit up.

"Yes, we were the first to welcome 'Abbas after his accession to the throne two years ago. We read him a poem – a very fine poem, but poetry isn't enough, not after this latest business with the British."

He seemed to be seething inwardly. Dora had heard reports of the khedive's eventful tour of Upper Egypt, like everyone else, but she didn't feel tempted to pursue the subject. Milo turned up in the nick of time, complete with smile, sweeping gestures, rolling sentences, and the latest gossip about the government. It took him only a minute or two to take charge of the conversation.

"I can tell you exactly what happened in Upper Egypt," he said to the young man. "I have it from an excellent source."

Seif frowned, poised to counter at once with his own version of the facts, but Milo was too quick for him.

"The khedive made a triumphal trip to Aswan."

"I know."

"The stations all along the route were decorated, the platforms lined with vast crowds. Horsemen mounted on magnificent beasts galloped ahead of the train, rivalling it in speed."

"I'm aware of all that," said the young man, eager to get to the heart of the matter.

"But first," Milo went on, assuming a mysterious expression, "there was an incident at Aswan of which no one has spoken. It happened during a visit to the hospital."

"I know."

"The khedive criticized the interpreter's Arabic pronunciation and condemned the incompetence of the British officer in charge of the establishment."

"He had every reason!"

"No doubt," said Milo, always ready to agree with a customer. "Anyway, things came to a head at Wadi Halfa, while the khedive was reviewing a battalion of Egyptian troops. 'These men are in a disgraceful state,' he declared. Then, turning to the commander in chief of the Egyptian army, he added: 'To be frank, Kitchener Pasha, I consider it shameful for Egypt to be served by such an army.'"

"Quite right too!"

"That was when General Kitchener tendered his resignation."

The law student jumped to his feet.

"Can you explain to me why the British have turned this minor incident into an affair of state? I know the reason: it was simply to humiliate the khedive."

"You're not wrong," said Milo. "Lord Cromer jumped at the opportunity. He'd been waiting months for an excuse to make the khedive pay for last year's government crisis, and also, no doubt, to demonstrate his power. Kitchener withdrew his resignation and 'Abbas was obliged to congratulate the commanders of the Egyptian army – in writing – on their men's excellent turnout."

Seif was outraged. "It's incredible!" he said. "The khedive actually apologized to his own army. He should never have given in."

"But he might have been deposed."

"Well, every patriotic Egyptian was disgusted by the affair, let me tell you. It's bound to have repercussions."

Dora, listening to them as she sorted out some invoices behind the counter, was struck by the young man's menacing tone.

"Perhaps you'd care to step into the studio," said the Photographer to the Consulates. "This way."

When they emerged twenty minutes later Dora was chatting with Norbert

Popinot, who had been passing. The businessman was smartly dressed in a dark suit and a bowler hat. Milo introduced his two customers to each other.

"Ah," said Seif, "you're French." Then, without more ado: "I can't understand why France failed to back the khedive in this latest dispute with Cromer."

Norbert Popinot was not a man to be easily flustered. "You can't?" he said suavely, all smiles. "For Egypt's sake, my dear sir, that's why. Our consul put it very neatly at a party the other night. His Highness's attitude, he said, must not be allowed to serve the British as a pretext for tightening their grip on Egypt. Remember last year's government crisis: Lord Cromer took advantage of it to send for an additional battalion of British troops."

Seif shrugged disdainfully. He was about to make some scathing rejoinder, Milo could sense it. To defuse the atmosphere he told of a newfangled contraption, invented by an American, that would shortly be on sale in Cairo.

"It's a treadle-operated phonograph — looks like a sewing machine. They say you can hear it play a cornet solo."

Seif 'Abdel-Latif was wholly uninterested in this subject. He took his leave, saying that he would pick up his photographs in two days' time.

Milo looked contrite when the time came: an error in the developing process had rendered the negatives useless. It was, he said, a genuine and almost unprecedented mishap.

"I shall take some more photographs of you," he told Seif. "You won't have to pay a piastre. My establishment presents them to you with its apologies."

The student was furious, having no time to waste on another sitting, but he could not resist the photographer's disarming tone. Milo, who had already sent Bulbul to fetch two coffees, ushered his visitor into the studio.

"Please sit down, this won't take long. Did you know that photographic studios in Europe are always situated on the top floor? Yes indeed, because of the light. In this part of the world we tend to have too much of it."

Seif refused to be mollified. "That French friend of yours came out with some strange arguments," he said after a while. "I mean, if French policy in Egypt amounts to keeping the British sweet in the hope that they won't behave any worse . . . "

"Quite, quite," said Milo, "but you really ought to have another chat with Norbert Popinot. He's a very nice man, and one who has numerous contacts in the French colony."

Milo was thinking less of Seif than of Popinot himself. He had sensed two days earlier that the Frenchman regretted being unable to pursue his conversation with this rebellious young man and convince him of his country's good intentions.

"Yes," he persisted, "you ought to have a talk with Popinot. I say, it occurs to me that he and his wife will be here on Wednesday evening. Why not come too? It's just an informal little gathering."

"I don't go to parties," Seif replied caustically. "I don't care for them. In any case, I have to study for my final examination."

"Head up a little, please. A little more. Perfect. Quite still now!"

"Your diploma comes first, of course," said Milo when they emerged from the sudio, "but you don't have to spend the whole evening with us. Look in for half an hour, say. That way I'll be able to hand over your photographs and save you further inconvenience. Our apartment is above the shop. Knock whenever it suits you."

Seif turned up at nine o'clock, at the same time as the Tiomjis, and stayed until midnight. A practising Muslim, he curtly declined to sample the chilled Muscadet the Popinots had brought and drank nothing but water or fruit juice. His observance of religious precepts was as strict as his political ideas were uncompromising. Doubtless because he was under Dora's spell, however, he more than once allowed himself to be carried away by the gaiety of the proceedings, which were enlivened by a Milo at the top of his form. Solange Popinot, who became bored by lengthy political discussions, took care to interrupt them with a few chords on the piano.

Without meaning to, Richard Tiomji made everyone weep with laughter by describing the problems he had with his ostriches.

"At first I thought the right thing to do was to build them some pens, but the stupid creatures panicked whenever their keepers made the slightest movement. They raced around like mad things and hurled themselves head first at the walls. It was an absolute massacre, damn them! I told myself I'd have done better to breed donkeys. I had to demolish the pens in a hurry and cut down all the trees. The birds were split up into groups of fifteen or twenty and confined in small enclosures to prevent them from picking up speed."

Someone asked Richard if it was true that ostriches hid their heads in the sand when cornered by hunters, so as not to see the danger that threatened them.

"Speaking for myself," Seif said gravely, "I deplore France's ostrichlike policy in Egypt."

There was a momentary hush before Norbert Popinot, like the good sport he was, cried, "Bravo, well said!"

17

The success of this gathering prompted Milo to hold regular Wednesday soirées. A dozen guests, or sometimes more, would assemble over the shop every week. These were not dinners properly speaking: Dora prepared some *mezze* and Popinot supplied the liquid refreshment. Impassioned arguments about the merits and misdeeds of the British alternated with charades and party games. There was always someone ready to recite a poem or sing a song. Conjured from the piano by Solange Popinot's nimble fingers, arpeggios rang out con brio, filling the room with joyous abandon. And, when Milo launched into an aria from one of his favourite operas, the pianist would utter cries of protest and laughingly accuse him of bursting her eardrums.

Milo was extremely proud of having French acquaintances. At Helwan he never failed to impress the family with his frequent allusions to Popinot, whom he referred to as "Norbert". He found their relationship reassuring, as if some of the impunity enjoyed by the European business-man rubbed off on himself. He admired Popinot for his sound financial position and regular income. Having lived from hand to mouth for years, the Photographer to the Consulates was beginning to see light at the end of the tunnel. The simple fact of consorting with a man like Popinot made him feel as if he were joining the privileged few.

To all this, Solange added a touch of modernity and panache. With her daring dresses, full-throated laugh and uninhibited language, the French-woman personified the Paris of Milo's dreams, nor was he insusceptible to her charms. As for Dora, she benefited from the presence of this childless and emancipated woman whose rather exceptional status enabled her, Dora, to seem less conspicuous. Besides, Solange was to do her a great service in the course of the coming months.

Although Dora liked her portrait of Milo very much, its defects became clear to her the more she delved into *L'Amateur Photographe* and a new handbook ordered from Paris. The line of the shoulders should have been horizontal. As for the left ear, it protruded in a rather unsightly manner. She ought to have left it in shadow.

In order to progress she needed to take more photographs of other subjects. Her friend Lita Tiomji would gladly have sat for her, but Richard was terribly jealous and could not endure the thought that his wife's picture might be exposed to eyes other than his own.

"He loves me too much, *chérie* . . . "

Dora then thought of Solange Popinot, who had already received her twice at her Manakh Street apartment. She didn't feel particularly at ease with the Frenchwoman, whom she considered a vamp and suspected of ogling men, notably Milo. Solange was the most readily available of her female acquaintances, however, so she decided after some hesitation to enlist her services. Ever eager to try anything once and thoroughly titillated by the idea of acting as a model, Solange agreed with alacrity.

In the studio Dora hung some plain fabric in the background: all that mattered was the person to be photographed. Unlike Milo, who seemed anxious to reproduce every stitch of the arabesque armchair, she began by seating the Frenchwoman on a simple, backless stool. She also dispensed with the neck-clamp, a device which in her view robbed a subject of all expression. The danger, of course, was that the photographs would turn out slightly blurred, but that didn't worry her.

The next day Solange turned up in a daringly low-cut dress.

"I'd like to try taking you on the ottoman," Dora told her.

Solange curled up on it like a cat. Dora took several photographs without ever uttering the fatal "Quite still, please!"

"I've brought a feather boa," said Solange. "Shall I drape it round my shoulders?"

"Why not? But this time, perhaps, sit down in the armchair."

This second series of shots took a good twenty minutes.

"And now, how about standing up?" said Dora.

While adjusting the camera she chatted to Solange about Nelly's milk teeth, the new hosiery stall in Khan al-Khalili, the next fair at Helwan.

"Forgive me," she said, "setting up this shot may take some time."

Solange had let go of her boa while waiting for Dora to complete her preparations. Bare-shouldered and with one hand resting on her cleavage, she seemed to be holding on to her dress to prevent it from falling down. And that was how Dora snapped her.

In the darkroom, detailed examination of Solange Popinot's full-length portrait revealed a few imperfections. Ought she to have reduced the intensity of the overhead lighting? The Frenchwoman's head was slightly lowered, as luck would have it, so the lighting didn't overemphasize her forehead and the bridge of her nose. In any case, the portrait's most striking feature was the subject's pose, or lack of it. Its originality lay in its spontaneity.

Milo got a shock when he saw this daring photograph, in which Solange seemed to be concealing her nakedness. He pronounced it indecent, not that he could tear his eyes away from it. Dora, who did not share his opinion, decided to show her model that shot only.

Solange was delighted with the portrait. She had it framed and prominently displayed in her drawing room. Since the Popinots entertained a great deal, many members of Cairo's French colony got to see it.

"Who took such a wonderful picture of you, my dear?" Solange was asked.

"The Studio Touta in Ezbekiyah Square," she replied. She made no mention of Dora, either because feminine coquetry prompted her to imply that she had charmed some man or other, or because she was at pains to advertise the services of the Photographer to the Consulates himself.

Whatever the truth, Milo built up a small French clientele in the months that followed. Among the new acquisitions he proudly listed were the librarian of the Archaeological Institute and the wife of the proprietor of the Pâtisserie Mathieu.

The saucepan lids clattered more often. On some days, thanks to all the photographs to be taken and developed, Milo could no longer afford to spend a couple of hours in the café, playing backgammon.

"Perhaps I could take some photographs when you're out," Dora suggested one night.

"Why not?" said Milo, after a moment's thought. "It might be amusing."

She threw her arms round his neck.

Thereafter she spent more time downstairs in the shop, developing her own negatives, than on the floor above. Milo congratulated himself. He had found an efficient collaborator who practised her profession with enthusiasm and attracted custom. He himself won more frequently at backgammon, as if his greater sense of freedom made him throw the dice with more élan.

Dora was careful to consult her husband as often as possible. She asked his advice whenever a photograph displayed special features or its development presented problems. He delivered his verdict in a categorical tone, not always advisedly, then dismissed the subject from his mind. Dora was not obliged to follow his recommendations. As time went by she learned to rely on her own instinct, even at the risk of making mistakes she would subsequently avoid.

Milo used to serenade her with the "Toreador" song from *Carmen*, modifying the words to accord with her new occupation. Dora was happy to be alive and very much in love. The young couple would sometimes exchange lingering kisses in the studio when a customer had left. On one occasion, when Bulbul was out, they even made love on the cushions at the foot of the ottoman, heedless of the gaze of the monster with the Cyclopean eye.

18

The shop's accounts began to look quite respectable. Now that he had no more real financial worries, Milo was in fine fettle. He excelled himself during family gatherings at Helwan, forever holding his audience spellbound with his revelations, comments, and bold predictions. The khedive's trip to Constantinople in the summer of 1894 was one of his tours de force, and everyone listened to it enthralled.

"The British tried to dissuade the khedive from paying the sultan a second visit, but 'Abbas was looking for an opportunity to thwart them with his overlord's support. Besides, he'd thoroughly enjoyed his first trip to Constantinople the previous year. The sultan had welcomed him like a son, showering him with gifts and decorations."

"The sultan can afford to shell out a few medals," observed Alfred Falaki, the jeweller. "Egypt pays the Sublime Porte an annual tribute of 750,000 Turkish pounds."

"Quite so! This summer the khedive inadvertently left his medals behind in Cairo. That's why he got such a chilly reception during the first banquet given in his honour at Yildiz Palace. The sultan barely favoured him with a glance. The atmosphere gradually relaxed, however, and 'Abdel-Hamid seated him on his right at the dinners that followed."

"But that's the grand vizier's place!"

"Exactly, so the grand vizier contrived to be absent. At table, whenever the sultan addressed him, the khedive rose and bowed low."

Milo's listeners were no longer in Nonna's dining room at Helwan, but in the sultan's banqueting hall at Yildiz, under the stern gaze of giants in gold-encrusted uniforms with big suns emblazoned on their chests.

"The sultan had permitted 'Abbas to smoke in his presence, but whenever the khedive tried to talk politics the Commander of the Faithful changed the subject."

Milo went on to describe, in a similar wealth of detail, the earthquake that had rocked Constantinople during this visit.

"It must have been just after noon, because the muezzins were calling the faithful to prayer from their minarets. 'Abbas was lunching with a dozen members of his retinue when a violent tremor brought the massive chandelier crashing down. Several people were injured. The khedive, who had never experienced an earthquake before, was panic-stricken. He shinned down a ladder into the garden and joined the sultan, who himself had taken refuge in the middle of the palace grounds. Meantime, in the city, the minarets were swaying and buckling. Some of them collapsed, taking the muezzins with them. Thousands of people fled from the bazaar . . . "

What a visit it had been, and it wasn't over even then. Milo kept the best bit — the subject that interested his listeners most — till last. He gave two versions of it, an expurgated one for the women and children, and another, more detailed one for the menfolk to relish over coffee in the smoking room.

"The khedive's mother was hell-bent on marrying him to an imperial princess. She had travelled to Constantinople ahead of him and put in weeks of hard work to that end. Her machinations were so successful that the sultan finally offered 'Abbas the hand of one of his own daughters. Overjoyed, the dowager khediva ordained three days of festivities. But 'Abbas didn't share her enthusiasm in the least: he was in love with Iqbal, a beautiful Circassian slave ten years older than himself."

Milo paused to let his listeners catch their breath.

"At that point, the grand vizier went to see the sultan. 'Your Majesty,' he said, "Almighty God will assuredly permit your beloved daughter to bear a son. What will become of the child? Will the British not be tempted to proclaim him Commander of the Faithful in your place?' The sultan realized that he'd been on the verge of making a serious mistake. Somewhat sheepishly, he sent word to 'Abbas that objections to the marriage had arisen. Overjoyed, 'Abbas hurried off to inform his beautiful slave."

"And the dowager khediva?"

"She was beside herself."

"I'm not surprised," said Nonna.

But the children were all on the side of lovely Iqbal, who, having borne the khedive a daughter some months later, persuaded him to marry her.

"In the khedive's place," said Dora, "I'd have married Iqbal right away, without waiting for the sultan to refuse me his daughter."

"What about his poor mother?" exclaimed Albert's wife, turning to Nonna in quest of approval.

The other sisters-in-law chimed in with similar expressions of amazement that any man could disregard his mother's advice in such a way.

But Nonna, swilling the ice around her glass of arrack, merely murmured, "Perhaps the young khedive was right after all."

Dora discreetly savoured her victory. She was aware that her sisters-in-law had a poor opinion of her, especially since getting wind of her photographic activities. One of them – René's wife – had felt emboldened to go to Milo and tell him how little she approved.

"Your wife is bringing the family into disrepute. People will think you can't afford to support her." Seeing him shrug his shoulders, she went on, "At the very least, you should forbid her ever to enter the studio alone with a man."

The family spoke of Dora's work in whispers, as if it were some shameful disease. Did Nonna know of it? On arriving at Helwan this time, the Mameluka had been struck by the old lady's grim expression and wondered if one of her sisters-in-law had maliciously put her in the picture. Relations between Nonna and her youngest daughter-in-law were complex enough as it was. Dora had displayed her independence on more than one occasion. The two women seemed to be engaged in mutual observation and appraisal. Theirs was a trial of strength, but they also appeared to understand each other with little need for words despite the forty-five years that separated them.

The wives of René, Albert, Aimé and Joseph called their mother-in-law "Aunt". Dora, who thought this custom ridiculous, had immediately adopted "Nonna", the children's name for her. The old lady did not take offence at this, nor did Milo, who felt closer to his nephews than to his brothers.

Even outside the family circle, the young woman's entry into the profession did not escape censure. One afternoon in October a new customer called at the shop to be photographed. A bulky Greek in a tarboosh, he kept dabbing at the big beads of sweat that trickled down his forehead. Without more ado, Dora invited the fat, perspiring man to step into the studio and sat him down facing the camera.

"Where's the photographer?" he demanded irritably, while she was adjusting the focus.

"I'm the photographer," she told him with a smile.

He leapt to his feet with a look of outrage. "Oh no, not that!" he cried, and, as he made for the door, "Dirty beasts! I should have been more careful! And I thought this was a respectable establishment!"

Bulbul's sudden guffaw convinced him that he was indeed in a house of ill fame. "You'll never get to Paradise! I shall report this to the consulate!" he bellowed as he slammed the shop door behind him.

Milo frowned when told of the incident. Dora was surprised by his worried expression.

"I shall lose the consulates' custom," he said gravely.

"The consulates' custom?" she protested. "But you've never had it!"

Milo took umbrage at this.

Dora put off telling her parents about her photographic activities. Léon Sawaya was quite capable of going to Milo and making a terrible scene. Although her brothers and sisters knew she spent long hours on their little terrace with the field camera, or even in the studio, they regarded this as merely a hobby.

Lita Tiomji was the only person to whom she could unburden herself, but even Lita had her doubts. "I don't know, *chérie*, if a housewife can afford to do what you're doing." She sighed before adding, "But then, you've never behaved like everyone else . . . "

That year the housewife added fuel to the flames by giving birth to a second child. Another girl, the baby was christened Gabrielle.

19

Captain Elliot had lost his heart to Dora at their very first encounter. He contrived to pay three more visits to the shop in the ensuing year, accompanied each time by a brother officer who wanted his photograph taken.

"Maloumian had better change his shop sign," chuckled Milo. "He can take the consulates and leave me the army."

Having learned on his most recent visit that Dora herself took photographs on Tuesday and Thursday afternoons, William Elliot decided to treat himself to another portrait. Attired in a dark blue uniform tunic adorned with a single row of buttons, he presented himself at the shop towards three o'clock one Tuesday afternoon in March. Dora was annoyed not only by the way he persisted in looking at her, but, in equal measure, by his casual and contemptuous treatment of Bulbul. He curtly ordered a coffee and tossed him a coin as he might have thrown a dog a bone.

The fact was, however, that this athletic young man in uniform flustered her more than she would have cared to admit, even to herself. It may have been because he was English. As a girl, she had often dreamt of marrying a European.

"I'm sorry," she told him, "but we've given up doing portraits in colour."

"Never mind," he said with a smile. "I prefer black and white anyway."

"In that case," she said, to hide her embarrassment, "let's go to the studio."

He sat down on the chair and struck a pose.

"No," she said, "there's no point in posing at this stage."

Surreptitiously observing him as she got the camera ready, she sensed that he was watching her every movement.

"Turn your head a little to the left," she said. "A little more. I'd prefer you to be looking into shadow. That's right. You can relax now. We'll adjust your pose when I've finished focusing."

As soon as she bent over behind the camera he slightly turned his head in her direction. They gazed at each other thus for a good twenty seconds, she with one eye, he without seeing her face. Feeling rather embarrassed, Dora tilted the camera downwards until it came to rest on his hands, which in turn were resting on his knees. They were strong, shapely hands with immaculate fingernails. The camera wasn't a barrier, as she had thought a year ago. On the contrary, the viewfinder brought her close to her subject – so close that she was almost touching him.

Slowly, the lens travelled upwards to the officer's chest, his throat, his chin . . .

"Do you mind about your uniform?" she asked.

His look of surprise prompted her to be more precise.

"I mean, do you want your uniform to show up in the photograph? I prefer to leave the details of a person's clothing in shadow, as a rule."

"You can do as you like with me," he told her, lowering his voice a little.

She wondered afterwards if those words had contained some double meaning, but she didn't know English well enough to be sure.

Dora was busy in the studio when William Elliot came to pick up his portrait two days later. Milo found him in exceptionally high spirits.

"I've heard some details of Slatin's escape," said Elliot. "It's an incredible story."

For days now, all Cairo had been talking of nothing but the Austrian Rudolf Slatin, who had managed to escape from the Sudan after twelve years in captivity. Barefoot and dressed as an Arab, the former governor of Darfour had turned up at an Anglo-Egyptian frontier post in the last stages of exhaustion, after twenty-four days on the run.

"Slatin was very harshly treated to begin with," Elliot went on. "A few hours after the fall of Khartoum, when he was already a prisoner, they brought him General Gordon's head wrapped up in a bloodstained cloth. However, the conditions of his imprisonment were relaxed as the years went by. Converted to Islam and renamed 'Abdel-Qader, he became a servant to the khalif, the Mahdi's successor. He spent his days outside the khalif's door, ate the scraps from his table, and ran barefoot beside his horse. Like all the khalif's entourage, he had to attend prayers in the great mosque at Omdurman five times a day. That was where one of our local agents managed to contact him. His escape was set for the night of 20–21 February. Slatin knew that his absence wouldn't be noticed until prayers at dawn, so he had a few hours to play with before the alarm was raised. When he presented himself at the frontier post twenty-four days later, he burst into tears and told them, 'I'm 'Abdel-Qader.' He was too overcome with emotion to give his real name. Our officers recognized him. They opened some bottles of beer and the garrison band struck up the Austro-Hungarian anthem."

Dora came out of the studio accompanied by an extremely ugly lady wearing a hat adorned with feathers.

"I hope you're pleased with your portrait?" she asked Elliot.

"It's remarkably good. I shall shortly have to have another taken to send to an uncle of mine in England."

"Really? They must have a whole album of you over there," Milo couldn't resist saying, although he wasn't in the habit of urging moderation on his customers. Then, still smiling, "When the Austrian arrives in Cairo, bring him to see me. He might go to Maloumian by mistake."

It was Jacquemart who took Rudolf Slatin's photograph.

Given a hero's welcome in Cairo and taken charge of by the British authorities, he was received in audience by the khedive, who elevated him to the rank of pasha. And, because a pasha could not be a junior officer in the Egyptian army, he was promoted colonel and granted twelve years' back pay. His mentor, Major Wingate Bey, took him to Jacquemart to have an official portrait made despite his scant liking for the French. It was hard not to have Slatin done by the palace photographer when Queen Victoria herself was eager to make his acquaintance.

Slatin Pasha's lecture to the Khedival Geographic Society on 30 April 1895 was one of the highlights of the season. Three hundred people attended it in the great chamber of the Mixed Courts, which had been lent for the occasion. Lord Cromer and General Kitchener were seated in the front row, amid elegant ladies who strove to combat the heat by energetically fanning themselves.

The speaker appeared to be in good health. His lecture, which had been drafted in German but translated into French, drew great applause. Although he read the text aloud in a calm voice, he stumbled over certain words. His knowledge of English and French had deteriorated during his years in captivity. Discounting his mother tongue, he seemed at ease only in Arabic.

Slatin presented a detailed account of the Sudan's various tribes. He spoke expertly of the Batahin and the Barabra, the Shilouq and the Danagla. William Elliot, who was at the back of the hall, listened intently, whereas the ladies in the first few rows were suffocating. Lord Cromer gestured to the attendants to open the windows wider.

The khalif's ex-prisoner passed swiftly over the circumstances of his capture and escape, promising to describe them at greater length in a book. To the ladies' relief, they saw him turn over the last page.

"Transported into the midst of civilized society," he said, "I have become a man among men once more. I often think back. I picture fanatical barbarians, the deserts of the Sudan, the dangers I have escaped, and I give thanks to God, whose protection has brought me here."

His thirsty listeners applauded him loudly, then made a beeline for the buffet.

"Slatin Pasha's book is an oddity," Milo disclosed some time later. "He writes in German, it seems, being an Austrian, but his draft is being translated into English by a Syrian — yes, a Syrian, we're everywhere! — before being rewritten in his own way by Major Wingate. It's also being retranslated in the other direction, because the final text will be published in German."

If the British authorities attached so much importance to the story of Slatin's captivity, it was doubtless to maintain the diabolical image of the Mahdists or prepare the public for a reconquest of the Sudan.

"We shall avenge Gordon," Captain Elliot declared on his next visit to the shop. "And Slatin Pasha will be the first to enter the fray and guide us to the khalif's lair."

"But would another war of conquest be really worthwhile?" Milo asked.

"Of course! Egypt needs to control the Upper Nile — everyone has known that ever since the time of the pharaohs. The masters of the Sudan could parch Egypt by diverting the river, just as they could swamp her by damming it and releasing all the water at once."

"That's a bit strong," said Milo. "Do you seriously believe the Mahdists capable of building dams?"

"Certainly not the Mahdists, but a foreign power could seize the Sudan. Unless Anglo-Egyptian forces retake the country, someone else will move in."

"France, you mean?"

"France, Italy, Germany, Belgium — everyone's interested in Black Africa these days."

"If I understand you correctly," said Milo, "we must expect to see another expeditionary force sent against the Mahdists."

"No, no, there's no question of sending a fourth column to be massacred in the Sudan. Next time it will be a genuine war of reconquest waged by all appropriate means. We must crush those savages once and for all."

20

William Elliot was not the only person to pay the shop an occasional visit. The photographic studio, which was conveniently situated in the heart of the city, had become a kind of natural port of call where people dropped in to have a chat and enjoy a cold drink or a coffee. Some used it as a rendezvous, others made new acquaintances there. That was how, one afternoon, Norbert Popinot came to have an unexpected set-to with one of Lita's uncles. The latter, a maladroit amateur photographer who ruined all his negatives, had brought some plates to be developed. Hearing Popinot's French accent, he expressed his admiration for Ferdinand de Lesseps, of whom a gigantic statue was to be erected at the mouth of the Suez Canal.

"Don't talk to me about Ferdinand de Lesseps!" Popinot exclaimed. "That individual deserves to be called a great Englishman, not a great Frenchman. His Suez Canal has guaranteed the British Empire total domination of the seas. But de Lesseps wasn't content to present it with that princely gift: he then went off to Panama to work for the Anglo-Saxons. Should a statue of such grotesque dimensions be erected in his honour on the very spot that marks our adversaries' triumph?"

Lita's uncle stared at him wide-eyed.

Milo valued this lively atmosphere, which lent his establishment an appearance of intense professional activity. The same could not be said of Jacquemart's studio, where clients arrived by appointment, one by one, to be greeted by a liveried commissionaire who ceremoniously opened the door for them. At Maloumian's, on the other hand, there were quite a lot of comings and goings. In addition to Britishers in uniform, his visitors had for some time included furtive, worried-looking Armenians in shabby overcoats. These survivors of the Turkish massacres did not come to be photographed by their compatriot. They were seeking employment or, failing that, letters of recommendation.

"They're down-and-outs," Richard Tiomji declared with a contempt that disgusted Dora. "They have no business in Egypt."

"Today it's the Armenians," she retorted curtly. "Thirty-five years ago, some of our relations fled here from the massacres in Syria."

"Well, I don't trust Armenians," Lita's husband said in a peremptory tone.

On such occasions Dora would happily have hurled something at his head.

Late one Monday morning in April, Solange Popinot caused a sensation by turning up at the shop on a bicycle. She entrusted her contraption to Bulbul, who looked thunderstruck, and begged for a drink of water. Her ride to Shubra Palace and back had left her dying of thirst, she said. She was wearing a boater, a waisted jacket, and, beneath her skirt, a pair of culottes tucked into some knee-length black leather gaiters. Milo thought she looked most amusing – very attractive, too, with her exertion-flushed cheeks.

For some months now, smart shops in Ezbekiyah had been displaying bizarre costumes imported from Europe and designed for cyclists of the fair sex. Ladies would pause in front of their windows and exclaim at the sight of Zouave trousers, hygienic corsets, or skirts convertible into culottes with the aid of knicker elastic, but few of them ever ventured into town in such outfits.

Donkey drivers had been dumbfounded to see the Frenchwoman pedal past. In Shubra Street, some young male cyclists had amused themselves by zigzagging round her, but without extracting a single cry of alarm.

"My legs are absolutely numb," Solange said gaily, having drained a whole jug of cold water. "I don't know if it's all my pedalling this morning or the ball at the French Agency two nights ago."

"Tell us about the ball," said Lita, who was fascinated by social functions.

"Oh, it was sensational! Norbert estimated that there were five hundred people present, including several princes of the khedival family. A big oriental tent with a wooden floor had been put up in the garden to serve as a ballroom, and leading up to the veranda were two staircases erected for the occasion. All the men had musical flowers in their buttonholes – they gave out harmonious chords when you blew on them. You should have seen all the ladies puffing at strange men as they walked past! It was an absolute scream . . ."

Meantime, Bulbul was circling the bicycle. "Stop prowling round that machine," Milo told him in Arabic. "Go and get the French lady another jug of water."

"The ball commenced at eleven with a quadrille of honour in which the consul general and Madame de Villebois had Madame Cogordan and the Duke of Saxe-Coburg-Gotha as their opposite numbers. The programme comprised eight waltzes, two polkas, a *pas de quatre*, a lancers, and, to end with, a grand cotillion. At four in the morning, tables and chairs were carried out on to the veranda, which was transformed into a supper room. The truffled pheasants *à la Périgord* were a trifle tough, perhaps, but Norbert found the Château Margaux exceptional, and you know how particular he is when it comes to wine . . ."

Lita's eyes had grown steadily wider.

"The cotillion began at about two, under the leadership of the Comtesse de Serionne. We indulged in some very amusing new steps and figures. A lady towing a cushion on a ribbon was pursued by several gentlemen, who tried to sit on it. The successful competitor earned the right to dance with her. How we laughed! In another figure, a fair-haired doll in a ball gown was placed in the middle of the floor beside a lady who chose one of two men as her partner. The other had to dance with the doll. Just imagine, Norbert got the doll! It made me feel quite odd to see him embracing that pretty, blue-eyed blonde . . . The cotillion concluded with the entrance of Mademoiselle Prévost in a magnificent sleigh filled with bunches of violets, which she tossed at all present. We didn't get home till five. Needless to say, I spent the whole day in bed."

Milo pictured the attractive cyclist flat on her belly and yawning into her pillow, buttocks bare.

"You'll be going back to bed, no doubt," he said with a rather dreamy expression. "Your bicycle ride must have tired you out."

"No, I'm going to treat myself to a bath at the hammam."

"The hammam?" Lita exclaimed in alarm. These European women were really incredible!

"I know a very clean hammam near the Qasr al-Nil barracks," said Solange, "but you have to get there early and avoid Fridays. The masseuses are unrivalled. They soap you, rub you down, make all your joints crack one by one. Then they anoint your body with sweet oils and knead you interminably. A divine sensation!"

Dora had gone over to the bicycle. "Would you let me try it some time?" she asked Solange.

Milo had difficulty getting to sleep that night. He was haunted by visions of Solange Popinot divesting herself in turn of her ball gown, her cyclist's outfit, and her nightdress, then entering a sweltering room, stark naked, and abandoning herself to expert hands whose touch impelled her to moan with pleasure.

21

After several invitations, Seif 'Abdel-Latif had ended by regularly attending the Wednesday soirées whenever his militant activities did not detain him elsewhere. The young lawyer, who had recently obtained his diploma, seemed to look upon the Toutas' salon as a political club. More earnest in his demeanour than ever, he continually reverted to the British occupation.

"Egypt isn't India," he declared one night. "In Bengal the British neutralized the rajahs by soaking them in alcohol. Here they have no hope of success. The Egyptians are a temperate race, they only drink the water of the Nile."

Richard Tiomji gave a raucous laugh. "That's why they catch bilharzia," he said.

Seif glowered at him. He had nothing but contempt for the ostrich farmer, with his hairy hands and shiny signet ring.

"Nile water is the best in the world," he retorted sharply.

"That's true," said Milo, who was anxious to avoid a row. "Did you know that Egyptian pashas take some with them to the Bosphorus whenever they spend the summer there? The sultan himself is reputed to have several flasks delivered daily for his personal consumption."

"Talking of drink," Popinot said to Richard, "try this burgundy."

The ostrich farmer sniffed his glass like a connoisseur, then dipped his bushy moustache into it. He wasn't the sort to deliver a qualified verdict on anything. His vision of the world was Manichean in its lack of complexity. To him, there were simply good wines and bad, respectable folk and beggars, well-made fans and trash, Greek Catholics and the rest of humanity. Despite his simplistic attitude, however, there were times when Dora found his presence reassuring and could better understand Lita's air of serenity. Her friend's children seemed to have found fixed reference points in this black-and-white world in which all had their role, each object its place, and every idea its diametrical opposite.

Although he refrained from arguing with Richard, Seif made up for it by listening to Milo's shop assistant with great attention and setting store by his most trivial remarks. "Bulbul tells me that a lot of Armenians have been calling on Maloumian," he would say, or, "Bulbul considers bicycles dangerous", or, "Bulbul fears a Mahdist offensive on the Sudanese border . . . "

"I really don't know what he sees in that imbecile," said Milo, who found this astonishing.

Dora thought she understood. Seif saw Bulbul as an embodiment of the people, as living proof of a deranged country on the road to regaining control over its own destiny — not that this prevented the personification of Egypt from guffawing whenever Seif addressed him.

The young lawyer spoke with great admiration of Mustafa Kamil, a former contemporary at law school whom the khedive had singled out and sent to complete his studies at Toulouse. Late in 1894 he had returned to Egypt even more of a militant nationalist than before, so the palace had discreetly given him some money and instructed him to go back to Europe, there to wage a propaganda campaign against the British occupation. Seif spoke of these things in a rather mysterious manner. It seemed clear that he was privy to secret meetings between Mustafa Kamil and the French of Cairo, the khedive's Swiss secretary, and possibly the khedive himself.

One Wednesday the young lawyer turned up in high excitement. He had just received excellent news from Paris: Mustafa Kamil had presented a picture to the president of the French chamber of deputies.

"A picture?" said Milo, raising his eyebrows.

"Yes, a picture of Egypt being oppressed by the British. I can actually show it to you, because six thousand copies of it were printed."

He put his hand in his pocket and brought out a folded sheet of paper. The drawing was so crude, it might have been done by a child. It showed a young woman in a long gown standing on the steps of a Greek temple.

"That's France, the liberator of oppressed peoples," Seif explained.

At the foot of the picture were several captives wearing chains and guarded by a lion. The leader of the Egyptian delegation, a young man in a tarboosh, was handing France a petition.

"Isn't it superb?" asked Seif, and he went on to claim that the French deputies had been most impressed by this *démarche*.

Dora refrained from commenting, but Milo loudly pronounced the drawing "very fine".

That night she had a peculiar dream. "My friend Mustafa Kamil is homesick," Seif told her in an ominous voice. "I must help him."

"You could give him a photograph," Dora replied.

"A photograph?"

"Yes, a photograph of yourself."

Seif thought for a moment. "That's a good idea," he said. "I'd like to be photographed with Bulbul."

Dora was forced to comply. She sat them down on the ottoman side by side. Seif, armed with a whip, insisted on the backcloth of rocks and stormy seas, but a Greek temple appeared in the lens. It was late, and the light was insufficient. Bulbul had hysterics whenever the magnesium flash went off.

22

Milo stared at me in bewilderment. "Reorganize? What do you propose to reorganize?" Prudently, I only mentioned the creation of a proper waiting room. That, I explained, was the only way of instilling a little order into the shop. Customers seldom came alone. Their companions would no longer disturb us at our work by waltzing in and out of the studio. They must be made to stay put somewhere, for instance by giving them photograph albums to look at. The room where Bulbul stored our equipment would do very nicely. "Jacquemart has a waiting room, and so does Maloumian,"I emphasized, knowing that this was the only argument likely to sway my husband. He mumbled something and left the room. I had won.

I negotiated the price myself with a small builder. While work was getting under way, I bought a sofa and two old armchairs from a second-hand dealer in the Moski and had them reupholstered. The future waiting room was furnished. All that remained was to frame a few Studio Touta portraits to brighten the walls.

The closure of the shop for a two-day public holiday enabled me to take an additional step — one that Milo had no good reason to oppose: the tidying of the darkroom. I had suffered for some time from his messy way of leaving things in heaps on the two wretched tables. These had to be cleared during every developing session to make room for the various dishes. Accidents often occurred during the fixing or alumizing processes. When flasks overturned, as they readily did, the walls of the darkroom rang with the operator's oaths.

"I'll leave you with the workmen," Milo told me when he learned of my intention to tackle the darkroom. "I've no wish to lose my temper, and my mother will be delighted if I pay a brief visit to Helwan."

With the help of Bulbul and a workman, I began by emptying the darkroom of all the furniture and objects it contained. Parts of the room were revoltingly dirty. The heavy chest of drawers in which various liquids were stored had never, from the look of it, been moved. We had to rip up the linoleum, which came away in shreds and had dissolved in several places. At my request, Bulbul swept the floor thoroughly and disinfected it twice with dilute carbolic. Finally, when the room was clean, I called one of the painters, who set to work at once.

Milo couldn't believe his eyes when he got back late that afternoon: the walls of the darkroom were dazzlingly white. "Are you out of your mind?" he shouted. "How are we going to develop our negatives?" I explained to him as calmly as I could that it was not only pointless but a positive disadvantage to have a darkroom with dark walls. All that mattered was the nature of the light emitted by the lantern. A dark wall was no protection against the actinic rays from an inappropriate form of lighting, whereas white walls diffused the light and avoided accidents. Milo chose to ignore these technical explanations, which meant nothing to him. "Very well," he told me, as if speaking to a child who had just made some crass mistake. "If the negatives are ruined, it'll be your responsibility. I don't intend to get involved in this business. Tomorrow I shall spend all day at the café."

Sounds of sawing filled the courtyard until noon the next day. I had given instructions for several work-tops and numerous shelves to be cut. One of these shelves was reserved for chemicals, another for tins of polishing powder, mirrors, plateholders, and various darkroom accessories. Yet another was to hold empty flasks, funnels, filters, graduated measures, and all the small utensils we used when mixing solutions. Part of the work table was taken up by a sheet of zinc with raised edges. This formed a kind of sink that enabled liquid waste to be drained off through an outlet pipe. Screwed to the wall was a reservoir equipped with a tap beneath which prints could be rinsed.

I spent the afternoon carefully labelling the jars and flasks. I inscribed the name of each liquid in capitals on glazed paper, using Indian ink and taking care to note the relevant formulae. I affixed these labels with gum arabic, then coated them with liquid paraffin to make them damp-resistant.

The "tidying" of the darkroom was complete.

I realize that all these measures – and those that were to come – may seem part of a very elaborate, carefully devised plan. Although some people said as much later on, I progressed by instinct alone, adapting myself to circumstances. It was the difficulties I encountered, some of them recurrent, that drove me to modify the scope of our work.

"While we're about it," I said to Milo one night, "what if we take the opportunity to modernize the studio itself?" He looked dumbfounded. Then he decreed that the studio was perfectly all right as it was. I replied, as gently as possible, that it could be improved, and that I had drawn a diagram.

I held out my drawing, but he didn't even look at it. "You mean you still haven't finished?" he shouted. "Are you mad, or what?"

I took my drawing in both hands and slowly, with a rather histrionic gesture, tore it in half – once, twice, three times, until it was reduced to confetti. Then I burst into tears. Milo stalked out of the room, fuming, and slammed the door.

I was already in bed when he returned an hour later. He undressed and lay down beside me without a word, quite prepared to accept the apologies I had no intention of making. At half-past midnight we were still lying there, gritting our teeth and unable to sleep. I was too proud to make the first move. He ended by resting his hand on my stomach in an ambiguous way. Loving, proprietory? It could have been either. Moments later, unable to restrain himself any longer, he pressed up against me. Our lips promptly sought and found each other. He smothered me with caresses through my nightgown. Then he undressed me with feverish haste, and I felt myself transfixed by the strength and warmth of him.

"You upset me earlier on," I told him softly, when the oil lamp was lit. He started to protest. "Will you really not take a look at my plan?" I whispered in his ear.

"But you tore it up."

"I might be able to recreate it."

Taking a pencil from the bedside table, I drew a sketch on the last page of the photographic diary from which I was never parted.

"As things stand," I said, "we can't move the camera back far enough. That makes group photographs very awkward. By moving this section of wall back into the storeroom I'd gain three metres." Milo shook his head in dismay. "What's more," I went on, "we need more sources of light. The only one we have at present is the glass roof. I suggest dividing it into an alternation of dark and light zones by means of opaque shades."

"You're out of your mind, honestly!"

"And here," I said, tapping the spot with my pencil, "I'd insert a frosted glass door opening on to the yard. With that as a luminous background, one could obtain some wonderful Rembrandtesque effects."

He was starting to lose his temper again. All these whims of mine would cost a fortune, he insisted. Far from it, I assured him: the builder had already given me an estimate. Mollified by our lovemaking, Milo shook his head and left it at that.

The workmen tackled the studio the very next day.

I used the little that remained of my dowry, together with my own savings, to fulfil another of my dreams: the purchase of various accessories essential to photography of high quality. Heedless of Milo's sarcastic remarks, I sent to Paris for two screen reflectors, a pinhole viewfinder, and some bifocal glasses. I also ordered a novel device called a photometer.

"The photometer enables you to determine the correct exposure time," I told my husband as I unpacked the instrument with care. It was a sort of miniature telescope, partly covered in morocco leather and ending in an eyepiece. "After focusing," I explained, "you get under the black cloth, place the photometer against the focusing screen, and centre your eye on the eyepiece. Then you turn the ring, like this, until the luminous patch seems about to disappear. All that remains is to read off the number of seconds indicated by the arrow."

But Milo had ostentatiously looked away. A professional of his calibre didn't need a telescope to photograph his customers.

23

The rearrangement of the studio enabled me to improve my portraits considerably during the early summer of 1895. In particular, I learned to adjust the lighting to accord with the personality of each subject. To do justice to a gentle cast of feature, for example, I carefully balanced my light sources. To emphasize the virility of a face, on the other hand, I accentuated the contrast between light and shade, even if the effect I obtained had to be corrected at the developing stage.

When purchasing equipment I had been reluctant to acquire an "eye-catcher" of the kind that was supposed to make one's subjects relax and hold their gaze. Jacquemart, who regularly photographed the children of Cairo's upper crust, had installed a clockwork bird that twittered when wound up. Adults were allowed a small, mobile mirror in which to adjust their expression and watch themselves while being photographed. Maloumian, who was less sophisticated, confined himself to holding the gaze of his military customers with a picture of St George slaying the dragon. For children he had installed a Punch puppet discreetly operated from behind.

On reflection, I dispensed with an eye-catcher for fear of its artificiality, that being the quality that worried me most. Similarly, I reacted against Milo's methods by making it a rule not to retouch my negatives. "That," I maintained, "is cheating."

I should add that my husband went pretty far in this respect. He even boasted, a few months after we married, of having brought a dead man back to life. On the day in question he was summoned to the Faggaala district of Cairo, where the relatives of a just-deceased paterfamilias wanted him photographed before he was consigned to his coffin. Milo was ushered into a darkened bedroom redolent of candlewax and roses. Without hesitation, he set up his camera facing the deathbed, drew back the curtains, and opened the shutters. Then he suggested turning back the hands of the clock to the exact time his subject had given up the ghost. The latter was dressed in a dark suit, and all his rings had been rammed on to his fingers. For once, the operator had no need to say, "Quite still, please!"

On taking delivery of their prints next day, the family evinced disappointment: the dead man looked a little too dead for their taste. Milo's suggestion that he should "open his eyes" was enthusiastically approved. He returned to the shop and closeted himself in the cubbyhole to perform this operation. I uttered a cry of horror when I saw the result of his retouching, but the family were so delighted that they paid the additional fee without demur.

My reasons for ruling out retouching on principle vanished the day I read an article signed by a talented photographer who had won an award at the Paris Salon. The camera, he explained, does not see as we do: it sees too well, so to speak, and thereby distorts reality. Its excessive precision deserves to be corrected by means of retouching. Why, for example, retain freckles invisible to the naked eye? Swayed by this argument, I took to spending time in the cubbyhole I had until lately used for colouring.

"I only retouch in order to tone down technical exaggerations," I used to say apologetically. "The subject must be protected from the camera's overly revealing eye." So I sometimes took the liberty of smoothing out a puckered lip, attenuating a prominent vein, preventing a dimple from showing up as a dark indentation, or eliminating the stray hairs that had escaped from a coiffure. On the other hand, I forbade myself to turn up the corners of a drooping mouth, or even to obliterate the shadow underlining the lower lid. By doing this, as he systematically did, Milo flattened the cheek and robbed the eye of its roundness.

Thinking back on the picture of myself as a child, I wondered why the painter had enlarged my mouth and thickened and reddened my lips. He had caricatured me, I realized on rediscovering the famous miniature in a boxroom at my parents' house, but this distorted image of myself had ceased to worry me. Indeed, I had hung it on the wall beside my dressing table and would sometimes contemplate it with affection.

Photographers were as capable as painters of caricaturing a face, I told Lita, but they could also emphasize its beauty and disguise its flaws by reproducing it from the best angle and in the most favourable lighting. "Not everyone is beautiful, *chérie*," she replied. "There's beauty in every face," I said. "It's up to the photographer to bring it out."

I was worried, for all that, by this enhancement of appearance. Wasn't enhancing a face tantamount to belying its true nature? The question nagged at me for some time. Then I realized that it was a false question. "I don't try to beautify faces," I wrote in my notebook one night. "I try to strip off their masks — to lay them bare, as it were."

This wasn't always easy. I sometimes felt I needed to wield a hammer and chisel to smash the screen behind which certain sitters of mine took refuge. I had some resounding failures. There were even two or three occasions on which I hesitated to show my customers photographs that struck me as disconcerting, but my personal tastes and those of the public were not necessarily the same. Conversely, it sometimes happened that a customer would refuse to pay because he failed to recognize himself without his mask.

One morning, twin boys were brought to me to be photographed on their eighth birthday. Not only were they dressed alike, but they made the same gestures and smiled simultaneously in an identical fashion. One was merely the mirror image of the other. I asked their mother to be good enough to wait outside while I took them into the studio. There I contrived to address them as individuals. Taken aback by this, they stared at each other, rather at a loss. I returned to the attack several times and persisted in distinguishing between them. They ended by reacting differently. One was amused by this novel situation, the other seemed to find it thought-provoking.

In the photograph, one of them wore a beaming smile while the other looked pensive, almost solemn. Their mother was furious. "What did you do to them?" she exclaimed when she saw the result some days later. I tried to defend my photograph, but she became more and more upset. Reluctantly, I dug out a plate I'd eliminated at the developing stage – one on which the twins were indistinguishable.

I did, however, derive a great deal of satisfaction in June 1895 from photographing a French academic whom we had met at the Popinots' two years earlier. He was the law school professor whom Milo had offended by his flippant response when questioned about the origin of the headgear worn by Greek Catholic priests. Directed to our shop by Solange, the old gentleman failed to recognize my husband and did not, thank heaven, think of inquiring his religious denomination. Prudently, Milo decided to leave him to me. On ushering him into the studio I was immediately struck by his monocle and resolved to construct the whole photograph around the eye behind the circular lens. Confronted by his portrait the following week, the old lawyer said nothing for several seconds. "Excellent, madame, excellent," he murmured at length. "You're an artist." I felt my cheeks glow with pleasure.

Milo's response when I told him of this verdict on the photograph was surprisingly offhand: "Was the old fool wearing his monocle, at least, when he saw it?"

24

Milo went for a stroll after dinner that night. He looked in at the Bar Bavaria, where he was sure to find his friend Ernest Zahlawi, whom Dora couldn't endure. A ledger clerk employed by the Société des Moulins d'Égypte, Ernest bivouacked there from seven o'clock onwards every evening, the whole year round. He claimed to be able to identify any make of beer, local or European, with a blindfold over his eyes. This was just about his only qualification.

Milo pushed the door open and entered in the wake of two rather tipsy English soldiers. The establishment was wreathed in tobacco smoke and smelt of burnt fat. The waiters' cries were echoed by the raucous laughter of several garishly made-up women seated side by side on a bench. An accordionist compounded the din by tormenting his instrument amid universal indifference.

Ernest Zahlawi was ensconced in his usual place beneath a big zinc chandelier. His goatlike face, with its elongated snout, lit up at the sight of Milo.

"Hello there, stranger! You picked the right day, *ya akrout*, a new beer has just come in. From Munich, no less!"

He stuck two fingers in his mouth and whistled for a glass and another bottle.

The bare-shouldered women on the bench laughed even louder and made eyes at Milo. He thought he recognized one of them as a prostitute who used to patrol the vicinity of the New Hotel some years before.

"Well," said Ernest, who had already sunk several bottles, "what do you think of this beer?"

They made merry and drank deep for the next two hours. One of the women made several attempts to perch on Milo's lap and drink from his glass, but he laughingly pushed her off. The waiters bustled around, shouting orders to the kitchen. Towards one in the morning an English soldier blundered into the accordionist on his way to be sick outside.

"I must go home," Milo said thickly, a little while later. "My wife will be wondering where I've got to."

"I'll come with you," said Ernest, having armed himself for the trip with another two bottles.

They only just avoided some British vomit as they emerged. The night air, which was much cooler than the fug inside the bar, made them shiver. On reaching the shop, Milo laboriously inserted the key in the lock. The oil lamp in the waiting room was alight. He picked it up and held it aloft. Bulbul was snoring on a mattress in his usual place beside the counter. Ernest went over to him, opened one of the bottles, and trickled some beer on to his face from a considerable height. Milo rocked with laughter. Bulbul sat up with a start, only to find himself face to face with his master. Milo put a finger to his lips and glared at him, whereupon Bulbul, thoroughly intimidated, took refuge beneath the covers.

Ernest headed for the studio with Milo lurching along at his heels. Seated side by side on the ottoman, they emptied the first bottle.

"What's this?" asked Ernest, picking up a reflector.

"It's for the light," Milo mumbled.

Drawing back his arm, Ernest abruptly hurled the reflector across the room. It struck the camera's handwheel and smashed.

They both roared with laughter. Ernest unbuttoned his flies and stationed himself in front of the fragments.

"Wait a minute!" said Milo, joining him.

They peed in concert, liberally watering the splintered glass.

The second bottle proved hard to open. Milo smashed the neck on the crank-handle, but the beer gushed out on to the carpet.

"And that?" said Ernest, pointing to something on a table. "What's that?"

"That," mumbled Milo, "is a p-pinhole v-viewfinder."

"A p-pinhole what?"

"A p-pinhole . . . "

They almost choked with laughter. Ernest picked up the viewfinder and gestured obscenely with it.

"No," said Milo, taking it from him, "not like that . . . "

And, with the little strength he had left, he hurled it at the opposite wall before collapsing, face down, on the sodden carpet.

Dora awoke at six that morning. Alarmed by Milo's absence, she lit the lamp, donned her dressing gown, and went downstairs. Bulbul was snoring loudly. Intrigued to see the studio door ajar, she peered inside and uttered an involuntary cry.

She stood in the doorway for a good minute, rooted to the spot. Tears welled up in her eyes. She put the lamp down, went over to Milo and shook him. He merely grunted, so she fetched a bucket of water from the yard and emptied it over him. Ernest Zahlawi received the same treatment. The two men struggled to their feet.

"You!" Dora shouted at Ernest. "Get out of here and don't ever come back!"

The ledger clerk departed with his flies still open, cannoning off the walls as he went.

Milo was clinging to the camera with his head hanging. Dora went right up to him and looked him in the eye.

"Never do that again," she said in a low voice, gritting her teeth.

Two hours later, when he had sobered up and Bulbul had finished clean-ing the studio, Milo paid a visit to the florist in Opera Square. He returned with a peace offering in the shape of an enormous bouquet. Dora was still too incensed to thank him. She left him to arrange the roses in a vase, which he did so clumsily that he pricked himself.

All Bulbul's sluicing and sponging could not eradicate the stains of the night. She felt like the victim of a rape committed jointly by her husband and a seedy third party.

Back in the apartment, she discerned a possible connection between Milo's binge and her own success of the previous day. "You're an artist," the elderly, monocled academic had told her. Could Milo's aberration have stemmed from that compliment alone? Perhaps he found her refurbishment of the shop more hurtful than she had thought.

"I don't feel at home here any more!" He had said that several times since the transformation of the darkroom, to which he now referred, with a hint of bitterness, as "the whiteroom".

Milo made genuine efforts to be pleasant in the next few days, and Dora's fears gradually subsided. He even wrote off to a Parisian supplier for a reflector and a pinhole viewfinder. When the parcel arrived a few weeks later, Dora was surprised to discover that it also contained an enlarger.

25

Their next encounter with Captain Elliot took place one August morning on the beach at Fleming. The young officer looked quite as elegant in his black, skin-tight bathing costume as he did in uniform. An involuntary tremor ran through Dora as he bent to kiss her hand in the French manner.

He was spending a few days' leave at his father's villa behind the dunes. Elliot Bey, deputy director of customs at Alexandria, had built the house in 1885, the year his son came out to join the Egyptian army. He had lived there every summer since losing his wife, alone except for a manservant and his black bulldog. He could be glimpsed in the distance at dusk, striding along behind his dog. "The Englishman of the Dunes" was a kind of sandman who frightened the children.

"I'm leaving tomorrow, unfortunately," said William Elliot. "Perhaps we could take tea together at the Casino San Stefano this afternoon? They'll be holding the floral bicycle competition."

Milo, never averse to any form of entertainment, accepted with pleasure. "It'll make a change for me. I used to photograph the competitors every year, but this summer I decided to take a proper holiday."

He no longer needed to work as a beach photographer. His expanding clientele had even enabled him to rent two rooms at the Hôtel Miramare instead of staying with his elder brother.

William Elliot's gaze lingered on Dora's bare arms. She looked delectable in her blue and white sun dress.

"Aren't you going to bathe?" he asked.

"Of course we are," said Milo, without even troubling to consult his wife. "We'll ask little Yolande to help the nursemaid look after the girls. She'll be delighted. Yola!" he called at the top of his voice. "Yola!"

Ten minutes later, having changed in their canvas bathing hut, they joined William Elliot at the water's edge. An excellent swimmer, he had already performed two dives and given a brief demonstration of the crawl to a group of admiring onlookers.

"Coming?" he asked, throwing back his wet hair.

"My husband will come with you," said Dora, who was christening a new bathing costume. "I can only just float."

"If you can float, madame, you're perfectly capable of swimming." He turned to Milo. "Would you permit me to teach your wife the breast-stroke?"

"An excellent idea!" Milo exclaimed. "I've tried, but she won't let me."

Half excited, half apprehensive, Dora waded in up to her waist. Milo looked on with a broad smile and the children ran up to watch with cries of "Mameluka! Mameluka!" Meantime, William Elliot had gone off to find a piece of driftwood.

"Hold it firmly," he said. "Rest your arms on it. No, not like that . . . "

Rather stiffly, she allowed herself to be guided by the young officer's strong hands. His touch gave her the strangest sensation, as if she were being publicly applauded for engaging in some forbidden act.

"And now, push the water away with your legs," said Elliot. "That's right, push!"

Dora was concerned less with her legs than with an approaching wavelet. Frightened of getting a mouthful, she raised her head as far as it would go.

"Don't be afraid," Elliot said. "I'm here."

"You must teach her to use her arms as well," called Milo. "Give me that plank."

Dora was even closer to Elliot without the plank between them. She clung to his wrists, feeling at his mercy.

"Relax," he told her gently. "It'll be fine, you'll see . . . "

The lesson was abruptly cut short by a babble of cries: little Gabrielle had swallowed a piece of cork, and the frightened nursemaid was clumsily trying to extract it. Everyone came running up.

"You must take her by the legs and shake her!" cried Milo, suiting the action to the word.

His mother had used the same method to save his own life at Helwan one Sunday, when he'd choked on a nut as a child. Nonna often recalled the incident, which had earned her a pat on the back from her brother-in-law, Dr Touta. "Never use your fingers to extract an object lodged in the gullet," he explained. "You'll only push it in further."

No sooner had Gabrielle been upended by her father than the fragment of cork fell out. Dora, with tears streaming down her cheeks, feverishly hugged the little girl to her damp bosom.

Milo's popularity at Fleming was such that fifteen or twenty cousins and friends joined the party that accompanied him to San Stefano for the floral bicycle competition. The table for three reserved by Captain Elliot was swamped by a cheerful, rumbustious throng. At first rather dismayed and put out by this band of noisy Levantines, the Englishman gradually allowed himself to be carried away by the atmosphere. He was soon feeling delighted with himself for having instigated such a successful outing.

In Cairo he consorted only with fellow Britons. The fact that he belonged to the Egyptian army rather than the army of occupation made no difference: British and Egyptian officers had separate messes, and it was considered a breach of etiquette for the former to be on personal terms with the latter. Each group lived apart and enjoyed a different status. "Natives" could not rise above a certain level in the military hierarchy and were paid less than their British counterparts, even when they held the same rank. Communication was rendered no easier by the language barrier. Few British officers spoke fluent Arabic. Theirs tended to be a literary Arabic acquired at Oxford before coming out to Egypt. It entitled them to extra pay but did little to promote everyday relations.

This was William Elliot's first encounter with Christians of Syrian stock, and he seemed bewildered by them. They were indefinable: neither Europeans nor genuine natives.

"How can anyone belong nowhere?" he inquired, after several glasses of beer.

Milo looked amused. "You've got the wrong idea," he said. "There are two sides to us. We're like photographic negatives, white and black in some cases, black and white in others."

The bicycles paraded past, smothered in flowers. The competitors' efforts attracted lively comments. Members of Alexandria's upper crust, they had decorated their machines with the greatest care. Among them was Rizqallah Bey Touta, a director on the San Stefano board, who was pedalling along in the midst of a rose bush.

"That fellow has overdone it a bit," said Elliot.

Milo laughed. "He's a cousin of mine – owns *Touta et Fils*, the chain of department stores. He married a very wealthy Jewess, one of the Aghions. It caused a terrible rumpus at the time, but his success has wiped the slate clean. Perhaps he'll do us the honour of appearing in this year's family photograph."

Rizqallah Bey, who had some sound business connections among the jury, was awarded third prize. Milo went over to congratulate him. Rizqallah, surrounded by admirers and deluged with compliments, shook his hand without seeming to recognize him.

"I've really taken to your husband," Elliot told Dora. "It would give me great pleasure to invite you both to a torchlight parade in Cairo next month. It's to be held at Qasr al-Nil Barracks, with the massed bands of both armies."

"A torchlight parade?" Milo exclaimed a few minutes later. "Wonderful! I'm very partial to displays of that kind."

He was even more partial, no doubt, to the idea of being a British officer's guest. They were standoffish, the British, and always gave the impression of avoiding, if not actively despising one. At a family lunch only the week before, Milo had greatly amused all present by reading out a new Egyptian police regulation: "Members of the local population will refrain from approaching inebriated British soldiers but are duty-bound to assist them in case of need." And he had mimed a passer-by hesitantly sidling up to a "redcoat" stretched out on the pavement.

More and more relaxed, William Elliot indulged in some jokes at the expense of his own government. Milo drew him aside.

"There's something I'd like to ask you – it's been bothering me. The first time you visited our shop – yes, the first time – why did you come to us, not Maloumian?"

Elliot chuckled. "You really want to know? I made a mistake, that's all. Someone recommended me to go to Maloumian in Ezbekiyah Square. I saw your window but omitted to look at the sign on the door. I've no regrets, though, believe me."

Dora was disconcerted by the covert glance he gave her after uttering those last few words.

26

That year, as every year, the Popinots departed for the cooler climes of Europe. Milo, Dora and the Tiomjis accompanied them to the ship laden with flowers. The scene on the quay resembled a social function. Smartly dressed ladies and gentlemen picked their way between mounds of luxurious luggage to bid farewell to the beys, pashas and numerous Europeans who were fleeing across the Mediterranean to escape the midsummer heat. Comments were passed on the wife of the Austro-Hungarian consul, whose attire included a hat of fuchsia velour adorned with rare plumes and surmounted by a stuffed bird with outspread wings. For his part, Prince Fouad was showing some friends the special hatbox he had ordered from Vuitton of Paris in which to transport his tarbooshes.

"We'll be back by 30 September at the latest," Norbert told Milo. "Don't hesitate to send for my coachman if you need him."

Solange, who viewed the forthcoming trip with a mixture of excitement and melancholy, alternately wiped away a tear and burst out laughing. She tripped over a parasol and saved herself by clinging to the lapels of a gentleman banker. Milo hailed an itinerant vendor and invited the whole party to glasses of tamarind juice.

Just after eleven o'clock the Messageries Maritimes steamship pulled slowly away from the quay, giving several blasts on her siren in token of farewell. Solange threw her friends a rose from the promenade deck. It fell short and was swallowed up by foaming water.

"Oh, how I'd love to see Europe some day!" cried Dora.

"You can go whenever you like," Milo told her jocularly. "The khedive has to go down on his hands and knees to obtain the sultan's permission."

In the cab that took them back to Fleming with the Tiomjis he amused himself by recounting the latest news — an affair the newspapers were treating with great discretion. Heaven alone knew how he had come by the details. He may only just have learned them by keeping his ears open on the quayside.

"The sultan didn't want 'Abbas running wild in Europe. Above all, he was afraid his vassal would seize the opportunity to meet with foreign heads of state and pose as an independent sovereign. But our khedive was itching to go to Venice and Divonne — Paris too, no doubt. He sent one of his physicians to Constantinople to plead his case. Dr Comanos Pasha informed the sultan that 'Abbas had put on weight, that he suffered from congestion and needed a change of climate. The sultan replied that his empire was large enough to provide all the climates anyone could desire, and that he would put a Black Sea palace at the khedive's disposal."

Richard Tiomji emitted one of his raucous laughs. "Speaking for myself, I'd have taken the Black Sea palace and spent some holidays there with Lita and my ostriches."

"Pressed by the doctor, who had a little pocket money to offer him, the sultan finally gave way, but only if the khedive's itinerary and means of transportation were specified by himself. 'Abbas was to sail aboard his own yacht, the *Mahrousa*, visit Italy and Switzerland only, and travel incognito."

"I'd have gone anyway," Dora said with a dreamy smile, "incognito or not."

So the khedive spent some weeks in Europe and some at Alexandria. Unable to endure the heat, he lived far from Cairo for part of the year, usually in the seaside palace he had built himself at Montaza. The magnificent estate was already planted with thousands of trees: palms, oranges, apricots, mulberries. Seif 'Abdel-Latif had been privileged to visit it that same summer, during the Popinots' sojourn in France. He went with a small party of former law students led by his hero, Mustafa Kamil, who had become the khedive's favourite and a *bête noire* of the British.

"His Highness was waiting for us on a huge terrace overlooking the bay," Seif recounted. "I didn't recognize him at first."

The handsome young man who had visited their law school three-and-a-half years earlier had become a corpulent figure in a tweed suit and yellow bootees. He greeted Mustafa Kamil with an embrace but extended his hand for Seif and his companions to kiss.

The khedive was very proud of his estate. He spoke to them of his tree nurseries, his rabbit farm, his cabinetmakers' workshops, and the special cable that enabled him to telegraph the whole of Europe without the British eavesdropping on him. This latter detail was the only one that interested Seif.

They lunched off a silver gilt service on the terrace. Afterwards 'Abbas took them aboard a small locomotive driven by himself and hitched to a carriage containing servants and teatime ices. This private line was only a few kilometres long, but the track would soon reach Lake Mariout. From there it was to link up with the railway line that would one day extend as far as the Tripolitanian frontier.

The khedive continued to sing the praises of his plantations, stables and workshops all the way. Seif felt that he was confronted by a sovereign who had given up and retired to his private domain. It was only on the return journey that Mustafa Kamil managed to engage him in a political discussion. 'Abbas then proceeded to vent his spleen on Lord Cromer and urged them to agitate in favour of an end to British occupation. Seif, who had been expecting so much of this visit, felt dissatisfied.

27

In October the Popinots returned from Europe with presents for everyone and a fund of anecdotes. Norbert never stopped talking about Captain Dreyfus' conviction, Solange had become a fanatical admirer of Debussy's music. They were the heart and soul of the Wednesday soirées, which Seif had taken to attending with a childhood friend named Ibrahim, who had also fallen under Dora's spell. A plump, cheerful young man, Ibrahim was a minister's nephew and the scion of one of Cairo's wealthiest Muslim families. Given his enthusiasm for painting, music, and fine wines, everyone wondered how the austere Seif could endure him. He was reputed to be a poet, and his one avowed activity was the composition of an Egyptian *Marseillaise*. Seif was always urging him to complete this anthem, which would, he hoped, do much to further the cause of independence.

"As soon as you've finished it," he told Ibrahim, "we'll have thousands of copies printed. We may have to translate it into English as well."

But the author seemed in no hurry. "I'm working on it, I'm working on it," he would say with an evasive smile, whenever anyone questioned him on the subject.

Ibrahim did not take himself seriously. He preferred to compose unpretentious little poems and read them aloud from the notebook he carried everywhere.

At one of the Wednesday gatherings, conversation turned — as it often did — to Lord Cromer.

"You call the British consul a despot," Richard Tiomji said to Seif. "If so, why is the Egyptian press so free?"

"It's a tactical device. Cromer maintains press freedom so as to know the state of public opinion. The newspapers provide him with a daily source of valuable information – information which he can readily verify later on. They also make it easier for him to keep an eye on the government's intrigues."

"You mean the papers should be silenced?"

"I didn't say that."

Their voices rose. Discussions between Richard and Seif always threatened to degenerate into altercations. Bored by the arguments on both sides, Solange struck up a polka. Ibrahim, leaning on the piano with a glass of wine in his hand, plied her with encouraging smiles. He waited for the piece to end before declaiming the following lines:

> We'll never be frightened of Cromer.
> His Lordship will threaten in vain
> while our khedive waters his flowers
> and plays with his little toy train.

Seif shot him a look of disapproval. "You'd do better to get on with your real work," he said.

Milo gaily broke into song:

> Allons enfants de la patrrr-i-i-i-eu
> le jour de gloire e-e-est arrr-ivé . . .

Solange put her fingers in her ears to blot out the false notes, then launched into a spirited rendering of the *Marseillaise*.

A little while later Seif read them a letter Mustafa Kamil had sent to Juliette Adam, the celebrated Parisian journalist and founder of the *Nouvelle Revue*.

"Toulouse, 12 September 1895," he began, punching out the words. "Madame, I am still young, but I cherish exalted ambitions. I dream of an Egyptian renaissance. People claim that my native land does not exist, but they're mistaken. I feel it living on within me with a love so strong that it will dominate all others, a love that prompts me to devote my youth, my strength and my life to my country's service. I am 21 years old and have just obtained my law degree at Toulouse. I wish to write, speak, and propagate the enthusiasm I feel for my country. People are forever telling me that I am attempting the impossible. It would be truer to say that I am *tempted* by it. Your own patriotism, Madame, is such that you alone can understand, encourage and assist me. I entreat you to do so. Yours respectfully, Mustafa Kamil."

"Very moving," said Solange. "How did Madame Adam respond?"

"She has promised to see him when he's next in Paris."

"Your friend Mustafa Kamil ought to found a political party," said Norbert.

"No, he's firmly opposed to that. His aim is to unite all Egyptians regardless of their political opinions."

Ibrahim smiled broadly. "That'll take him a while!"

A great admirer of the Impressionists – he owned two Monets and a Sisley – Ibrahim refused to concede that photography was an art.

"Armed only with a brush and some paints," he remarked to Dora one evening, "the painter brings his canvases to life. Photography is merely the product of a mechanical and chemical process."

They were almost the words she herself had used when debating the subject with Milo a few years before. But the rather poor arguments her husband had then advanced were of no great help to her now. An aesthete like Ibrahim was far more exacting.

"It's feelings that make an artist," she retorted, "not processes."

The young Egyptian thought for a moment, then shook his head. "No," he said, "photography was born of science. It'll never lose that original taint – in fact I think its status will only decline as time goes by. The greater its technical perfection, the more remote it will become from art."

"It could be the other way round."

"No, no, photography depends for its very existence on an extremely complicated device. It's art without an artist."

Seeing Dora's face darken, he realized that he had gone too far.

"Don't be offended," he went on quickly. "Let's say that photography is an art like hunting or navigation. It isn't one of the fine arts. Call it a scientific art, if you like."

"Why shouldn't photography be an art in its own right, like painting, drawing or architecture? Anyway, what *is* art, in your opinion?"

Ibrahim shrugged. "Art is a form of creation. It creates beauty and arouses emotion."

"Very well, photography fits that definition perfectly. At least, some photographs do."

"You see?" said Ibrahim, his eyes lighting up. "*Some* photographs, you said. No one would dream of saying that *some* pictures are works of art."

"No?" she retorted quickly. "You really think *all* the canvases displayed in the Moski are works of art?"

He burst out laughing. "All right, point taken, but you've sidetracked me. Let's get back to the subject. Why should a camera, which reproduces reality by mechanical means, invest its operator with the status of an artist? That's too easy."

Dora was beginning to enjoy this rhetorical duel.

"If I understand you correctly," she said, "your definition of a work of art depends on how difficult it has been to produce."

"Oh no, you won't lure me down that blind alley!"

"Contrary to what you appear to believe, my dear Ibrahim, photographers aren't copyists. They don't produce replicas of reality. It's they, not their cameras, that choose to emphasize particular aspects of their sitters, dispense with details they consider superfluous, and light their subjects in such and such a way. They don't show you only what they've seen, but how they've seen it."

Still sceptical, the poet resolved to answer her in verse at the earliest opportunity.

28

"Would you photograph my uncle?"

Dora found it hard to conceal her surprise when Ibrahim came out with the question, point-blank, one Wednesday evening.

"Your uncle the minister?"

"Yes. It would really tickle me to get him taken by a woman."

"He'd never consent."

"He won't know. He's very short-sighted."

Dora was reluctant to lend herself to a practical joke of this kind. Ibrahim's suggestion proved that he didn't take photography seriously, or even that he despised it, but Milo was highly amused by the idea when she told him about it. Besides, he couldn't contain himself at the prospect of numbering a minister among his customers.

"Just think of it, a minister! All right, so a minister carries much less weight than a European consul, but all the same, it's a step in the right direction."

Ibrahim offered to go and broach the idea to his uncle the very next day. The pasha was minister of education, but, like all Egyptian cabinet ministers, he was flanked by an omnipotent British adviser who took most of the decisions. His huge office, whose walls were hung with pink silk, was open to all comers. Visitors thronged it all day long, sipping hot or cold drinks that were constantly replenished by a clerk. The minister, who must have weighed a hundred and twenty kilos, half sat, half reclined on a sofa. Looking bored, he would lend an ear to one or another of his petitioners, who rose and presented his request with a host of flowery phrases. The pasha would listen absently, then turn to someone else. The visitor sat down again, ready to resume his performance at the smallest sign from His Excellency.

From time to time, with a twitch of the eyebrow, the minister would summon one of the aides who hovered beside a door in the background. Bent double, the official would hurry over to receive His Excellency's august instructions. Everyone's gaze converged on the man in anticipation of some gesture, and the game began anew. When the minister's British adviser was in conference with him, the room was cleared and the doors were shut.

Ibrahim was firmly resolved not to wait and anxious to obtain his uncle's consent to the portrait on the spot, but he turned up just as a secretary was submitting a decree for his signature.

"Has the British adviser initialled this?" demanded the minister. The secretary replied in the affirmative, whereupon the pasha aimed a limp finger at the seal on the desk in front of him.

"There's the minister," he said. "Get him to sign it."

Ibrahim took his uncle's arm and steered him into the studio. It was true: the pasha could hardly see across the room. Dora, having been told that he was very short and exceedingly fat, proposed to flatter her subject by photographing him beside a piece of furniture even bulkier than himself: the chest of drawers from the drawing room, which Bulbul had carried downstairs with the help of the porter from the neighbouring apartments.

Dora adjusted the focus while Ibrahim and Milo danced attendance on the minister. Every now and then she would whisper some instruction to her husband, who politely conveyed it to their illustrious customer.

"Not full-face," she muttered. "He'd look quite monstrous."

"Your Excellency," purred Milo, every inch the Photographer to the Consulates, "might I take the liberty of suggesting that you turn slightly to the right?"

Another muttered instruction: "And get rid of that treble chin for me!"

"If you wouldn't mind lowering your head a little, Excellency, just to help you to relax . . . "

Dora made the pasha's features look less gross by accentuating the shadows as much as possible. Then, for fear of having overdone things, she exposed another two plates with different lighting. Only half of his face was lit in the photograph she selected the following day.

Ibrahim, who had come to view the result of the session, pronounced it superb. He had never seen his uncle look so dignified and, all things considered, so handsome. Milo accompanied him to the minister's office the same day, complete with the prints. It was the British adviser's time of day, unfortunately, so they had to spend forty minutes waiting outside in the corridor with a crowd of evicted petitioners. As soon as the doors reopened, however, Ibrahim managed to get in ahead of everyone else.

The minister was delighted with the portrait and congratulated his nephew on having shown such initiative. "The first intelligent suggestion you've ever made," was his considered verdict.

He was so pleased with the photograph that he ordered fifty copies. A few hours later, a messenger brought Milo the fee and, in token of the pasha's appreciation, a box of South American cigars. Ibrahim, rocking with laughter, extemporized:

> Cigars for a lady? Good lord!
> Why not give her a rifle or sword,
> a moustache cup, tiepin or razor?
> Dear uncle of mine, you'll amaze her!

But Milo soon ceased to be amused by the affair. He was irritable and short with Dora in the days that followed, as if resentful of her success, not that she ever preened herself on it. In her eyes, the matter was closed.

One afternoon, when the shop was empty and the doors were open, the sound of Gabrielle's sobs carried to the darkroom.

"The little girl's crying," Milo said reproachfully.

"I can hear her," said Dora, as she went on inserting some sensitive plates in their holders.

"It's because she never sees her mother," he grumbled.

She felt herself blush like a guilty child..Given that she regularly rebuked herself for sacrificing her daughters to her profession, nothing could have wounded her more. It should be added that none of her friends sought to reassure her on the subject. Lita Tiomji was forever reminding her of her maternal duties.

"Yes, I can hear her," she repeated in a faltering voice. She put the plates away and hurried upstairs to the apartment.

She had never seen Milo look as inscrutable as he did at supper that night. Had his pointed allusion to the little girl been deliberate? Dora found herself wondering more and more about the thoughts that troubled her husband and his reaction to her success. He was proud of her, gratified that he had converted her to photography, and delighted to see his business expanding, of that there was no doubt. But there were times when she sensed that he felt hurt and humiliated, as if aspersions had been cast on his manhood.

29

I was astounded yet again by Milo's ability to attract an audience. He arrived at that party at the home of Richard Tiomji's brother knowing no one. A quarter of an hour later he was surrounded by a dozen guests, all of them enthralled by his stories and sticking to him like glue.

"As the minister of education — a client of mine — was telling me the other day . . . " I was just as staggered by the audacity with which he made capital out of Ibrahim's uncle. Torn between admiration and annoyance, I didn't blame my husband for claiming all the credit. It was only natural, after all: no one could be allowed to know that the minister had been hoodwinked; it might have come to his ears and caused a scandal. For all that, I thought it a little excessive of Milo to invent statements and put them in the pasha's mouth: "His Excellency was quite categorical: there won't be any military operations in the Sudan in the near future."

Bombarded with questions, he responded with the evasive air of an official spokesman who knows all the answers but is not at liberty to divulge them. Needless to say, this only whetted his listeners' curiosity.

It was when the buffet opened that I unexpectedly ran into the man who had blighted my childhood. I recognized him by his big hands, with their blunt fingers and grimy nails, which were resting on an immaculate white tablecloth.

The painter had hardly changed in the twelve years since our last encounter. He was still as stocky and thickset, still resembled a lumberjack astray in a drawing room. The one difference was the white hair that contrasted with his bushy black eyebrows. I went over to him.

"Are you a painter?" I asked.

"I paint," he growled. Then, in the same gruff voice: "How did you know?"

I told him that I was.Léon Sawaya's daughter, and that he had once painted my portrait.

He stared at me blankly. "Really? It's possible." Clearly, he had no recollection of the miniature he had produced twelve years earlier. Heaven alone knew how many of those little portraits, and how many victims, he had been responsible for in the course of his life.

The man reached for one of the dishes in the middle of the table, picked up a stuffed vine leaf, and conveyed it to his mouth. He chewed with deliberation, smacking his lips.

"I used to do a few watercolours some years ago," I said, to keep the ball rolling. "These days I'm a photographer."

The painter went on chewing impassively, like the uncouth boor he was. After a moment or two, without thinking, I said, "If the idea appeals to you, I could do *your* portrait."

Afterwards, I wondered more than once what had possessed me. Had I wanted to compel him to speak? To decipher that luminous, rather oblique gaze? Or had I been tempted to exchange roles after an interval of twelve years and efface the scar left by the miniature?

We made an appointment for two days' time.

The man was seated in the chair facing the camera, leaning forwards. I studied him through the lens, far more closely than I had been able to at the party two days earlier. He must have been about fifty-five. His heavy features radiated a kind of suppressed violence.

I recalled the time when I myself had sat for him. He didn't utter a word, merely came over to me from time to time and raised my head, ungently taking my chin between his rough fingers. "This gentleman is going to paint your portrait," my father had told me. "You're expected to sit still." Having seen my mother maintaining a similar pose in equal silence two weeks before, I wondered if the entire family was going to sit for this taciturn painter.

All at once, the image in the lens went blurred. I had no time even to wonder why. The man had come over and was clasping me round the waist with a lecherous expression. "Well, really!" I exclaimed, straightening up in a hurry.

We were face to face and only inches apart. One of the hands with grimy nails closed on my bosom. I suddenly felt very frightened. "No, really, let me go!" I cried, trying to free myself.

The painter was still wearing the same salacious smile. Prompted by my resistance, he clamped his hand over my mouth to prevent me from crying out. My arm struck the camera's crank handle as I struggled with him. He glared at me and tightened his grip, seized my bodice and tugged at it twice in quick succession, ripping it open. In my terror I snatched up the first object that came to hand, a reflector, and brandished it at him, simultaneously shouting at the top of my voice – shouting as I'd never shouted before. Disconcerted, he backed off with an oath and hurried from the studio, colliding with Bulbul on the way.

"What happened?" Bulbul asked. "Get out!" I shouted, shielding my bosom with the camera's black cloth. Bulbul just stood there with his mouth open and his arms dangling. "Get out, I said!"

I decided not to mention the incident to Milo, who was at the café playing backgammon, for fear of causing a scene. I felt I was to blame, having invited the man to come and be photographed. He must have misconstrued my intentions.

Upstairs in the apartment I began by washing myself all over. Then I scented myself and put on one of my best gowns. While making up at the dressing table I caught sight of the miniature reflected in the mirror. Calmly, I took it down, removed it from its frame, and held it over the flame of the lamp. It buckled, caught fire, and was reduced to ashes.

"Did you have trouble today?" Milo asked me that night. "Bulbul spun me some incoherent yarn about a peculiar customer who broke things in the studio."

"Bulbul's the peculiar one," I said. "To the best of my knowledge, nothing in the studio got broken."

When tidying the studio a little earlier I had found a small penknife with a discoloured handle lying on the carpet. It summoned up a vision of my parents' drawing room twelve years before: the painter had laid aside his brush and cleaned his nails with the tip of a penknife. Was this the same one? I almost kept it, then changed my mind and consigned it to the dustbin in the yard.

I had the same nightmare twice the following week. I was a little girl again. The painter left his easel, came over to me, and clamped his hand over my mouth to prevent me from crying out. "It serves you right!" said Mother Marie des Anges, jingling her big bunch of keys. My father made no attempt to intervene, simply looked on with a smile.

For some time afterwards I felt rather nervous when alone in the studio with a customer. I would even, on occasion, violate all my principles by leaving the door ajar. But the memory of that grotesque scene soon faded. The painter's victim had been a little girl, not a young woman – the victim of a painted stigma far more wounding than an attempted assault of which nothing remained but a faint bruise on my arm.

"Did you hurt yourself?" asked Milo, stroking the brownish mark with his finger. "It must have been you," I replied archly. "You're a regular beast at nights." His only response was to nibble my neck.

Who had introduced the painter to us twelve years earlier? My father wasn't the type to consort with artists, still less with an artist as uncouth as this one. Only my mother could have been responsible for the famous miniature. Odette Sawaya, née Falaki, was regarded in her youth as a person of taste devoted to all forms of art, and even as an artist herself. Lita Tiomji used to say, "I shall never forget your poor mother conjuring such beautiful music from the piano while we were playing together in your room."

She might have been speaking of a dead woman, and it is true that my mother, whose emaciated features betrayed the smallest stirring of emotion, had been a recluse for years. Some people thought her mad, but it was simply that her thoughts were elsewhere. She daydreamed whole afternoons away on a divan, puffing at her long ivory cigarette holder. She could recite entire odes by Ronsard or de Musset, wreathed in blue tobacco smoke and heedless of those who came near her.

I cannot say that I thought of my family with much pleasure. My father seemed incapable of understanding me and my mother was just as uncomprehending. As for my brothers and sisters, I hardly knew them, doubtless because of my long years at boarding school. None of them had shown any real interest in my photographic activities; their sole reaction was surprise.

My father had at first been indignant to hear that I spent part of the week in the studio, but I cut him short and made it clear that I had no intention of turning the clock back. The poor man mumbled something and left it at that. His own wife's strange behaviour precluded him from lecturing anyone on a woman's role in the home. I could have been gentler with him and more persuasive.

I made desperate efforts to strike up genuine conversations with my mother. My third daughter, Marthe, was born in February 1896. All I got for my pains, when I brought her the baby to see, were vague smiles and curious references to the moon and the wind. I was mortified.

At Helwan, Nonna reacted in a far more traditional manner: she took her grandchild in her arms with cries of *"Wihsha! Wihsha!"*

Yet another girl . . . "Fourth time lucky," Milo's aunts and sisters-in-law told him consolingly, but he seemed far from disappointed that heaven had presented him with another replica of the Mameluka. It was a treat to see him smiling down at little Marthe with our other two daughters clinging to his shoulders.

30

Seif was beside himself with indignation. "Imagine, the khedive was only told of the Sudan campaign at the very last moment. They came to inform him that he'd declared war on the Mahdists!"

To remedy this deliberate omission, Lord Cromer had gone to the palace to offer a purely formal apology. The infuriated 'Abbas was presented with a fait accompli and had no choice but to salute the troops who were leaving for the front. He was left with only one regiment and his personal guard. The rest of the Egyptian army, with some British battalions in support, went off to fight in the Sudan under the command of General Kitchener.

"Did you know," the young lawyer went on, "that villages near the Sudanese frontier are being raided and peasants forcibly hauled away to recruitment centres? There they have cords fastened around their necks with lead seals. 'You're in the army now,' they're told. 'That's the khedive's seal. If you break it and try to run away you'll be punished as deserters.' The poor wretches' wives and mothers go to the compound, but are refused entry. They cling to the bars, they weep, they shout, they roll on the ground and cover their heads with dust. The recruiting sergeants drive them away with whips."

"The real scandal," said Norbert Popinot, "is the half-a-million pounds Lord Cromer proposes to withdraw from government reserves to finance the operation. Everyone knows that those reserves are meant to guarantee the repayment of Egypt's national debt. And who are the holders of

Egyptian government bonds? French citizens, for the most part! Britain intends to retake the Sudan with our money, ostensibly on the khedive's behalf!"

"Just a minute," said Richard Tiomji. "Who said anything about retaking the Sudan? May I remind you that the purpose of this campaign is to go to the aid of General Baratieri's Italian troops, who are in difficulties at Kassala?"

"The British couldn't care less about General Baratieri!" Popinot retorted. "Their aim is to retake the Sudan. You need only look at the map to see that. If *I* were heading for Kassala, I wouldn't go via Dongola."

And he launched into an account of British tactics.

"It's more than seven hundred kilometres from the Egyptian frontier to Omdurman. In that intervening space the Nile describes two huge loops and negotiates six cataracts that render navigation impossible. Kitchener is going to cut across those loops in the desert by means of the railway line, which it has just been decided to extend. The British have cured themselves of makeshift operations. This time they'll advance step by step, like the Romans, never losing touch with their supply depots."

Milo drew Richard Tiomji's attention to the fact that, if the Sudan were retaken, caravans would resume their activities and supply Egypt with ostrich feathers. The resulting competition might well prove formidable.

"I don't give a damn about Sudanese ostriches!" bellowed Richard. "My birds' feathers are incomparable!" He snatched Lita's fan and held it under Milo's nose. "I defy anyone to produce articles of this quality at the same price."

William Elliot called at the shop in a state of high excitement.

"I'm off. We're going to avenge Gordon at last."

He implicitly confirmed that the aim was to reconquer the whole of the Sudan. Appointed to command a cavalry squadron numbering eighty sabres, he couldn't wait to get to Omdurman.

"Slatin Pasha is coming with us. He'll be able to show us the route."

Taking advantage of a few moments alone with Dora, he addressed her in an undertone.

"Would you allow me to write to you?"

She didn't know what to say, she was so taken aback, and he interpreted her silence as an affirmative.

"We've always been told that it was vital to control the waters of the Nile," Ibrahim said nonchalantly, leaning on the piano with a glass in his hand. "Egypt has either occupied the Sudan or been ejected from it ever since the time of the pharaohs. I don't see why we shouldn't try to recover those lost provinces today."

"Every Egyptian patriot wants the Sudan retaken," Seif said solemnly. "Indeed, the Nile Valley can only have one master, but we've never wanted and would never wish to retake the Sudan under British command."

Ibrahim shrugged. "What's the difference?"

"All the difference in the world. Their presence at the head of the army is intended to drive a wedge between the Sudanese and ourselves. This latest campaign is a British operation launched under Egyptian colours."

"Egypt and Britain are so closely united," Norbert put in sarcastically, "that the rights of the one are inseparable from the ambitions of the other."

But Ibrahim persisted in playing devil's advocate. "In that case," he said, "tell me why the British have waited all this time to intervene in the Sudan. It's eleven years since Khartoum was captured by the Mahdists."

"That's easy, my friend," said Norbert. "In recent years it's been in Britain's interest *not* to retake the Sudan: by pointing to the illusory Mahdist menace, she could pose as Egypt's protector and justify her continued occupation. Now that other European armies have intervened in Africa, however, circumstances have changed. The purpose of this military campaign is to forestall the other powers. Under the pretext of coming to Baratieri's assistance, the British mean to shut out the French, the Belgians, the Germans — even the Italians themselves. What do you think! Queen Victoria has her sights set on territories far beyond

Omdurman. She dreams of a British Africa running from Alexandria to the Cape. If the British have decided to extend the railway line, it isn't just to keep General Kitchener's troops supplied!"

Solange Popinot, who was beginning to find this discussion rather protracted, played the opening bars of the *Marseillaise*. They were a nod in Ibrahim's direction. "Yes, yes," he said with a laugh, "my work is coming along. You'll see . . . "

Milo burst into song:

> Contre nous de la tyrrr-annie-eu
> L'étendard sanglant-t-élevé
> L'étendard sa-a-anglant-t-élevé . . .

"Spare us, spare us!" cried Solange, pretending to stop her ears. But Seif pursued his train of thought in an earnest voice.

"In 1884 the British forced Egypt to abandon the Sudan. That was illegal: only the sultan could have ordered the khedive to make such a withdrawal. Today the British are compelling Egypt to drench the Sudan in the blood of her sons. That's illegal too: only the sultan can decree a military operation. The truth is, the British wanted Egypt to give up the Sudan so as to reconquer it for their own exclusive benefit."

"I'm completely lost," said Solange.

"It's quite simple," Milo said with a simulated air of gravity. "The Sudan belongs to Egypt, so it belongs to Britain. But, since Egypt belongs to the Ottoman Empire . . . "

31

William Elliot's first letter was discreetly delivered to the shop by a soldier in civilian clothes. Dora slipped it into her bodice without mentioning it to Milo. She waited until that evening to read it by lamplight, while nursing little Marthe.

Firket, 10 June 1896

Dear Friend,

If this letter causes you to think, if only for a moment, of a dust-caked officer in the furnace heat of the Sudan, I shall be overjoyed.

Permit me to dedicate our first victory, which I hope will be the first of many, to yourself.

We had concentrated our forces at Akasha, some ninety miles beyond the frontier: ten battalions of infantry, seven squadrons of cavalry including my own, and elements of the Camel Corps. Reported to be facing us were 30,000 Dervishes! Without hesitation, General Kitchener formed two columns. The first, under his personal command, advanced upstream. Our own was instructed to cut off the enemy's line of retreat by crossing the desert and occupying the high ground above Firket. On 7 June we marched on the Dervishes' camp. Many Arabs were killed in the course of a brief engagement, among them Emir Hammouda, whose body was identified by Slatin Pasha. Do you realize that this one victory has extended Egypt's territory by 450 miles?

Thank you for not forgetting me.

Yours,

William Elliot

There could be no question of showing this letter to Milo. Although Dora might have destroyed it right away, she decided to keep it long enough to reread it, so she locked the envelope in a blue velvet casket and hid the key. She had no reason to reproach herself, after all. How could she have prevented the Englishman from writing to her? She couldn't even forbid him to write again.

Three months later, on her return from Fleming, she received a second letter via the same messenger. Its tone was more direct, more intimate.

Dongola, 23 September 1896

My dear Dora,

Will you forgive me for not having written to you before? We weren't allowed to send any mail until after the capture of Dongola, which has now, thank God, been completed in accordance with the Sirdar's plans. The Egyptian flag has been flying over the town since yesterday.

The crossing of the Second Cataract was a genuine feat. Just imagine: in order to negotiate the rapids, each of our gunboats had to be towed upstream by 2000 men hauling on huge ropes! Half of them were replaced every quarter of an hour.

Then, in frightful heat, we marched across the desert to Sadin-Funti. A sandstorm threatened us with disaster, but the Dervishes did not, as luck would have it, put in an appearance.

After various incidents, the whole of the expeditionary force assembled not far from Asbara, whither supplies of food, equipment and ammunition had been transported by dhows and steamers. Our advance on Dongola could commence.

On 19 September the Dervishes were driven out of Hafir, then cut to ribbons by our artillery shells. After that the entire column crossed over to the west bank of the Nile. Number 4 Squadron, commanded by Captain Adams, charged some Baggara cavalry. Adams fought hand to hand with their commander. Both men were unhorsed and the squadron rode over them, but Adams escaped without a scratch!

The battle of Dongola was relatively easy in spite of the continuous fire of the Dervishes, who were better armed than we had thought. Pursued by the Egyptian cavalry, they abandoned their children in the sand. Not long afterwards our artillery wagons came trotting into Dongola laden with black babies!

Dear Dora, I often think of the torchlight parade you attended with your husband at Qasr al-Nil Barracks. You looked stunning in that emerald velvet cape. It was that mental image which sustained me during the assault on Dongola. I wanted you to know, that's all.

I hope you had an enjoyable holiday in the cool sea air at Fleming. What wouldn't I give for a swim right now! I shall write to you again at the earliest opportunity — that's a promise.

Yours,
William

32

The war against the Mahdists wrought no changes in Cairo's cultural and social life. The opera, in particular, was more active than ever. Although the theatre season lasted only a few months, it kept the European colony occupied all year round. In newspapers and drawing rooms alike, interminable controversies raged over the choice of programmes, the quality of the performers, and the manager's dynamism. No subject was taken more seriously than the theatre, and none aroused such passion.

Norbert Popinot, who held a season ticket for the Khedival Opera, where boxes were expensive and evening dress was *de rigueur*, used to hold forth at length on the relative merits of the Alexandria and Cairo companies.

"The Alexandrians are privileged," he would say. "They have the Zinzinya, the Alhambra, the Alcazar, and the 'Abbas Theatre — and all available to fewer than six thousand people capable of appreciating Verdi or Bizet! In Cairo we're limited to the Opera and that pathetic open-air theatre in the Ezbekiyah. It's only natural that our standards should be more exacting."

Each of the two cities possessed a theatre committee whose members included several pashas. These gentlemen regularly went prospecting in France and Italy with a view to engaging the best companies. It sometimes happened that the more frivolous of them — or the more generous — offered their protection to some pretty young singer desirous of becoming acquainted with Egypt during the season.

At the Wednesday soirées Popinot never failed to give a detailed account of the performances he had attended with his wife. He described the costumes, the music, the audience's applause or catcalls.

"Ah, that scene!" he would exclaim. "The quartet in Act III sent the whole house into raptures, and everyone wept at poor Mimi's death in Act IV."

Dora, whose knowledge of opera was confined to Milo's falsetto solos, listened to these effusions in a dream. She luxuriated in Popinot's comments, which were those of a true connoisseur:

"Madame Lacombe's voice displays a few weaknesses, especially in the upper register."

The Frenchman was hard on artists of whom he expected much better things:

"As a tenor, Monsieur Bucognani can hold his own. His voice has the fluidity of an oboe. But, although he sings well enough, he can't act. He's no thespian."

In other cases he could be more indulgent:

"Mademoiselle Labarrère was suffering from a slight cold last night – she lacked her full vocal resources – but she bravely soldiered on and scored a triumph."

The manager of Cairo's Khedival Opera, the celebrated Monsieur Morvand, came in for much criticism. Norbert Popinot was not the only one to call for him to be relieved of his coveted post:

"Monsieur Morvand does his utmost to court disaster. He engaged some performers at random. That *Werther* was absolutely hopeless – unco-ordinated movements, noise, confusion, no music. The claque applauded in vain; the audience didn't even try to respond. His Highness left after the first act, which isn't a good sign. When the performance ended, several people sought out Morvand and demanded an explanation."

The season's programme, too, was criticized by some of the Opera's regular subscribers.

"For years now, they've selected nothing but works from the French repertoire," said Ibrahim, whose family rented one of the curtained boxes reserved for Muslim ladies. "As a genre, it's almost played out. They'd do better to go looking for some Italian operas with big ballet divertissements."

Two petitions began to circulate concurrently, one in favour of French opera, the other in favour of Italian. Norbert Popinot was torn between his patriotic sentiments and his desire for a change of programme and manager. Several of his friends experienced a similar division of loyalties. At the Cercle Français, the Opera controversy provoked crises of conscience more complex than the Dreyfus affair, in which each had chosen his side spontaneously.

At this difficult juncture, Milo – with thoroughly oriental flexibility – fed Popinot a crumb of consolation.

"My dear Norbert," he said, "you stand up for French opera, which is only natural. You also call for Italian opera, and the repertoire genuinely needs an infusion of new blood. Where's the problem? If I were you, I'd sign both petitions."

Popinot stared at him in perplexity. On reflection, however, this compromise appealed to him. He mooted it to his friends, hesitantly at first, but his self-assurance steadily grew with every favourable response he received.

"Art transcends patriotism," he went so far as to murmur, with an audacity which he himself found impressive.

Several members of the Cercle Français decided to sign both petitions, and Italian opera won by a short head.

The new manager, Luigi Gianoli, included forty works in the next season's programme, among them several by Puccini, Rossini, and Verdi. Though not dissatisfied with the repertoire and the artists, the Opera's season-ticket holders became convulsed by a new controversy: shouldn't ladies be prohibited from wearing hats of excessive size during performances?

"It's quite unacceptable," Popinot declared one Wednesday evening. "The other night I was prevented from seeing three-quarters of the stage by a monstrous basket of fruit. It was attached, heaven alone knows how, to the head of the president of the charity ball."

Popinot's small stature — he was several inches shorter than his wife — was insufficient to account for this visual disability, which was shared by many other occupants of the stalls. Solange, who detested hats, also complained of her female neighbours' headgear.

Some of the Opera's regulars had taken to arming themselves with a cushion to boost the height of their seats. Others brought two to be on the safe side, but this was not appreciated by the operagoers behind them. The hat dispute threatened to be compounded by a cushion fight.

Halfway through the season it was rumoured that a group of sixteen youngish gentlemen were planning reprisals: they had ordered some fourteen-inch tarbooshes and were threatening to wear them on the opening night of *Rigoletto* unless the ladies came to heel. The conspirators' names were to remain secret until the last moment, but Popinot claimed to know several of them.

The threat did not materialize. *Rigoletto* was a success, and the season continued relatively smoothly thanks to the diplomatic skill of Signor Gianoli, who was much esteemed by the fair sex and prevailed on the more recalcitrant of the ladies to replace their set pieces with modest creations.

"Signor Gianoli," declared Popinot, "has shown exceptional courage and perspicacity in this matter. There's talk at the Cercle Français of forming a committee to recommend him for the Légion d'honneur. We're to meet next week to decide."

"You'll tire yourself out again," said Lita Tiomji in her rather soft, lilting voice. She was adept at polite little remarks of a purely formal nature.

Aida had played at one or another of Alexandria's theatres every year since 1871, when it was first presented in Cairo to mark the opening of the Suez Canal, and season-ticket holders never tired of seeing Verdi's work performed by new artists recruited in Europe. That was how Mademoiselle Valentine Mendorioz came to arouse her audience's enthusiasm at the Zinzinya, in the course of a memorable evening for which Ibrahim made a special trip to Alexandria.

Ovation succeeded ovation throughout the performance. The stage, pelted with flowers from Act I onwards, was littered with them by the end of Act III. During the interval the diva received a number of little poems bearing the initials of well-known local dignitaries.

Members of the public awaited her at the stage door, torch-bearers surrounded her carriage, and a band of amateur musicians escorted her back to her hotel. The next day she found herself the recipient of numerous gifts: a ring, sundry bracelets, a set of engraved silver coffee cups, and even some envelopes containing cheques. It was reported that Rizqallah Bey, owner of the *Touta et Fils* department stores, had sent her a magnificent bronze-framed mirror two metres high. The day she sailed for Europe, Mademoiselle Mendorioz received an album containing all the verses composed in her honour, notably a quatrain signed "Ibr":

> *Whate'er thy role — Aïda, Desdémone,*
> *or doleful Mimi, racked with coughing dire —*
> *it is the magic of thine art alone*
> *that nightly thrills the audience entire.*

"Bravo," cried Solange Popinot, when Ibrahim read out his poem to the Wednesday circle, "you've surpassed yourself!"

"What about that *Marseillaise* of yours?" demanded Seif, who was nettled by such trivial distractions.

33

"Oh, no! This time I'll leave him to you."

Milo had just caught sight of Oscar Touta, swathed in a black cloak, crossing the square on his way to the shop. His sexagenarian uncle thrust the door open with his walking stick.

"Today, uncle," Milo said in his most honeyed tones, "Dora will be taking your photograph. Yes, yes, Dora, my wife. She takes excellent portraits, you'll see."

Oscar Touta, who had barely heard, was already heading for the mirror to adjust a rebellious wisp of hair with his finger. Milo seized the opportunity to go and play a game of backgammon in the local café. He could always be sure of finding an opponent among the tarbooshed idlers seated at the tables noon and night, puffing at their *shishas*. Dora would know where to find him in an emergency.

"A day without backgammon," he used to say, "is like Mass without Communion."

Except that Milo took backgammon a good deal more seriously than Communion. Each of his throws was accompanied by earnest, almost theological comments if he was winning, and by fearful oaths if luck had the effrontery to desert him. A small crowd always gathered round the table to watch these three-piastre games. Some players moved their mother-of-pearl pieces silently, sliding them across the board. To Milo, by contrast, backgammon was inconceivable without crashes and exclamations. He picked up the pieces and slammed them down on the board as if trying to shatter them.

As soon as the Photographer to the Consulates entered the café, the one-eyed bootblack came hurrying over. He knelt down, removed Milo's shoes, and bore them off, leaving him in his socks on the sawdust-strewn floor. A quarter of an hour later the shoes were returned, shining like twin suns.

Bulbul came to summon his employer halfway through the second game: Oscar Touta wanted him in the shop.

"How much do I owe you?" Oscar inquired.

"Owe me? For what?"

"For the photograph of me your wife just took, of course!"

"What! You mean she actually took your photograph, uncle?"

"What did you expect her to do, idiot?" Oscar said testily. "What is this place, a hairdressers', a Turkish bath?"

Milo couldn't get over it. Oscar tendered a banknote and he pocketed it, looking foolish. Dora emerged from the studio a moment later. It was all she could do not to laugh.

"Honestly, I must be dreaming!" Milo exclaimed when his uncle had closed the shop door firmly behind him. "How did you manage it?"

"How?" Dora feigned surprise. "I took his photograph, that's all."

"Come on, tell!"

In the studio, privately cursing Milo for his backhanded concession, Dora had told Oscar Touta on impulse that the camera had developed a fault, so she couldn't photograph him. He looked relieved. She then proceeded to explain how sensitive plates worked. He listened with only half an ear and took in very little of what she said, but his nervous tics subsided. Having "repaired" the camera before his eyes, she then took a photograph. He seemed delighted.

"I think he'll come back for more," she told Milo.

Oscar's photographic adventures had amused the Touta family for years. Everyone used to weep with laughter at Milo's impressions of Oscar's abortive visits to the studio, so his "cure" threatened to deprive them of a treasured piece of family folklore. But Milo was never short of stories. His fund of hilarious anecdotes increased as his clientele became more numerous. One could be forgiven for assuming that all the crackpots in Cairo filed past his lens. To the children of the family, his photographic studio seemed a magical place, a veritable Aladdin's cave. Even Dora laughed uproariously at Milo's tales of Gilbert and Alphonse.

Alphonse ("Alphonth") and Gigi, of whom the former had a lisp that only endeared him more to the latter, were a couple of fifty-year-old bachelors who had long shared an apartment opposite the Telegraph Company building in Emad ed-Din Street. They regularly came to be photographed on the ottoman, side by side, but each was apprehensive of the result.

"No, I don't want to thee mythelf!" Alphonse would say. "I'm far too ugly."

"Stop it!" Gilbert would retort. "If *I* were lucky enough to have a nose like yours . . . "

Milo had devised a good way of showing them their double portraits. Masking the print with a small piece of cardboard, he showed Alphonse the half that depicted Gilbert and Gilbert the half that depicted Alphonse. This evoked cries of delight.

"Thuperb!" Alphonse would say. "You've captured him perfectly!"

"*Ayyuh!*" Gilbert would exclaim. "He's handsomer than that tenor at the opera the other night."

Then came the rather awkward moment when each was confronted by his own face on the other half of the photograph. That was Milo's signal to come out with his *pièce de résistance*:

"Honestly, Monsieur Gilbert, I've never seen a more piercing gaze in eight years behind the camera . . . Monsieur Alphonse, I can't get over it: you could be mistaken for the Prince of Wales."

Milo was adept at including the children and young people of the family in his world. They felt they knew its inhabitants without ever having set eyes on them. His friends and customers were benchmarks and points of reference — sometimes, even, like saints and angels, unseen observers capable of judging or being disappointed by their behaviour. Seif made a particular impression on them. Although the lawyer did not know them and they themselves would have found it hard to recognize him in the street, Yolande was heard telling a cousin of hers one day, "You mustn't say such nice things about the English in front of Seif!"

Milo's nephews had a soft spot for Ibrahim. Reassured by his poor showing at school, his bad habits and sarcastic remarks, they often mentioned him to their friends and proudly pointed out that their uncle was on close terms with a minister's relation – a poet, moreover, who was writing the Egyptian *Marseillaise*. They had invented a game that consisted in replying to each other in rhyme, a practice at which Yolande excelled. Not that she admitted it, she was head over heels in love with Ibrahim.

The Popinots occupied a special place in the family imagination. Thanks to them, or to Milo's descriptions of them, the young Toutas got to know a France that was gay and frivolous, if not downright saucy – a France that did not, of course, figure in the lessons taught them by the Frères des Écoles Chrétiennes or the nuns of the various congregations to which their innocent souls had been entrusted. Thus, the native land of Charlemagne and Joan of Arc expanded to include the Moulin-Rouge, Réjane, and *la belle* Otéro . . .

Milo had never been to Europe. He followed events in Paris through the medium of what Norbert and Solange Popinot told him about them. But how enthusiastically he transmitted those items of information to his nephews! The arcades in the rue de Rivoli, Sarah Bernhardt's latest triumph, preparations for the World Exhibition, the flower festival in the Bois de Boulogne, the incredible elegance of Boni de Castellane . . . The boys lapped up every word he uttered. To them, Paris at third hand was a place of enchantment.

In return, the Popinots became acquainted with an Egypt of byways and back streets unknown to the majority of Europeans. Milo, who accompanied Norbert on his visits to banks and government departments, initiated him into the science of *bakshish*:

"No official leaves his desk drawer open by accident. You would offend him if you slipped a guinea straight into his hand . . . "

Solange had the delicious feeling that contact with the lower orders was leading her into dissolute ways. She was hugely amused by Richard Tiomji's Arabic oaths and demanded immediate translations of them. "May God hang him!" she would exclaim, with one of her full-throated laughs. "May the pepper of envy scorch him!" She was the first to applaud when Seif invited them all to attend the wedding of one of his brothers, which was to take place in five weeks' time. "A Muslim wedding!" she kept saying, overcome with delight.

The marriage-broker consulted by the young lawyer's family had proved remarkably efficient. When submitting the results of her research a few days later she sang the praises of the prospective bride, allegedly a young person of exceptional qualities and sheltered upbringing, discreet as a shadow and breathtakingly beautiful. She received a sceptical hearing. Accompanied by five of his sisters and sisters-in-law, Seif's mother went to assure herself of the accuracy of this information at a party given by the womenfolk of the opposing camp. Returning home convinced, she gave her son a richly adjectival account of the merits of the fifteen-year-old girl in question, and it was decided to sign the marriage contract.

"But your brother still hasn't seen his future wife," Solange protested.

"He'll see her on their engagement day," Seif replied. "It'll be a pleasant surprise, I'm sure."

The fiancé's mother criss-crossed the city all day long, paying calls on the ladies of her acquaintance. Each of them showered her with congratulations, questions, and kisses.

The betrothal took place one Thursday. Seif described how the wedding presents had toured the whole district, escorted by mounted policemen and preceded by musicians. In the open carriage were some twenty caskets with glass sides that enabled everyone to see their contents: not only silverware, china, embroidered gowns, silk chemises, parasols, fans, and beaded slippers, but crystallized fruit, chocolates, and sweets of all kinds.

"In the *salamlek*," Seif went on, "the fiancé and the girl's representative removed their shoes before sitting down on the carpet, facing each other.

They made their proposals of marriage in turn and joined hands. Then the *qadi* placed his hand on theirs and recited some verses from the Koran. Finally, they signed the contract that specifies how much money is to change hands."

"Ah, the dowry," said Norbert. "At least that's the same as with us."

"Yes," Ibrahim put in mockingly, "except that it's paid by the husband."

34

It was about nine o'clock when Milo and I turned up at the wedding night party. The whole of the small square to which Seif had directed us was occupied by a multicoloured marquee some ten metres high. Guests were greeted at the entrance by musicians playing flutes and tambourines. Inside, the tent poles were almost hidden by lamps, flowers and palm fronds. Running along one of the canvas walls was a platform with two gilt chairs on it.

The Tiomjis, already seated at one of the tables with Ibrahim and the Popinots, beckoned to us to join them. Seif, looking very smart, came over soon afterwards. "Permit me to introduce my brother," he said. The young bridegroom, attired in a black *stambouline* and a white waistcoat, was going the rounds of the tables. He shook hands, thanked us for our gifts, and suggested that the ladies might care to go into the house and inspect the wedding presents, which were laid out upstairs. Solange Popinot rose at once, all excited, and swept us – Lita and me – along with her.

There were only women upstairs. Several of them had clustered round the bride, a mere child on the verge of tears, and were busy adjusting her white satin gown. In order to enter her husband's home some hours earlier, she had been obliged to step over a pool of blood – steaming blood still warm from the water buffalo calf whose throat had been slit in her honour.

We were privileged to visit the bridal chamber under the supervision of one of Seif's aunts. Part of the room was occupied by an enormous four-poster. Two pairs of new, neatly aligned slippers awaited their owners. Draped over some divans were several nightgowns of fine cambric, together with the shirts, undergarments and socks presented by the bride to her future lord and master. "How very original," said Solange, rather at a loss for words.

During our absence the bridegroom had gone to the mosque with his friends to pray. The procession wound its way through the alleyways of the district, lit by lanterns and flaming torches. When he returned an hour later the marquee was filled with the scent of roast meat. The guests were seated in groups of eight or ten around low tables, each of which bore a huge copper tray with a whole roast sheep on it.

Richard Tiomji, who was famished, tore off a piece of meat with his hairy, pudgy fingers and gallantly tossed it on to Solange's plate. She gave a little cry of delight. "Wait, I'll get them to bring you some forks," said Seif, who was passing our table. "No, no, don't dream of it," said Solange, sinking her teeth in the meat with gusto.

Lita and I, who would have welcomed the aid of a fork, exchanged a surreptitious glance. Every now and then Richard wiped his greasy hands on a napkin embroidered with gold thread, took a swig of fruit juice, and went back for more. Norbert Popinot would happily have wet his whistle with a glass of burgundy or bordeaux, but he resigned himself to cold water and even made an effort to drink it by the jugful.

A sweet dish was brought, followed by some fish. Salt and sweet courses alternated. When the rice pudding finally arrived I admitted defeat and went off to wash my hands in a copper basin carried by one of the servants.

A zither player wrung some plaintive notes from his instrument. Then a singer launched into a nasal melody whose refrain was taken up in unison by a group of women:

> *Ya leili, ya layali*
> *Ya leili, ya layali . . .*

"What about you?" I asked Ibrahim. "Doesn't marriage appeal to you?"
"I'm too busy," he said gaily. "My *Marseillaise*, you know . . . "

Popinot asked a question about polygamy. Seif, who had joined us, surprised the French by defending the custom. "In the East every woman is provided with a husband, whereas your European households are cluttered with elderly spinsters. Polygamy was instituted to guarantee women a home and their children a father whose identity they could be sure of. Isn't that better than the disguised polygamy you practise in Europe, where men conceal their mistresses' existence?"

It was hard to picture Seif with several wives — or even, to be honest, with one. Nothing seemed capable of distracting him from the political fray, neither the joys of family life nor the pleasures of sex.

There was a sudden commotion at the end of the marquee nearest the house: the bride was entering to the sound of shrill ululations from some women in black. "Watch," Ibrahim chuckled. "They're scattering pinches of salt on her head to ward off misfortune."

I scarcely recognized the child of a short time before. She was smothered in jewels, and the little one could see of the face beneath the veil seemed heavily made-up. She kissed her mother-in-law's hand, then climbed the steps to the platform and joined her husband, who was already seated on one of the gilded chairs. Meanwhile, stridently accompanied by the musicians, the crowd began to sing more loudly than ever:

Ya leili, ya layali
Ya leili, ya layali . . .

Belly dancers undulated to the furious rhythm of the *daraboukkas*. They were joined by a woman in peasant costume, who proceeded to wriggle her hips and make obscene gestures. Everyone roared with laughter except the bride, who demurely lowered her eyes.

The young couple soon left the platform and made for their private quarters. There followed a little more warbling and one or two cries of "*Ya leili*"; then the guests began to take their leave. It was nearly midnight. "To wash this whole feast down," said Popinot, "I'm inviting you all to a cognac at Shepheard's."

Lita had no time to object.

* * *

The famous hotel had just been renovated and equipped with electric light. I had never before set foot inside. All I knew of the place was the terrace and its two little sphinxes, which anyone could see from the street. Surrounded by all those Europeans, who looked thoroughly at home, one didn't seem to be in Egypt at all. We seated ourselves in a luxurious lounge with a ceiling of carved wood, and Popinot ordered a bottle of the finest cognac.

"I've just heard something quite incredible," he said. "Imagine, the Thomas Cook agency included an invitation to the Khedival Ball in its current programme – just like that! Naturally, the palace's masters of ceremony refused to issue any tickets. The English tourists are furious. Some of them have protested in writing to Lord Cromer."

"It's not as incredible as all that," Milo said. "Under the last khedive, the agency's tour of Cairo included a visit to the vicereine. A request for an audience was submitted, and the British consulate persuaded her to grant it. Whole gaggles of English ladies and their daughters descended on the harem and were presented to the khediva. They peered at everything, fingered the silver plate and silk curtains, and then hurried off in search of other amusements – the bazaars, the Pyramids, the museum, et cetera."

Popinot shook his head in dismay. "The Cook agency runs this country. You need only pass its offices in Kamil Street and see the tourist guides on duty to realize that. What with their violet silk pelisses, their turbans and curved sabres, they're far more impressive than those wretched Egyptian policemen with holes in their shoes."

Conversation reverted to the wedding and the nightgowns and under-garments displayed in the bridal chamber. After the third cognac, matters began to get out of hand. "Do you know," asked Popinot, "why all the obelisks are on the east bank of the Nile and all the pyramids on the west?" None of us had registered this fact. In any case, the French couple were the only members of the party to have visited Upper Egypt. "You mean you don't know? Why, because the obelisk is a phallus and the pyramid symbolizes woman!"

"I don't see how pyramids resemble women," Richard Tiomji said thickly.

Popinot and Milo burst out laughing.

"The pyramid is the breast of Isis," said Popinot. "But it could also be a more intimate part of her anatomy."

"An inverted pyramid, if you like," Milo remarked to Richard.

Lita found it hard to conceal her embarrassment, I was amused to see. She looked like a frightened doe, just as she used to at boarding school when she saw me reading a prohibited book. She was little different from the adolescent of those days. Slim, impeccably turned out, her wrists adorned with gold bracelets, Lita had the rather frigid charm of a woman unlikely to derive much pleasure from lovemaking. "Hardly surprising, with that great ape of a husband," I told myself, rather fuddled by the fumes from my brandy glass.

Talk of monuments and sex continued, punctuated by exclamations. Richard hooked a finger in Popinot's waistcoat pocket. "Male ostriches have whoppers, did you know that? You should see the things! That's why they mate properly, unlike other birds."

Lita didn't know what to do with herself. Even I was becoming embarrassed, so I drew Milo's attention to the fact that it was nearly two o'clock in the morning, and that Marthe had been running a slight temperature when we went out.

The little girl seemed restless when we got home. The nursemaid was fast asleep beside her bed, and the oil lamp was smoking dangerously. When I picked her up she had a sort of fit and passed out — not the first time this had happened. "Quick," I called to Milo, "fetch the sulphuric ether from the darkroom!"

He almost tumbled down the stairs with the lamp in his hand. Dashing to one of the cupboards in the darkroom, he grabbed a bottle. Realizing as he hurried back upstairs that it was the wrong one, he swore and retraced his steps. The baby had recovered consciousness by the time he returned. I made her some camomile tea. A quarter of an hour later she seemed quite calm and her temperature had gone down a little.

"They're simple spasms, not convulsions," Doctor Touta had told me.

"She's a very sensitive child. I think she's trying to attract your attention."

Milo sat up with her till daybreak. Now and then he would pick her up and cradle her in his arms. Half asleep, I heard him singing:

Ya leili, ya layali
Ya leili, ya layali . . .

35

Not everyone was lucky enough to have a father like Milo. His nephews, whom he had charmed since childhood, envied his daughters and conceived of their existence as one long playtime – nor were they wide of the mark.

Once a month if they had been good – though children were always good, if not too good, in Milo's estimation – he would take the two older girls, Nelly and Gabrielle, on a "Swaress trip". Nothing delighted them more than a ride in one of the omnibuses that took their nickname from their owner, Count Suarès.

The driver, perched high on his box, whipped up the horses after every stop and cursed them roundly. The Swaress passed the Mixed Courts and skirted the Rossetti district, then drove all the way along Clot Bey Street to the station. After crossing the railway line it turned into Shubra Street, a handsome thoroughfare flanked by giant sycamore trees. Ahead lay open countryside.

"We'll get out here," Milo told the driver.

Nelly and Gabrielle gazed at the elegant carriages that paraded up and down the avenue from dawn to dusk. Sometimes the khedive himself put in an appearance, preceded by cavalrymen in gold sashes. Milo would then launch into a regular fairytale: how the young prince had been summoned back to Egypt on the death of his father; how he'd had to brave a storm aboard the decrepit Austrian warship that was bringing him home; how he'd fallen in love with a beautiful slave when the sultan intended him to marry his daughter. Gabrielle, who was only two, understood little of this story, but Nelly adored it. In any case, its telling delighted the storyteller himself.

Another omnibus conveyed them back to their point of departure outside the Ezbekiyah Gardens, and the outing was always rounded off by a pistachio ice cream at the Pâtisserie Mathieu.

Dora was happy to let the little girls go with their father, knowing that he would derive as much amusement from such excursions as they did. "I sometimes tell myself that Milo is the mother of my daughters," she confided to Lita, her feelings of affection mingled with pangs of conscience. Her friend would either refrain from commenting, eyes fixed on her embroidery, or sigh faintly and change the subject.

On Sundays, when the shop was shut and Marthe in the care of her nursemaid, Dora's solitude enabled her to complete some job in the dark-room or go and daydream on the terrace. She needed to be alone with herself, whereas Milo found it impossible to live without other people. Even at Mass on Sunday mornings he was incapable of restraining himself for five minutes without making some whispered remark to his immediate neighbours.

On the terrace Dora would look through her photographic notebook. At this stage, faithful to the instructions in *L'Amateur Photographe*, she still made daily sketches of views, poses and simple lighting effects for future reference. This virtuous practice irritated Milo, but she pretended not to notice. There were even times when she deliberately overdid her assiduity in a spirit of provocation that wasn't the least of her faults.

Milo lost interest in the Swaress during the autumn of 1896. Thereafter his attention was focused entirely on trams, the first of which had just begun to operate between 'Ataba al-Khadra Square and the Citadel. Everyone in Cairo was fascinated by these electricity-fed serpents on rails, for which Belgian engineers had gouged endless grooves in the thoroughfares. Crowds of onlookers gathered whenever a tram passed by. These gleaming machines, with their merrily clanging bells, were a universal topic of conversation, not only at the Turf Club but in the humblest of Arab cafés.

Solange Popinot pronounced the subject tedious, unlike Ibrahim, who rebuked her in verse:

> Madame, you really should not rue
> the advent of a godhead new
> surpassing Buddha or Vishnu.
> Applaud this novelty, madame,
> for Christendom and ev'n Islam
> are bowing down before the Tram.

By the following year, controversy was raging. The newspapers published irate letters denouncing the casual attitude of the *wattmen*, or drivers, to whom timetables meant absolutely nothing. They not only expressed their mood of the moment by braking inopportunely or accelerating abruptly, but sailed past request stops and ignored the signals of prospective passengers whose faces didn't appeal to them.

"I waved my hat and stick like mad," Norbert Popinot protested in outraged tones, "but did he stop, the dirty dog? Not on your life!"

He waxed even more indignant about passengers who jumped on between stops or clung to each other on the running boards. Their bad manners were more than he could stand.

"Imagine, the other day I found myself next to someone who not only dug his elbows into my ribs but persisted in eating that dried fish with the overpowering smell."

"*Fisikh,* you mean?" said Milo, hooting with laughter.

"It wasn't funny, believe me. As for the passengers who sit cross-legged, the better to pick their toes . . . "

Popinot resolved never to take the tram again, but the horrible beast appeared to have it in for him. One morning, when his coachman was driving down the middle of Muhammad Ali Street followed by a tram descending from the Citadel, the horse took fright at its bell. It shied and bolted, knocking down a pedestrian as it went. Popinot very nearly ended up beneath the wheels of his own carriage.

Milo, for his part, welcomed the tram with the same enthusiasm as he had hailed the coming of cinematography. The Lumière brothers' early works, which were shown in a Cairo café, thrilled him to the marrow. He had seen *L'Arroseur arrosé*, *Les Chutes de Niagara* and other, similar shorts no fewer than three times, and three times he had come home with eyes alight and superlatives on his lips.

He was spellbound even by technical innovations capable of impinging on his own profession. The Eastman Company was conducting an aggressive advertising campaign for its Kodak camera: "Each shot requires only two movements. First, depress a lever; secondly, turn a key. If you can wind your watch, you can use a Kodak."

Milo ordered a Kodak as soon as he could. The relatively heavy box that was delivered to him guarded its secret closely. There was no question of opening the case for a peep inside: the sensitive element would have been ruined. This consisted, not of plates, but of a flexible film propelled by a winding mechanism.

Milo christened his Kodak in the Ezbekiyah Gardens. He snapped his family and the Tiomjis, who were also there with their children. Then, as instructed, he mailed the whole camera back to Europe to have the negatives developed.

"It isn't very practical," was Dora's verdict.

The Kodak returned after several weeks, together with some prints so dark that the children couldn't recognize their own faces.

"And Lita looks like an ostrich," said Richard, with his customary tact.

Clearly, the Kodak revolution still had some way to go. Milo was very disappointed, but his ultimate emotion was one of relief. "The button-pressers," he declared, "present no threat to professionals like us."

The Kodak was simply a toy. The Photographer to the Consulates would never have dreamt of using one to take the annual family photograph. His subjects would have felt cheated. After all, how could such a rite be worthily performed without a black cloth, sensitive plates, and a tripod?

36

That summer, however, the members of the Touta family were entitled to two photographs, not one. The announcement was made by Milo:

"Dora will take over from me in a minute; then I'll be able to come and pose with you."

The rest of his remarks were drowned by youthful cries of delight.

Proceeding in the time-honoured way, he marshalled his sixty-odd relatives in rows outside Dr Touta's villa. Children under the age of twelve sat on the sand in front. Behind them came a row of cane chairs for the elderly. The rest of the family were disposed on the steps in perfectly symmetrical tiers.

Maggi, Yolande's little sister, would not stay put. She not only kept turning round but sometimes stood up to see what was going on behind her. Other children followed suit, and all Milo's powers of persuasion were required to induce them to sit still and face the front.

The grown-ups, too, succumbed to a certain amount of disorder. Aunt Angéline, no longer able to endure the confines of the chair that had been assigned her, suggested swapping places with her daughter Rose, who was situated at the other end of the steps. This change of position threatened to upset the photographer's careful arrangement. In the end it was Marguerite's wicker chair, a receptacle the size of a hip bath, that had the privilege of accommodating Angéline's cramped posterior.

There followed a few more negotiations and final adjustments. Milo regularly emerged from under the black cloth to ask someone to close up or someone else to move slightly to the left or right.

"All right, everyone," he called at last. "Quite still now!"

The Touta clan donned a fixed smile and froze for what seemed an eternity.

Dora took over amid a babble of exclamations and laughter. Additional confusion was caused by two old aunts who had not been informed of the second part of the programme. Milo cupped his hands around his mouth.

"Stay where you are, all of you!"

Although rather nervous, Dora was not displeased by the confusion that had set in. "Children," she called to the front row, "you can get up and mingle with the grown-ups."

She would have liked to inject some novelty into the picture by siting the camera at the top of the steps, or even on the first-floor balcony. This being her first family photo, however, she dared not carry originality too far. She had given the matter a great deal of thought, naturally. Her photographer's notebook was full of peculiar diagrams in which the tops of silhouettes formed curves, triangles, or inclined planes. In the event, she arranged the family in a semicircle, inviting several dark-suited men to form a group on one side with some women in pale dresses standing in front of them. Everyone was amused by these unexpected instructions, which came as a welcome break after the official photograph. Albert's eldest son, who liked a joke, climbed on a chair for long enough to get some laughs.

Then silence was abruptly restored by a clatter of hoofs. Everyone turned to see an opulent landau bowling along the road.

"Well I'm damned!" cried Milo. "It's Rizqallah!"

The owner of the *Touta et Fils* department stores had, in fact, announced his intention of coming the day before, but no one had expected him to turn up. This would be his very first appearance in a family photo. The carriage door opened and the great man, attired in a superbly cut suit of bronze satin, alighted. At once, several people hurried over to him.

No member of the family was more assiduously courted and pampered than Rizqallah Bey. He was always being buttonholed by some uncle or aunt. "Rizqallah, *habibi*," they would ask, "do you by any chance sell black mantillas (or pink quilted housecoats, or hem-stitched cretonne)?"

The owner of *Touta et Fils* would then produce a visiting card from his waistcoat pocket, scribble a few words on it in his big, spiky handwriting, and hand it over with a condescending smile. "Of course I do! Go to the lingerie (or hosiery, or haberdashery) department. They'll give you a nice discount."

Old Dr Touta was one of the few people not to be impressed by his nephew, whom he remembered as a humble twenty-year-old dragoman employed by the French consulate in Alexandria. He could not refrain from chiding him now and then. "Take care," he used to mutter, "gold weighs you down."

Several of the menfolk insisted on surrendering their places to Rizqallah for the photograph. They made a great fuss about it, adopting a peremptory, spuriously familiar tone and punctuating their demands with oaths:

"Sit there, I tell you! Sit there, may God hang you!"

A powerful fragrance emanated from Rizqallah's person. A spicy perfume with a gum benjamin base, it annihilated every other scent in its vicinity and could only have been worn by a man of his distinction.

The department store tycoon went to say hello to Dr Touta, who was seated, grumbling, in the middle of the front row. Then he sat down on the vacated chair beside him – the place of honour, so to speak.

Dora was growing impatient. All the men had risen to their feet and were looking in the same direction. She asked them to turn and face one another as though engaged in conversation.

"And you," she called to Aimé and Albert, "don't turn your backs on each other. You'll look as if you've had a row."

"Well, I declare!" boomed Rizqallah. "So we're to have our picture taken by a pretty young woman!"

A burst of laughter greeted this happy turn of phrase. The Mameluka's irritation mounted.

"You'd look better standing up," she told him rather curtly. "That's right, please mingle with the other men, it'll be better that way."

"I always obey pretty young women!" cried Rizqallah, and his gallant rejoinder earned him another laugh.

Dora disappeared under the black cloth. As soon as she had exchanged the focusing screen for the sensitive plate, she released the shutter.

Milo managed to include Rizqallah in his own photo by dint of some skilful retouching. He never hesitated to employ this device on behalf of absent relatives anxious to associate themselves with the family ritual, so he contrived to insert his distinguished cousin in a vacant space between two aunts. Indeed, on the print destined for him personally, the owner of the *Touta et Fils* department stores appeared in the very front row, the jeweller Alfred Falaki having been banished to make room for him.

The difference between the two photographs was striking. Milo's showed a group of frightened people staring fixedly at the lens as if some terrible event were unfolding before their eyes. The print was dappled with pale patches, these being disembodied hands that should properly have been concealed.

On Dora's photograph, only Aimé and Albert had a stiff and unnatural air. Their wives, on the other hand, seemed deep in conversation, and Maxime Touta was exchanging confidences with Nada Mancelle. Even Alfred Falaki, who usually resembled a shop window dummy, with his big, sparkling ring and gold watch chain, had been captured at an expansive moment.

Dora was dismayed when she saw the two negatives developed side by side in the darkroom. With an embarrassment verging on panic, she wondered briefly whether she shouldn't give up photography altogether. The superiority of her work was too glaring to escape Milo, who simply laughed it off. Did he regret having suggested the taking of a second photograph, a practice repeated the following year at the unanimous request of young and old? It was the first time the Photographer to the Consulates had pitted himself against the subscriber to *L'Amateur Photographe*.

37

In the north of the Sudan, Anglo-Egyptian troops commanded by Sirdar Kitchener were advancing slowly but steadily, with the inexorability of a steamroller. Hundreds of soldiers had been assigned to construct the railway line that bypassed the Nile's convolutions by cutting straight across the desert. Over a mile of track was laid every day, even at the height of summer.

"That's all very well," said Norbert Popinot, "but who's going to foot the bill?"

Britain's plan to finance the military campaign out of the national debt had resulted in a clash with the French and the Russians, who were suing the khedival government in the Mixed Courts.

"This beats everything!" thundered Seif. "The British decide to invade the Sudan without even consulting the khedive, and now his government is being sued for having financed the operation!"

Harsh comments were passed on the celebrated "national debt case" at the Toutas' Wednesday soirées. Popinot opened the champagne on two occasions: once when the court ruled against the government and again when the latter lost its appeal. No sooner had judgment been given, however, than the British surmounted this obstacle by granting Egypt a special loan of £800,000 to finance the war in the Sudan. Seif was almost apoplectic.

"Eight hundred thousand pounds plus interest! How are we going to repay it? By accepting this loan we're fettering ourselves to the occupying power. The Sudan expedition will cement Britain's annexation of Egypt for evermore."

"Some people are never satisfied," grumbled Richard Tiomji. "You complain even when people lend you money."

He never spoke a truer word. Two years later, when the British government wrote off the debt as an ostensibly magnanimous gesture, the young Egyptian lawyer published a vitriolic article in two Arabic-language newspapers. "The cancellation of this debt," he declared, "is the foulest trap the occupying power could have set us . . . "

Abu Hamid, 10 August 1897

Dear Dora,

We arrived outside the walls of Abu Hamid on the 7th. The Dervish garrison was a thousand strong and resisted bravely, so we had to take the place by storm. Our victory cost us twenty-one dead, among them my good friend Edward Callaghan, who was serving under General Hunter's command.

The capture of Abu Hamid will enable us to extend the railway line this far, and, consequently, to replenish our supplies — not that we're short of anything as it is. The absence of our friends is all we find hard to endure . . .

The other day I sighted the photographic wagon attached to our headquarters. With you in mind, I put a few questions to the officer in charge, who is assisted by five men from the School of Military Engineering at Chatham. They photograph fortifications, entrenchments and views of various kinds, but also soldiers and prisoners of war. They are further called upon to enlarge, reduce or copy the plans and maps of which a certain number have to be distributed. The wagon is fitted out as a darkroom. One of the two cameras is such that it can be loaded on to a pack horse or mule, complete with plates and lenses, when the terrain is too rough for the wagon to negotiate. It seems that the process used for making prints is a warm platinotype bath (???) I don't think I'm betraying a military secret by telling you this.

Mail reaches us quite easily. I've heard from my father in Alexandria and my family in England, but not from you. May I hope for a few lines? The messenger who delivers this letter could forward yours in the opposite direction.

Your devoted
William

38

No, I simply couldn't send William Elliot a reply. Receiving unsolicited letters was one thing; writing back was another. I should have felt I was deceiving Milo.

My conscience pricked me sometimes. I wondered if I ought to have told my husband when the first letter came, but it was rather late for that. He would have asked to see the letters, and I couldn't have borne him to read them. Anyway, how could I prove that I'd never written back? The resulting scene would have had adverse repercussions on the young officer, of that there was no doubt.

To be honest, I derived a certain pleasure from the situation. Captain Elliot's letters aroused the sort of romantic daydreams I'd indulged in at boarding school. I was so obsessed with my imaginary Prince Charming, a Visigoth cavalier with golden locks, that I ended by admitting all in the confessional and earned myself a penance of thirty rosaries.

William Elliot's letters related to my private life, after all, and everyone is entitled to a few secrets. Husbands and wives aren't obliged to tell each other everything. "Once you've told each other everything, you've nothing left to say." Having read that equivocal statement somewhere, I clung to it as I did to Milo's shadowy past. He was always very vague about his youthful conquests prior to our marriage. Had he resisted the advances of the brazen creatures who haunted the lounges of the big hotels? I'd felt an involuntary pang of jealousy when I spotted one at Shepheard's the night Popinot entertained us there.

No, husbands and wives couldn't be expected to tell each other everything. I myself had only vaguely alluded to the miniature that had blighted my adolescence. That mouth . . . I was chary of mentioning it even now, for fear that Milo would spread the word. I should have felt as if a hundred pairs of eyes were forever scrutinizing my lips.

Every letter from William Elliot set my heart racing. I would prolong the pleasure by leaving the envelope unopened for several hours. Then, having read and reread the contents, I would lock it up in the little blue velvet casket.

Abu Hamid, 20 September 1897

Dear Dora,

The hours crawl by under a burning sun. Enforced inactivity is getting on my nerves. Sometimes, at dawn or dusk, I kill time by going for a solitary gallop in the desert. Our commanders have decided not to take any risks. This method has paid off perfectly, so far, but you know how impatient I am. Or do you, if the truth be told? What do you know of me?

What, for that matter, do I know of you?

We've lately been joined by a Sudanese battalion. I watch them every day, those black soldiers who loathe the Mahdists and are exemplary fighting men. Their courage and powers of endurance are unsurpassed. We have no difficulty in enlisting them in return for a uniform, a rifle, and fifteen piastres a month. You should see how lovingly they take possession of their guns! They finger them, fold them in their arms, sleep with them clasped to their chest. But they wouldn't dream of going off to war without a wife, those simple souls, so the military authorities' first concern is to get them married. Having enlisted some men, the recruiting officers round up a number of women or seize them from passing caravans and assemble them in camp. The men are then sent for one by one, beginning with the noncommissioned officers, and invited to take their pick. Finally, a qadi is summoned to marry them all in a body. Every wife is entitled to half-rations. The black soldiers take their meals and spend the nights in their tents, each in the company of his wife. They're more fortunate than us!

Still no news of you, my dear Dora — not a word. Does that mean you find

my letters tiresome? At least let me know if I'm not permitted to write to you
any more . . .

That time I almost wrote a note and entrusted it to the messenger in civilian clothes, who always contrived to hand me the envelopes discreetly.

I sometimes managed, during the day, to escape in spirit and picture William Elliot's existence in the scorching heat of the Sudan. My memory of his face had faded a little. I refreshed it by studying the photograph filed in our studio records. He was as handsome as I remembered.

It was a reinvigorated William who wrote to me the following April. I wondered with a twinge of jealousy if some Sudanese woman from the neighbouring battalion was helping to give this British warrior, too, a good night's rest . . . The letter had been sent from Atbara, which he called "Fort Atbara":

> *. . . At dawn, after bivouacking in the desert, we reached the Dervish camp at Shendi. Two hours later we bombarded it. The enemy responded with a brisk fusillade, and we were obliged to storm the place. The Egyptians and the British competed to see who could enter the fortified camp first. That honour went to the Cameron Highlanders, who drove the Dervishes back, trench by trench. The Egyptian cavalry had only to pursue the fugitives. We took a thousand prisoners including Emir Mahmoud himself, who was hiding under a bed.*
>
> *The savages left over 3000 dead on the battlefield. Our own losses were minute by comparison: fourteen dead and 200 wounded. I don't include myself in that number despite a scratch on the arm from a swordpoint, which will take some weeks to heal . . .*

39

Norbert Popinot commented derisively on the British victories. He attached far more importance to the exploits of a French expeditionary force dispatched to the Upper Nile under the command of Captain Jean Baptiste Marchand. Consisting of only 150 Senegalese riflemen, this had already crossed vast tracts of unconquered territory and succeeded in transferring a river steamer, the *Faidherbe*, from the basin of the Congo to that of the Nile. Popinot paid daily visits to the Cercle Français to consult the latest Paris newspapers and follow Captain Marchand's peregrinations step by step.

"We French," he proclaimed, "do not need an army of twenty thousand men to extend our influence in Africa."

Situated opposite the Ezbekiyah Gardens, the Cercle Français comprised a lecture hall, a card room, a billiard room, a drawing room, and a large terrace. This place of relaxation had become, in Popinot's phrase, "a focus of resistance to our adversaries", namely the British, whom he accused of shamelessly reaping all that the French had sown in Egypt since Bonaparte's day.

"Perfidious Albion," Popinot used to say, "has never deserved its name more richly than on the banks of the Nile."

For proof of this statement he had only to brandish any edition of his favourite daily paper, *Le Journal Égyptien*. Its French editor, Barrière Bey, printed a daily reminder at the head of page one that the British had reneged on their undertaking to withdraw from Egypt.

"You simply can't trust those people," was Popinot's verdict on them. He delighted in reading his wife the column entitled "Moustiques", which was devoted to British misdemeanours. "Listen to this, my dear," he would say. "The 'Mosquitoes' have distinguished themselves yet again . . . " He rejoiced at the smallest grain of sand that got into British cogs, for example:

Admiral Hopkins presided over the unveiling of Queen Victoria's statue at Port Said yesterday. All the bigwigs had assembled on the Quai Eugénie. The admiral gave a signal and the veil fell. What then came to light was a pathetic object in plaster, barely one metre high and reminiscent more of a saint's statuette than the effigy of a sovereign. While the Maltese band was striking up "God Save the Queen", one corner of the veil wrapped itself round Victoria's right arm and snapped off her hand. Admiral Hopkins gazed in horror at his mutilated sovereign . . .

Having been educated by French nuns, and belonging as she did to a community that regarded France as the natural protector of oriental Christians, Dora was susceptible to Popinot's acerbic remarks about the British. However, she found it hard to share his conviction that they were guilty of every sin under the sun. Like most members of the Syrian community – most Egyptians too, in fact – she had always adopted an ambivalent attitude towards the occupying power, and William Elliot's irruption into her life had confused her perception of the British still further.

She considered it rather endearing that the English ladies of Cairo should have founded a society for the protection of animals. Like them, she was revolted by cruelty such as that inflicted on a poor little dog whose forepaws had been severed by a passing tram. Some laughing urchins had picked it up and left it, oozing blood, outside the portals of the Mixed Courts.

The hospital set up by these ladies could accommodate as many as a hundred and twenty patients. Any animal found in poor condition on a public thoroughfare could be brought there. The society had become the bane of the capital's donkey-drivers, who feared being hauled off to the police station at any moment. Even their major competitor, the tramway, worried them less.

"The British would do better to take an interest in human beings," growled Seif.

"For all that," Dora pointed out, "it's thanks to them that slavery has been abolished in Egypt."

"What's the use of abolishing the enslavement of individuals, only to enslave a whole nation?" the young lawyer said darkly.

At the Wednesday soirées Dora listened in some perplexity to the arguments on both sides. The charges levelled at Britain by Popinot and Seif often drew sarcastic rejoinders from Ibrahim, though no one ever knew exactly what he was thinking. As for Richard Tiomji, he defended the British occupation in his blunt, commonsensical way, pointing out that Egypt had never been as peaceful and prosperous.

"You can say what you like, it's figures alone that count. The census has just shown that Egypt's population has grown from six-and-a-half million in 1882 to nine-and-a-half today – by a third, in other words. That would never have happened without the public health measures instituted by Cromer."

Richard shook his head apprehensively whenever Seif went into political or humanitarian considerations. It particularly annoyed him when the young lawyer quoted his hero, Mustafa Kamil, whose notoriety was steadily increasing, not only in Egypt but – thanks to Juliette Adam's support – in France as well. Seif never failed to enliven the Wednesday soirées with readings from the celebrated French journalist's letters to Mustafa Kamil and the latter's lyrical replies. One of these began: "Dearest Madame, I most respectfully kiss your hands and lay my most respectful tributes at your feet . . . "

"Don't you think he might have left her feet out of it?" Ibrahim said drily.

One Wednesday night, almost before he had entered the room, Seif saw Richard Tiomji bearing down on him with his eyes bulging.

"What right does that farmyard orator have to insult us?" Richard demanded.

Some days earlier, in a speech that attracted much attention, Mustafa Kamil had inveighed against "intruders in the pay of the occupying power" and accused them of spitting on the country that had made them so welcome. The Syrians found no difficulty in identifying themselves with this offensive description, on which several newspapers had commented.

First surprised by Richard's onslaught, then furious at having been treated to such a reception, Seif made for the door without a word. Richard caught him by the sleeve and drew back his fist.

"Stop it!" cried Lita, and Milo stepped between them.

"Come, come," Popinot said in a conciliatory tone. "If I had to come to blows with my Scottish neighbour every time the British committed some outrage . . ."

A little while later, when tension had eased, Milo drew Seif aside. "Try to understand," he said. "Mustafa Kamil's speech upset us a great deal. The Syrians have founded newspapers and businesses in Egypt. They hold many government posts."

"But Mustafa didn't denounce all the Syrians in Egypt," Seif said angrily. "He was only referring to certain profiteers. In any case, he'll make that clear in an article to be published tomorrow."

Popinot had just poured Richard, who was now at the other end of the room, a big glass of Saint Émilion. "Profiteers like me, you mean?" snarled the ostrich farmer.

"Please, Richard!" said Milo. "If Mustafa Kamil puts things right in his article, the incident will be closed. By the way, I haven't yet told you about Eldon Gorst's incredible trip to the province of Guirga."

"Who is this Gorst?" asked Lita, ready to do anything to disperse the storm clouds.

"Eldon Gorst is the Ministry of the Interior's strongman. The other day, the provincial governor who was supposed to meet him at Guirga failed to show up. Thoroughly put out, Gorst boarded his boat again. Just then the deputy *mudir* came running up, frantically waving his handkerchief from the bank. Gorst ordered the boat inshore again and picked up the perspiring little man, who apologized profusely. A little way downstream he put in at a deserted islet in the middle of the river and ordered the native official ashore. And that's where he left him, marooned in the middle of the river!"

"They've no manners, those people," was Popinot's comment.

40

Without a doubt, the only time Norbert Popinot approved of the British authorities was during the Muslim pilgrimage in the spring of 1898. "One doesn't trifle with the plague," he told Milo gravely.

Inveterately curious, Milo never failed to attend the departure of the Sacred Carpet for Mecca. In April each year he would take a party of young relatives to watch this rather peculiar ceremony, which attracted substantial crowds.

The pilgrims took thirty-seven days to cross the desert. They returned after three months, somewhat fewer than when they had set out, having lost the frailer of their number to heat, fatigue, or disease en route.

"No Muslim could hope for a finer death," said Ibrahim, who was as amused by this as he was by most things.

But death was prowling more busily than usual during the spring of 1898. There were alarming reports that the plague, which had been raging in India for some time, had reached the Hedjaz and was threatening to infect the pilgrims. Summoned to an emergency meeting in Cairo, the public health authorities had suggested banning the pilgrimage, and Popinot thought them justified.

"This business concerns us all. The expatriate communities are right to be worried. Egypt has always been a gateway for epidemics from Asia."

Seif, who vigorously advocated that the pilgrimage be allowed to proceed, argued that Muslims should not be prevented from fulfilling their most sacred duty.

"But there could be an epidemic!" Popinot said angrily. "Surely you don't want the plague to spread."

"The plague is in India, not the Hedjaz," Seif retorted. "The British are the masters of India; they need only close its borders. The Turks haven't been forbidden to go to Mecca by the sultan, the Commander of the Faithful. There can't be two rules inside the same empire. To forbid some Ottoman subjects a privilege permitted to others would be a treaty violation."

The Frenchman shrugged his shoulders, far from convinced by this quibble.

"Take care!" said Seif, growing heated in his turn. "To ban the pilgrimage would be to sow the seeds of hatred in Muslim breasts. Our people would bear a grudge against all Europeans, everything Christian . . . "

Propagated by the Cairo newspapers, this controversy intensified as the days went by. The Egyptian cabinet, greatly embarrassed by it, ended by issuing a compromise edict in which pilgrims were warned of the risk they ran. In order to obtain a passport, applicants had to undertake not to return to Egypt prior to the complete disappearance of any epidemic that might declare itself in the Hedjaz. Accordingly, they were required to prove that they had sufficient funds to meet their needs for at least six months.

"That's reasonable," said Popinot, somewhat relieved.

"Outrageous, you mean!" Seif cried. "This regulation means that only the rich can visit the holy places."

The danger assumed even clearer shape in the days that followed. The epidemic sparked off riots in Bombay, and several cases of the plague were reported in the Hedjaz.

"You see?" said Popinot.

"The reports are false," Seif snapped. "The Sherif of Mecca has given an assurance to that effect."

"But it's in the Sherif's interests to deny the existence of an epidemic that would reduce his takings."

Milo came back from Khan al-Khalili with some unpublished information: "On arrival at Jeddah all the pilgrims will be confined to the hospital for twelve days. After that spell of quarantine they'll be put aboard special boats and landed at an uninhabited spot on the coast. From there they'll be conveyed to Mecca by healthy camel drivers whose beasts have been disinfected in advance."

"What a delightful prospect," said Solange, and Ibrahim was moved to recite another of his quatrains:

> To part is like a taste of death, they say,
> so let us die with fervour and élan.
> Pilgrims, if you with fire resolve to play,
> a place in heav'n is yours from this time on.

An immense crowd thronged the streets of Cairo on 10 April. Milo had assembled his little party at an early hour and conducted them to Roumila Square, at the foot of the Citadel, but without Dora, who preferred to finish off some work in the studio. This was the young Toutas' first sight of the Popinots. Norbert had only decided to turn up at the very last moment, as if he suspected the pilgrims of carrying the plague already, but his wife, ever greedy for novel sensations, was in the highest of spirits. The youngsters of the family hovered round this alluring Frenchwoman, who had deemed it her duty to honour the Sacred Carpet by christening a gown with a plunging neckline — much to the amazement of the veiled women who watched her from their windows.

Milo had rented a rather decrepit balcony on the first floor of an uphol-sterer's workshop.

"It's the best possible vantage point," he assured Popinot. "We'll be exactly on a level with the Mahmal, the famous palanquin."

"Why a palanquin?" asked Popinot, eyeing the crowd apprehensively.

"It's in memory of a very beautiful woman, Shagaret-ad-Durr, who became sultana on her husband's death at the beginning of the Mameluke era. She ruled Egypt for eighty days before acquiring a new husband and going off on the pilgrimage in a sumptuous litter carried by camels. The Mahmal has accompanied the Kiswa ever since."

"And what, pray, is the Kiss-me?" Solange Popinot's question evoked universal laughter.

"The Kiswa," Milo told her with a smile, "is a silk cloth embroidered with verses from the Koran. The Egyptian sovereign sends it to the Sherif of Mecca every year, to cover the Ka'aba. Now you're going to ask me what the Ka'aba is . . . "

Members of the government and religious dignitaries were awaiting the khedive on a platform screened by multicoloured hangings. A salute of twenty-one guns greeted 'Abbas's arrival. His landau, flanked by mounted guardsmen, came into view.

Solange derived great entertainment from watching the crowd. The young Toutas, for their part, preferred to look at her plump, bare shoulders and picture the breasts beneath her bodice. When she raised her arm to point out some object of interest, they could see her shaven armpit glistening with a film of perspiration.

The procession entered the square soon afterwards, preceded by soldiers attired in white uniforms and tarbooshes. The pilgrims' tents, waterskins and prayer mats were carried by big camels decked out in palm fronds for the occasion. Strapped to the back of one animal was the chest containing the money that was to cover the caravan's expenses. Bringing up the rear were groups of Dervishes in turbans of various colours, who sent the crowd wild by performing weird dances to the rhythm of fifes and tambourines.

Cheers greeted the chief camel driver, a fat, bare-chested man swaying gently along on the back of a beast adorned with hangings and feathers. More cheers greeted the pilgrims' leader, who was to conduct the trek through the desert on his gorgeously caparisoned horse. Members of the caravan's military escort followed in their smart uniforms, equipped with brand-new carbines.

There was a buzz of excitement at the far end of the square. It swelled to a roar:

"*Al Mahmal! Al Mahmal!*"

The camel-borne palanquin, a litter with a sloping canopy, rocked to and fro as it threaded its way through the vociferous throng. Heaven alone knew what benefit they hoped to derive, but all were eager to approach it, touch it, put their lips to it. Protected by two ranks of mounted police-men, the sacred object made three circuits of the square accompanied by gunfire and the strains of a brass band.

"That old man at the rear," Milo explained to Popinot, "is Abul-Helawat, the so-called father of sweetness. He's never without his whip. It's his job to rouse sluggish pilgrims at dawn every day."

The procession turned down one of the streets that led off the square, followed by a joyful and disorderly crowd. As it passed them, some women behind the upstairs *mashrabiyas* tried to touch the Sacred Carpet by lower-ing scraps of cloth on lengths of string.

The young Toutas had struck up a conversation with Solange Popinot. She asked them various questions about Muslim religious festivals: Ramadan, the Moulids, Greater and Lesser Bairam. They answered rather haphazardly, laughing as they did so. She laughed too, with every sign of pleasure. The boldest of the boys contrived to take her hand and help her down the upholsterer's rickety stairs. She even saved herself by leaning on his shoulder with a little cry of alarm, having almost tripped and fallen. This incident was destined to preoccupy the youths of the family for some weeks to come.

"Now you've seen how people celebrate the pilgrims' departure, imagine what it's like on their return!" Milo said to Popinot. "Some families go out into the desert to meet the caravan, taking food and new clothes. They go from camel to camel in search of their fortunate relative, who will bear the illustrious title '*hagg*' from now on. Sometimes he's nowhere to be found, and they can tell from the other pilgrims' mournful expressions that some misfortune has befallen him. Others simply meet the new *hagg* at the gates of the city and escort him home with music and banners. In three months' time the khedive will return from Alexandria to welcome the Mahmal back. This square will witness scenes of jubilation even wilder than today's."

"The khedive may return," Popinot replied stiffly, "but *I* won't. For a dose of the plague? No thank you!"

41

The following Monday – an exceptionally rainy April day that was turning Cairo's streets into a vast quagmire – Milo dashed up the spiral staircase and burst into the nursery.

"Something extraordinary has happened," he gasped to Dora, looking quite distraught. "Something quite extraordinary – disastrous, in fact!" Without pausing to catch his breath, he went on, "An emissary from the palace was here. He only just left."

"From the palace?"

"Yes, the palace!" he spluttered. "Just imagine, the khedive saw the portrait of Ibrahim's uncle and fell in love with it. He wants me to photograph him too!"

It took Dora only a moment to gauge the extent of the disaster. Milo would never be able to produce as good a portrait of the khedive as she had of the minister. Unlike her, he didn't know how to play around with the lighting or exposure times. He was incapable of sensing the best angle or bringing out a sitter's personality – and, for all his braggadocio, he knew it.

"What on earth are we going to do?" he moaned.

Dora thought for a moment. "There's only one thing for it," she said. "I'll have to go to the palace."

"You, a woman? Are you mad?"

"But I won't be a woman."

He stared at her aghast.

"I'll disguise myself as a man."

Milo recovered from his momentary stupefaction. "This is no joking matter!" he snapped.

"I'm not joking," said Dora. "We'll go to the palace together. I'll be your operator."

"Don't be silly, it would only need someone to ask you a question and you'd be found out."

"Then I'll be dumb – yes, deaf and dumb. In the meantime, don't mention this to anyone. Not a word to Richard or Seif, let alone Ibrahim."

Milo was dismayed, not only by what had happened but also by his inability to cry it from the rooftops. He, the walking newspaper and purveyor of gossip, was condemned to keep mum about a sensational occurrence.

After discussing the matter until the small hours, they decided to solicit at least one outside opinion by confiding in Norbert and Solange Popinot.

"It's a big risk, my friends," said the Frenchman, looking worried. "Such decisions aren't to be taken lightly."

But he had no alternative to suggest. Solange uttered cries of enthusiasm. She would happily have accompanied them to the palace in male attire.

"Let's think it over till tonight," said Popinot.

It wasn't a Wednesday, as luck would have it, so their little group would not be meeting. When evening came, the four of them gathered over the shop. Milo, normally so fond of pranks and practical jokes, was in a terrible state. Popinot's caution perturbed him, but Dora concealed her own anxiety and promptly seized the bull by the horns. She announced in resolute tones that, having carefully considered the matter, she had decided to disguise herself as a man and photograph the khedive. Solange flung her arms round her neck, then sat down at the piano and dashed off the first few bars of a triumphal march.

The couple rehearsed their act in every detail. It was agreed that Dora would perform all the operations that did not require the khedive's cooperation – adjustments to the lighting, for instance. Any instructions to Milo would be conveyed by means of gestures or grunts.

Dora studied the official photographs taken of 'Abbas by Jacquemart. She found them technically perfect but soulless. The day before the session at the palace she jotted down the following resolutions in her notebook:

Above all, don't try to make him look regal. Be bold and capture his natural disposition. A's reserved expression is only skin-deep. His eyes yearn to smile.

Milo lay awake all night. Popinot's remark kept echoing inside his head: "It's a big risk, my friends. Such decisions aren't to be taken lightly." The khedive was reputed to be irascible, even violent. He'd ordered erring servants to be flogged before now, so it was said. Milo could already see himself in chains. He thought with dread of the convicts of Abu Za'abal, breaking stones on the banks of the Nile. They were forbidden even to watch their sovereign pass by. When the khedival barge drew level with them they had to form up, present their backs to the river, and bow their heads in submission.

That morning Bulbul was sent off on an errand that would take him to the other side of Cairo. A little notice on the shop door stated that the premises were closed for repairs. The Popinots turned up in good time, and Solange, in high excitement, saw to Dora's disguise under her husband's rather apprehensive gaze. The jacket, trousers and bootees fitted her perfectly, and her shapely hands were concealed by a pair of light gloves the colour of fresh butter. Solange gummed a thin false moustache to her upper lip and thickened her eyebrows. Her hair was pinned up into a bun beneath her tarboosh, which she would not be removing.

"Very practical, tarbooshes," remarked Popinot, trying to sound jocular. "You aren't expected to remove them, unlike hats – in fact it's very bad manners to do so. In Europe, my dear Dora, the man you purport to be would have had to bare his head, especially in front of royalty."

The Popinots' coachman drove them and their equipment to 'Abdin Palace. Dora's lips trembled involuntarily, and Milo was only partly reassured by the rather too vigorous and virile way in which she helped to carry the reflectors and the tripod on arrival.

They were conducted up a lateral staircase to the first floor. After making their way along a number of passages and traversing some sumptuously appointed reception rooms, they were ushered into a kind of spacious boudoir flanked by two french windows.

"I'll leave you to install yourselves," said the chamberlain who had accompanied them. "His Highness will be with you in half an hour."

Dora drew two deep breaths to steady her nerves. She was feeling even more apprehensive than she did before every photographic session, but she didn't show it.

Leaving Milo to unpack the camera, she experimented with the ebony chair on which the khedive was to sit. Having tried it in several different positions, she decided that it should face the light some three metres from one of the french windows. Then she set up her reflector and pulled the curtain cords this way and that until she obtained precisely the desired effect.

"Sit down on the chair," she told Milo in a low voice.

He firmly shook his head, but she insisted that he do so, enabling her to adjust the focus in advance.

When the khedive came in with the chamberlain in attendance, Milo stepped forward, bowed, and uttered a few flowery phrases. The operator in the tarboosh continued to stand impassively beside the camera.

"All is in readiness, Highness," said the Photographer to the Consulates. "If Your Highness would care to . . . "

'Abbas seated himself in the ebony chair and Dora bent over the camera. She adjusted the khedive's position with a series of little gestures, which Milo ceremoniously translated.

After exposing the four plates that accorded with her original intention, she was not entirely satisfied. All things considered, the khedive's other profile was the one she preferred. She intimated as much to Milo, but he failed to grasp this change of plan and merely looked aghast when she persisted, grunting at him inarticulately. She proceeded to clarify her meaning with two or three little taps on the cheek, inadvertently dislodging one side of her moustache.

"Madame seems to have a minor problem," said the khedive.

Milo froze. He exchanged a terrified glance with the chamberlain and stammered something unintelligible.

The Mameluka slowly peeled off the remainder of her moustache, removed her tarboosh, and shook her hair loose.

"Forgive us, Highness," she said in a tremulous voice. "At the studio, I'm responsible for portraits. My husband specializes in group photographs and landscapes."

Milo stared transfixed at the chamberlain's face, which was suffused with anger. Then his own face brightened: the khedive had uttered a gleeful laugh.

"Be good enough to look at me, Highness," said Dora.

And she pressed the bulb.

Of the five photographs Milo brought him in a morocco-bound folder, it was the fifth the khedive preferred. His unwonted smile was quite spontaneous. No longer the viceroy of Egypt, he was a roguish young man of twenty-four, and handsome despite his portly figure. One might have been seeing him for the first time.

"Convey my heartiest congratulations to Madame Touta," said 'Abbas.

That afternoon a courtier came to the shop bearing a velvet jewel case. Dora, for whom it was intended, found it to contain a diamond necklace which Alfred Falaki, Milo's jeweller uncle, valued at over 400 Egyptian pounds.

42

Within days, all Cairo knew of the portrait affair. The gossip column of *Le Journal Égyptien* reported in its own inimitable way that "a man-and-wife team of photographers" had tried to hoodwink "a senior member of the government". Neither the khedive nor the Toutas were mentioned by name, but this only whetted the public's curiosity and very soon helped to identify the perpetrators of the felicitous hoax.

More than a dozen new customers presented themselves at the shop the following Monday. For the first time ever, Milo had to turn away business and start keeping an appointments book. Many of those who turned up had no special requirements; they simply wanted a closer look at the photographer and his wife.

"My word," exclaimed the Photographer to the Consulates, filled with wonder at what had happened to them, "we're becoming positively famous!"

Days went by, and still the customers flooded in. Overwhelmed with work and bombarded with questions, Dora and Milo could not keep up and decided to take on an assistant. They were recommended a thirty-year-old Copt who had spent some time in Jacquemart's studio. This discreet and punctilious individual was assigned to develop their plates. Nick- named "my ghost" by Milo, he spent all his days in the darkroom, where Dora visited him from time to time to issue instructions.

It was Milo who had the idea of exploiting the famous portrait. He broached it one Sunday night, in the train that was taking them back to Cairo from Helwan.

"Why don't we print some picture postcards of the khedive?" Dora stared at him in surprise. "Well, why not?" he said eagerly. "Picture postcards, like Disdéri's of Napoleon III."

Dora frowned and shrugged her shoulders. She had come to distrust her husband's sudden crazes, which often led him down expensive blind alleys. What about his rash and ill-considered print order for "personalized greetings cards" two years ago? No one had wanted the things, and three whole crates of them were mouldering away in the shed behind the shop.

This time, although he had every confidence in his khedival picture postcard idea, Milo needed the consent of the person concerned. Fearing that he would meet with a refusal if he went to 'Abdin Palace himself, he suggested sending Dora instead.

"Never!" she said. "I'd feel I was prostituting myself."

Milo persisted, but she remained adamant. Having abandoned his attempts to win her over, he thought of asking Seif, who had some good contacts at the palace. However, he knew the young lawyer too well to present the matter in a commercial light.

"The khedive," he told Seif the next day, "needs to draw closer to his people, just as the people need to draw closer to their khedive. Can any tie be closer than a likeness carried in one's wallet or kept on one's bedside table? Napoleon III made his picture postcard an aid to governing France. I could sell 'Abbas's for a mere ten piastres. Everyone would want one, even Bulbul . . . "

Seif was enthusiastic. He hurried to the palace to drum up support for the picture postcard. Rebuffed on all sides, he requested an audience with the khedive himself. 'Abbas received him briefly the following week, but without evincing any more interest than his underlings. Seif did, however, obtain a personally signed letter authorizing the sale of his portrait.

Having thanked the lawyer warmly on behalf of the Egyptian people, Milo set to work at once. He envisioned his product as a rectangle of heavy card measuring nine centimetres by six, with a stylized "T" for Touta in the small blank margin beneath the photograph. This, he explained to Dora, was how Nadar, the famous French photographer, signed all his picture postcards:

"Nadar's 'N' has become as celebrated as Napoleon's!"

The Touta studio had no means of running off the hundreds of copies Milo had in mind. He decided to call on Maloumian, who, in addition to being the photographer to the army of occupation, had plenty of equipment at his disposal. He went to see the Armenian, plied him with compliments on the portraits that adorned his shop window, accepted a coffee, recalled the Turkish massacres with tears in his eyes, and proceeded to engage in some arduous haggling. Maloumian asked for four piastres per photo; Milo offered two. The Armenian swore on his wife's head that, even if the entire army of occupation marched over his prostrate form, he would never accept any such offer. At six that evening they concluded their business with an honourable compromise: three piastres ten milliemes, pasteboard not included.

"But Milo," said Dora, "Seif will choke if he discovers that the khedive's portrait is being printed by the photographer to the army of occupation!"

"Don't worry," said Milo, "I'll explain it to him."

And he went to inform the young militant of the defeat they'd just inflicted on the British:

"The effective fighting man makes use of his enemy's weapons."

Sales of the picture postcards got off to a slow start. Milo found it very hard to place his merchandise with the shopkeepers of Cairo. What was more, Maloumian insisted on payment in advance. Dora took a pessimistic view.

"You'd better abandon the scheme."

"On the verge of success? Don't you believe it!"

She was furious when he told her he proposed to sell the necklace the khedive had given her.

"It belongs to me, after all!"

Milo's face darkened, and she realized that she had wounded him deeply.

"Forgive me," she said, bursting into tears.

The next day Milo took the jewel case to Alfred Falaki. The jeweller offered him 300 pounds, claiming that this was a "family price". A stormy scene ensued.

"But Uncle Alfred," Milo protested, "a few months ago you yourself valued this necklace at 400 pounds."

"Yes indeed, *habibi*, but that was a few months ago. The state of the market has changed . . . "

An improvement set in over Christmas. The first six hundred copies sold out and another thousand had to be printed urgently. Maloumian demanded a higher price on the grounds that he would have to engage another assistant.

By the end of April six thousand picture postcards of the khedive had been sold. Several shops in Alexandria were clamouring for them. One order even came from Assiut and another from al-Mansoura. Milo's gamble had paid off.

"I might be able to buy the necklace back," he said to Dora one night. She threw herself into his arms.

He went off to Falaki's with 300 pounds in his pocket. Old Alfred greeted him with tears in his eyes. Very solicitous, he sat him down in the best chair in the shop and insisted on treating him to two cups of coffee.

"Alas, if only I'd known," the jeweller said, looking downcast. "I've promised the necklace to a customer, unfortunately. He's bringing me 400 pounds this afternoon."

Fuming, Milo had to pay 350 to recover his property.

43

The Touta family were hugely amused by Milo's account of this epic scene, in the course of which Alfred Falaki almost got two *mazbout* coffees in the face.

"I said to him, 'But really, Uncle Alfred, you yourself bought the necklace from me for 300 pounds – you assured me it wasn't worth any more.' And you know what he replied, the wry-mouthed old scoundrel? 'How dearly I should have liked to accommodate you, *habibi*! I'd make you a gift of that necklace if I hadn't already promised it to a customer . . .'"

Milo was quite capable of making the same audience weep with laughter at the same story for weeks on end, but he had no time to dwell on the scene in the jeweller's shop. He became wholly preoccupied with a far more spectacular event that occurred during the same spring of 1898: an attempt on the life of Prince Fouad, destined one day to become king of Egypt. No one followed the episode more closely than Milo, and none could recount it with greater skill.

A delicious breeze was blowing that late afternoon in May. Norbert Popinot, leaning on his balcony in Manakh Street, watched it ruffle the leaves of the acacia trees. In the absence of Solange, who was spending a few days with some friends in Ismailia, he had intended to dine at the Cercle Français before playing a hand or two of whist. The dinner would doubtless be marked, as it had been the night before, by one of those fierce arguments about the Dreyfus affair, of which the French colony never tired.

A sudden report made Popinot jump. Two more followed in quick succession a few seconds later. Almost simultaneously he heard shouts issuing from the Khedival Club, which was situated on the other side of the street. A man came rushing out on to the first-floor balcony.

"Stop him! Stop him!" he yelled in Arabic.

Dumbfounded, Popinot stared down at the almost deserted street. A favourite haunt of Cairo's high society, the Khedival Club was the last place one would have associated with such an hullabaloo. He decided to go downstairs and investigate, but not before changing his jacket, adjusting his tie, and renewing his eau de cologne.

A small crowd had gathered outside the building. Some uniformed *shaw-ishes* were already marching a young man off to 'Abdin police station in handcuffs.

"It's Prince Seif ad-Din," said someone. "He just killed his brother-in-law, Prince Fouad."

"Who's Prince Fouad?" asked Popinot, who got mixed up between all these Egyptian luminaries.

"One of the khedive's uncles."

Popinot walked quickly down the street to hail a cab on the corner. Without really knowing why, he told the cabby to take him to Studio Touta in Ezbekiyah Square.

Milo thanked him on hearing what had happened. "You did well to inform me," he said briskly. From his tone, he might have been the Reuters correspondent or Cairo's security chief. "Let's go," he added, hurrying out of the shop.

The Khedival Club had never known such a commotion. Figures were entering with urgent tread or emerging at a run. The crowd was being held at bay by a cordon of policemen armed with whips.

Milo, with Popinot at his heels, managed to worm his way to the front. He rose on tiptoe and craned his neck to watch the arrival of the officials for whom a passage had been kept clear. Catching sight of Ibrahim's uncle, the cabinet minister, he hastened to greet him warmly. The *shawish* on duty, seeing him in such exalted company, let him through.

"I think I'll leave you," called Popinot, who was still in the crowd.

"They're expecting me at the Cercle."

"Carry on," Milo called back. "I'll tell you about it later."

And he strode into the Khedival Club in the wake of the short-sighted minister, who had failed to recognize him. Although he was prevented from ascending the stairs, he was able to question several people coming down them. Their accounts of what had happened were not always identical. Like a professional storyteller with his audience in mind, Milo retained the most sensational of them. On returning home two hours later, he knew considerably more than the inhabitants of Cairo would glean from their newspapers on the morrow.

Prince Fouad was not dead. He had, however, been hit by two bullets, one in the thigh and the other in the chest. His condition precluded him from being moved from the reading room where the attempt on his life had taken place.

"The prince was out on the balcony with Nicolas Bey Sabbag," Milo recounted, "when he saw his brother-in-law Seif ad-Din entering the club. 'Could he by any chance be coming here to kill me?' Fouad said jokingly. He never spoke a truer word!"

Although not a member of the club, Prince Seif ad-Din was a relative of the khedive's, so the porter was wary of forbidding him to go upstairs. Once there, he produced a five-shot revolver from his pocket.

"Fouad had gone into one of the reading rooms. Seeing that his brother-in-law was armed, he hid behind Abani Pasha, the war minister, gripping him by the shoulders. Then he dashed into the poker room. That was where the first bullet hit him in the buttock — yes, yes, the buttock, not the thigh, as it says in the newspapers! He collapsed on the floor. Seif ad-Din fired twice more, hitting him in the chest. 'Finished!' said the would-be assassin. He then went downstairs again. But the porter, hearing cries of 'Stop him! Stop him!', had shown great presence of mind and locked the outer door."

Milo went on to describe how Prince Fouad, a plump young man of thirty, had lain there groaning. "'I'm dead, done for,' he kept saying. 'I'm dead, they're going to bury me.' His mother hurried to the club with several doctors and tried to talk some sense into him. 'You're a soldier, Fouad – you wanted to take part in the Sudan campaign. Imagine if you'd been wounded in battle. Console yourself by reflecting that you're not being nursed in some sweltering tent. You're in a comfortable room, surrounded by the love of your friends and relations . . .'"

Next morning Manakh Street was choked with harem carriages. Several princesses had come to inquire after the patient, who was being attended in relays by ten physicians of divers nationalities.

"The club has been transformed into a regular pharmacy," said Milo, who spent most of the day there with a crowd of curious spectators. So as not to miss anything, he even dined on the spot at Norbert Popinot's apartment. Dora thought this a little excessive but refrained from saying so.

During the next few days, both in the shop and at the café, Milo delivered veritable lectures to audiences fascinated by the affair. He revealed that Fouad had been maltreating his wife, Princess Shivekiar, and that she had been sending her brother Seif ad-Din despairing messages begging him to rescue her from the palace where Fouad kept her a prisoner.

"Seif ad-Din adores his sister," said Milo. "He denounced the pasha's intrigues to all and sundry. He even took his complaints to the British consulate."

"Is it true, Monsieur Touta, that Seif ad-Din was insulted by his brother-in-law in Arabic and Turkish when he got to the club?"

"I can't confirm that. But if he shouted 'Finished!', it means he really did intend to kill his brother-in-law, not merely wound him, as he now claims."

"And how *is* Prince Fouad, Monsieur Touta?"

"Better, much better." Milo almost expressed his gratitude for this inquiry. "The doctors have extracted the bullet lodged in his buttock, but they've abandoned their attempts to remove the one in his chest. It doesn't hurt him or threaten his life. However, its presence causes him to emit a sort of bark now and then."

And, much to the delight of all present, Milo demonstrated this phenomenon.

* * *

Seif ad-Din was tried before the native court at Bab al-Louq the follow-ing month. The chamber being a small one, it proved necessary to issue dignitaries and members of the press with special tickets. Milo failed to get in, for all his efforts, but that did not prevent him from describing each session with a host of details that must have escaped the journalists present.

The French counsel for the prosecution and defence requested permis-sion to plead in their own language. The senior judge objected on the grounds that "in a native case, everything must be native", so the whole of the hearing was to be conducted in Arabic.

"In Arabic?" Popinot said angrily. "Where do they think they are?"

In the course of the trial, the judge asked Abani Pasha, the principal witness of the dramatic incident, to act out the attempted murder. Seeing the minister of war pick up the revolver and point it at the judges, an ill-informed princess almost swooned with terror. A moment of pure hilarity ensued when Abani Pasha, behind whom the victim had hidden at the crucial moment, was asked a pointed question by one of the lawyers:

"Is it true that the accused said to Your Excellency: 'Get away from in front of Fouad Pasha!'?"

Seif ad-Din's counsel drew attention to the rather deranged young man's hereditary background, "the lack of any moral guidance in childhood that might have developed his awareness of right and wrong", and "vicious habits denoting the perversion of his senses". He was sentenced to serve seven years in prison and pay £1845 to cover the fees of the ten medical experts who had given up trying to extract the bullet from Fouad's chest.

"His appeal will be heard after the summer holidays," Milo announced.

The weather in Cairo on 28 June was already hot, and all the city's nota-bles were in a hurry to take the train to Alexandria or sail for Europe.

"I'll write to you if there are any developments," Milo told Popinot on the quayside. His tone was that of a lawyer with a watching brief.

44

Dora was not, to say the least, obsessed with the Seif ad-Din affair. For her the spring of 1898 was marked by some far more exciting events in which family and professional concerns were closely mingled.

In the first place, there was her father's portrait. Léon Sawaya's attitude had changed completely since the khedive's gift. Congratulated by several of his clients, the estate agent gave them to understand that he had always fostered his daughter's artistic talents and had provided her with painting materials from her fifteenth birthday onwards.

So Léon had turned up at the studio and struck a flattering pose, thumb in waistcoat pocket, without heeding the operator's suggestions. The result, a banal photograph of which Dora felt ashamed, was enlarged, framed, and displayed — far more conspicuously than the ill-omened miniature — in the Sawayas' drawing room.

As for Odette Sawaya, she wanted nothing of her daughter and had received the news of her success with characteristic indifference. She would doubtless have consented, without batting an eyelid, to be photographed at home on her divan. Her ghostly, smoke-wreathed face would have made a wonderful subject, but Dora refrained from capturing that image because she would have felt she was, in a sense, stealing it. She made her mother's refusal to come to the studio a pretext for not photographing her.

That excuse was doubly invalid because she had just surprised her in-laws by bringing the field camera to Helwan one Sunday. The children, who thought she meant to take a group photograph, were delighted until they learned that Nonna would be the only subject. Milo's mother had always declined to be photographed – "I've no wish to see myself in such a mirror" – on the grounds that she was too old.

It should be added that Nonna was the great non-participant in the annual family photograph. She never went to the seaside, having laid it down, once and for all, that the sulphurous waters of Helwan were superior to those of the Mediterranean, which she pronounced excessively salty.

Dora's professional activities certainly embarrassed Nonna *vis-à-vis* the ladies of the neighbourhood, who laughed them to scorn, and she avoided referring to them in the family circle. Dora was merely Milo's wife and the mother of his "three little chicks". She did not, however, treat her like her other daughters-in-law. Though younger, the Mameluka attracted fewer rebukes and was treated with more formality. The two women kept their distance, and the passing years had brought them no closer.

So why did Nonna decide to grant Dora what she had always refused her favourite son? Milo had never, in fact, been very insistent. He was too well acquainted with the nasty surprises of the darkroom and too well aware of his own limitations to risk producing a distorted image of his mother.

Dora, for her part, knew what she could make of that keen-eyed, ever watchful face. She had already photographed it a hundred times in her head. Taking Nonna's portrait would be one way of testifying to the growth of an affection she found it hard to express.

Much to the children's disappointment, the photographic session was to take place in private the following morning, not on Sunday itself. Dora, who wanted to work in an atmosphere of calm, had resolved to spend the night at Helwan. She and Nonna dined alone for the very first time.

"Milo wasn't born to be a photographer," the old lady remarked in the course of conversation. Surprised and faintly embarrassed, Dora looked at her inquiringly. "He'd have made an excellent businessman or lawyer, don't you think?" Without waiting for a reply, she went on abruptly, "He nearly died when he was a boy. He'd swallowed a nut. I picked him up by the feet."

"Yes, I know."

"Everyone needs shaking by the feet now and then – it gets rid of their inhibitions, don't you agree?"

They looked at each other for a moment, then burst out laughing.

The camera was set up under an arbour in the garden. Dora had risen early and prepared for all eventualities, even bringing out a parasol in case the sun became too strong and shone through the bougainvillea.

"I'm stifling here," Nonna told one of the servants. "Bring me a glass of arrack."

She fidgeted around on her wrought-iron chair, incapable of holding a pose. For once, Dora heard herself say, "Quite still, please!" Nonna got up as soon as the photograph had been taken. No, she didn't want to try another pose. One was quite enough.

"I really would like to take another," Dora told her. "Just to be on the safe side."

"No, my dear, really not. I'm worn out."

Dora's photograph of Nonna smiling with a glass of arrack in her hand was considered scandalous by one section of the family. Was that the way to show a respectable matriarch? Her sisters-in-law were outraged. Milo seemed to have mixed feelings.

Nonna's opinion was the only one that counted with Dora, but she didn't quite know what to make of it. A rather puzzled smile came over the old lady's face when she saw herself. Then she kissed Dora on the forehead and bore the photograph off.

Dr Touta, who was visiting Helwan, displayed more enthusiasm than anyone. "This photograph shows you as I've always known you," he told his sister-in-law, and the sincerity in his voice was unmistakable.

Dora felt slightly reassured. She welcomed the prospect of seeing the old doctor at Fleming in a few weeks' time.

"If you photograph me too," he said mischievously, "I give you fair warning: I shall make a point of wearing a bathing costume."

45

Reinforced by a second British brigade, General Kitchener now had at his disposal twenty-seven thousand men supported on the Nile by ten gun-boats and fourteen steamers. His depot at Atbara was crammed with food and equipment. The Nile was in spate, too, so the Anglo-Egyptian expeditionary force could begin its long-awaited march on Omdurman, the Mahdist capital.

Captain William Elliot was stirred by the solemn, almost silent ceremony at which the Sirdar reviewed his troops before they set off. Then the order to strike camp was given. The men marched along the river bank with the flotilla matching their rate of advance. Thousands of Dervishes had been reported in the vicinity, but no one sighted any.

William's excitement mounted as the days went by. Not for the first time, he felt surprised that Her Majesty's government had taken so long to reconquer the Sudan and avenge General Gordon. It was thirteen years since Khartoum had fallen into the hands of the Mahdists — thirteen years since the looted and abandoned capital had ceased to exist and been superseded by Omdurman, on the other side of the river.

William had an opportunity to meet Slatin Pasha when they were seated around the fire in a makeshift camp one night. The Austrian came out with one or two reminiscences of his captivity that did not appear in his book. He said that blocks of sandstone from Gordon's residence at Khartoum had been used to build the Mahdi's tomb at Omdurman. The dome of this white mausoleum, which dominated the city's low buildings, was visible for miles around.

"It'll make a perfect target for our artillery," exclaimed a gunner colonel who was warming his hands at the fire.

William greeted that remark with a nervous little laugh.

On 1 September 1898 the Anglo-Egyptian forces took up a position ten kilometres north of Omdurman, the Nile at their backs and the vast Kerreri Plain, flanked by hills, to their front. The moored boats had trained their guns on the Mahdi's mausoleum, which could be clearly seen through binoculars. The Sirdar estimated that fifty thousand Dervishes, or possibly more, were preparing for battle and might debouch into the plain at any moment.

William could not sleep a wink that night. His men started up at the smallest sound, poised to leap on to their horses. The steamers' searchlights kept scouring the plain to flush out potential attackers and overawe the khalif's men, who possessed no such equipment.

At three-thirty in the morning, well before dawn, the soldiers stood to in absolute silence. William was as good as ready, not having removed his uniform. He buckled on his belt, slid his sabre into its scabbard, and satisfied himself that his revolver was fully loaded. Then he donned his khaki cap with its gilt crescent and star. His second in command was waiting outside the tent.

The Sirdar's troops formed a semicircle. On the left, overlooking the Jebel Surgham, were British battalions bearing prestigious names: Warwickshires, Seaforths, Camerons, Lincolnshires. The Egyptians were deployed on the right, facing the Kerreri Hills.

"We're in danger of waiting too long," said William, who was reining back his charger. "They won't be crazy enough to hurl themselves into our jaws."

Dawn was just breaking when some shadowy figures detached themselves from the Jebel Surgham: ten men, then twenty, then a hundred. They were coming! A distant hum began to fill the plain. On the Anglo-Egyptian side, brief commands were passed down the line. William readied his men for action.

To the sound of their war drums, the Dervishes advanced at a run flanked by horsemen brandishing banners. The Anglo-Egyptian forces, shielded by low walls constructed the previous day, came under a hail of bullets. The Sirdar let the attackers come well within range before giving the order to fire. At once, all hell broke loose, the crack and thud of field artillery mingling with the rattle of Maxim guns.

The Dervishes' front rank was almost entirely flattened. The survivors continued to come on at a run, vaulting over the bodies of those who had fallen, and were soon joined by other fighting men armed with rifles or spears.

"They're brave bastards, these savages, but their tactics are hopeless!" shouted William's second in command.

William and his men kept up a continuous fire. Some of their carbines became overheated and jammed. Meantime, the artillerymen were emptying water bottles over their guns to cool them down. William was so deafened by all the noise that he failed to hear the enemy's bullets whistling past. Stunned to see his second in command collapse, hit in the temple, he bellowed an order which no one heard, then gestured urgently to his men to take cover.

To their front the attackers continued to advance, only to fall prey to the merciless chatter of the Maxim guns. Not one of them managed to reach the Anglo-Egyptian lines. The hundreds of green, red and white banners carried by the khalif's cavalrymen disappeared one after another.

At eight o'clock the fusillade ceased. Nothing happened for several minutes. William surveyed the smoking plain in a daze. Behind him, stretcher-bearers were attending to a handful of casualties.

There was an unexpected resumption of hostilities soon afterwards, when a fresh tide of humanity came pouring down the slopes. Some British cavalry, who had been unwise enough to advance, were forced to beat a retreat under covering fire from the gunners. Very soon, however, the same scene was repeated, and whole ranks of Dervishes were mown down in mid charge.

Another long silence ensued. So many white robes littered the plain below the sandy hills, daubed with blood, that they resembled a snowfield. Then came the order to march on Omdurman. As the leading ranks of the Anglo-Egyptian force stepped over the enemy corpses, some wounded Dervishes scrambled to their feet and, summoning up their last reserves of energy, loosed off a volley of spears. Few of the men on the ground survived after that, most of the wounded being shot or bayoneted.

A colonel came galloping up to William. "The Dervishes are getting away over those hills. We must stop them from reaching Omdurman. Take your squadron and join the lancers of the 21st!"

William promptly mounted his charger, calling to his men to follow him.

Some four hundred horsemen headed for the hills at a gallop. Once on the other side, they were startled to find themselves confronted by three thousand Dervishes hidden in a fold in the ground. They came under heavy fire. William lost several of his men, and his horse very nearly threw him.

Still in a state of shock, the Anglo-Egyptians found it hard to regain the initiative. Then the officer commanding the 21st Lancers gave the order to charge. Enemy horsemen were converging from several directions. Without hesitation, William charged them at the head of his squadron. The impact was violent in the extreme. Sabre clashed against sword, horses streamed with blood. A British corporal, hit in the chest and swaying in the saddle, was ordered to leave the ranks. "Never!" he yelled, brandishing his bent lance. "Form up and follow me, No. 2 Troop!"

The Anglo-Egyptian cavalry succeeded in regrouping a few hundred metres further on. They formed up as if on parade, ready to charge once more, but were ordered to dismount and open fire while awaiting rein-forcements.

An hour later, when the last Dervishes had fled, William rode across the plain. It was one immense charnel house. Many of the white-robed dead looked as if they were asleep. Others, who had fallen forwards in a kneeling position, seemed to have been caught unawares while at prayer. Mutilated corpses and severed limbs lay strewn across the sand, which reeked of blood and cordite.

"To Omdurman!" cried someone.

It was Sirdar Kitchener, holding the khalif's black banner on high. He rode past William at a jogtrot. Ahead of them, all resistance had ceased.

The Anglo-Egyptian commander and his staff, guided by Slatin Pasha, found the city deserted on entering it. There was no one left to welcome the victors but a handful of European prisoners: one Austrian, one German, and some Greeks. They later came across several Italian nuns who had been forced to marry during their years in captivity.

William was struck by the stench that emanated from the city, which was littered with dung and dead animals. But could it be termed a city? Omdurman was more like an immense, dusty village whose reddish soil was covered in places with sand. In the centre, squat hovels crouched at the foot of the great mosque. Only the khalif's palace had more than one storey. Gibbets had been erected in many of the squares, not far from some sinister-looking, windowless huts. Their stout doors, laden with chains, betokened that they had served as prisons.

The dome of Omdurman's mausoleum had been badly damaged by shellfire, but the guards, who preferred to die than allow the infidels to enter, were still at their posts. General Kitchener ordered the Mahdi's tomb to be opened and his remains thrown into the Nile – all except the skull, which was sent to Gordon's nephew prior to being cremated.

Two days later, to the sound of the Highlanders' bagpipes and the Grenadiers' fifes and drums, the Sirdar crossed the river to Khartoum accompanied by his senior officers and representatives from the various regiments. William knew that the city, which had been uninhabited since 1885, would be in ruins, but he was surprised to see so many trees. Extinct or not, Khartoum abounded in fruit. Thoughtfully, he picked a few figs.

Queen Victoria's message of congratulations to the Sirdar informed him that, from now on, he was Lord Kitchener of Khartoum. The same day, William Elliot learned of his promotion to the rank of major.

A moving ceremony was held in memory of Gordon. I can't find the words to describe it, dear Dora. A guard of honour comprising representatives from every regiment was drawn up in front of the former governor's residence. A twenty-one-gun salute was fired, followed by fifteen volleys. The Union Jack and the Egyptian flag were hoisted. Three clergymen — one Anglican, one Presbyterian, and one Catholic — held a service in the course of which the band played Gordon's favourite hymn, "Abide with Me". That, I don't mind admitting, was when I piped a tear or two.

46

"Over ten thousand Dervishes killed within a few hours!" exclaimed Norbert Popinot. "The retaking of Omdurman was a massacre, not a battle. The British have no cause to preen themselves on such butchery. If they *hadn't* defeated the Mahdist hordes, with all their technological resources, it would have shattered one's faith in the superiority of the white race!"

Details of the battle had only reached Cairo in dribs and drabs. In default of proper accounts, the newspapers were publishing a series of brief and sometimes inconsistent dispatches. It was nonetheless known that General Kitchener had ordered the Mahdi's tomb to be desecrated and his remains scattered. That was quite enough to disgust Seif.

"The British weren't satisfied with blood," he said darkly. "They had to kill the dead twice over."

Popinot nodded. "Kitchener may be an officer," he declared in solemn tones, "but he's certainly no gentleman."

This verdict could not have been original. It was just the sort of dictum relished by the members of the Cercle Français, and must already have been applied to more than one son of perfidious Albion.

Seif deplored the khedive's absence at a time when a new page in Egypt's history had just been turned. 'Abbas was on holiday somewhere between Paris and Constantinople, after making a cure at Divonne, above Lake Geneva. Throughout the preparations for the battle of Omdurman, the Cairo newspapers had published ludicrous pieces about the titular commander in chief of the Egyptian army: "The khedive takes a shower every morning . . . His Highness is massaged by François, the shower attendant . . . After partaking of lunch and going for a walk, the viceroy sits down at the piano . . . He takes another shower before dinner . . . "

Ibrahim commented on these reports in jocular verse:

> Stop the water teeming down,
> Monsieur François, or I'll drown!
> That's no shower, you buffoon,
> it's a cascade or monsoon.
> Shower Kitchener instead,
> for his hands with blood are red.

Dora had been in an agony of suspense for several days because the newspapers announced that the battle of Omdurman had cost the Anglo-Egyptian expeditionary force some dozens of dead and hundreds of wounded. She almost kissed the soldier in civilian clothes who turned up at the shop on 9 September with a buff envelope addressed in William's handwriting. "William Elliot might have dropped us a line," Milo had grumbled only the day before. "Greetings cards apart, we haven't had a word from him in over two years."

Dora was incapable of defining her feelings for this British officer who, although she scarcely knew him, had written her some fifteen letters.

In the drawing rooms of Cairo, Omdurman had already been eclipsed by Fashoda. No one spoke of anything but the dispute between France and Britain at this Sudanese outpost on the Upper Nile.

"If the British want war," Popinot said excitedly, "they shall have it!"

Although the details of the affair were still unclear, it was known that General Kitchener had left the Sudanese capital and sailed for Fashoda with a flotilla of five gunboats. There he came up against the celebrated contingent commanded by Captain Marchand, who had been occupying an old Egyptian riverside fort for the past two months.

"Those gentlemen can't forgive us for having stolen a march on them," Popinot declared. "But Marchand isn't a tourist — he doesn't travel under the auspices of Thomas Cook: he's France's representative at Fashoda, and there he'll remain. Egypt abandoned that territory in 1885. It doesn't belong to her any longer, still less to Great Britain!"

Although she said nothing, Dora was far from unacquainted with what was happening at Fashoda. She had the benefit of a first-hand account sent her by someone personally involved in the operation:

> *Our flotilla entered the fort's channel at about ten in the morning. The guns were unlimbered and their crews stood to. I was with my unit on board one of the big two-deck barges being towed by our gunboats. Facing us on the bank in full dress uniform were a handful of Frenchmen. A dinghy was sent to pick up Captain Marchand and ferry him across to Lord Kitchener's steamer. The Sirdar politely informed the Frenchman that he had just reconquered the Sudan in the khedive's name, and that Fashoda formed part of the Sudan. In a high and mighty tone, Captain Marchand replied that he was occupying Fashoda on the orders of the French government. He would be delighted to welcome the victor of Omdurman in the name of France, but he refused to leave. It's a ridiculous attitude, dear Dora, and cannot be tolerated . . .*

While awaiting instructions from their respective governments, the British and French forces remained encamped, face to face, at Fashoda. London newspapers inveighed against Marchand, whom they referred to as an "explorer", and there was much sabre-rattling at Cairo's Cercle Français. Popinot dropped in there morning and evening to scour the newspapers and discuss at great length the strategy his country should adopt.

"We shall fight for Fashoda!" he kept saying, drawing himself up to his full five feet two inches and throwing out his chest.

"Did you know that Norbert used to fence at law school?" Solange asked everyone.

But France, embroiled in the Dreyfus affair, was slow to take a firm stand.

"I hope," Popinot muttered in his more dejected moments, "that diplomacy will enable France to escape the cruel humiliations to which our enemies hope to subject her. The absence of news from Fashoda strikes me as an ominous sign. Something underhanded must be going on there."

The British, being in control of the Sudanese telegraph cables, released only such information as suited their book. All Marchand knew of the political debates raging in Paris was what the adversaries encamped opposite chose to tell him. Tiring of this situation, he decided to leave his men for a while and seek information in Cairo.

Word of his impending arrival sent the members of the Cercle Français into transports of excitement. Late in the afternoon of the day in question, over fifty of them assembled at the station an hour before the train pulled in. Cheers rang out as soon as the captain appeared at the carriage window. "*Vive Marchand!*" the gentlemen cried, waving their hats. "*Vive le brave commandant!*" A short, slim man with a black goatee, the hero of Fashoda had just been promoted to the rank of major, and the officer's cross of the Légion d'honneur glinted on the tunic of his blue and white marine uniform. The French consul general, Monsieur Lefèvre-Pontalis, who had been instructed to extricate him from the crowd, ushered him along a private passage to his waiting carriage. Instantly, all the cabs outside the station were taken by storm and sped along 'Abbas Boulevard in an attempt to reach the Agency at the same time as Marchand.

"I think I was the second person to get there," said Popinot, more flushed with excitement than anyone had ever seen him.

Major Marchand spent part of the night perusing the latest cables from the Quai d'Orsay. He greeted the dawn pale as death. The order to evacuate Fashoda struck him as all the more outrageous because of the spurious grounds on which it was based: he, Marchand, had never requested permission to quit the place for reasons of ill health.

The news spread quickly. Norbert Popinot was speechless. He almost tore up the newspaper that concurrently reported General Kitchener's triumphal homecoming. In London the new peer had been presented with a magnificent sword whose solid gold hilt bore the Egyptian and British flags on the back, united for better or worse.

"And the blade?" cried Popinot. "What of the blade? Is it stained with Sudanese and Egyptian blood?"

He chose to wear a black tie for the reception in honour of Marchand at the Cercle Français. On the same occasion he also refused to shake hands with the consul, poor Lefèvre-Pontalis, who was just as appalled as his compatriots. When his health was drunk, the hero of Fashoda responded to the toast in forceful terms:

"The longer these dark days continue, the nearer draws the dawn of proud aspirations finally fulfilled. The granite sphinx that dreams amid the sands not far from here, a witness to the passing of Bonaparte and his exploits, Lesseps and his work, has yet to utter its last word . . . "

"Everyone wept," Popinot reported.

Some days later Marchand paid a ceremonial visit to the Collège des Frères des Écoles Chrétiennes at Khurunfish, where he was greeted with a fanfare and the *Marseillaise*. Led by the Brother Superior, a thousand Christian and Muslim pupils, most of them Egyptian, cried "*Vive Marchand! Vive la France!*"

Marchand subsequently climbed the Great Pyramid and did some sightseeing in the streets of Cairo. He was eagerly acclaimed wherever he went – indeed, some harem ladies were seen to raise their veils as he passed in a signal token of respect.

The British residents of Cairo, being good sports, decided to appoint Major Marchand an honorary member of the Turf Club.

"Much good that'll do us!" grumbled Popinot.

At Fashoda on 11 December the bugles sounded "to the colours" for the last time. The tricolour slowly descended the flagpole and an Egyptian captain stepped forward to take possession of the fort. France's Nile adventure was at an end. She would henceforth steer clear of the great river just as Germany, Belgium and Italy had done before her. The British were masters of the Nile.

Norbert Popinot developed a high temperature and kept to his bed for three whole days. On medical advice, his wife not only applied leeches but administered sudorific herbal teas and footbaths. He almost suffered a relapse the following month.

"Abandoning Fashoda means handing Egypt to Britain on a plate!" Seif declared in his presence. "France has adopted a policy of *laissez-faire* and *laissez-aller*. It'll cost her very dear, I'm afraid. Did you know that pupils already enrolled in French classes at government schools are applying to switch to English?"

47

This time the soldier in civilian clothes had delivered a brief note, not a letter, and he was waiting for a reply.

Cairo, 8 February 1899

Dear Dora,

I've been granted a short spell of leave. I shall be in Cairo till tomorrow night, and I'm longing to see you. Fix the time and the place — any time, any place.
Yours impatiently,
William

I felt myself go weak at the knees. The man who had been writing to me for two-and-a-half years was here in town — only just round the corner, perhaps. I was panic-stricken, irresolute as a compass needle swinging this way and that.

It was almost a summons. Would William Elliot have taken such a liberty if there was nothing between us? I had never answered his letters, admittedly, but this one-way correspondence had been enough to create a mutual intimacy of which he felt he could take advantage.

When could I contrive to meet him? Only one possibility occurred to me: very early in the morning, at an hour when I sometimes went down-stairs to work in the darkroom, leaving Milo still asleep in bed.

"Tomorrow, 5 a.m., outside the north gate of the Ezbekiyah Gardens."

Trembling, I scrawled those words on a slip of paper and handed it to the messenger.

William Elliot in Cairo! I had, of course, pictured his return several times, especially since the battle of Omdurman. I knew that he would announce his arrival sooner or later or turn up unexpectedly at the shop, but this curt summons to a clandestine assignation took me quite unawares.

The man had insinuated himself into my life like a housebreaker. I hadn't been able – or willing – to stop him. Although William's letters perturbed me, they also made me daydream. Hadn't I more than once removed them from the blue casket and reread certain passages? They sometimes conjured up disturbing images: a bare-chested young officer with his hair all wet, washing on the banks of a river . . .

For the rest of the day I displayed an absent-mindedness that was quite unlike me. I forgot to buy the girls some sweets I'd promised them, and I almost ruined the portrait of a lawyer from the Mixed Courts by omitting to draw one of the curtains over the window. I just succeeded in remedying the effect of this excessive light while developing the negative.

I was afraid of failing to wake up in time and too agitated to doze off in any case, so I didn't sleep a wink that night. I rose at half-past four, cursing the cockerel on the terrace next door, which threatened to disturb Milo's slumbers. He grunted two or three times and turned over, but remained in the land of dreams. I got dressed in silence and set off down the spiral staircase, taking care to avoid the treads that creaked. Bulbul was blissfully snoring on his mattress in the shop downstairs.

I opened the outer door with extreme care. The air struck chill in spite of my cape. It was still dark, and the trees were wreathed in wisps of mist. My heart pounded as I hurried to the Ezbekiyah Gardens, realizing as I did so that I had forgotten my gloves, or possibly dropped them.

All at once, a shadowy figure emerged from a doorway. I gave an involuntary cry of alarm. "You're early," said a voice. Torn between excitement and embarrassment, I couldn't think what to say. William Elliot absolved me by bending to kiss my hand. "Thank you for coming," he said, and, a moment or two later, "I never heard from you."

I detected reproach in his voice, but did I have to explain myself? "I'm well, as you can see," I replied with a smile, evading the implied question.

His shoulders seemed broader than I remembered, perhaps because of the military greatcoat he was wearing. His demeanour, though, had changed. He looked more mature, even if he did preserve the easy self-assurance of a youthful empire-builder whose efforts had been crowned with success.

"You'll catch cold," he said. "Can't I take you somewhere more congenial?" I told him that this was impossible, that I didn't have much time. His face fell a mile. What had he been expecting — that I would spend the whole day with him?

"We could at least get into the cab that brought me here," he said. Without waiting for a reply he opened the door, brusquely instructing the cabby to stay where he was. He took my hand and helped me on to the step, then got in himself, shut the door, and sat down opposite on a folding seat. The cab's interior was illuminated by the glow of a gas-lamp some distance away, enabling us to see each other quite clearly.

"Are you still taking photographs?" he asked, having first made polite inquiries about my family. "I don't take photographs," I said, "I'm a photographer." He smiled faintly.

To hide my embarrassment I congratulated him on his promotion. He beamed, less with pride, no doubt, than because of my implicit acknowl-edgement that I had read his letters. I realized this a moment too late. But, after all, wasn't it obvious? I should hardly have kept this appointment had I consigned all his letters to the wastepaper basket unopened.

"You could have sent me a note, a sign," he said in the same reproach-ful tone as before. "A sign of what?" I replied, trying to re-establish the distance between us. His face froze. As if afraid of what I might have added, he went on, "I haven't stopped thinking about you for two-and-a-half years, no matter where or when, day or night . . . "

He wasn't telling me anything I didn't already know, in a sense, but to hear it from his own lips and spoken with such sincerity . . . A shiver ran down my spine. With downcast eyes, I went on listening in silence and made no attempt to withdraw my hands when he clasped them in his own. "You're still cold," he murmured. On the contrary, my face was on fire. I scarcely knew where I was any more.

"Dora!" he said feverishly, gripping me by the shoulders. Our faces were almost touching, and I could feel his breath on my cheek. "No, please don't," I said, releasing myself.

He stared at me in dismay. I stood up, opened the door, and got out of the cab. Once outside I turned to him and asked, rather unsteadily, when he would be returning to Egypt for good. He said nothing for a few moments, then, "I don't know if I shall, not now."

Words failed me. "I'm sorry," I said. "I have to go."

"I'll walk you home," he said dully.

"No, it wouldn't be wise. Safe journey, William."

I said his name after a moment's hesitation. I uttered it like a gift or an apology – or, perhaps, a promise. My lips continued to shape it, again and again, as I almost ran back across the square.

48

The Wednesday night set had acquired a new member: Maxime Touta, editor of the *Sémaphore d'Alexandrie*. A year ago Milo would not have ventured to invite his cousin, who was older and far better established, but the studio's notoriety was lending him wings. Besides, Maxime himself must have been intrigued by the Mameluka's growing reputation and eager to become more closely acquainted with the woman whom he had glimpsed a few times during family reunions at Fleming. Having accepted Milo's invitation without more ado, the journalist made a wholly informal appearance one Wednesday in February. Isis, his dark-haired wife, came too.

"Isis is a Copt," Milo told the Popinots. "She scandalized everyone at the time of her marriage some twelve years ago by studying medicine. A woman doctor – imagine the outcry!"

"I don't see why," said Solange. "After all, your wife's a photographer."

Dora, captivated by the newcomer's elegance and grave demeanour, took to her at once. Isis told her in the course of the evening that she was much in demand among ladies who declined to expose so much as a square inch of their bodies to male scrutiny. "So you see," she said, "most of my patients are my very worst enemies."

Isis and Maxime, who were regarded as a modern couple, maintained a complex relationship. The sporadic smiles they exchanged seemed expressive more of friendly understanding than of amorous intimacy. Although their manner conveyed no hint of discord, it was hard for anyone seeing them together not to be reminded of the rumour that Maxime was having an affair with Nada Mancelle.

"The Mancelles live at Ismailia," Milo explained. "They own a villa at Fleming, and that's where Maxime and Nada meet every summer."

The editor of the *Sémaphore*, a clear-eyed fifty-year-old with greying temples, was a courteous, elusive man. He congratulated Dora on her portrait of the khedive, but even more so on that of Dr Touta, which she had taken at Fleming the previous summer.

"Those old man's wrinkles and that young man's gaze . . . I thought I knew my father, but you've made me rediscover him."

He went on to ask Dora's opinion of the few photographs that appeared in his newspaper.

"Many of them are useless," she said bluntly. "The text conveys more than the pictures that accompany it, which are very dull."

Maxime Touta seemed impressed by this remark. He told her that he would like to discuss the matter further another time.

"Tell us about the Aswan Dam," someone asked. "I gather you were present when the foundation stone was laid."

Unlike Milo, who might have been announcing the end of the world whenever he embarked on an anecdote, the journalist expressed himself with moderation. He appeared supremely well-informed, but he never strove for rhetorical effect; without seeming to, he merely detonated an occasional bomb in passing. Now, leaning on the piano, he described how the Duke of Connaught had used a silver trowel for the occasion. Afterwards, the Nubians had given him a sample of their aquatic skill by swimming across the foaming cataract. Lunch was served on board the khedival yacht. Meanwhile, the Italian workmen refreshed themselves in the temple of Philae, which was destined to be half submerged by the waters of the dam.

"The temple of Philae, imagine!" Norbert Popinot said indignantly. "For twenty centuries, all the conquerors of the Nile Valley have wanted to leave their mark on it: Persians and Ptolemies, Arab caliphs and Turkish Mamelukes – all of them in turn. Now the British want to follow suit. 'Why shouldn't we leave our mark here as well?' they say. Some mark, by heaven! They're planning to drown one of the masterpieces of the Pharaonic age."

Richard Tiomji, looking dumbfounded, asked Popinot if he was being serious. "Don't tell me you prefer a few old stones to a dam that'll enable us to store vast quantities of water?"

"Certainly I do, my friend! What's a hideous dam compared to a superb temple like that?"

The ostrich farmer was outraged. To him, nothing was more absurd than the puerile passion Europeans seemed to cherish for relics of interest to no one else. If only they could be practical for a change! When some sensible soul had suggested equipping the Great Pyramid with a cable railway to facilitate its ascent, howls of protest went up.

Solange Popinot's contribution to the debate was characteristically vehement. "A single column from the temple of Philae," she proclaimed, "is worth more than all the cotton fields in Egypt!" Her throaty voice took on a special vibrancy whenever she became heated.

Richard Tiomji deemed it pointless even to reply. Refilling his glass with the Cahors Norbert had brought along, he sniffed and swirled the wine before tasting it. "A trifle rough," he remarked to Popinot, who nodded.

From the khedival yacht, conversation turned to the khedive himself.

"He can't be relied on any more," Seif declared. "He was under no obligation to congratulate his old enemy so warmly. When one recalls that it was Kitchener who humiliated him in 'ninety-four, before the expedition to Upper Egypt, by compelling him to extend a public apology to his own army!"

"Times are changing," said the editor of the *Sémaphore*. "Now that 'Abbas's relations with the sultan have deteriorated, he's making up to the British. His current ambition is to be received in London by Queen Victoria."

"He's quite capable of going there, more's the pity," growled Seif.

The Wednesday regulars had never heard him speak like that before. The young lawyer had, in fact, become steadily more disillusioned in recent months. By this time, although the scales had been slow to fall from his eyes, his indignation was boundless.

"'Abbas," he went on, "is only interested in feathering his nest. Did you know that he has seized the assets of several princesses?"

Maxime Touta smiled. "Are you positive of that?" He went on to dispel Seif's last remaining illusions by identifying the khedive as the principal beneficiary of the traffic in orders and decorations that was rife in Cairo. Seif found this all the more infuriating because the palace was covertly continuing to finance the nationalist movement. Could dirty money be supporting so noble a cause?

Milo defused the atmosphere by bringing conversation round to some gossip picked up in Khan al-Khalili.

"'Abbas is capable of extravagance, but he can also be extremely stingy. Just imagine, to economize on paper he saves the blank pages from some of the messages he receives."

That night, for the first time ever, Seif held out his glass for Popinot to fill. Three mouthfuls of wine, and his head began to swim. He went over to the window for some fresh air. Dora waited a moment, then joined him.

"I'd like to photograph you some time," she said.

He hesitated briefly, taken aback. "Very nice of you, but I don't see the point."

"Not everything in life has to have a point," she replied in a low voice.

49

Seif's face looked blank as he confronted the camera two days later.

"You're miles away," Dora told him.

He raised his eyebrows.

"Yes, you are. How do you expect me to work under these conditions? It takes two to make a photograph, you know."

His eyes glinted with impatience.

"There you are at last!"

Moments later, however, he was as impassive as before. Either his lack of expression was a product of self-control, or his thoughts were genuinely elsewhere. All that lent his face a modicum of life was the slight angle at which he wore his tarboosh.

Dora resolved to wear him down. She had discovered that, after a lengthy session, some of her subjects ended by dropping their masks and baring their souls, as though restored to themselves. Accordingly, she spun out the preliminaries and took care not to engage Seif in conversation. Ten minutes went by, but still the young man's face remained devoid of expression. In desperation, Dora broke the silence.

"I really don't see why people are so critical of the British. Egypt abandoned the Sudan. They helped her to get it back."

Seif's eyes flashed. "How can you say that!" he protested. "In 1884 the khedive was compelled to relinquish the Sudan by a combination of circumstances and the British. Besides, he didn't abandon it, he temporarily evacuated it. He couldn't have renounced his rights over the Sudan even if he'd wanted to. As viceroy of Egypt, he's merely the sultan's representative. He has no authority to abandon or cede any of the territory entrusted to him at the time of his accession."

Dora, who was adjusting the focus, listened with only half an ear. "You're splitting hairs," she said, "and well you know it."

He jumped to his feet, his face contorted with anger. "How can you —"

"Please sit down," she said. "You're lucky you didn't hurt yourself. Other photographic studios use neck-clamps. Even here, my husband —"

"Neck-clamps be damned!" he snapped. Then, resuming his seat, "Forgive me, but you really do say some incredible things. To think that you, of all people . . . But I hate arguing like this. Why not take the photograph and get it over?"

It was taken already. Dora had tripped the shutter a few seconds before, just as that mixture of surprise and anger came flooding into his face. She thought it better not to tell him, however, and decided to take a second photograph. With her eye glued to the lens, she squeezed the pneumatic bulb almost mechanically and remained motionless for several seconds, unable to tear her eyes away from the face that was eluding her once more.

Of all the portraits Dora Touta produced at this period, Seif's was undoubtedly the most original. It owed its originality to the subject's irate expression. By hardening his youthful features, the photograph revealed the personality of a rebel — a man devoted heart and soul to an ideal.

"Thank you," the lawyer said politely when Dora gave him two prints of the first negative. "I'll make good use of them."

She knew he would simply put them in a drawer and forget about them.

At his friend's home some days later, Ibrahim caught sight of the two photographs lying on top of a stack of files. He stopped short.

"What are those?" he asked.

"Nothing. Just some photographs."

Ibrahim couldn't tear his eyes away from the first portrait. He inquired who had taken it, though he already knew what the answer would be. He and Dora had engaged in a long argument about artistic creation only the week before.

"A work of art is unique," he had maintained. "You can't conceive of another *Mona Lisa*, whereas a photograph can be reproduced ad infinitum."

"Reproduced but not retaken," she had retorted. "No one photograph is the same as another."

But Ibrahim had plenty of ammunition. "Artistic creation is a time-consuming process," he said. "That's as true of painting as it is of music or poetry. A photograph takes only a second to produce."

"No, it doesn't. You have to set up a photograph and then develop it. I like the verb develop. If you develop something you widen its scope, enable it to attain its fullest extent. You also reveal it."

Ibrahim shook his head. "You'll never rob me of the idea that a photograph is an imprint. It merely reproduces reality with frightening precision. The painter is quite at liberty to modify the landscape in front of him — at liberty to ignore it, even. He can paint as his feelings alone dictate, contenting himself with the images in his head, whereas the photographer can't operate without some person or thing in front of his lens. No subject, no photograph. Photographers are prisoners of reality."

"Why speak of imprisonment?" Dora replied. "Every photograph is the vestige of something, I grant you, but isn't that just what constitutes its value?"

That night she made an entry in her notebook:

> *Photographs are not just imprints of space; they're imprints of time as well. By capturing the moment with a camera and recording it on paper, they eternalize it.*

But Ibrahim had returned to the attack. "You'll never convince me that photography is the equal of painting," he said. "Is there a photographer in the world who would dare to compare himself to Michelangelo or Rembrandt?"

She didn't reply, brought up short by this argument.

"You see?" the poet pursued with an air of triumph. "Photography is to painting what prose is to poetry."

"And, since you only set store by poetry . . ."

"I consider it superior, that's all. Unfair or not, the fact remains that the most untalented painter comes closer to art than any photographer, even one as sensitive and gifted as yourself."

Dora had been wounded by that remark. Ibrahim realized this and apologized. He regretted it all the more, no doubt, on seeing Seif's portrait.

"May I have a copy?" he asked his friend.

The lawyer shrugged his shoulders indifferently, then asked his ritual question: "How's your *Marseillaise* coming along?"

Ibrahim discreetly entrusted Seif's portrait to a member of the Khedival Opera committee who was leaving for France. That autumn Dora was astonished to learn that she had been awarded first prize at the Salon de Photographie in Paris. The following Wednesday, Norbert Popinot opened several bottles of champagne and everyone commented on the enthusiastic articles that had appeared in the *Sémaphore d'Alexandrie* and the *Journal Égyptien*.

Seif might have resented the use of his portrait had he not received a letter from his hero, Mustafa Kamil, congratulating him on having upheld Egypt's honour in an artistic competition:

> *The photograph of you in a tarboosh, which has appeared in several French publications, is the finest tribute you could have paid our beloved country. May the future hold further blessings in store for us!*

50

Customers now had to book sittings several weeks in advance.

"I'm very sorry," Milo would say with a broad smile, turning over the pages of his appointments diary, "we're full up this month."

He could, however, make exceptions and would always find room for a wealthy old codger or yield to a pretty young woman's look of entreaty.

The studio gradually adjusted itself to this steady improvement in its fortunes. Operators had to be engaged in addition to the darkroom assistant, first one and then another. Bulbul had been promoted. Although he was still a factotum, his length of service lent him a certain superiority vis-à-vis the newcomers.

It was Milo who made the customers welcome, and he did so with characteristic zest. Having entertained them to coffee and titbits of gossip that sometimes made them roar with laughter, he conducted them to the studio, where one of the operators would be on duty. Dora could have limited herself to taking a hand at the last moment, like Jacquemart, who merely made final adjustments to pose, lighting and focus, but she refused to take the easy way out and worked by appointment only. Thus, ordinary photographs were taken by the operators, whose technique improved week by week under her supervision. To avoid harming the studio's reputation, however, it was ordained that only the finest specimens, selected by Dora herself, would be signed with the red "T".

The couple's finances were flourishing thanks to this influx of customers. They now rented a villa at Fleming for the entire summer, not far from the one owned by the Tiomjis. Two or three times a week Milo threw boisterous parties in his drawing room overlooking the sea, where he clowned around until the small hours.

One unmistakable sign of his rise in the world was an invitation to dine at Rizqallah Bey's town house in Nabi Danial Street, Alexandria. The owner of the *Touta et Fils* department stores sat Dora on his left, the place on his right being reserved for the wife of the Greek consul. Though awed by his wealthy cousin's furniture, paintings and influential connections, Milo made Bella, Rizqallah's Jewish wife, laugh heartily at table with an amusing and unpublicized episode from the trial of Prince Seif ad-Din.

On Norbert Popinot's advice, and despite the rather steep price he was obliged to pay, Milo had bought the shop and apartment he rented in Cairo. The adjacent premises came vacant at almost the same time, so he acquired those too, on credit, and knocked the two buildings into one by demolishing some party walls. Dora at last had the studio of her dreams, complete with a room in which to store equipment, plenty of shelf space, and even a dressing room.

The latter, which boasted turquoise walls, a dressing table and a cheval mirror, enabled female customers to titivate themselves before a sitting. It was also patronized by gentlemen solicitous of their appearance, who would have been disconsolate had a strand of hair become displaced at the last moment.

"Would you care to visit the dressing room?" Milo would inquire in ceremonious tones. His response to customers who said yes: "Quite right, it's always wise to carry out a last-minute inspection." To those who said no: "Quite right, you look perfect as you are. Don't change a thing, whatever you do."

Big leather-bound albums, their covers encrusted with mother of pearl, reposed on the tables in the waiting room. Customers never failed to consult them, either to kill time or as a source of inspiration. "I'd like the same type of portrait as Sakakini Pasha," they sometimes said, or, "Give me the same sort of look as Madame Avierino."

"We'll do just as you say," Milo would purr.

Dora merely smiled. "People are ugly only when they try to be beautiful," she said to Ibrahim. "I have a hard time persuading them to be themselves."

"They aren't themselves in everyday life," said the poet. "Why should you expect them to be so in a studio with that cannon trained on them? Photographers ought to conceal the tools of their trade, like dentists."

Beneath his flippant and casual exterior, Ibrahim was becoming more and more interested in the Mameluka's work. Delighted to have helped her win a first prize and more fascinated by her than ever, he often questioned her about it.

"Do you try to make your portraits good likenesses?" he asked one day.

"Likenesses of what? My concern is to do justice to the character, the underlying nature of the persons facing me — to photograph their soul, so to speak. But you're forcing me to use big words. It's simple, really . . . " She paused for a moment or two. "A photograph enables one to show people what they're usually incapable of seeing. That's as true of a portrait as it is of a landscape."

"What about you? Do you see all that at first glance?"

"Of course not."

She would have liked to give him an example, but how to describe the continuous process of observation, the almost imperceptible movements that preoccupied her before, during, and even after a shot?

"I always observe my subject before entering the studio. Sometimes a simple turn of the head can tell one more than a stream of words. When developing a negative I often discover details that have escaped me. It's almost embarrassing at times. A photograph enables one to see people as they don't see themselves. It reveals unexpected sides of their character."

"In other words, it's a form of rape."

"How you do go on! Let's say that, with my eye glued to the camera, I sometimes feel I'm peering at my subjects through a keyhole."

Ibrahim chuckled. "That metaphor appeals to me," he said, already searching around for a word that rhymed with "keyhole".

* * *

The studio was unrecognizable. Dora had consigned all Milo's old bric-à-brac to a storeroom: the Roman column, the fake staircase with four steps, the armour, the stuffed crocodile. The décor now comprised some genuine, tastefully chosen pieces of antique furniture set off by a huge Persian carpet. There was even a baby grand.

"Won't you play me something while I get the camera ready?" she asked a very nervous young woman whom she knew to be a moderate performer on the piano.

The sitter's nervousness degenerated into panic. After playing a few bars and receiving Dora's congratulations, however, she found the sitting an easy matter.

Oscar Touta turned up to have his portrait taken three or four times a year. He asked for Dora every time he entered the shop. "Where's your wife?" he demanded imperiously. "I've come to have my photograph taken." He might have been a brothel habitué insisting on the services of one particular inmate.

Dora soon tired of this. "We have a new operator," she said. "You'll find him quite satisfactory."

Muttering to himself, Oscar reluctantly yielded to this suggestion. He followed the operator into the studio but bullied him for fifteen solid minutes.

"Take me full-face — yes, full-face, what else? I pay the going rate. I want a proper portrait complete with two eyes and two ears. I didn't come here to have my left ear photographed. And make sure you show my watch chain. Don't think you can short-change me and get away with it!"

Thrusting out his chest and striking a pose, he opened his mouth and smiled broadly at the lens. The unfortunate operator was at a loss to disguise such an ill-fitting set of false teeth.

51

To the great delight of the younger members of the family, whose knowledge of him stemmed largely from Milo's humorous anecdotes, Oscar Touta was invited to Helwan on 1 January 1900. Nonna had insisted on welcoming the new century with a special lunch for sixty-odd people.

Sternly ignoring the grand-nephews who were introduced to him, Oscar seemed uninterested in anything but his precious person.

"That operator of yours is a fool," he growled at Milo, without so much as bidding him good day or wishing him a happy New Year. "If I were you, I'd fire him on the spot."

"But uncle," said Milo, feigning dismay.

"A fool, I tell you! And a swindler! Why does he never manage to show my tie-pin?"

Dora dared not look at Milo for fear of laughing out loud, but someone behind her tittered, and everyone within earshot was instantly convulsed with irrepressible mirth. Fortunately, Oscar had already turned on his heel and was complaining to their hostess about the dearth of cabs at Helwan station.

Nonna surveyed her guests with a look of wonder. "I never thought I'd be lucky enough to see the new century!" she exclaimed.

"Nor I," said Dr Touta, who was blithely approaching his eighty-ninth birthday.

The older persons present were still the freshest of all, not having attended any of the riotous parties that had gone on till dawn in certain

Cairo establishments. As though afraid of missing the turn of the century, people had made it their duty to celebrate New Year's Eve even more frenetically than usual.

In Alexandria the *Touta et Fils* stores had remained illuminated all night long, and Rizqallah Bey had held a banquet for a hundred people at his mansion. At midnight every guest found a silver medallion engraved "1900" on his or her plate. The "sale of the century" was scheduled to last until 31 January. Milo's illustrious cousin had placed advertisements in several of the capital's newspapers encouraging Cairenes to pay a special visit to Alexandria in mid winter. Anyone armed with a return ticket was entitled to an additional discount of ten per cent in all departments.

Ibrahim had greeted 1 January 1900 after his own fashion:

> *The dying century, my friends, deserves a toast,*
> *the age of Hugo, Rimbaud and Verlaine.*
> *Of all its sons 'twas they who pleased us most,*
> *so let us rise and drink to drown our pain.*

Milo was describing his New Year's Eve festivities to some youngsters who had clustered round him.

"You should have seen Richard Tiomji leading the farandole with streamers draped all over him! He was still dancing at four in the morning, I promise you! As for Ibrahim, the minister's nephew, he was well away! At one stage he could be seen chasing Solange Popinot round the room with a big fork, threatening to eat her alive. Solange almost choked, she was laughing so much . . ."

Dora confirmed her husband's account of these nocturnal dissipations with a half smile, having only half enjoyed them. Solange's behaviour, in particular, had annoyed her. She clung rather too tightly to Milo in the course of certain waltzes, and he himself seemed not unaware of her alluring décolleté.

Maxime Touta, who was seeing in the New Year on shipboard in Upper Egypt, had sent Nonna a charming letter of apology for his absence, but his brother Alexandre had come to Helwan with his family. As for Alfred

Falaki, the jeweller, he and his buxom wife Angéline were seated opposite Dr Touta midway down the big table.

"Where are my three little chicks?" Nonna asked at regular intervals, turning to look for Nelly, Gabrielle and Marthe, all of whom were dressed in white.

"'Smallah, 'smallah!" said Angéline Falaki, fanning herself. "They remind me of my own three blossoms."

One or two surreptitious smiles greeted this dubious compliment. Rose, Marguerite and Violette, who had married the Dabbour brothers, were not conspicuously attractive, but their husbands – civil servants all three – had more than fulfilled their conjugal duties. How many pregnancies could the couples boast between them? On the annual family photograph their impressive progeniture had to be represented by a delegation only. Now in their fifties, Rose, Marguerite and Violette were a rather faded bunch of blossoms.

Dora cherished other ambitions for her daughters. Nelly, the eldest, sometimes trailed after her into the studio and watched her every movement, whereas Gabrielle, the next in order of age, loved nursing her dolls. There was nothing to prevent her from becoming a doctor some day, like Isis. All Milo's nieces and second cousins basked in the reflected glory of the Salon de Paris prizewinner and her growing reputation. Some, like Maggi, dreamt of becoming explorers and following in Stanley's footsteps; other, more sensible girls like Yolande wondered if it wouldn't be better to dedicate themselves to their future homes and families. Their mothers, who naturally nudged them in that direction, considered Dora a dangerous influence. "Go on misbehaving this way and you'll end up like the Mameluka!" Albert's wife had been heard to tell her youngest daughter.

Nonna was incensed by this remark when it came to her ears. The following Sunday, instead of kissing its author, she proffered a chilly cheek and asked her why she persisted in wearing floral dresses too young for her. They made her look fat, she added unkindly.

A gala meal had been prepared in honour of the new century. Dr Touta, who was in brilliant form, regaled the table with some historical reflections on a grand scale:

"On 1 January 1800 Egypt was under French occupation. Today, 1 January 1900, she's under British occupation. It would intrigue me to live another hundred years and find out where she'll be on 1 January 2000."

Everyone hazarded a forecast. Alfred Falaki predicted occupation by Germany. Alexandre, the father of Yolande and Maggi, inclined towards Russia. Albert Touta thought that a political convulsion in Turkey would bring the country back under strict Ottoman control.

Dora recalled the toast proposed by Seif the night before. "To Egyptian independence!" he had proclaimed, raising his glass of lemonade on high. Richard Tiomji had greeted this toast with an ironical shake of the head, and Ibrahim shared his scepticism. "That toast, at least, costs nothing to say," he said jocularly.

A mountain of honey cakes had just been deposited on the table when Nonna abruptly closed her eyes and fainted. A moment's panic ensued.

"*Ayyuh!* She's dying, she's dying!" Angéline Falaki kept repeating stupidly. The maidservants, overcome with terror, converged at a run.

Dr Touta's proximity was a blessing. He firmly and promptly took charge, told everyone to stand aside, and had his sister-in-law carried upstairs to her bedroom. Dora caught Milo's eye. She felt very close to him at that moment.

Fifteen minutes later the old doctor returned to the dining room. "It's nothing," he said. "Just too much exertion or excitement. She needs rest."

To lighten the proceedings he described how, late one night some fifteen years ago, he had been summoned to Fleming by the manservant of the Englishman who lived behind the dunes. He'd been ushered into a bedroom in which a fair-haired young man lay shivering in the throes of a high fever. The mother was weeping; the father, Elliot Bey, had preserved his usual impassive, bulldog demeanour and said nothing. Having diagnosed pneumonia, Dr Touta had administered a purge and applied vesicatories.

"A handsome young man, William Elliot — you know, the one who became an officer and served in the Sudan. I saw him at Fleming four or five years ago, just before he left for the front. Yes indeed, a really handsome young man."

Dora, under the impression that everyone in the room was looking at her, felt her cheeks burn. She had never heard tell of this incident, which had occurred some years before her marriage. Milo must have known about it. Perhaps he had mentioned it after William Elliot's first visit to the shop, but at that stage the Englishman was just another customer with a portrait photograph to be tinted. She unobtrusively left the table and went to join some of the other ladies at Nonna's bedside.

The absence of the mistress of the house wrought a change in the atmosphere at the lunch table. Milo's sisters, alarmed by their mother's indisposition, remained upstairs with her. This gave their sisters-in-law free rein. The wives of Aimé, Joseph, René and Albert assumed an unwonted air of importance: they bustled to and fro, signalling to the servants to clear away the plates and serve coffee. No one had ever seen them look as self-assured at Helwan before.

Early that afternoon the children were permitted to visit Nonna's bedroom in turn. She received them in her big four-poster with the mosquito net raised, sitting up but looking very frail. Her bedside tables were cluttered with a motley assortment of objects: a bonbonnière, some curling tongs, an enema syringe . . . In one corner of the room a pitcher and a chamber pot reposed beside a bathroom stool. The children felt they were entering forbidden territory.

A little earlier Dora had been startled to see her photograph of Nonna prominently displayed on one of the bedside tables. The whole family must have seen it, or would do so in due course. A faint smile had illumined the old lady's wrinkled face when Dora came in, and she'd tried to raise her hand in greeting.

Encircling the black crucifix above the bed was a rosary discoloured, no doubt, by long disuse. Milo's mother, who was regarded as an unbeliever, had always come to her own arrangements with heaven.

"The Almighty understands me," she used to say with a knowing smile, as she swilled the ice around her glass of arrack.

Dr Touta, too, seemed to understand her. He had more than one characteristic in common with his sister-in-law, notably a look of thoroughbred distinction that was rare in either family and had certainly not — to judge by a photograph on the wall — been shared by Nonna's late husband. With his bristling moustache and bulging eyes, Shafiq Touta might have been mistaken for a coachman. It was hard to believe he was Milo's father.

This rather blurred portrait was the first to have been taken by Milo in his Ezbekiyah Square studio. Shafiq, who had provided the wherewithal for his youngest son to set up shop there, had come from Helwan to inspect the premises. Milo got him to pose in the arabesque armchair but failed to coax him into the neck-clamp. Part of the Roman column was visible in the background.

"I was so looking forward to the turn of the century," muttered Nonna, "and now I've ruined my New Year's lunch."

"You haven't ruined it at all," Dr Touta told her. "Your guests are in high spirits — they're sure to stay to dinner. Some of them have gone off to hire donkeys for an excursion to the Tourah quarries. I advised them to take some candles."

The old doctor drew Milo and his brothers aside when he came out of the bedroom.

"Her condition worries me. She'll have to take great care of herself, but there's no reason to deprive her of her glass of arrack at mealtimes."

52

Nonna's state of health apart, 1900 began under the most favourable auspices. In the middle of January, for the second time in eighteen months, a gentleman-in-waiting turned up at the shop. He had come to deliver an invitation, addressed to "Monsieur et Madame Touta", to the khedive's annual ball at 'Abdin Palace.

The thick card was engraved with 'Abbas's coat of arms. Milo cradled it in his hands for minutes on end, bursting with pride. For the next few days he contrived to acquaint each of his customers with the honour that had been done him:

"Your prints will be ready in ten days or so, Labib Effendi, but please don't come at the weekend — we'll be rather pressed for time. Yes, the khedive's ball . . . "

He inundated Dora with remarks about what would be, as it was every year, the social high spot of the Cairo winter:

"Thirteen hundred invitations have gone out, but not just to all and sundry. The guests are carefully handpicked. Not even the Popinots have received a card."

Rather than hiring evening dress, he went to an Armenian tailor with whom he sometimes played backgammon and chose a length of the finest English cloth.

"After all," he said with the air of a palace habitué, "I don't want to have to hire a tailcoat every year."

Lita Tiomji, who collected Parisian fashion plates, promptly offered her services to Dora, but the Mameluka, in keeping with her quirky reputation, proposed to design her own ball gown.

"You're mad, *chérie*," Lita kept saying.

Purchased at Mayer's and accompanied by a sketch, the cloth and trimmings were entrusted to a dressmaker the same evening. Dora had her first fitting a few days later. She smiled as she inspected herself in the long mirror to cries of admiration from Lita and the dressmaker.

The more imminent the fateful Saturday, the greater the suspense in the shop. Bulbul, although he couldn't really fathom what his employers would be doing at the palace, was as excited as anyone. Hurrying from room to room, he moved things around, dusted the furniture furiously, and greeted the least remark with a loud guffaw.

The Popinots had insisted on lending the couple their carriage and coachman. The latter had still not appeared by ten o'clock that night. Milo, in a fever of impatience, was about to hail a cab when the carriage drove into the square at a leisurely pace.

"We're going to the palace!" he called anxiously.

"Like the last time, you mean?" the turbaned coachman replied.

Milo couldn't help laughing. Their destination was indeed the same, but they'd come a long way since then!

The entrance of 'Abdin Palace was aglow with electric lights. A footman in ceremonial dress opened the carriage door. Young ushers in tarbooshes were greeting guests, all smiles, and offering their arms to the ladies as they ascended the great marble staircase, which was strewn with flowers.

Conversation ceased when Dora entered the first reception room. She looked dazzlingly beautiful. The khedive's necklace that sparkled at her throat went perfectly with the earrings Milo had given her when they married.

The Dutch consul general was leading the quadrille in an adjoining room. "Forward, two . . . Ladies into line . . . " Flanked by gentlemen in evening dress and British officers in uniform, bevies of graceful femininity were moving in time to the orchestra. "Forward, four . . . and sway . . . "

The farandole wound its way across the floor in obedience to the caller's commands. Now and then, while the line of dancers was entering the room next door, the owner of a ball gown would utter a little cry — drowned by the music — as someone trod on her train.

"Dora, you look magnificent," said Maxime Touta, bending to kiss her hand. The editor of the *Sémaphore d'Alexandrie* seemed very much at home in this gala setting, if a trifle remote from the throng that populated it. "It amuses me to watch. Take that harem over there . . . "

In response to their look of inquiry he drew them to the far end of the third reception room, which was shielded by latticework panels of carved wood. Issuing from behind these *mashrabiyas* could be heard the twittering and laughter of the ladies of the court, who were permitted to attend the party without being seen.

The farandole ceased abruptly, to be followed by the khedival anthem. "'Abbas must have made his entrance," said Maxime.

Applause rang out, then conversation resumed. Dora was bemused by the lights, the music, the shimmering colours. One little sip of Milo's champagne, and she already felt drunk.

"Can this be my photographer?" said a voice beside her.

She nearly fell over backwards. The khedive, accompanied by several notables, inclined his head in greeting. She promptly sketched a curtsy of the kind she'd once been taught at boarding school, but 'Abbas, who was wearing a plain black *stamboulina* devoid of orders and decorations, preserved a friendly, almost familiar tone.

"I'm very honoured, Madame Touta, to welcome to this palace a person as talented as yourself. I trust you'll find the occasion an enjoyable one."

He quickly shook hands with the editor of the *Sémaphore d'Alexandrie* before resuming his progress through the room. Milo, who had barely recovered from his surprise, realized with a twinge of regret that the khedive hadn't spared him a glance, doubtless because he hadn't even noticed his presence.

"Aren't you going to ask me to dance?" said Dora, knowing how capable he was of being hurt by this incident.

The orchestra was playing a slow English waltz. She rested her head lovingly on Milo's shoulder, as if to demonstrate to the world at large that he was her husband, her lover, the only man in her life. When the music stopped he left her in Maxime's care and went off to pay his respects to Ibrahim's uncle, who had just arrived. A liveried flunkey came up, bearing a salver.

"May I get you a glass?" Maxime asked. Almost immediately, he went on, "I should very much like to publish a photographic report on the reconquest of the Sudan, but I'd need a talented photographer. Someone like you . . . "

She smiled. "With all the work I have here? Our clientele is growing month by month. We're taking on a second darkroom assistant next week."

They sighted Lord Cromer in the distance. Very much a centre of attraction, the British consul general was talking to a personage with a flowing beard. The latter, tightly buttoned up in a tunic covered with decorations, was standing with one hand resting on the hilt of a cavalry sabre.

"That's the Ghazi Mukhtar Pasha, the sultan's envoy," said Maxime. "A lover of the language of Molière. I'll wager he's speaking French with Cromer."

The buffet opened at midnight. Dora glimpsed a series of horseshoe tables covered with damask cloths and a wide assortment of dishes. Stuffed vine leaves and truffled galantines rubbed shoulders with whole roast lambs.

Hungry dancers had taken the tables by storm. Elderly ladies in heavy velvet gowns complained of being unable to move in their direction. One of them almost slapped the face of a young British officer whose spurs had torn her lace hem.

"Permit me to introduce myself, madame. I'm the Dutch consul general."

Dora, with a plate in one hand and a glass in the other, could only smile at the person who had accosted her, an elegant man in his fifties.

"I'm told you take magnificent portraits. Might I have the honour of sitting for you?"

"But of course, monsieur," said Milo, who had trampled on two ladies' feet in his haste to join them. "I'm Émile Touta."

Dora effaced herself as far as possible and left the beaming Photographer to the Consulates to fix an appointment with his first customer from the diplomatic corps.

Ibrahim was vigorously beckoning them from the far end of the buffet. They threaded their way over to him. "What a crush!" said the poet, chuckling. "And to think this palace is so big. Do you know the winter garden?"

"No, I don't believe I do," Milo replied with the air of one who had frequented 'Abdin Palace from the cradle on.

Ibrahim led them up a staircase with a crystal balustrade. The winter garden, which occupied an entire overhead gallery, boasted a superb collection of ferns and palm trees. Rounding a clump of vegetation, they came face to face with Jacquemart, the photographer to the princes, who was strolling along with a pasha attired in black and gold. The Frenchman treated them to a haughty stare and continued on his way.

"I'm sure that dirty swine knows who we are!" Milo exclaimed. "Believe me, the next time we meet I'll say, 'Good evening, colleague, can I send you some customers? I'm snowed under.'"

Dancing had recommenced by the time they came downstairs, and the orchestra was playing *The Blue Danube*. A British officer bowed to Dora. She accompanied him on to the floor in the second reception room, thinking of William Elliot.

"Madame Touta?" said another English officer, just as she was about to rejoin Milo and Ibrahim. She assumed he was a would-be dancing partner and almost said no, but he went on quickly, "I'm on Lord Cromer's staff. His Lordship would like you to take his photograph. Could you see him at eleven next Friday morning?"

"Friday at eleven?" she repeated in a daze.

"Yes. I'm very sorry, but it's the only time he can spare for weeks to come."

He thanked her and melted into the crowd.

"You must have dreamt it," Milo kept saying as the coachman drove them home. "Who is this officer? What's his name?"

She didn't know what to say.

"You don't imagine Lord Cromer is going to turn up at a place he doesn't know, just like that! Are you sure he said 'Cromer'? It wasn't 'Keller' by any chance? Besides, Keller's not a lord . . ."

Even Dora was beginning to have her doubts. Had the officer really said "His Lordship"? Milo's persistent questions only added to her uncertainty.

She found it hard to sleep that night. She had a confused dream in which she was Cinderella. During a waltz, William Elliot made a secret assignation with her in the palace winter garden, the route to which ran through Nonna's bedroom.

Late next morning a note addressed to Madame Touta and bearing the seal of the British consulate general confirmed that Lord Cromer would come to the studio to be photographed by her at eleven a.m. on Friday.

53

I'd never seen Milo in such a state. "It's out of the question!" he exclaimed. "We can't have him here with the place looking like this!" In order to give Lord Cromer a fitting reception, he proposed to have the entire shop repainted. I shrugged and told him firmly that Cromer wouldn't care two hoots about our paintwork, which was only a year old in any case. But Milo absolutely insisted on charming the eye of our illustrious customer. He sent for a decorator and asked him to rejuvenate our shop window in double-quick time.

The blood-red paintwork gave me a shock when I saw it next day, but I refrained from commenting. Milo himself realized that his window looked rather incongruous and instructed the decorator to overpaint it pale green.

He shook his head when the job was done. "No, it's too pale. I'm going to pick out a navy blue instead."

"You're not being very discreet," I told him irritably. "The neighbours will be wondering what's up."

"So what? All the better – let the whole of Cairo know! You surely don't think we're going to conceal the fact that the most powerful man in Egypt has chosen to be photographed in Émile Touta's studio?"

Something else had been preying on my mind for the past two days. How would Seif take Lord Cromer's visit to our shop? He wasn't employing the photographer to the army of occupation, not this time. This was a far more serious matter: our studio was offering its services to the very symbol of the

British occupation. "We're not going to deny ourselves a customer of that calibre to please Seif," Milo retorted. "You'd do better to decide what refreshments we're going to offer Lord Cromer. Yes, yes, refreshments! We're not going to treat him like some beggar off the streets."

On Wednesday evening, feeling very embarrassed, I took the initiative and told Seif our news. I expected him to turn pale — even, perhaps, to sweep out and slam the door. Much to my surprise, the young man's face brightened. "But that's wonderful," he said. "I'll be able to have a word with him. Will you allow me to be present the day after tomorrow?"

"Certainly not!" snapped Milo. "I don't want a scene. Lord Cromer is my customer, and I insist on my customers being respected."

"There won't be any scene, I assure you," said Seif. "I'd simply like to ask him a question."

"Perhaps I could sing him my *Marseillaise*," said Ibrahim.

"Drop the subject," I told Seif in an undertone. "We'll arrange it somehow." Then, to the room at large, "The *mezze* are hot, help yourselves. I'm sure Milo's dying to tell you all about our evening at the palace."

All was in readiness. The third coat of paint had dried, and the door bore a notice informing customers that the shop would be shut on Friday morning. Bottles of every description were already arrayed in the waiting room, from which one or two bulky armchairs had been removed. Even the red jacket that Bulbul would be wearing — an idea of Milo's — had been ironed and draped over a hanger in the lobby.

But my husband couldn't sleep. His thoughts continually reverted to Seif. The young lawyer's satisfaction on learning of Lord Cromer's visit struck him as extremely suspicious. What outrage was he preparing to commit? All at once, Milo sat bolt upright in bed. "My God!" he cried. "He's planning an assassination!"

"What did you say?" I asked feebly, half awake by now.

"An assassination! He's planning an assassination!"

I reassured him as best I could. Then I went back to sleep.

* * *

Milo persisted in harping on his anxieties at breakfast. "You'll upset me if you go on like this," I told him angrily. "I'll make a hash of Cromer's photograph." At that, he more or less forgot about Seif and concentrated on the final preparations.

Bulbul looked like a clown with the red jacket buttoned up to his chin. He never stopped gazing at himself in the big mirror, utterly transfixed.

Milo rearranged the photographs in the window yet again, popping feverishly in and out of the shop. His goings-on ended by attracting several onlookers. "There's nothing to see!" he yelled at them.

More curious spectators converged. Two men in turbans actually sat down on the pavement and waited for something to happen. Seeing Bulbul in his fancy dress, they proceeded to tell their amber beads.

"Go and fill the buckets in the yard," Milo told Bulbul.

"But they're full, *ya bey.*"

"Then empty them, you fool!"

The Popinots, the Tiomjis, Seif and Ibrahim turned up at ten o'clock, as arranged. "Your presence will make the shop look busier," I'd told them. "I can't see us confronting Lord Cromer on our own."

Ibrahim, wearing a bright pink shirt, was his usual jovial self. He inquired if he ought to kiss the British potentate's hand. "At the opera the other night, his carriage was preceded by a groom who cleared the route with cries of 'Make way for the Lord! Make way for the Lord!'"

Popinot told us of something Cromer had recently confided to a European passing through Cairo: "If there were a dozen men in Egypt capable of governing the country, we'd clear out at once." This remark had prompted bitter comments at the Cercle Français. Seif nodded but did not, for once, look incensed. He was smartly dressed in a dark suit and a polka dot tie. Milo, who had been watching him closely ever since his arrival, failed to detect any suspicious bulge that might have concealed a weapon.

I was expecting Lord Cromer at eleven precisely. We locals had abandoned our elastic notion of time since the start of the British occupation, even though William Elliot used to complain that "the natives" still had a long way to go before they learned the meaning of punctuality. Dr Touta said that, prior to 1882, three different times had existed in Cairo: railway time, hotel time, and cannon time. The latter was the only reliable indicator. When a loud report from the Citadel made the houses shake, one knew that it really was noon. Invitations to official functions used to read "at 9 o'clock by the cannon". This custom had been dropped since the arrival of the British. Military time was now the rule, and guests who turned up late ended by not being invited any more. However, a wide gulf separated parties at the British Agency from the rest of the country!

So Émile Touta and his staff expected to see Lord Cromer appear on the first stroke of eleven. In fact, the shop door opened twenty-five minutes early. It was the Englishman who had accosted me at the ball.

"Madame Touta, His Lordship is expecting you at the Residency."

I couldn't conceal my surprise. "Wasn't it intended that the sitting should take place here?" I asked.

"My apologies," he said. "That was a ruse adopted for reasons of security. Arrangements have been made for the sitting to take place at the Residency."

"But I won't have my equipment!"

"You'll find some equipment there very similar to yours, madame. I'm told you use a Zeiss. In any case, you can bring any requisites you like. We'll transport them for you. Don't worry, they'll be handled with due care."

Ten minutes later, when Milo followed me out and was about to board one of the two carriages waiting outside the door, the Englishman politely intervened.

"I'm sorry, only Madame Touta is expected at the Residency. I'm not authorized to bring anyone else."

I was already in the carriage when I caught Milo's look of dismay. For a moment I wondered whether to decline to go under such circumstances, but my desire to take this photograph won the day.

I had an attack of incipient panic on the way there. Would my portrait of Lord Cromer be a failure? No such fear had possessed me in the case of the khedive, I was so concerned to avoid discovery. This time, dizzy with apprehension, I came within an inch of asking my escort to take me home.

The Residency's heavy portals, emblazoned with the royal coat of arms, opened to let us pass and the sentries on duty saluted. I entered Lord Cromer's office just as a big clock chimed eleven. My head was still whirling when the British consul general bade me welcome and apologized for the change of plan. A majestic-looking man of sixty, he had an exceptionally penetrating gaze. I knew at once that I would photograph him in three-quarter profile with plenty of shadow, tilting the camera a little so as not to emphasize his baldness.

Lord Cromer congratulated me on my portrait of the khedive. "You managed to make His Highness look quite likeable," he said, a malicious glint in his eye. The son of a City banker, he bore the modest title consul general like his European colleagues, but everyone was conscious of the power he wielded, which seemed infinite and eternal. He had already ruled Egypt for seventeen years, having previously served in India and Jamaica.

"Our French consuls take it in turns," Norbert Popinot used to say bitterly, "whereas no one in London would dream of replacing Lord Cromer. He may be popular in his own country, but only because he's adept at manipulating public opinion. Why else do you think he publishes his annual reports on the situation in Egypt and makes such a song and dance about them?"

A camera as big as the one in the studio had been set up in the office, and a mobile screen offered a selection of several plain backgrounds. I had no need even to unpack my reflectors and my pinhole viewfinder: instruments similar to my own were lying ready on a low table.

My subject humorously consented when I asked him to turn away a little from the light. "I can do no less than Queen Victoria. In the special studio Her Majesty has installed at Windsor Castle, she's as obedient to her photographer as she is to her physician."

I did not, in fact, have to give Lord Cromer many instructions. He neither struck a pose nor assumed a forced smile. Motionless without being stiff, his face commanded attention of itself.

Used to chatting with my sitters while focusing the camera, I asked if he ever had the time to indulge in his well-known love of poetry. "I begin every day by reading a page from the Greek or Roman poets," he said, and proceeded to recite a passage from the twelfth book of the *Iliad*, a favourite of his.

I relaxed. In this peaceful room, face to face with this all-powerful man who was reciting Homer to me, I felt far removed from all that was said about English arrogance. "They despise us," Seif used to say. "They regard us as savages." One day, by way of consolation, Popinot told him, "Don't worry, they despise us too. To the English, Africa begins at Calais."

The light on Lord Cromer's face was rather too strong, so I went over to the french windows and drew the curtain halfway across. Before exposing the last plate I took my courage in both hands.

"I know a young Muslim who would give anything to be in my shoes at this moment," I said, "so as to have a few minutes' conversation with you. He's a genuine patriot, a lawyer . . . "

"Leave his name with my secretary," Cromer replied. "I'll see him when I've a moment to spare."

Though touched by my initiative, Seif intimated that he wouldn't seek an interview. "I wouldn't want to be mistaken for one of those journalists who go fishing for information at the British Residency. If ever I'm obliged to speak to Lord Cromer, it'll be on Egyptian territory."

"Or, better still, on liberated Egyptian territory," said Ibrahim. "But for that you'll have to wait a little longer."

Lord Cromer's portrait, which was to appear in more than one illustrated book, occupied a central position in our shop window alongside that of 'Abbas Hilmi. By effecting this bold rapprochement, Milo was in tune with the times. The khedive had just been humiliated by the sultan, who had compelled his yacht to leave Rhodes and take refuge in British Cyprus. Rejected by Constantinople after being disappointed by Paris, 'Abbas was tempted to turn towards London. He was said to be desirous of maintaining excellent relations with the Prince of Wales, who might succeed his eighty-one-year-old mother at any moment.

Lord Cromer thanked me warmly for the photographs. At Milo's insistence, I delivered them in person and asked if he would authorize the studio to market them. "Why should I object to the dissemination of a picture that flatters me?" he replied with a smile. "Not, I suspect, that many people in Egypt will wish to buy my portrait."

His Lordship was mistaken. Over the next two years, that picture postcard adorned with the red "T" sold almost as well as the one of the khedive.

54

From now on, who could have disputed Émile Touta's right to style himself "Photographer to the Consulates"? With Lord Cromer in his window, he seemed even to be erring on the side of modesty.

Passers-by paused spontaneously to look at the consul and the khedive exchanging stares. A small notice announced that copies of these postcards were on sale within for 10 piastres, or less, depending on the number purchased. Many customers, intending to dignify their family album with the presence of Cromer *and* 'Abbas, bought one copy of each.

The Émile Touta studio, without any doubt, initiated the picture post-card revival in Cairo that year. Numerous unknown individuals ordered a hundred or two hundred copies of their portraits overprinted on the front or back with their names and addresses. In order to guarantee production on this scale, it was no longer in Milo's interest to subcontract Maloumian, who could not in any case satisfy demand. Accordingly, he equipped the studio with various accessories including a camera with six lenses. He also engaged a third operator whose only job was to turn out picture postcards.

"You ought to sell albums as well," Norbert Popinot suggested one evening. "Print a 'T' on the covers, and I'm sure they'd be a success."

Milo was thrilled with this idea, which gave him another chance to demonstrate his business acumen. He went at once to two printers in the Moski, invited them to quote against each other, lost his temper with each in turn, and ended by opting for the more expensive, who at least had the merit of being a Greek Catholic. Adorning the shop window several weeks later were some albums in coarse-grained leather reinforced on the back with four nickel-plated studs. Available in dark red or Prussian blue and furnished with gilt edges and a spring clasp, they sold for eighty-nine piastres. Preliminary sales were so substantial that the price was increased the following month.

Milo also hit on the idea of filling his window with such photographic trinkets as Alfred Falaki was finding it hard to dispose of in his jeweller's shop. The titanic haggling to which this gave rise was ultimately successful, because each party did quite well out of it. Thus, the albums were joined by photograph frames, medallions, brooches, charm bracelets, and even silver tiepins capable of accommodating tiny miniatures.

Money came pouring in so fast that Milo had to deposit it at the Imperial Ottoman Bank every two or three days. Armed with a small Gladstone bag, he had himself driven there by his recent acquisition, a coachman. Nothing gave him greater pride than his carriage, which stood outside the shop all day long, and which he gladly placed at the disposal of privileged customers.

"Certainly not, Lutfi Bey, I can't have you going home on foot . . . No, no, Madame 'Ayrout, I insist. My coachman will take you . . . "

Flattered by these attentions, his customers brought the studio some additional publicity by spreading the word. But Milo did not refrain from resorting to more traditional advertising methods. Like Jacquemart, he inserted little notices in the papers: "Émile Touta, Photographer to the Consulates. Portraits in Every Style." Contrary to Dora's advice, he added: "First Prize, Salon de Paris."

To reach the apartment, Wednesday night guests no longer had to go through the shop and sprain their ankles on the spiral staircase. A liveried *sufragi* greeted them at the door of the adjacent building purchased some months earlier, which opened on the street. Although the soirées were attended by many more people than in the old days, they preserved their informal and rather impromptu character. Some dishes were supplied by the Pâtisserie Mathieu, others prepared on the spot by the Toutas' cook. Norbert Popinot still chose the wines, but he merely recommended vineyards and vintages to Milo, who ordered them by the case.

Now that it had almost trebled in size, the apartment boasted two spacious, adjoining reception rooms. Their walls were not covered with little framed photographs in the manner of some Cairo interiors. Dora had selected only two, which were displayed on a Louis XVI chest of drawers: one of her three daughters wearing big straw hats on the beach at Fleming; and, despite its imperfections, her very first portrait of Milo in an open-necked shirt.

Everyone much enjoyed the way the master of the house enlivened these soirées. Solange Popinot wasn't the only one to weep with laughter at his account of the gymkhana held near the Pyramids in the presence of the Duke of Saxe-Coburg-Gotha, which had included "a donkey race for ladies and gentlemen holding hands". Milo had the knack of introducing his guests in a flattering way and putting them at ease with one another. Thanks to him, there was never a dull moment on Wednesday evenings. Conversation ceased only when Solange or some other lady sat down at the piano. A small chamber orchestra performed on occasion. Sometimes, again, Ibrahim would recite a few poems in default of his *Marseillaise*, which was still far from finished.

Isis was among the new Wednesday regulars. Generally unaccompanied by Maxime, she liked to hold forth on a subject close to her heart: how to improve the lot of Egyptian village women. For months now she had been bombarding the public health authorities with requests that rural midwives be given basic training.

"The British are proposing to administer first-aid training to the barbers who carry out circumcisions. That's all very well, but it's the mid-wives who need training. Their influence in rural areas is immense. Only they could persuade women not to give birth to twelve or fifteen children, most of whom will die before they've learned to wield a mattock."

Dora had grown increasingly fond of Isis, who was now a close friend of hers. Neither Solange Popinot nor Lita Tiomji could provide her with conversation of this kind. Although she discussed art with Ibrahim, her exchanges with the young Copt were of a deeper and more general nature

— more intimate, too. Few women in Cairo could have understood each other as well as these two dissidents.

"By pursuing a profession," Isis said one day, "you've committed a crime like mine, but even more heinous: all my patients are women; you photograph men."

"And I've been criticized for it plenty of times!" Dora said angrily. "I sometimes feel as if I'm guilty of taking obscene pictures." She thought for a moment. "I envy you in a way. People come to you to have their bodies attended to. That's straightforward, at least. Me, I'm expected to remedy their outward appearance. It's unfair."

Isis reverted to the subject a few days later. "When you come down to it," she said, "people can't forgive us for working. We're lucky to have such understanding husbands, the two of us. Not many men would react as they do."

"I'm sure that's truer of you than it is of me," Dora said pensively.

The portrait she took of Isis that winter bore witness to their growing intimacy. Half reclining on a sofa with her hands clasped behind her head and a defiant smile on her face, Maxime Touta's wife made an almost immodest impression. One sensed that she was perfectly in accord with the photographer who had captured the pose.

55

What with his carriage, his coachman, his cook, his three maidservants, and his suits made by the best tailor in Cairo, Milo cut quite a dash. Gone was the young bohemian with the waggish air who relied solely on his charm and glib tongue to help him make his way in life. Although his behaviour sometimes verged on the nouveau riche, he escaped ridicule because of the amusement with which he continued to regard the world and himself. In his heart of hearts, he considered the image of success more important than success itself.

He still derived as much pleasure from his three-piastre games of backgammon at the café on the corner, but how proudly he deposited an Egyptian pound on the table when playing against Richard Tiomji! He was equally proud to announce to all and sundry that his daughters had been invited to take part in some amateur dramatics by one of the wealthiest families in Cairo.

"The big drawing room had been converted into a theatre. All the upper crust were there, including Prince Hussein and Prince Toussoun. Someone banged on the floor three times, and the curtain rose on a celestial landscape. Gabrielle was playing the part of a dove. You should have seen her hovering beside Fairy Bonbon . . . "

While lunching at Helwan he mentioned in the same tone of voice that Dora had been invited by the ladies of the French Charity Committee to run a stall at their annual event.

"The ponies were supervised by Lady Palmer and Lady Rogers. Flowers, confetti and streamers were on sale. The lady collectors kept rattling their boxes at some pashas. Three witches in a tent were in direct communication with Lucifer and would make prophecies for ten piastres. The prettiest of them predicted that I would very soon go on a long journey. 'To Europe?' I asked the *katkouta*. 'Another five piastres and I'll tell you,' she said. A little further on the Comte de Serione, dressed up as an Arab, replied in verse to every question he was asked. The takings amounted to 700 pounds."

"Excellent!" commented Alfred Falaki, who always relished a good round figure.

Dora was very vague when questioned about this charity bazaar. The truth was, she had found it grotesque and resolved never to take part again.

"Why do you consult witches?" Nonna asked Milo sternly.

Embarrassed smiles greeted this outburst. The old lady had not been herself since her indisposition on New Year's Day. She sometimes made incoherent remarks and got her own children's names mixed up, but she could also, as of old, summarize her thoughts in one deadly phrase. In contrast to those who had considered Milo too quixotic to succeed in life, Nonna had always believed in her youngest son's lucky star. Now, when his success seemed complete, she was being strangely reticent.

She sometimes exchanged a look of concern or annoyance with Dora when Milo was describing one of his social exploits. The two women had never been so close, even though one was wreathed in glory and the other lapsing into the mists of old age. This intimacy manifested itself in an occasional, furtive gesture: Nonna's habit of clasping Dora to her when they kissed, or the affectionate way in which the young woman would bend over her mother-in-law and ask, in a low voice, if she would care for some orange-blossom tea.

"Get me some arrack," Nonna would mutter. "It'll perk me up."

Wednesday night guests often referred to Dora as "the Mameluka". Solange had uttered the nickname in front of a French woman friend, and it promptly went the rounds of Cairo. Hitherto confined to the family circle and close friends, it passed into the public domain. Encouraged to do so on all sides, Dora joined in the game. After all, she was as much the queen of those soirées as of the dinners given by the Popinots or other prominent residents of Cairo.

Men would do anything to please her. To mark her twenty-eighth birthday, which was celebrated with a memorable masked ball, Ibrahim composed no fewer than twenty-eight verses each of twenty-eight alexandrines.

"I feel as if I've used up all the words in the dictionary," the poet confided to Norbert Popinot, with the weary but triumphant smile of a marathon runner breasting the tape.

One Tuesday morning, Dora took delivery of an alabaster table with rosewood legs, a gift from a Jewish antique dealer whom she had briefly met at a party the night before. The next day, the same admirer sent her a silver filigree coffee service formerly owned by one of Muhammad Ali's grandsons. She was obliged to return the second gift the same day for fear of receiving still more.

An Italian banker from Alexandria, who fell madly in love with Dora, sent her ardent letters that remained unanswered. He travelled to Cairo every weekend, purely on the off chance of seeing her as she came out of church after Mass at Darb al-Geneinah. It was later rumoured that he had tried to slit his wrists in his office with the entire board of directors waiting for him in the room next door.

The interest shown in the Mameluka was not unequivocal. To men, the very fact of being alone with her in the studio fostered dreams and fantasies. Some ill-informed male customers, in hopes of heaven alone knew what, mistook the studio for the darkroom.

Dora was reputed to have a number of lovers, among them a European consul and a prince of the khedival house. She was also the subject of unpleasant tittle-tattle, not all of which, fortunately, came to her ears or Milo's. It was insinuated by some that her relations with Isis were reprehensible. This calumny was accompanied by a play on words: Isis and Dora became "Isidora". Evil tongues strove to devise riddles like "Why doesn't

Isidora ever share her husband's bed?" The answers varied from day to day: "Because the lady's hard at work" or "Because no one can be in two places at once."

One anonymous individual courageously saw fit to inform Milo of this in writing. He read the letter and flew into a violent rage. For once, it wasn't Bulbul who suffered in consequence but a customer who had the misfortune to express surprise at the length of time it was going to take to develop and print his portrait.

"You've come to the wrong place!" yelled Milo. "If it's military punctuality you want, go to Maloumian across the way. Yes, Maloumian, official photographer to the army of occupation. He photographs officers, but don't worry, he also takes private soldiers – even deserters!"

Alarmed and uncomprehending, the customer made a hasty exit.

Milo, who was convinced that the rumour emanated from Jacquemart's studio, threatened to knock the Frenchman's block off with the whole neighbourhood looking on.

"Take care," Popinot warned him. "My compatriot is not without influence. If you laid into him, he'd be quite capable of taking you to court and doing you a lot of harm. Besides, you've no proof of his ill will."

Milo's sisters-in-law conceived of Dora as a woman eaten up with ambition – one who had skilfully played her cards for years, one after another: colouring prints, learning to take photographs and develop them, reorganizing the studio, entering for the Salon de Paris . . . To them she was a careerist who had planned her every move from the outset, having married Milo with the sole aim of usurping the studio and attaining notoriety.

Milo was well placed to deny the existence of this implacable scheme. He had followed his wife's development, discoveries and hesitations step by step, just as he had shared her surprise at the momentum of her professional advancement. This did not, however, prevent him from becoming more and more jealous of her success. At night after dinner he sometimes remonstrated with her because some European, intellectual or magistrate had spent too long chatting with her or kissed her hand in an overfamiliar way.

"What about you!" she would retort. "Don't imagine I didn't see the way you were dancing with the niece of the manager of the Ottoman Bank . . ."

Although she realized only too clearly that her professional success was disrupting their married life, she felt as borne along by it as others are by misfortune: it was an unstoppable process that fed on itself. One triumph led to another, and the higher she climbed the more humiliated Milo felt.

True, he could boast of having devised the scheme to print picture postcards of the khedive and Lord Cromer, which were bringing in good money. It was he, too, who had steadily increased the studio's prices in proportion to its fame. But, although a red "T" now cost more than a portrait by Jacquemart, this did not prevent Dora from being regarded as the mainstay and symbol of the business. The "T" bore a strong resemblance to a "D".

Milo's jealousy was all the keener because he had little cause to reproach his wife. Although a trifle intoxicated by her growing reputation, Dora refrained from bragging about it and left others to become aware of her photographic prowess or the tributes that were paid her. They learned of them in the end, and that had a far greater effect than anything they could have heard from her own lips. Had her sisters-in-law been shrewder, that was the Achilles' heel they could have laid bare: a feigned modesty that disguised great personal satisfaction.

Nevertheless, honours and prestige meant less to her than the pleasure she derived from producing work to her taste. She put her whole self into every portrait, every time with the same emotion.

"As a photographer," she told Ibrahim, "I transmit my emotions to my subjects. I dominate them throughout the sitting, almost as if I were pointing a gun at them. Those moments are very intense, very disturbing. My photographs – the successful ones, at least – convey what I was feeling when I took them. They're almost self-portraits."

56

One Thursday afternoon, when Dora was at home with her daughters, the Italian consul general – a hunchback with a goatee beard – presented himself at the shop. Milo was most attentive. He offered to photograph him right away, without an appointment.

"I'll attend to you myself," he said effusively.

"Very good of you," said the Italian, "but I'd like to be photographed by Madame Touta."

Milo controlled his trembling lips with an effort and went to fetch Dora. That evening he made an embarrassing scene over a trifle.

"You left the appointments book in the studio. I looked everywhere for it. It's intolerable! I can't work in these conditions!"

She apologized and left it at that, attributing his sudden outburst to fatigue. Milo had been nervous and touchy for some time – he flared up for no reason at all. Twice in the course of the last few weeks he had joined the appalling Ernest Zahlawi at the Bar Bavaria. Although not drunk, he had come home slightly tipsy. Dora hadn't dared remonstrate with him for fear of triggering an explosion.

The following night he didn't address a word to her. "What's the matter with you?" she demanded, growing impatient.

"That photograph of the Italian consul is an absolute disaster," Milo said coldly. "We'll have to offer him another sitting free of charge."

Dora, her own sternest critic, was speechless. She had been delighted by her photograph of the man with the goatee and congratulated herself on having caught the mischievous twinkle in his eyes. The portrait made one forget his deformity. She had asked him to lean forward with his elbow on the arm of a chair. In that position he looked no more hunchbacked than anyone else.

"Anyone can make a mistake," Milo added in the same tone of voice. "I'll call at the consulate and explain. He'll understand."

"But —"

"But nothing!" he snapped. "You don't think I'm going to put my name to that rubbish, do you?"

Dora was stunned and close to tears. He had never spoken to her like that before. She left the room without a word.

That was not the first tantrum Milo had thrown. Every time Dora took some major initiative in the studio or did something strikingly successful, his manner became strange: sometimes sarcastic, sometimes spiteful, but always remote. They used to end by making it up with kisses and caresses, laughter or tears — by attaining mutual fusion and regaining a measure of equilibrium. That equilibrium had now been upset for quite some time, and Dora felt incapable of re-establishing it.

Feeling the need to discuss this with someone, she found an attentive and tactful audience in Isis. More than just an audience, in fact, because the young Copt had also confided in her and hinted at how distressed she was by her husband's affair with Nada Mancelle. Listening to her helped Dora to see her own worries in perspective. Hers, after all, were only professional in origin. Would they have arisen had she not pursued the same occupation as Milo?

He had sometimes failed to congratulate her as warmly as she deserved. After the Salon de Paris, for example, he had ignored the quality of the photograph that had captivated the jury and reserved all his praise for Ibrahim's discreet initiative, his skill and ingenuity, as if Ibrahim himself were the prize-winner. But never before had he poured such scorn on his wife's work.

The Italian consul, who looked in at the shop the following day, was so delighted with his portrait that he ordered three hundred copies of it in postcard format. His wife, who was with him, begged Dora to grant her an appointment during the week: she was even prepared to sit for her during the lunch hour.

"And we should be delighted," the Italian wound up, "if you and Monsieur Touta would share our box at the opera one night."

Although reassured on the subject of her work, Dora was all the more puzzled by her husband's attitude. She recalled certain other incidents she had failed to interpret at the time, for instance Milo's unaccountable refusal to take part in the first photographic exhibition at the Hôtel-Casino San Stefano in Alexandria. All the leading Egyptian studios, Jacquemart's included, were showing examples of their work. The khedive had announced his intention of opening the show, which featured several views of the Montaza estate of which he was so proud. Milo had received a more than cordial invitation from the San Stefano management. What sweet revenge for the young man who, only a few years earlier, had set up his tripod outside the casino in the hope of obtaining some orders at the floral bicycle competition! The Mameluka's works would have had every reason to be the exhibition's focal point, especially as a rhapsodic article about her, written by the Cairo correspondent of the Paris newspaper *Le Temps*, had just been published and widely quoted in the Egyptian press. Could it have been her predictable success that had put Milo off?

He maintained that the best way of distinguishing themselves was not to turn up at San Stefano at all: the photographs exhibited by the studio would be lost among so many others, and the wisest policy would be to wait a few months before holding a private exhibition devoted to Dora's work alone.

That argument could, at a pinch, be defended. The fuss over the Italian consul, on the other hand, seemed unjustifiable. Dora refused to stomach it, but she was too proud to demand an explanation. She simply informed Milo of the order for picture postcards.

"Three hundred?" he exclaimed on hearing the news. "These Italians! They're regular woman-chasers!"

57

Milo cancelled the following Wednesday's get-together on the pretext that he was ill. It seemed unlike him. Solange Popinot looked in the next day to satisfy herself that it was nothing serious. Bulbul explained in sign language that his master was playing backgammon at the café and his mistress busy with a customer in the studio. Solange bumped into Milo on the pavement as she left the shop. Concerned to see him looking so tense, she asked what the matter was. Her solicitude suddenly made him feel genuinely ill.

A quarter of an hour later they were sharing a table in the Pâtisserie Mathieu, on the far side of the square. Milo described the rigours of his early days as a photographer, laying it on with a trowel. He told how he had spent whole nights shivering in the darkroom in winter. The ether fumes had made him dizzy. As for the mercury vapour that escaped from the box in which the plates were developed, it had almost robbed him of his eyesight . . . He described himself in summer, streaming with sweat beneath the studio skylight. A big block of ice had to be placed in a bucket in the middle of the room to cool the air a little. The stifling heat used to give him palpitations . . . Milo retouched the story of his beginnings in photography just as he retouched his customers' portraits. It might not be authentic, but it rang true and made the listener yearn to believe it.

Solange let herself be lulled by the mellifluous, low-pitched voice that had charmed her at their very first encounter eight years earlier.

"You look feverish," she told him, while the waiter was bringing another pot of tea.

"I'm feeling a little better," he replied, fixing her with a velvet gaze. "Thanks to you."

They arranged to continue their conversation in the same establishment the following afternoon.

"Don't trouble to send word if you're ill," said Solange. "I shall come anyway — it'll make a nice outing for me. And if you haven't appeared after fifteen minutes, I'll understand . . . "

The next afternoon Milo got to the Pâtisserie Mathieu ten minutes early. Solange soon turned up, spry and scented, in a pink dress that boldly hugged her bosom.

"Indian tea as before?" said Milo as he rose to greet her.

"By all means, it was excellent."

Having ordered, Milo sent her into fits of laughter by telling her about his very first attempt at developing a negative in the darkroom: the portrait of his father, which had stubbornly refused to appear on the sensitive plate. He recalled the solutions he'd mixed in the wrong proportions, the dishes he'd upset. There was something profoundly sensual about Solange's husky laugh.

Milo went on to speak of his first school photograph for the Jesuits. With brazen cheek, he'd presented himself at the porter's lodge one morning and offered his services. Not only had he come without a letter of recommendation, but it was his misfortune to have been a pupil of the Jesuits' competitors, the Frères des Écoles Chrétiennes.

"We already have a photographer," a monk told him gruffly.

"Yes," said Milo, "but you pay him."

"Of course. What of it?"

"With me it's the other way round." The monk looked puzzled. "I'll pay you one pound per photo," Milo said grandly. "Then I'll take orders from the boys' families. In addition, I'll supply the school with five free copies for its own requirements."

He was engaged to photograph the junior classes.

Solange Popinot's plump hand looked irresistible as she picked up her teacup and conveyed it to her lips. Milo experienced a burning desire to kiss it. Still speaking, he caressed the Frenchwoman's wrist with his forefinger. She gave a little start but raised no objection. He was emboldened to seek her knee with his beneath the table. She lowered her eyes.

They were now speaking in an undertone, their conversation interspersed with meaningful silences and low, suppressed laughter.

Soon afterwards she discreetly joined him in a room at the New Hotel. Their mutual desire was only intensified by the audacity of this rendezvous in the middle of town and in broad daylight. Milo unhooked Solange's dress with an ease that surprised him. She undid her corset herself, releasing two breasts of dazzling whiteness. Milo could hardly believe the evidence of his hands: this was a Frenchwoman, born in France, who was moaning under his caresses. He carried her over to the bed.

Solange was not the sort of woman that erupts like a volcano in company but proves strangely extinct in the intimacy of a bedroom. She clung to Milo's brown body and wrapped her legs around it, emitting prolonged, plaintive moans that steadily rose in volume as pleasure pervaded her. She concluded their embrace, which left her perspiring on the almost undisturbed bed, with a series of full-throated cries.

Had they been audible outside the room? On emerging into the passage a little while later, Milo thought he detected a congratulatory expression on the face of the floor waiter. But perhaps that was merely wishful thinking.

58

Dora found Milo remote and inscrutable in the days that followed. He got one of the operators to stand in for him at the reception desk and spent long hours in the café. He put in token appearances at lunch and dinner, but his conversation was limited to a few monosyllables.

The three girls were distressed by this atmosphere. Marthe had a recurrence of her fits, abruptly losing consciousness for a few moments, then coming to as if nothing had happened.

"She's trying to attract her father's attention," Dora told Isis.

Nelly, who would soon be eight, could not understand why Milo had forbidden her to enter the studio, whereas the operators would allow her to watch from a corner during certain sittings. She was doubly surprised by this change of heart because he had never refused her anything in the past.

But it was Gabrielle, the youngest, who seemed most affected of all. "Why is Papa sad when he laughs?" she asked one morning.

"Don't talk nonsense," Dora replied, avoiding her eye.

Milo had taken to addressing his wife in a brusque tone of voice. He lost his temper over trifles – a plate too hot, a door left open – and steered clear of any subject that might, if only indirectly, have enabled her to tackle him about the real reasons for his unpleasant manner. At nights he studiously kept to his own side of the bed as if afraid of some infection. In recent months his lovemaking had amounted to the perfunctory embraces of a man in need of sexual relief. Dora seldom responded to them. All she would have liked was to feel him lie against her with his fingers in her hair and no special end in view, as he used to in the early days of their marriage, when they lingered in bed with sunlight streaming into the room.

"Someone's calling downstairs," she would say, straining her ears. "I think it's Bulbul. We must have a customer."

"He'll come back," Milo would reply, kissing the hollow of her neck, "or he can't be a genuine customer. Look at Uncle Oscar: he always comes back for more."

It was impossible for Dora to discuss such things with Lita. Her childhood friend felt nothing but indifference, or even disgust, for the act of love. She was one of those virginal matrons who seem to have conceived with their eyes shut. As for Isis, she approached these matters with the unselfconsciousness of a doctor, but also with the frustration of a discontented woman. She listened and sympathized but could provide no answers.

Milo looked almost unrecognizable at lunch the following Tuesday. His lips were trembling, his eyes bloodshot. Dora was not to know what had just happened in the shop.

A new customer had come in and asked him, quite innocently, "Aren't you the one they call the Mameluke?"

Milo, never short of repartee as a rule, stood there open-mouthed. It was a brutal insight into the way some people saw him: he was merely the Mameluka's husband, collaborator and shadow – her bag-carrier. Without a word to the customer, he had turned on his heel and retired to the little terrace, where he paced to and fro.

To fill the silence once the *sufragi* had served the main course and left the dining room, Dora talked about the children. Nelly, who was already looking forward to her next birthday, had asked for a portable camera. There could be no question of giving her such a bulky article, but Dora wondered if a "Photo-Éclair" would fit the bill. This was a miniature French snapshot camera such as practical jokers concealed beneath their waistcoats so as to photograph people unobserved.

Milo promptly raised the roof. "Why not a photographic revolver while you're about it? I don't want my daughter turning into a slut!"

Dora stared at him in amazement.

"You'd do better to teach her how to sew," he bellowed. "Yes, you heard me, sew! And cook, for that matter, so her husband isn't obliged to eat shit!"

Dora folded her napkin and rose without a word. He jumped to his feet.

"Where are you going? I didn't give you permission to leave the table."

She walked off, still without a word. Dashing after her, he caught her fiercely by the arm.

"Let me go," she said in a low voice.

At that he slapped her face as hard as he could, three times in succession.

Shocked and dazed, she stood rooted to the spot for several seconds, then ran to the bedroom and double-locked the door. She leant her back against it, trembling all over.

She would never have thought him capable of such an act. The day Mother Marie des Anges had tried to slap her for impertinence at boarding school, she'd yelled so loudly that the nun stalked out and slammed the door behind her.

She inspected herself in the mirror on the dressing table. Her lower lip was bleeding. It made her mouth look huge — daubed with red like the miniature. She moistened a piece of cotton wool and dabbed it with a shaking hand. Then she turned away so as not to see the tears in her eyes.

Milo spent the afternoon at the café, playing backgammon. He seemed in high spirits, as if some weight had been lifted from his shoulders. The loss of the first game didn't upset him in the least; he even congratulated his opponent on his luck.

At four o'clock Bulbul came to fetch him because a customer had requested his presence in the shop.

"One of the operators can attend to him," Milo said. "I haven't finished my game."

The game had started badly. He was bound to lose and insist on at least one return match, but that didn't blight his good humour. He jocularly asked his opponent where he'd learned to play with loaded dice.

Forty minutes later Bulbul was back. Guffawing loudly, he announced that an important customer had come to complain about a defective print.

"Go away, damn you! My wife can deal with him."

And he threw the dice with a snap of the wrist, as if hoping to conjure up a double six. Another poor throw. He let out a regular backgammon oath that drew chuckles and grunts of appreciation from the onlookers clustered round the table.

When Bulbul appeared a third time, looking stupefied, night had already fallen. Milo almost hurled the board in his face.

"It's the lady," Bulbul said haltingly. "She's gone."

An unwonted silence reigned in the house. The wardrobe in the bedroom was open and half empty. All the scent bottles on the dressing table had disappeared. The tearful maidservants told Milo that their mistress had packed her belongings in several suitcases and called two cabs. She had left, taking the children with her.

59

Dora had not confined herself to taking her personal effects and those of the girls; loaded into the second cab, in addition to their suitcases, had been the field camera that was only used at Fleming in the summertime.

Her first words, on being shown into Maxime Touta's office, were, "I'm ready to go to the Sudan."

The editor of the *Sémaphore d'Alexandrie* looked dumbfounded.

"It was your suggestion," she went on.

"Indeed it was, but . . . I didn't think you'd be in a position to go."

"I am now."

"You'd go there by yourself?"

"Yes."

He asked no more questions, just pronounced himself absolutely delighted by this opportunity to publish an illustrated report, the first of its kind to appear in his newspaper. Various articles on the new Anglo-Egyptian administration had come out since the fall of Omdurman. The readers of the *Sémaphore*, as of other daily papers, had been able to see a few photographs of Khartoum undergoing reconstruction, but they were very commonplace pictures. They lacked an artist's eye, said Maxime. He pointed to two prints on the wall.

"Ismailia, my very first piece. I wasn't even a journalist at the time — I had to sign it with a pseudonym. That's the Place des Consuls in Alexandria in ruins. I was lucky enough to be there during the bombardment of 'eighty-two. That time, they simply had to hire me . . . The *Sémaphore* reopened in Cairo soon afterwards, but it kept the name that had made it famous. Five years later, youthful newcomer and non-European that I was, I became editor in chief."

Dora was well acquainted with Maxime Touta's career, which had gone down in the family annals. Her husband's cousin must have known that he was telling her nothing she didn't know already. She concluded that he was trying to put her at her ease or gain time for thought.

"What do you expect of me?" she asked.

"Nothing specific. That's to say, anything you think worth photographing. You'll have to abandon your speciality and produce something other than portraits."

"It'll make a nice change."

"But I wouldn't say no to a portrait of Wingate, for example."

Sir Reginald Wingate, formerly British intelligence chief in Cairo and organizer of Slatin Pasha's escape, had just been appointed commander in chief of the Egyptian army and governor general of the Sudan in succession to Lord Kitchener, who had been posted to the Transvaal to direct the campaign against the Boers.

"All civil and military powers are concentrated in Wingate's hands," Maxime explained. "No one is fooled by the Anglo-Egyptian condominium over the Sudan. That's just a formula devised by the British to cloak their annexation of Mahdist territory, pure and simple. But you may find the place in something of a turmoil when you get there. The 14th Sudanese Regiment mutinied, had you heard?"

She shook her head, so he enlightened her. It seemed that a British major had seen fit to throw two or three men into the Nile to compel them to swim. This method did not appeal to the soldiers, who rebelled.

Maxime went on to discuss the various subjects Dora might tackle in the Sudan. He obviously had faith in her, being convinced that his newspaper could only gain prestige from a signature like hers.

"Are you sure you won't need some help on the spot?" he asked. "The *Sémaphore* was long thought to be biased in favour of France, but the British have found it more acceptable since Paris and London came to terms. If you like, I could —"

"No, that won't be necessary. I'll manage."

One of the newspaper's staff would buy Dora's train ticket and cable Khartoum to book her a hotel room.

"The *Sémaphore* will naturally take care of your travelling and living expenses," said Maxime, "and you'll be free to market your photographs once we've published them. As for your remuneration . . . "

"I'm sure I can count on you to do the right thing," Dora said, getting up.

"What of my cousin?" asked Maxime, as he was seeing her off. "Is he well?"

Dora didn't answer, just gave him a little wave and climbed into the waiting cab.

Milo had begun by walking from room to deserted room in disbelief. Exasperated by the maidservants' lamentations, he swore at them, came close to hitting them, and finally told them to make themselves scarce. Bulbul who was roaming the shop like a dog bereft of its master, attracted a violent diatribe of his own.

"Did she pay you to keep quiet? Well, out with it! No? Not even that? It's true, you're too stupid. And you went and called a cab, you moron? *Two* cabs? Why not a tramcar?"

Neither Bulbul nor the maids knew where Dora had taken the girls. To her parents, no doubt. Milo couldn't see himself knocking on his father-in-law's door; their relations were on the cool side. "You haven't seen my wife, by any chance?" He'd sooner die. Léon Sawaya had always made Milo feel he despised him. Would he have consented to marry his daughter to a humble photographer if his name hadn't been Touta? During the early years, the estate agent had found it intolerable that Dora should work to help her husband keep the wolf from the door. His objections to a woman working had vanished once she became well-known and charged high prices for her portraits. Indeed, he all but accused his son-in-law of having married her for the money she earned.

Milo's anger soon gave way to dejection. He spent all evening dinnerless and in darkness. The glass of gin he poured himself left an acrid taste in his throat, but he persevered, almost forcing it down. Now and then he was overcome by an insane urge to burst in on the Sawayas, overturn their furniture, smash their china, and drag Dora off by the hair. He finally fell asleep towards four in the morning, slumped in an armchair with the empty gin bottle on the floor beside him.

Dora's first, instinctive thought had been to take the girls to Helwan. She would probably have done so had Nonna been less enfeebled by her circulatory disorder. One never knew how she would react since her illness. The old lady could behave quite normally, just like her old self, but she could also be surprisingly incoherent. She made uncharacteristic remarks about photography, crediting every portrait with a kind of human reality or magical power. She was convinced, for example, that people could be hurt at long range by pricking their likenesses with a pin. She cited the case of her husband, who had died at Alexandria only hours after his photograph had been accidentally knocked off the bedroom wall at Helwan and fallen to the floor, buckling the frame and smashing the glass. Dora's photograph of her was still prominently displayed on her bedside table.

Having abandoned the idea of taking the train to Helwan, Dora turned up at the Tiomjis' early that afternoon. She left the three girls in Lita's care and set off for the *Sémaphore* offices less than an hour later. Lita was appalled.

"Of course I'll look after them, *chérie*, but what about you? How are you going to manage? Surely you don't mean to travel on your own? They're savages, those people!" Dora's childhood friend was alarmed by the chill determination in her eyes. "But you don't know anyone in Khartoum . . . "

"I know William Elliot."

"Elliot? That tall, fair-haired Englishman who came to be photographed by you?"

"The very same."

"But *chérie —*"

"Please, Lita!" Dora said firmly, and that was the end of it.

Next day she boarded the train at Bab al-Hadid station with two suit-cases, the field camera, and a bag crammed with photographic equipment.

Richard Tiomji called on Milo late that morning. The servant who answered the door explained that his master was ill and unable to see anyone, but the ostrich farmer insisted on coming inside even so. Milo appeared, looking pale.

Richard, thoroughly ill at ease, informed him that the three girls were at his home with Lita, but that Dora had just caught a train to Khartoum.

Milo's jaw dropped. "Khartoum?" he exclaimed.

Richard hated having to undertake this mission at Dora's request. As he saw it, the whole business had boded ill from the start. He would never have permitted his wife to devote herself to any form of professional activity. "Women must be kept on a tight rein," he used to say, mashing out his cigar in an ashtray.

But neither would he have dared voice such a maxim in front of Dora. She overawed him more and more, and he'd raised no objection when entrusted with this errand the day before.

"Thank you," said Milo. He almost hustled Richard out of the house and shut himself up again.

On the way home, Richard wondered uneasily if Milo's thank-you had been a veiled accusation of treachery. He nervously lit a cigar, rehearsing the scene he would make that night if his wife dared to plead a headache and refuse him.

60

"To begin with," the editor of the *Sémaphore* had told me, "I advise you to sit on the right of the compartment, so you can see the Pyramids. At al-Minya, on the other hand, you should sit on the left for a view of Beni Hassan and the Nile Valley. Then back on the right till you get to Aswan. After that, I don't know."

Right, left, right . . . I recalled the advice I'd been given by Maxime, the only member of the Touta family to have travelled as far as the Sudanese border, as the train picked up speed on the outskirts of Cairo. Thanks to the railway line constructed during the reconquest of the Sudan, the last section of which had just been opened, I would be going much further afield.

"The journey from Cairo to Khartoum should take about fifty hours," I'd been wearily informed by the guard as he supervised the weighing of the baggage on the platform. "Fifty hours — possibly sixty or seventy. We always get there in the end, God willing." I mechanically slipped a coin into his hand to reward him for this invaluable information.

The first-class compartment was empty. I congratulated myself, feeling disinclined to tell anyone my life story. I'd brought several books, among them a copy of *Fire and Sword in the Sudan*, Slatin Pasha's account of his captivity, which William Elliot had given me. I'd never thought I would some day open it, and the pages were still uncut. William, who had made it his bedside book, declared that "every civilized person" ought to read it, but at the time I couldn't have cared less about Slatin or the Sudan.

As we passed the Pyramids at Giza I recalled my first photographic excursion eight years before. It seemed so long ago. To think I'd used the very same field camera that was accompanying me now! Only a few accessories had been replaced. I recalled how the black cloth had fluttered in the wind that day beside the Pyramids, and how the Bedouin had gathered round to watch. I recalled the trip back to town and the interminable hours in the darkroom. I also recalled the night that followed. Never had our bodies seemed better attuned . . . I felt the tears well up and threaten to engulf me.

I tried to immerse myself in Slatin's book, but without success; my thoughts strayed, and I kept breaking off in mid sentence. The Austrian described how he had been captured by the Mahdi's warriors. Held in chains for eight months, he was given nothing to eat every day but a few grains of maize. General Gordon and his men were besieged in Khartoum throughout that time. One day Slatin heard a noisy crowd approaching his cell and three men burst in, laughing derisively. One of them was carrying a bloodstained cloth. It contained General Gordon's head.

The blood rushed to my head, and my heart seemed to stop beating; but with a tremendous effort of self-control I gazed silently at this ghastly spectacle. His blue eyes were half-opened; the mouth was perfectly natural; the hair of his head and his short whiskers were almost quite white . . .

I put the book on my lap and looked out of the window, thinking of my daughters but forbidding myself to cry. "Why aren't you taking us with you on your long journey?" Gabrielle had asked. "We wouldn't get in the way, I promise." I coughed several times, my throat irritated by the dust that was seeping into the compartment. "It's worse in second class," Maxime Touta had told me. So what could it be like in a third-class carriage, from which sensation-hungry Solange Popinot had once been ejected, in company with her husband, because it was out of bounds to foreigners?

At Samalout station I got down on the platform and proffered my glass to a water-seller.

Continuing on its way, the train skirted some fields of sugar cane and cotton. On the banks of the Nile I sighted the famous "bird mountain". The multitude of sails on the river made a splendid picture. Under other circumstances I would have regretted my inability to photograph it, but photography was the last thing on my mind at that moment. With an effort, I returned to my book.

Rudolph Slatin's lot improved after the Mahdi's death: Khalif 'Abdullah, the Sudan's new master, appointed him a member of his household staff. Despite the menial nature of this post, Slatin found it preferable to guard the khalif's door and walk before his horse than to crouch, shackled, in the confines of a prison cell. After two years 'Abdullah presented Slatin with a horse: Gordon's erstwhile lieutenant and governor of Darfour was a porter and factotum no longer; he was even assigned a house of his own. In recompense for his services the khalif gave him an occasional slave girl. The Austrian contrived to sell any such gifts for a few coins.

> The Khalifa has four hundred wives, four of whom are legitimate. This large assortment of ladies varies in colour from the darkest black to the purest white. They are divided into groups of from fifteen to twenty, each of them presided over by a female superior ... Occasionally the Khalifa holds an inspection of his entire household, and makes use of such opportunities to rid himself of those of whom he is weary in order to make room for new attractions. Those disposed of in this way he generally passes on to his near relatives, his special favourites, or his servants.

Lulled by the swaying of the train, I ended by dozing off. I didn't wake up until we pulled into Assiut station. Instantly, I was overcome with sadness. The events of the last few days came flooding back: the look in Milo's eye, his brutal tone of voice, that slap in the face ... Then it occurred to me that I'd forgotten Maxime Touta's advice to sit on the left of the compartment.

Some colourfully attired Europeans were waiting in a bunch on the platform. "Thomas Cook!" called the self-important courier who was accompanying them. The words might have been a magic spell: the guard deferentially stood aside. "Until Aswan," Maxim had warned me, "two potential disasters lie in store for you: the dust and Thomas Cook. After Aswan, I couldn't say . . ."

The English tourists got into the compartment. The guard made sure they were all comfortably installed before blowing his whistle. They began by singing a song, interspersed with loud laughter, in memory of the wretched *dahabiya* that had carried them up the Nile from Cairo to Assiut. Then they gave three cheers.

I tried to read but soon gave up. "Are you Egyptian?" asked the woman beside me, a fat redhead with a blotchy complexion. I replied in French that I was an Egyptian Syrian, which clearly meant nothing to her. "You're a *native* and you're travelling *alone?*" the fat woman exclaimed with the avid expression of a tourist who has just discovered a curiosity.

That was as far as our conversation went. A little while later, when the whole horde trooped off, still singing, to invade the dining car, I decided not to follow suit. I limited myself to dipping into the basket of food that Lita had prepared for me.

At Luxor I had to change trains. I was stiff after sitting for sixteen hours, and the dust had made my eyes and throat sting. I would not have continued my journey with the Thomas Cook tourists for anything in the world. Fortunately, they were not going any further.

Until Aswan I shared the compartment with an elderly, turbaned village dignitary who slept from start to finish. His snores eventually merged with the monotonous rumble of the train. I too dozed off several times, but had a nightmare and awoke with a cry. Slatin's book was directly responsible for this. He described the savagery with which the Khalifa had rid himself of a rebel tribe:

> Arrived at the marketplace, a terrible scene awaited us. The unfortunate Batahin had been divided into three parties, one of which had been hanged, a second had been decapitated, and a third had lost their right hands and left feet . . .

I didn't manage to sleep a wink between Aswan and Halfa. I kept thinking of the way Milo had slapped me. He'd hit me twice more, while I was

still dazed from the first blow. But it wasn't physical pain I felt, even then
— even when I'd recovered my wits; it was more shame or rage. What had
really appalled me was the reflection of my face in the mirror, the sight of
my bleeding lip.

I hoped to be able to sleep a little better in the luxury train that was
supposed to transport us from Halfa to Khartoum in twenty-seven hours.
My first-class sleeper not far from the dining car made a very comfortable
impression. The brand-new train had no fewer than four classes, the
fourth being reserved for Sudanese.

I saw a thin man in clerical garb and little round glasses with blue lenses
making his way along the platform towards my compartment, followed
by a black man carrying his open sun umbrella and suitcase. "I have a
second-class ticket," he told the inspector in English, "but I'll pay the
supplement . . . No, no, no sleeper. The others can sleep. I shall sit up."

My fellow passenger introduced himself as the Reverend Mr Peter
Richardson. Eyeing me sternly, he asked first if I was travelling in company,
then if I was going to join my husband in Khartoum, and finally if I
was a widow. My three negative replies caused him to look sterner still.
Although the rest of the compartment was deserted, he took up a place
of authority directly opposite me.

The Reverend Mr Richardson informed me, at the very outset, that his
trip to the Sudan had no connection with tourism. He was going to join
an Anglican mission that had at last been authorized to install itself some
sixty miles south of Khartoum. "As a rule," he said, "it's missionaries and
traders who pave the way for civilization, whereas soldiers merely join
them in the course of time. In the Sudan the contrary has happened. The
military were the first to tread the soil of Omdurman, but, strangely
enough, they prevented any missionaries from following them there."

He seemed outraged by the attitude of Lord Cromer, who had done
his best to oust men of the cloth from the newly reconquered Sudan. The
British consul general had invoked the insecurity that still prevailed in
the country, but also the danger of rekindling Islamic fanaticism by

proselytizing too openly. Mr Richardson found this appalling. "Cromer gave a major speech at Omdurman after the victory. He undertook not to challenge Islam – indeed, he promised to encourage the building of mosques. I ask you!"

I had no opinion on the matter, nor had I any wish to debate it with my travelling companion. I asked him to excuse me, got up, and made my way to the dining car.

From Halfa to Abu Hamid the railway line constructed by Anglo-Egyptian troops cut across the great loop of the Nile and traversed the desert in a straight line. Eight stations numbered two to nine had been established on the route. I recalled the letter in which William Elliot had described the construction of this stretch of track, which was nearly 200 miles long:

> Our engineers are directing operations with remarkable vigour. Under a scorching sun, dozens of rails are being laid every day . . .

It occurred to me that I knew whole passages from that missive by heart.

I amused myself during lunch by watching some gazelles bounding along beside the train, and did not return to my compartment until we were pulling into Station No. 7. The train came to a halt, axles squealing. There was nothing to be seen on either side of the track but endless expanses of desert.

"I was speaking of Cromer," said the Reverend Mr Richardson. "Did you know that, for years now, we've been collecting the wherewithal to set up a Gordon Mission in the Sudan? We were ready to install ourselves there even before the battle of Omdurman, and we weren't alone. Presbyterians and Catholics were also eager for the fray." I tried to open my book, but he continued in the same lugubrious tone of voice. "No, I simply don't fathom Cromer. Islam is a barbarous and dangerous form of fanaticism. It's every Christian's duty to fight it to the death, as Gordon did. His heroic act of self-sacrifice has been an example to British youth."

I didn't know what to say, but he wasn't expecting me either to comment or signify approval. His voice rang out like that of a preacher in the pulpit of an empty church. "We are empire builders. The victory at Omdurman was ordained by God. It was a recompense for the innate superiority of the British people, who have been summoned to bear the white man's burden. God is asking us to take control of the Sudan – to deliver it from obscurantism and barbarity for no reward other than the knowledge that we have done our duty."

I retired to my sleeper soon afterwards, leaving the clergyman to commune with the Almighty. I devoutly hoped not to see him again until as late as possible the next morning.

Desert sand seeped into the compartment all night long. I awoke to find the seats covered with a yellowish film, as were my hair and clothes.

Awaiting the handful of passengers on the platform at Damer station were some Sudanese armed with big feather dusters. One of them hurried over and proceeded to dust my face and dress. I let the man have his way and gave him the coin he expected.

From Damer to Khartoum I did my utmost to avoid further conversation with the Reverend Mr Richardson. I sat in the corner of the compartment, turned my back on him, and deliberately immersed myself in Slatin's book.

Towards the end of our journey, when we were level with the Sixth Cataract and the countryside was becoming more and more verdant, he came over to me and recited some English verse that referred to the white man's burden. "Do you know who wrote that wonderful poem?" he asked. "He composed it especially, to mark the battle of Omdurman." When I shook my head, the reverend gentleman inscribed seven letters on the dusty seat with his forefinger: KIPLING.

61

I felt rather bemused on leaving my sleeper after such an interminable journey. The peaceful platform at Khartoum, which was guarded by a few British soldiers, had nothing in common with the lively bustle of Bab al-Hadid station in Cairo, but the chill morning air woke me up. Having said goodbye to the Reverend Mr Richardson, I followed the three porters who had taken possession of my baggage.

The sight of the Blue Nile overwhelmed me. Its azure waters traversed by big white sails and agleam with brilliant winter sunlight, the majestic river thoroughly merited its name. I felt happy for the first time since setting out on my journey.

I was conducted to the landing stage in company with a sullen-looking European who didn't open his mouth until we reached the other side. The two-storeyed hotel, which had balconies running along its façade, seemed to be floating on the water. One of its wings was still under construction. Seeing us approach, the labourers stopped work and waved vigorously.

The proprietor was waiting to welcome us on the landing stage. "The hotel is new, like every building in Khartoum," he said. "All General Kitchener found when he arrived here eighteen months ago was an expanse of rubble. Those savages had done their best to destroy everything before establishing themselves in Omdurman, on the other side of the river. They forgot to cut down the fruit trees, fortunately. You'll find we have some excellent fruit here."

My room was on the first floor. Spacious but sparsely furnished, it was redolent of new paint — a pleasantly symbolic smell to one who, like me, felt the need to start afresh. My balcony afforded a view of the river stretching away into the distance. A white, high-decked steamer was gliding slowly past the hotel. It hooted once as though to greet our arrival.

My first thought had been to send William Elliot a note informing him of my presence, but I changed my mind. It seemed better for me to settle in, rest a little, and, in a manner of speaking, regain possession of myself. I may also have wanted to savour the delay, just as I used to when I received a letter from him and slipped it into my bodice to open later on.

It wasn't until mid afternoon that I handed an envelope to one of the hotel staff. Prior to that I sat on my balcony and read Slatin's horrifying description of the great famine of 1889, during which he had seen two women on their knees beside a dead donkey, devouring its entrails raw. I shut the book and leant on the balustrade.

William Elliot came panting into the hotel lobby less than half an hour later. I hadn't been expecting him so soon, and my heart lurched when I sighted him from the balcony. A bareheaded figure in khaki service dress, he looked even more attractive than my mental picture of him.

I waited for a bellboy to knock at my door before going downstairs. In the lobby William hurried over and lingeringly kissed my hand. "You here?" he said incredulously.

The Sudanese sun had tanned his chiselled features and intensified the blue of his eyes. "You here?" he repeated.

We couldn't just stand there in the middle of the lobby with the hotel staff looking on. "Do you have time for a cup of tea?" I asked.

"Time?" he said. "Now you're here, I've all the time in the world!"

The big veranda was deserted, so we chose a table at random. William's shoulder straps bore the insignia of a new rank, I noticed: the gilt crown and star betokened his promotion to lieutenant colonel.

Anticipating his questions, I explained that I had been commissioned to produce an illustrated report for the *Sémaphore d'Alexandrie*. I made no mention of having left Milo. He listened in disbelief, still unable to accustom himself to the idea that I was there in the flesh. He reproached me for not having warned him of my arrival. "It was a last-minute decision," I told him. "What about you, how have you been getting on? Tell me."

I hadn't heard from him for eleven months. Having, with a heavy heart, resolved to forget me after our clandestine meeting in Cairo, William had sent me a kind of farewell letter informing me of his intention to remain in the Sudan. His comrades and his family found this quite understandable: in London and Cairo alike, British officers were lining up for a chance to serve in this mysterious land, which was still wreathed in glory by the victory at Omdurman. In the light of William's military exploits, his request for a local posting had been granted without hesitation. The military authorities had put him in charge of the market at Omdurman.

"Could you get me an introduction to one or two influential people?" I asked.

"Of course. I'll do my utmost, Dora, but every door is bound to open to you of its own accord. There are so few women here, let alone pretty women."

I pointed out that I wasn't a European. "What does that matter?" he exclaimed. "Anyway, you're famous. I got a shock the other day when I saw a postcard of Lord Cromer bearing the signature of your studio. A brother officer brought it back from Cairo with him. 'That's a portrait by Dora Touta, the best photographer in Egypt,' he told me. You can imagine how surprised I was – and how proud."

To familiarize me with the town, William asked a waiter for a pencil and a sheet of paper. I watched his hand while he drew a rough sketch map, the well-manicured hand that must so often have taken up a pen to write to me.

"There are really two towns at the confluence of the Blue Nile and White Nile," he said. "Omdurman, the native town, faces the desert and backs on to the river, which the Mahdi and his fanatical disciples regarded as the infidels' route of access. Khartoum, the colonial town, has lush vegetation. The place will be another Cairo once our town planners have finished redesigning it. It follows a chequerboard pattern, with avenues at right angles and one or two diagonal streets – like this." He laughed when he noticed my quizzical smile. "Yes, its layout resembles the Union Jack, but the street names pay due respect to the Anglo-Egyptian condominium. Here, for instance, Victoria Avenue is intersected by Khedive Avenue." Still chuckling, he went on, "The only real link between the colonial town and the native town is sport. The golf club is on this side of the river, the polo club in Omdurman."

William offered to show me everything, starting on the morrow. Remembering what the editor of the *Sémaphore* had said, I queried the possibility of disturbances in town. "Order has been restored," William told me reassuringly. "A few native officers were found guilty by a court martial and compelled to surrender their swords. They've been taken to Cairo under escort and locked up in the Citadel to await the khedive's return. He's off gallivanting somewhere, as usual. In this place, my dear Dora, the only language people understand is force. The Mahdists used force. We use it too, but in a civilized manner."

"Can the use of force ever be civilized?" I murmured. He gave me a puzzled stare.

When he took his leave at seven, William kissed my hand even more lingeringly than before. I concealed my emotional turmoil behind a rather set smile, but the touch of his lips on my wrist remained with me for the rest of the evening.

62

We had arranged to meet at nine in the morning. I changed my clothes three times after breakfast, finally settling on a close-fitting princess gown with flounces. William turned up five minutes early, beaming happily. "Everyone in Khartoum goes around on donkeyback or in rickshaws, but I've managed to get hold of a gig." He invited me to climb up beside him and took the reins.

Khartoum looked like a sleeping city with its squat buildings and deserted avenues. We passed the future site of Gordon's bronze statue: the hero was to be shown on camelback with a small cane in his hand. "That's where he was killed," said William, indicating the governor's palace, a large white building with arcaded verandas and the Egyptian and British flags flying over it side by side. Part of the frontage was hidden by some impressive palm trees. The Sudanese sentries in front of the entrance, lanky men with spindly legs, were wearing very tall tarbooshes adorned with pompoms.

"And this is the Gordon Memorial College," William announced. We were nearing a big building site. The air was filled with the sound of picks and hammers. Walls of dark brick had already risen from the ground, and workmen were preparing to erect the roof timbers. "This school will symbolize the coming of civilization to the Sudan." Noticing my sceptical air, William went on eagerly, "Yes, civilization. Our mission isn't simply to restore order, rebuild Khartoum and combat epidemics. We're also here to abolish slavery and found schools."

I told him of my encounter with the Anglican missionary. "Oh, those missionaries," he said. "They were asked to concentrate on the pagans, not the Muslims. They belong in Fashoda, not Khartoum. In any case, their efforts would be futile. We shall have to civilize the Sudanese before making Christians of them." The British would find it easier to civilize the Sudanese than the Egyptians, William explained. "Here we can act without let or hindrance, whereas in Egypt our task is complicated by the presence of a cosmopolitan community of Europeans and Levantines. They disrupt our relations with the natives."

"In other words," I said, "we're in your way."

"Oh no, Dora, not you! Not you!"

He made a detour through the residential district on the banks of the Nile to show me some villas under construction. Then he turned into a street of small houses surrounded by bright green lawns, each of them bearing the name of an officer and his official function. When he pointed out his own, I complimented him on it for form's sake.

We were then ferried across the river to Omdurman. The White Nile did not flow as fast as the Blue; its waters had a brownish glint and looked stagnant by comparison. Once ashore on the other bank we hired some donkeys, and William led me off into a maze of narrow streets that debouched into a dusty square. The Mahdi's celebrated mausoleum was a quadrangular building pierced by ogive windows and surmounted by a dome. One side of it was pitted with holes made by shells during the battle of Kerreri. I asked William if it was true that General Kitchener had had the Mahdi's remains dug up and thrown into the Nile. He not only confirmed this but added that it had been a necessary measure. "You'll turn him into a martyr," I said. "No, no, Dora," he replied briskly. "You talk like the kind souls at home in England who know nothing about the Orient. If we hadn't exhumed the Mahdi the Sudanese would have inferred that we were frightened of him, even in death, and it would have fostered fanaticism." I conveyed with a shake of the head that I was far from convinced by his arguments.

Next I was shown the house Slatin Pasha had occupied during his captivity, now the telegraph office. After that William took me to see a big building piled high with various relics of the Mahdist period. Apart from a motley collection of headdresses, swords, pistols, harquebuses, and several old bronze cannon, it contained a carriage that had belonged to Gordon, and even his piano. "Tomorrow we can visit the battlefield at Kerreri," said William. "The Thomas Cook Agency has included it in its future tourist itinerary. You'll be able to see the bones of Dervishes bleaching in the sun." I was wholly uninterested in such things, being impatient to meet some living people. Since we were in Omdurman, I asked William to show me the market.

The stalls, which lined the river bank, consisted for the most part of simple squares of matting laid on the dusty ground. Pungent smells arose from this heterogeneous conglomeration, where a hundred varieties of spices, herbs and perfumes rubbed shoulders with saltpetre and dried meat. Native policemen clicked their heels and saluted as William passed them. "This is the biggest market in the Sudan," he told me. "It's supplied by boats and caravans. Slaves were sold here before our arrival."

I said I'd gained the impression that there were many women in Omdurman. "It's not just an impression," William told me. "There's a shortage of men here. Over ten thousand of them were killed during the battle of Kerreri alone, don't forget."

Returning to the hotel at about two, we lunched together in the restaurant. This gave me another opportunity to admire the hands that had set my pulses racing the day before. I was finding William more and more attractive. At that moment, I couldn't have cared less about his imperialist's arrogance or his attitude toward the natives.

He ordered champagne, then treated me to an amusing account of Khartoum's Saturday night dances, which were as short of women as Omdurman of men. He also told me that, although a police regulation obliged Sudanese women to cover their breasts, local policemen would order dancing girls to drop their veils in return for a modest *bakshish* from a foreigner.

Even though I didn't appreciate that kind of story as a rule, I never stopped laughing. It was many days since I'd had a light-hearted conversation with anyone, and the champagne was ever so slightly going to my head.

After lunch, when William was standing very close to me in the lobby, reluctant to depart, I came within an ace of inviting him upstairs to my freshly painted room.

63

After three days of dejection, during which he had no desire to see anyone, Milo was galvanized by self-pride. So the Mameluka had gone? Very well, he would do without her! He'd show people who was the studio's guiding light, its backbone and real motive power.

His first step was to go to the Tiomjis and reclaim his daughters. Lita could hardly refuse him. She had in any case assumed that she would have to return the three girls to their father if he showed any sign of wanting them back.

Timidly, she asked Milo if he wouldn't find it difficult to look after them. She would be happy to keep Gabrielle, Nelly and Marthe for as long as necessary, she said, provided she could engage one or two additional maids. Milo took umbrage at this, expressing surprise that anyone could want to "separate a father from his children", but he ended by pronouncing this a practical solution. He would exercise his paternal rights on Sundays by taking the girls to Helwan, to the zoo, or to the puppet theatre in the Ezbekiyah Gardens.

"I'm sure your wife will have returned by then," said Richard.

"She'll return when I permit her to!" Milo retorted grandly. And, to demonstrate that nothing in his life had changed, he told the Tiomjis that he would expect them next Wednesday evening.

The Popinots had been very embarrassed by this affair, especially Solange, who wondered if her brief affair with Milo lay at the root of this conjugal drama. Unable, for obvious reasons, to discuss the matter with her husband, she worried about it for several days. Then Milo himself dispelled her fears by gaily reminding them to turn up on Wednesday evening.

The shop almost ran itself, thanks to the four operators and darkroom assistants, but Milo was keen to assert his authority. He supervised their work continuously, showering them with useless pieces of advice, and insisted on taking certain portraits himself. It was a long time since he had been so much in evidence at the studio, so busy and self-assured.

Clients who expressed surprise at Madame Touta's absence were informed that she was away. Some of them said they would prefer to cancel their appointment and book another for after her return. Milo compelled them to reconsider their position.

"I'm booked solid for several weeks," he told them firmly. A French banker from the Crédit Lyonnais, who stood by his original request, was offered a provisional sitting on 25 June. It was then March.

Léon Sawaya, who had been advised of his daughter's departure by Lita, called on Milo to demand an explanation.

"If she'd consulted me before leaving," Milo said with a sorrowful smile, "I would have condemned the idea in the strongest possible terms."

"But I'm told that it was your cousin, Maxime Touta, who sent her off to Khartoum."

"I've nothing in common with my cousin. In any case, nobody forced her to go."

"And you've had no word from her?"

"None."

Léon Sawaya went away fuming, the more so since tongues had begun to wag and all kinds of rumours were going the rounds. How, he wondered, could a lone woman survive in the Sudan? By way of reassurance, Lita had told him that his daughter knew an English officer stationed at Khartoum. Léon didn't know what to make of the affair. An English officer was better than a mediocre photographer, to be sure, but he'd appeared on the scene nine years too late.

On Wednesday night several people cried off at the last moment. They sent

Milo brief notes pleading indispositions, unforeseen and urgent family or business commitments.

The diminished soirée resembled those of the early days. Norbert Popinot brought the wine and Milo ordered the *mezze* from a caterer. The Tiomjis, who, for reasons they themselves failed to fathom, had turned up with a magnificent bunch of gladioli, tried hard to be cheerful. Ibrahim wore a perpetual, sarcastic smile, whereas Seif seemed bowed down beneath the weight of British colonialism. The Popinots enlivened the start of the evening by unwrapping a present for Milo from Paris.

"A walking stick?" he said with a smile. "You're giving me a walking stick?"

With an air of mystery, Norbert unscrewed the handle. "The roll of film is here. The button that releases the shutter is under the handle. That's the winder. There's even a magazine designed to hold three spare rolls."

Milo seemed delighted with his toy. He would have liked to try it out on the spot if the light had been adequate. "When electricity is installed," he said, "I may be able to photograph my guests secretly, without a magnesium flash. I've been promised it very soon."

Seif spoke of the disastrous Nile floods, which were causing the peasants great concern.

"It was a waste of time reconquering the Sudan," said Popinot. "After all those stories about the value of knowing the state of the river upstream . . . For several weeks now, the British engineers on the spot have been sending alarming cables. Where does that get us? Sometimes the river forgets to rise; at other times, like now, it takes a malicious pleasure in overflowing its banks. Knowing about it in advance makes little difference."

Conversation languished. Richard Tiomji embarked on a long account, which interested no one, of his ostrich-farming activities.

"People often ask me what ostriches eat. That's easily answered: they live on beans and *berseem*. But they're very unusual creatures — they also like to swallow pebbles. Yes indeed, pebbles! You'd find whole bucketfuls in their stomachs if you performed an autopsy on them. To be absolutely frank, ostriches also eat pieces of wood, glass or copper. Yes, yes, copper! The fact is, all these objects aid their digestion. I expect you're going to ask me how . . . "

Ibrahim was scribbling furiously in his notebook. Popinot asked him what the matter was.

"I can't finish my poem. I'm stuck."

"Read it to us," said Solange. "We'll help you."

Ibrahim complied with bad grace.

> *Has it struck you, engineers,*
> *that the Nile is never right?*
> *It has always kindled fears*
> *that it won't attain a height*
> *suitable for irrigation . . .*

"That's where I got stuck."

"You need a word ending in 'ation'," said Solange.

"Thank you for nothing!" growled the poet.

"How about *'and enough to feed the population'*"?

"It doesn't scan. Too many feet."

She counted on her fingers: "*'suitable for irrigation'* . . . eight. *'And enough to feed the population'* . . . ten. You're right. You'll have to change the line that comes before it."

"Certainly not," said Ibrahim, shutting his notebook. "That's no way to write a poem."

"Your poems are getting on our nerves!" snapped Seif.

Norbert Popinot deemed this an appropriate moment for everyone to sample a burgundy famed for its exceptional bouquet. Milo insisted on opening the bottle himself. He had three attempts at it and ended by ruining the cork. As a gesture of friendship towards the master of the house, Seif consented to moisten his lips, but he very soon reverted to his real concerns.

"It defeats me why the khedive was so quick to condemn the Egyptian officers who mutinied at Khartoum," he said angrily. "Or rather, I understand him only too well: all 'Abbas can think of is his forthcoming trip to England."

Everyone ignored this. If there was one subject *not* to be discussed, it was events at Khartoum. Quickly changing the subject, Popinot mentioned a book devoted to the emancipation of Egyptian womanhood. It was causing a stir in the drawing rooms of Cairo because it attacked polygamy, instant divorce, and the wearing of the veil. This had at once brought down the wrath of the ulemas on the head of the author, one Qasim Amin.

"At last a man courageous enough to denounce the medieval world in which we're living!" exclaimed Ibrahim. "Our sisters and cousins are still brought up the way they were a thousand years ago. They spend their lives closeted at home and lolling on divans, smoking or nibbling sweets. It's a stupefying way of life. It not only harms their constitution but robs them of all intelligence."

"Well said! Well said indeed!" Popinot said briskly, trying to liven things up.

Seif took issue with Ibrahim. As he saw it, the book in question was upsetting Egyptian society to no useful purpose. The Egyptians had other, more important battles to wage.

"Don't you think your womenfolk would look more attractive without the veil?" asked Solange Popinot.

"No, I don't. Quite apart from its acknowledged moral virtues, the veil is extremely useful. It enables a woman to conceal her facial imperfections and enhances the depth and brilliance of her gaze."

"You sound like a sheikh from al-Azhar!" Ibrahim said impatiently.

"I espouse the same point of view as Mustafa Kamil!" Seif retorted.

"The same as the khedive, you mean. 'Abbas has forbidden the author to set foot in the palace."

"Not unnaturally."

"Make up your mind! You condemn the khedive when he makes overtures to Queen Victoria and defend him when he slams the door on Egyptian womanhood."

Solange weighed in with a spirited tribute to sexual equality. She pointed out that in France, for the very first time, one woman had just joined the Bar while another pioneer, the Duchess of Uzès, had obtained her driving licence. Richard Tiomji intervened in his turn: a woman's place, he declared, was in the home – "in the home and nowhere else", what was more.

"You're right," Milo said gravely.

His remark cast a chill. Silence persisted for a few seconds. Then Solange played some Brahms to dispel the feeling of uneasiness that had settled on the drawing room.

64

Ten days went by, and Dora still hadn't taken a single photograph; she hadn't even unpacked the camera. William expressed surprise at this. "I'm just looking," she told him in a dreamy voice. "I'm trying to take it all in."

William didn't complain – far from it. He hoped her stay in Khartoum would be a long one, especially as she was very vague about its duration and never alluded to what she proposed to do in Cairo on her return. He ended by wondering, without daring to believe it, if she had made up her mind to remain in the Sudan for good. It seemed too much to hope for. Many were attracted by this virgin land where everything had still to be built and all seemed possible. Greek and Syrian merchants were already in Darfour, awaiting permission to carry on their trade in the south of the country, but what did Khartoum have to offer a photographer who was not only married but far from her children?

William had gathered from a few brief remarks that Dora and her husband were no longer on good terms. Though secretly delighted by this, he didn't really know what to make of it. He was afraid that, if he questioned her, he might antagonize her or elicit some terribly disheartening response.

Dora would go to Omdurman market every morning, accompanied by a Sudanese guide found for her by the proprietor of the hotel. There beside the Nile, seated a little apart on a sack of cotton or maize, she would watch the barges being unloaded. At first she was accosted by inquisitive locals who heard her reply in Arabic – an Arabic different from theirs but intelligible — and engaged her in conversation. In the end, when her presence had ceased to surprise them, they brought her gifts of dates or milk.

The peaceful throng became quite animated whenever a camel caravan arrived after trekking across the desert for days on end. Everyone clustered round the weary travellers as they laid out their wares on the ground — gum arabic, ivory, ostrich plumes — and bargaining commenced.

Dora would rise and stroll round the stalls. Although she occasionally bought something, these occasions were more an opportunity to mingle with people.

"But you see the same thing every day," said William, who found her behaviour surprising.

"Yes," she replied, "but not necessarily with the same eyes."

The stallholders' children who came over and talked to her reminded her of her daughters, and her eyes would grow moist. Nelly, so well-behaved in the studio . . . Marthe's tears the night before she left . . . And that remark of Gabrielle's when being put to bed:

"Are you going away because you don't love us any more?"

At last, two weeks after her arrival, Dora asked William if he would accompany her on a day-long tour of Omdurman and its environs, this time complete with camera. He had only to get another officer to stand in for him, so he agreed with alacrity.

William Elliot proved a perfect guide throughout this excursion. If he didn't know the way, he made inquiries. He could name various forms of vegetation such as the mustard tree or soap tree, and there was nothing he didn't know about the gum acacia or the asclepiad, with its large, veiny, sugary leaves. He was a pleasant, attentive, interesting companion. On two or three occasions Dora was shocked by his arrogant attitude towards the natives and didn't hesitate to tell him so, but he clearly found it hard to behave in any other way.

She knew exactly what she wanted to photograph, as if she had already picked out the locations, assembled her subjects, and studied their mannerisms. No sooner were they in front of her lens than she tripped the shutter without giving them any precise instructions. She used only a dozen sensitive plates during the day. William, accustomed to army photographers and their extravagant ways, couldn't get over it, but Dora seemed quite content with her day's work when the light faded.

"Are you really satisfied?" he asked her twice, like a lover worried about his latest performance.

She reassured him with a smile.

The day after this photographic outing, William handed Dora an invitation to a ball at the governor's residence.

"Ball is putting it a bit strong," he told her. "They do things very simply here, you'll see — these parties are quite unlike the soirées in Cairo. Besides, you'll get a chance to meet everyone in Khartoum who matters — Sir Reginald Wingate, for a start. You'll even see Slatin Pasha, who arrived here yesterday. He's making a brief stop before setting off on some expedition to the back of beyond."

Dora did not put on any of her jewels that night. She limited herself to a very plain emerald gown that set off her dark, glossy coiffure.

Sir Reginald, a powerfully built man with silver hair, was wearing all his medals. He seemed to take genuine pleasure in speaking French. Having welcomed Dora with the utmost courtesy, he introduced her to the guest of honour, his friend Rudolf Slatin, whom he had wrested from the clutches of the khalif while head of British intelligence in Cairo. Dora remembered that Wingate was suspected of having strongly influenced the Austrian's account of his adventures for propaganda purposes.

A dashing figure in his mid forties, Slatin Pasha was younger than she had imagined. The Mahdi's erstwhile prisoner had been removed from the Sudan after the battle of Omdurman and was counting on his friend Sir Reginald to obtain him another government post. Meantime, he had joined a private expedition that was prospecting for gold and silver in the Nubian highlands.

Laughingly, the Austrian told Dora that he was the only member of the present distinguished gathering to have prayed in the great mosque at Omdurman five times a day for several years in succession.

"I know," she said, and quoted a passage from his book, which she had just finished. Slatin looked duly flattered. "I'm a photographer," she added. "Could I take advantage of your stay in Khartoum to photograph you outside the mosque and in the various places where you were held prisoner?"

"For a woman as attractive as you," Slatin told her with a bow, "I'm prepared to postpone my departure."

The band struck up a waltz, and Dora opened the ball in Sir Reginald's arms. The two hundred-odd guests stood and watched them with approving murmurs, then applauded. There could not have been more than fifteen women present. Several officers partnered each other with plenty of verve, much to the amusement of the ebony-skinned servants in their immaculate livery.

Dora granted Slatin a waltz, then danced with two strangers. William was awaiting his turn. She pulled an embarrassed little face at him by way of apology, but he smilingly conveyed that she wasn't to worry.

The quadrille was heralded by several blasts on the trumpet. Sixteen couples, three or four of them consisting of men, gaily took their places. William managed to station himself opposite Dora, and the first figure commenced. The dancers moved rhythmically to the strains of the piano, flute and violins, then speeded up in the pastourelle. Dora laughed heartily, as she used to during boisterous parties in the villa at Fleming.

"Careful with the finale!" called the colonel who was directing the quadrille.

The band surpassed itself. Six trumpets and two trombones drowned the dancers' exuberant cries and the pounding of their feet on the floor.

"Forward, four!" yelled the colonel.

The dance ended in a wild cavalcade that left Dora bathed in perspiration. She slumped into a wicker chair just as the buffet was opening.

The food was not as delectable as it had been at 'Abdin Palace, but Sir Reginald had done his best, and the wine flowed freely. A small group of people had gathered round Slatin Pasha, who was on brilliant form. He recalled that the Mahdi, his original captor, eschewed strong drink but was very partial to date syrup flavoured with ginger, which was served him in silver vessels formerly owned by Catholic missionaries.

"The women of his harem fought to get near him. They would kiss his footprints – they even drank the water he'd washed in. They massaged his body, using precious essential oils with a sandalwood base. He was coated in them from head to foot. The smell was overpowering, believe me . . . "

Dora strolled out on to one of the verandas, glass in hand. The governor's palm trees were stirring in a gentle breeze from the river. Khartoum's low buildings lay spread out beneath a starry sky.

"I hope you aren't bored," William said softly from behind her.

Startled as if by a caress, she remained silent for some moments. "No," she said. "I'm seldom bored. I might be, if I were blind."

"Would you grant me this waltz?" he asked with a respectful bow, as though they were strangers.

Dora smiled to hide her emotions. In William's arms, she let herself be whirled away across the floor. She felt his chest against her bosom, felt the strength of his body, and it made her happy.

"May I get you something to drink?" he murmured a little later.

"No, I think I'd sooner go."

On the way back he stopped the gig in a dark avenue flanked by orange trees. She didn't move when he rested his hand on hers. Then, slowly, she turned towards him and sought his lips with her own.

"I'm taking you to my place," said William, who was holding the reins in one hand and embracing her with the other arm.

Her only response was to nestle still closer.

Two hours later, in that overly narrow bed with its coarse, ill-ironed sheets, Dora was staring up at a ray of moonlight on the ceiling. She had clasped that fair-skinned body to her in a paroxysm of desire, kissed it, licked it, raked it with her nails. Now it was over, and she felt nothing any more –

none of the boundless contentment that had so often filled her when she and Milo made love.

Outside, some bird emitted a strident, unfamiliar cry. Dora dissolved into tears. With her face buried in the pillow, she strove to blot out the memories that were crowding in on her.

65

On 5 April 1900 a photograph signed by Dora Touta appeared in the *Sémaphore d'Alexandrie.* It occupied the centre of page one, and beneath it was a brief caption: "Sudanese women near Omdurman". Despite the poor reproduction, this photograph was cut out by numerous readers who called at the newspaper's Cairo and Alexandria offices in the hope of buying a print on albumen paper. The *Sémaphore* had to publish a small announcement to the effect that prints were not yet available, but would probably, subject to the photographer's permission, be offered for sale at a later date. Meantime, only Maxime Touta possessed a decent print, to wit, an enlargement which he hung on his office wall alongside his two photographic "mascots" of Ismailia's Champollion Square and Alexandria devastated by shellfire.

Dora's photograph showed six bare-breasted women facing the camera. Five of them had pitchers on their heads and were steadying them with one hand. The unencumbered arms of the central figure, a strikingly beautiful girl, formed a perfect arc because she was loosely clasping the thumb of her left hand with her right. This gesture alone lent her an extra-ordinarily natural, lifelike air. Several little girls were seated in the dust in the foreground, one of them hugging her pitcher as if it were a doll. Every face seemed expressive of boundless melancholy — more reminiscent of a millennially wretched existence than a hundred newspaper articles.

Milo, who had cut out the photograph himself, couldn't tear his eyes away from it. He felt as if he were seeing his wife through the medium of that young black woman with the bare breasts and full lips. She brought back memories of his wife's lips — the lips he had so much loved to look at, caress with his fingertips, and kiss . . .

He had been living alone for over a month now. As the days went by, his artificial euphoria had given way to mounting tension. He reprimanded his employees for no reason at all, and had even been known to lose his temper with customers. One of them was the daughter-in-law of the owner of the bazaar, a shy young woman who had been intimidated by his peremptory manner and couldn't bring herself to face the lens despite his injunctions. In the end, Milo's patience ran out. "Come on," he yelled at her, "smile, for God's sake!"

Ten days later the owner of the bazaar came to complain, having seen his daughter-in-law's frozen smile captured on film — at great expense, since the photograph bore the celebrated red "T". Milo had to agree to retake the portrait, but he retaliated by entrusting it to an operator.

Two Sundays in succession he failed to appear to take his daughters for an outing. Lita became concerned.

"Would you like me to take them to Helwan myself?" she asked.

"No, no, I'll come next Sunday," Milo told her in an edgy voice.

But he didn't. What was more, he cancelled the Wednesday soirées, saying that he was tired out by all the work the shop was giving him. Several times that spring he caroused at the Bar Bavaria with Ernest Zahlawi, his boon companion of evil memory, who persuaded him to try a new beer or sink a bottle of gin with him. Returning home blind drunk, he entered by the shop door, as of old, and knocked over some chairs on his way through. Bulbul was awakened by his imprecations but hid beneath the covers, knowing that there was nothing to be done.

Everyone was very disappointed not to see Milo at the Easter lunch party at Helwan. Nonna was unable to supply a reason and seemed completely uninterested. Some weeks earlier, her sole response to the news of Dora's departure, uttered between two sips of arrack, had been, "A fine to-do!" No one knew whom she blamed, her youngest daughter-in-law or her favourite son.

[295]

The Popinots made three or four attempts to invite Milo to their home, but he declined on a variety of grounds. Norbert even failed to interest him in the World Exhibition that had just opened in Paris. Newspapers reaching the Cercle Français were filled with enthusiastic accounts of modern marvels: the impending inauguration of the Métro, the Palais de l'Électricité, the Château d'Eau, the Pont Alexandre III, the moving platform, the upside-down manor house resting on its turrets . . . In normal times, all these curiosities would have thrilled Milo and given him an opportunity to retail them in countless different versions. But he uttered no exclamations and asked no questions. All Norbert elicited were a few indifferent nods.

Ibrahim, for his part, thought he was doing the right thing by sending Milo the first three verses of his *Marseillaise Égyptienne*. He did not even receive an acknowledgement.

Even Seif, so uninterested in anything not directly connected with the British occupation, grew worried. Anxious for news of Milo, he called at the shop one Sunday afternoon but barely got beyond the doorstep. He gave up and left.

"In Milo's place," Richard Tiomji told his wife one night, "I'd have caught the first train to Khartoum and dragged Dora back by the scruff of her neck."

Lita, exasperated by his braggadocio, couldn't restrain herself. "You get train-sick," she muttered, "you know that perfectly well."

He was so furious, he mounted two assaults on her that night.

66

"It's a personal letter for Madame Touta," said the young British officer.

Milo, who was standing behind the counter, put out his hand for the envelope.

"No, I'm sorry," the young man said, turning puce, "I'm supposed to deliver it to Madame Touta in person."

Milo got on his high horse, a frequent habit of his in recent weeks. "And who do you think I am, if not Monsieur Touta? You've run your errand. You may go."

He snatched the envelope away. The officer hesitated for a moment, then turned on his heel and, in a sudden fit of pique, slammed the door behind him.

Milo dashed outside and seized him by the arm. "Hey, you little whippersnapper!" he shouted. "Do you know who you're dealing with?" He levelled furious forefinger at the shop window. "That's Lord Cromer — yes, Lord Cromer, a customer of mine. I can go and see him any time without an appointment. I can walk into his office and ask him to reduce you to the ranks. He'll tear off your lousy pips on the spot!"

A small crowd had gathered. It was unprecedented to see a British officer being tongue-lashed in this way; the boot was on the other foot as a rule. The young man mounted his horse without a word and disappeared round the corner.

"Who does he think he is!" snarled Milo. A number of shopkeepers, though ignorant of what had happened, were already congratulating him.

Once back behind the counter, he opened the letter. It had been written in Fashoda and was, bizarrely, dated January of the previous year. A note scrawled on the envelope stated that it had been inadvertently delivered to the wrong address and returned to the Sirdar's headquarters.

Dear Dora,
I've never stopped thinking about you since my last letter. Would you forgive me
if I told you that your memory haunts me all the time? I shall do my utmost
to obtain some leave in the next few weeks and come to Cairo . . .

Milo felt stunned. He left the shop and made for the Ezbekiyah Gardens, where he walked aimlessly for two or three hours, sometimes retracing his steps along the same path. His fury subsided, but his thoughts were in a whirl. All at once, he understood everything and nothing.

He had a vision of William Elliot in his black bathing costume on the beach at Fleming. "Would you permit me to teach your wife the breast-stroke?"

"The swine!" Milo muttered to himself as he passed the deserted open-air theatre for the third time. "The rotten swine!" he added in the same tone of voice.

The Mameluka . . . "What's the derivation of the word 'Mameluke'?" Norbert Popinot had asked one day. "The Mamelukes were former slaves who became princes of Egypt," Ibrahim replied. "In Arabic, 'mamluk' means someone who is owned or possessed."

Milo turned this over in his mind. The Mameluka was his possession — a woman who had once been his but was so no longer. A woman whom he would never possess again . . .

He not only could but should have acted differently from the very first. He hated photography, if the truth be told — hated spending hours on end in the darkroom developing plates as Dora used to do before her departure. What interested him was greeting customers and exploring new markets — indeed, he found that fascinating. He sensed that he excelled at the commercial side of the business and was brimming with ideas on how to expand it. In addition to the albums and knick-knacks in the window, he would have liked to display photographic equipment for amateurs: portable cameras, exposure meters, sensitive plates . . . Not only that, but technical handbooks and photographic magazines imported from France – and, while he was about it, why not metal tripods and lanterns, test tubes and funnels as well? So as not to mix up the different lines he would, of course, have needed another shop where the albums and knick-knacks could also be accommodated. It just so happened that a shop was for sale on the other side of the square, a stone's throw from Maloumian's. Milo pictured the sign: ÉMILE TOUTA, PHOTOGRAPHER TO THE CONSULATES. PHOTOGRAPHIC EQUIPMENT AND ACCESSORIES OF ALL KINDS.

He would also have liked to hold an exhibition of Dora's work – in a room at Shepheard's, for instance. Art would have come within her domain, all else within his. However, none of those things was feasible without Dora herself. Dora, who haunted his days and nights. Dora, whose concerns and emotions he had been incapable of sharing for months, if not years.

That night, after waiting for his employees to leave and dismissing Bulbul, Milo went into the darkroom. His mind had been made up since noon. All that had given him pause for thought was how to phrase his farewell letter. In the end, however, he had decided not to explain his course of action in writing. Everyone would understand, Dora most of all.

He had planned a theatrical scene that would lend his demise greater impact. He would go to the shed in the yard and retrieve the arabesque armchair his wife scorned to use. That was how he would await his death, seated facing the lens. He would also install a background: the rocks and the raging sea, in memory of the beach at Fleming.

His throat was smarting. Despite its improved ventilation, the dark-room still gave off an acrid smell of ether and soot. He lit the lantern and went over to the page from *L'Amateur Photographe* that had been pinned to the far wall. Carefully removing the four drawing pins as if anxious not to disturb anything, he took the page over to one of the desks and sat down.

The chart, which was very detailed, comprised four columns: the name of the poison, its physical effects, the symptoms it induced, and potential antidotes.

Ammonia was unsuitable; the most its fumes could do was inflame the lungs. At Fleming the previous summer, Dr Touta had been called out in the middle of the night to treat a case of that kind, and his patient had survived.

Milo moved on to the next line, which was devoted to sulphuric ether. Its effects sounded imprecise: they were "similar to those of chloroform". But what exactly did chloroform do, apart from putting you to sleep? He recalled the early months of their marriage. "No," he used to protest, "I don't snore. Don't you dare accuse me of snoring!" The result would be a pillow fight, followed by hilarious laughter, followed by . . .

Where potassium oxalate was concerned, the chart cited four grammes as the smallest recorded lethal dose. Milo knew where to find some: every jar was carefully labelled and identified in Indian ink. As a first-aid antidote to potassium oxalate, *L'Amateur Photographe* recommended magnesium. There was no magnesium handy, and it would in any case be several hours before anyone entered the shop. Oxalate caused "a burning sensation in the throat and the pit of the stomach, together with vomiting and cramps . . ." Milo couldn't picture himself vomiting on the arabesque armchair in the studio. He ruled out potassium oxalate.

That left potassium cyanide. The flask was labelled LETHAL in bold capitals. He need only ingest fifteen centigrammes of the stuff to be rid of his loathsome existence. "I can't understand," Nelly used to say, "why Muhammad Ali shot the Mamelukes in the Citadel. He'd invited them to dinner, so he could have poisoned them instead." The thought of his daughter pierced Milo to the quick. The Mamelukes, the Mameluka . . . Vomiting . . . He was too soft-hearted for his own good. "Cyanide induces laboured breathing, dilated pupils, and spasmodic clenching of the jaws," the chart stated. He thought of Gabrielle and Marthe, their trepidation at the zoo, their delight at the puppet theatre. "There is no known remedy," added *L'Amateur Photographe*. Abruptly assailed by a vision of himself with dilated pupils, he banished it from his mind.

He restored the chart to its place, blew out the lantern, and left the darkroom. "I'm good for nothing," he told himself. "I'm not even capable of putting an end to myself." He felt infinitely, mortally sad.

67

Nonna died, like Khedive Tewfiq, on a Thursday. Her last words were intended for Milo, but she made several deathbed allusions to "that girl in the Sudan". At noon, with the ladies from the neighbouring houses in attendance, she feebly asked for her customary glass of arrack. For whatever reason, they denied her request. She gazed at them imploringly, overcome by a momentary fit of panic. Then she closed her eyes and expired.

Milo was a universal focus of attention during the funeral Mass in Cairo, which was heavily attended. A dry-eyed, preoccupied figure seated in the front row with his brothers, he looked very forlorn. Of whom was he thinking, Nonna or the absent wife who was the subject of so many whispers in the pews behind him? Items of news from the Sudan were few and far between, but the Mameluka was rumoured to have enslaved the whole of Khartoum. Senior officers prostrated themselves at her feet, ready to comply with her smallest whim, and she swept into the governor's residence as if she owned it . . .

Milo seemed a shadow of his former self while members of the family were receiving condolences after Mass. Usually so dapper, he appeared to be two sizes too small for his dark suit. He shook some people by the hand and proffered a feverish cheek to others, but he was miles away.

His sisters-in-law, who were in full mourning, looked almost indecent by comparison, with their tearful, bloodshot eyes. She was no more, the woman who had bullied and sometimes terrorized them throughout their married life. Yes, they wept sincerely, the wives of Albert, René, Aimé and Joseph, their feelings of relief mingled with the sensation that a great void had opened up.

Rizqallah Bey, who travelled by train as readily as others by cab, could have come from Alexandria for the occasion, but he had limited himself to sending one wreath in his own name and another on behalf of the *Touta et Fils* department stores: two gigantic, garish wreaths that put all the others in the shade.

The Popinots, with their dark attire and appropriately solemn expressions, looked perfect. They conveyed just the right amount of sympathy for Milo without seeming affected. This was their first contact with the family since meeting some of its younger members when the pilgrims departed for Mecca two years earlier. Jeannot, the youngster who had taken Solange's hand to help her negotiate some stairs, passed the Frenchwoman without daring to relive his memory of the incident.

When Ernest Zahlawi drew level with Milo he gave him a familiar pat on the cheek, but Milo merely blinked at him. Ernest had poured himself into a tight black suit and was looking presentable for once. All he seemed to lack was a pair of clerk's shiny oversleeves.

Oscar Touta mumbled something as he passed his nephew. He was quite capable, even on this occasion, of complaining about the operator at the studio or the draught from the church door, which someone had omitted to close.

Yolande, who had once had a crush on Ibrahim, thought she spotted him in the crowd. The poet was wearing a green silk shirt. He was fatter and older than she remembered. Doubtless feeling ill at ease in such a gathering, he shook hands with Milo and quickly slipped away.

The Tiomjis were true to form: he a bulky, perspiring figure with a bristling moustache; she, with her peculiarly ivory complexion, more sylphlike than ever. They were accompanied not only by their own five children but by Nelly, Gabrielle and Marthe, all dressed in black — "my three chicks", as Nonna used to call them.

Old Dr Touta, looking very erect and dignified, stood beside his nephews to receive the mourners' condolences. He was as affected as anyone by the death of his brother's wife. They had seemed two of a kind in more than one respect — indeed, he may secretly have been in love with her. Although aware for some weeks that Nonna's days were numbered, he had refrained from telling anyone.

"Your mother was a great lady," he told Milo, taking him in his arms. Then, and then only, did Milo shed a tear.

A rather embarrassing incident occurred at the cemetery. Just as the undertaker's men were nearing the open grave, one of them tripped and let go of the coffin, which struck the ground. Looking contrite, the man straightened up, his trousers white with dust, while his colleagues hurriedly remedied the situation.

"Dora never did bring Nonna good luck," René's wife commented acidly.

Everyone went home after the ceremony. If the funeral had been held at Helwan, the whole family would have foregathered at the big house, a house deprived for ever of its owner. It had yet to dawn on anyone what Helwan would be like without Nonna. Summer had begun, and the Touta family's thoughts and dreams were exclusively focused, this year as every year, on the sea.

68

It seemed clear that, for the first time in recent memory, there would be no family photograph this year. The field camera was in the Sudan and Milo had not procured another. In any case, he seemed far from eager to convene the Touta clan, or even to show his face in public. His daughters were staying at the Tiomjis' villa; he lived alone in his.

He wasn't the Milo everyone knew. Thin and ill-shaven, he forgot to smile and had lost his love of words. The children — thirteen-year-old Maggi, for example — felt abandoned, but the older ones were no less baffled. Having left the shores of childhood behind, they usually maintained a kind of camaraderie with their uncle. For two summers now, he had taken them to tea dances at the Casino San Stefano. He had personally extracted permission from their mothers, who were very strict with their daughters but unable to resist him. Yolande's delight on hearing the news had been unbounded.

This time, Milo limited himself to collecting his daughters daily and — as if it were a duty — treating them to a donkey ride on the beach. To the surprise of the children and adolescents of the family, for whom it was an unprecedented occurrence, Nelly, Gabrielle and Marthe seemed bored. The only time they laughed at all was when the donkey-driver swore at his wretched beast.

The beginning of summer was marked by the khedive's official visit to England. For the first time since his accession, 'Abbas was spared the gibes of the English-language press. "Although His Highness has taken some time to find the right road," the *Egyptian Gazette* perfidiously commented, "that only reinforces his conversion."

The khedive was ill by the time he reached the English coast and could not go ashore right away. Having at first suspected diphtheria, his doctors finally diagnosed a bad attack of tonsillitis. However, it may simply have been excitement at the prospect of meeting Queen Victoria.

The *Sémaphore d'Alexandrie* did not deprive its readers of a single detail of the khedive's ceremonial welcome: an interview with the Prince of Wales at Marlborough House, Lord Jersey's garden party, a concert at Buckingham Palace, lunch with Lord Rothschild at his Piccadilly mansion . . . Maxime Touta's paper stated, tongue in cheek, that the Royal Victorian Order with which 'Abbas had just been invested was "a new decoration reserved for persons who have rendered Her Imperial Majesty particular service."

"Just imagine how furious Seif must be!" said one of Milo's nephews.

Yolande shrugged her shoulders as if to convey that Seif no longer existed. What did Milo's friends matter to them now?

The *Sémaphore* published the menu of the royal banquet held in the khedive's honour: clear turtle soup *à la reine*; fillet of salmon *à la genevoise*; vol-au-vent *à la financière*; *chaud-froid* of chicken in aspic; fillet of beef *à la paysanne*; quail *aux petits pois*; asparagus with hollandaise sauce; *gâteau de riz à l'ananas*; fruit jelly *au champagne*; Parmesan croquettes . . .

Although the *Sémaphore* acquainted the holidaymakers at Fleming with every aspect of the khedival jaunt, they missed the sounds, colours and smells that went with it. They missed the gleeful excitement of Milo, who would have dashed out on to the beach and set the sun umbrellas quivering:

"You'll never guess what happened in England the other day!"

And all who heard him would instantly have imagined themselves at Windsor or Buckingham Palace . . .

Dora's absence was much debated by day on Fleming beach and at night in the Casino San Stefano. Everyone had his or her own pet theory about it.

"No wife and mother deserts her husband and children because of a little slap," Alfred Falaki remarked sagely.

Then someone mentioned an English officer, and the rumour spread like wildfire from villa to villa. Some said he was a lieutenant colonel, others a general. Even the Sirdar's name was mooted. After all, hadn't Sir Reginald taken up his post as governor general of the Sudan only a few weeks before Dora's departure for Khartoum? Because it gave rise to such extravagant hypotheses, however, this rumour about a putative lover lost all credibility.

Some subscribed to quite another theory. "Her husband's affair with the Frenchwoman was more than she could endure," they maintained.

Rose Falaki's eldest son was acquainted with one of the receptionists at the New Hotel, and the latter had been only too pleased to inform him that his uncle, Émile Touta, had spent an afternoon there in the company of a European woman. The description he gave exactly tallied with Solange Popinot's appearance. It was clear to all the youngsters who had hovered round that alluring creature two years before that Milo had sacrificed himself in her service – in fact they would have thought him foolish not to. But that still didn't account for Dora's disappearance. Would a wronged wife really have abandoned her children and renounced her legal rights in order to vanish into the Sudanese inferno?

There remained another hypothesis. Yolande put it this way: "Perhaps the Mameluka felt drawn towards a land of mystery."

Back in Cairo, Solange Popinot espoused the same theory. The Frenchwoman seemed to sympathize with the absent Mameluka, and even to envy her. She mused aloud about the Sudan, its wild beasts, its big black men with their glossy limbs . . .

People recalled that Dora owed her nickname to her fabled escape at boarding school. Had she tried to escape once more and succeeded yet again?

"Escape from what, pray?" fat Angéline Falaki exclaimed. "She lacked for nothing – her husband waited on her hand and foot. I know of more than one young woman who would have married Milo like a shot."

"Perhaps she found life *too* easy," Dr Touta muttered one night after a game of whist.

Asked to explain what he meant, the old man merely shook his head. Was he voicing a simple conjecture, or had he got it from Isis, Maxime Touta's wife, his youthful fellow physician and close friend?

69

Khartoum, 25 May 1900

Dear Isis,

Forgive me for having taken so long to respond to your affectionate letter and the questions it contained, but I simply didn't feel like writing — nor, I suppose, like putting the replies you wanted into words. I wonder if you'll find them in this letter, which may strike you as rather mystifying.

I've done a great deal of thinking in the last few weeks. A great deal of weeping, too. I didn't know it was possible for a person to shed so many tears.

You either know or guess the fundamental reasons for my wounded state. I needed to be alone, and for that I had to go far away. Besides, my presence was becoming too much of a burden — I was beginning to find myself insufferable. I suppose I also needed to indulge my temptations to the full.

Do you remember our long conversation in the studio one Sunday afternoon? We agreed that, in life, one has to remain oneself but change gear at regular intervals. Well, I think I'd been tired of my success for some time. It wasn't enough for me to be "the most sought-after portraitist in Cairo", as you so kindly put it. I had to try my hand at something else — something more difficult, no doubt.

Some photographers are interested in landscapes. I am more attracted by people. And, by dint of observing them through my lens, I've learned a little bit about them. What people, though? A tiny segment of the population of Cairo, that's all! It was Seif who alerted me to this one day, quite unwittingly, by displaying an unexpected interest in Bulbul, our shop assistant. I realized that I knew nothing about the men and women who wade through the mud of the Nile Valley. The only

Arabs with whom I'd come into contact since childhood were the Bulbuls, the servants or tradesmen who lead a more or less cheerful existence. Having toured the villages for so long, you know what I'm talking about. You're acquainted with these people. I had to reach the age of twenty-eight and go all the way to Khartoum before I encountered them.

I'm not saying I've lost interest in the world of the "consulates" (and I weep as I write that word, albeit for different reasons . . .). It gave me pleasure to photograph Slatin Pasha in front of the great mosque at Omdurman and Sir Reginald wearing plus fours in the garden of his residence, but I could never be satisfied with that kind of clientele alone, not now. Besides, I prefer to take unposed photographs.

You mention my daughters. I miss them terribly, as you can imagine. They must be finding their mother's "long journey" very long, but I think it's their father they miss most of all.

You also mention the man whose name I can't commit to paper without weeping, and I'm deeply distressed by what you tell me of your own situation. What can I say, dear Isis? I've had only one love in my life, and now it's over — over because of me. Ought I to have reacted sooner? Undoubtedly, but how? I'd have found it as unthinkable to give up photography as you would to give up tending the sick. And I'm not sure even that would have been enough. I'm a photographer and always will be. If I still had a chance of resuming my former place, however, I'm convinced I'd behave differently. By that I mean that I would pay as much attention to other people as I do to my sitters. But you're bound to find this all very confused and confusing.

I've been at the end of my tether for days now. I miss so many things: the shop, the house at Helwan, mornings on the beach at Fleming. I miss the sound of the sea, the smell of seaweed, the lights of San Stefano when darkness falls. Above all, I miss the man in whose company I was never bored, and whom I didn't know how to love as he deserved . . .

I know where I belong and dream of returning there, but I'm afraid it's too late.
All my love,
Dora.

70

No one knew, of course, that Milo had purchased a gun. If the least hint of it had got out, Dr Touta would have gone to his nephew's villa in person and demanded an explanation.

It later transpired that he had bought it from a gunsmith in Alexandria, Dimitriou of Sesostris Street. He accepted the first thing he was offered, making no attempt to haggle. It was a so-called "Bulldog", a central percussion revolver with a cross-hatched grip of imitation ebony. The cylinder held six rounds, but he reflected that it would take only one to put him out of his misery. The gunsmith, who noticed his customer's haggard expression and trembling hands, was loath to sell him the weapon.

It was only just eight o'clock on the morning of 6 July when Maggi started shouting, having just run the length of the beach.

"Milo, Milo!" she kept calling.

Although Maggi was known to be overexcitable, she had never shouted like this before. There was something exceptional about her shrill, breathless, imploring cries.

She reached the villa and hammered on the door, but in vain. She made three more attempts, banging away at it with all her might in a kind of impotent fury. Giving up, she collected a handful of pebbles and threw them at the first-floor window. Her aim was good, but nothing happened. Disheartened and apprehensive, she started to sob.

"If there's no photograph this year," she had told her sister Yolande the day before, close to tears, "I'm never coming to Fleming again. Never, you hear!"

Upstairs, the shutter over the french window creaked open and Milo's tousled head appeared. He emerged on to the balcony.

"Come quick!" Maggi called breathlessly. "The Mameluka's here!"

As though turned to stone, Milo continued to lean on the balustrade for several seconds. Then, having donned a shirt and a pair of slacks, he came downstairs without even putting on his shoes. Maggi took his hand and they headed for the shore.

The beach was still deserted – deserted save for the distant figure of a woman sitting beside the sea.

Milo walked on in a kind of dream, shadows looming before his eyes. Some long-forgotten words came back to him: "You reinvent the sea, mademoiselle? I reproduce it exactly." He repeated them to himself as they buzzed insistently in his ears, clung to them like a drowning man. At times it seemed there was nothing in front of him but the boundless blue sea. He saw nothing, felt nothing but his feet sinking into the sand. Then, quite suddenly, it was as if he had taken wing. The white figure was nearer and more distinct. "You reinvent the sea, mademoiselle?" With Maggi's hand clasped tightly in his, he walked on and on, faster and faster. "I reproduce it exactly . . . "

Dora was seated on one of her suitcases at the water's edge, wearing a pale muslin gown and a broad-brimmed straw hat. Her bootees were lying on the sand beside her. The sea was as smooth as a millpond. Nothing broke the silence save the splash of an occasional wavelet.

Milo, who had let go of Maggi's hand, neared the shore. Dora turned towards him, her eyes misted over with tears. They were now only a few paces apart. Maggi saw Milo's face light up beneath his three-day beard. Tactfully, she turned and walked back towards the villas.